THE SINGULARITY

THE SINGULARITY

Keith Mutter

Writer's Showcase

San Jose New York Lincoln Shanghai

The Singularity

Writer's Showcase
an imprint of iUniverse, Inc.

For information address:
iUniverse, Inc.
5220 S. 16th St., Suite 200
Lincoln, NE 68512
www.iuniverse.com

ISBN: 0-595-22527-6

Printed in the United States of America

To Marilyn and Swami Vinayagananda

Contents

TRACER

Lua watched the tracers cascade down onto the blue and white planet, as their craft hung in the darkness of space. A composite global map lay in front of her, a holographic copy of the planet they had journeyed through space and time to reach. This was Earth at the beginning of the second millenium. She felt a tingle of excitement, an expectation of the unknown.

Next to her sat Daljit, her friend and colleague, and beyond her Carter, both with eyes glued on their map grids. The rest of the team sat around the globe mesmerised by the image of the planet.

They had traveled a vast distance in search of an unknown individual. All they knew about this person was a bio-ethereal read-out. The tracers' job was to seek them out amongst a population of six billion souls, like picking up the frequency of a radio station. And find him or her they would; the question was how long would it take? Their window of opportunity for the jump back to their time frame was not a long one, and this unknown factor was the cause of some concern. They had one other consideration—how old would the owner of this bio-ethereal read-out be? Old enough they hoped, old enough to help them out.

Lua's section of the map included southeast United States, Central, and part of South America, and the string of Caribbean islands. Whoever's set of tracers found their target would be assigned the mission of making first contact. It could take days. Each knew the languages and the customs of their section of the grid.

A bright light flashed on above the globe and all eyes on deck looked up in unison, startled, and in disbelief. They had only just started, yet the tracer had locked on and confirmed the read-out. In a few seconds they would know who the lucky one is. No one said a word.

A beam of light then issued from above, slowly making its way down to the globe and pinpointing their target on a tiny island in the Caribbean. Lua's heart raced for a second. She quietly stood and started off for the Captain's quarters, pausing a moment to hold Daljit's hand, then a brief wave to the cheers of her crew-mates.

When the door slid shut behind her, Lua jumped and punched her fist in the air. "Yes!" she hissed. The tingle in her guts was now a tsunami of passion.

CONTACT

Kel lumbered over to his spot, sat down, and secured his cold beer in the sand. He leaned back and propped himself against the now familiar backrest of the sloping palm tree, and stared out to sea. The sun was a few degrees above the horizon, and the colour of the sky slowly changing—a few clouds to add the spectacular to the burning plumes of the sinking sun. The trunk of the tree veered away from the sea so there was no danger of a falling coconut interrupting his constant musings about life, as the play of memory danced in his brain. This was Kel's favourite time of the day as light gave way to dark, as if a light switched on in him that made him more aware and alive.

Nearby was a beachbar run by a Rastafarian named Shakey, not a true Rasta though, since he served and drank beer. He certainly liked to smoke grass, and was one of those friendly souls who inhabit the Caribbean whose philosophy embraces the simple message, 'smoke a joint, reminisce, hug and kiss'. He now danced around the bar to an old reggae tune, crooning out the words like a well-worn engine, as if talking to himself.

"Oi, Kel!" called Tattoo Jack, gliding by on the beach. He beamed a smile of such friendly charm it could have gained him entrance to the sanctum of a nunnery.

"Oi, Tattoo Jack!" Kel yelled back. "Why don't you feed that dog of yours? He was at my heels again last night!"

"He's just playing man, just playing."

"Yeah sure, give him some corned beef and ganja, cool him down a bit," called Kel, as he watched this charmer's slow progress down the deserted beach. There was very little of anything happening on the island, and he was beginning to enjoy these occasional territorial encounters with Bruno. Tattoo Jack had recommended he call out the dog's name to initiate a friendship, but this gross invasion of privacy had had the opposite effect, and the occasional squirmishes continued.

The sunset's colour show kicked in and feasted Kel's eyes. He took a long swig of cold beer and lit a cigarette. The first puff made him dizzy and his heart raced.

His thoughts ebbed and flowed, his head toasted by this habitual jolt to his nervous system. Ten years ago he had been a businessman travelling the world selling some or another product as a sales representative, mostly in Japan. He had quickly tired of this and dramatically changed his life-style, becoming a massage practitioner, learning some esoteric techniques and practicing in Japan and Europe. This he also tired of, so he sold everything he had, kissed his Japanese girlfriend goodbye, and arrived on these lazy sun-drenched shores some six months ago. He had suffered proportionately to the love he had lost, and the sting of separation from a romance gone stale had now abated. It was over, though a tinge of loneliness occasionally swept from his heart to his abdomen and back again, like the ebb and flow of the tide before him.

This tiny island, as yet relatively unspoilt by the ravages of tourism, had given Kel much joy. The people were tough and friendly, and lived an austere life, preserving folklore, legend, and close inter-social relations that characterise a people living in close community for some generations. They were attached to the soil and the sea, and having a fair idea of what was going on in the world chose to stay where they were.

Such societies produce eccentric individuals, not to be shut or hid away as they had been in our desperate attempt to regulate life, but to be enjoyed as part of the warp and woof of human society. One such character now approached Kel with the inky sea, and the dying embers of the sun as a backdrop.

"That you Kel?"

It was Ken-eye, who was very short sighted and looking for a beer, a joint and a chat.

"It's me Ken-eye, what're you up to?"

"Following my nose." After a few seconds of silence, when neither beer nor joint were offered, Ken-eye made his way carefully, almost sideways like a crab, over to Shakey who would most surely indulge his desires. He lead, with his left hand out in front of him, feeling his way through the air. Ken-eye liked to philosophise—and a great philosopher he was—but now was not the time for talk, and Kel settled back into the silence of the sunset.

Kel was in his forties, still trim and fit, but supping a few too many beers of late, and enjoying a few too many smokes to go with them. But he had surrendered himself to this lazy way of life, finding that disciplining himself was a waste of time and effort, resulting in a few days of purity followed by an almighty binge. This was where he was at, and so far so good. No burning bush had told him to do otherwise, and he kidded himself that there would be plenty of time for an ascetic approach once his body had expired. Occasionally, in the morning when his head was a little heavy, his conscience would prick at him, and he had become adroit at ignoring it.

He was born English, the product of middle class suburbia, and in his youth had tired and sickened of the judgmental nature of some of his countrymen, their constant preoccupation with how you talk, how you act, who you know. This great nation had somehow managed to temper its intellectual ability into a weapon of Narcissus, sometimes wielded as a haughty and proud superiority, and at others as a groveling means to obtain the approval of the ruling classes. It had taken him many years to be able to watch English news interviews with any degree of objectivity that overrode his conditioned response to accent, dress, and demeanour. Such are the collective sins of parents upon their children, 'Oh England! Land of judgements'. Kel took a long draw on his cigarette and looked around him quickly, spat in the sand, sat back, and resumed his nightly thought-watch.

As with most Englishmen who have become nomadic, Kel had ditched the quaint Englishman act. He had spent some time in and around San Francisco, America's most liberal city, where the real meets the unreal, and somehow had become acutely aware of his own act, albeit a good one, but an act. Neurosis counts for very little in such a place, what you do being more important than how you act. Overall it had been a great and liberating experience for him, and he had found Americans a relaxed and friendly people, if somewhat sad and alone in the empty triumph of consumerism. He remembered the night he had caught himself surfing around and around over a hundred television channels in an unconscious plea to make contact with something meaningful. Bloody madness! he thought, and took a swig of his beer.

His restless bulldog mind now veered towards a new critique of this or that, but he caught himself in time and forced his attention into the present, turning his gaze upward to the stars, which were starting to peer through the darkening night. Shakey turned on the sparse lights that hung lazily from the gangling palms around the bar. He looked over at Kel, wide-eyed and smiling, spreading his hands and fingers in mock surprise, and gratitude for the pure magic of electricity. Meanwhile, Ken-eye, oblivious to this brief lapse of his companion's attention, continued to expound on one or more of the truths of life.

Kel occasionally yearned for his homeland—the country pubs, the lush green hedgerows, the passion for football, and even the unbelievable measure of leisure in a five-day cricket match and its meditative slowness. England had been born of such a painful past, as have most European countries, and the rights of the working man had been hard won by. We deserve the government we get, he thought, and winced at the remembrance of the particular Prime Minister who had spurned his move to get the hell out of the so called United Kingdoms. He tried to force this thought out of his mind, but like all cynical socialists, it was indelibly etched there.

England now reeled in his brain and he suddenly remembered a talk he had had with his grandfather many years before. Apparently filth and noise had characterised Victorian cities. Filth from the trains, the chimneys of factories and houses, and the horses…noise from the carts and carriages, and their hooves on the cobblestones. When motor transport had begun to replace horses in the early twentieth century, his grandfather had said, everyone noticed how relatively quiet and clean town centres became. Quiet in London? A memory from his childhood, the vision of a trolley bus, a red double decker, flashed through his mind.

A loud guffaw of laughter at the bar briefly lifted him out of his nostalgia, but he was locked into it as the beer slowly nursed his emotions, and edged him back to his youth.

He remembered the soot and terrible fogs of London, of hardly being able to see his feet on the edge of the kerb on his way to that drab Victorian edifice, a concentration camp they called school. Line up, shut up and prepare to be molded into the work place. Through the coal laced fog with rasping lungs he walked to such a place as if in a bad dream. A sand crab approached and tapped Kel's toes, benevolently lifting him out of the fog, and this particular barrage of thoughts assailing his mind. He flared his toes at this intruder and it scuttled away like a robotic dinky toy, and then dug his feet into the sand and scrunched the grains together between his toes. I love the beach, he thought, as the cold beer sizzled at the back of his throat; another jolt of nicotine and the continuing foray into the past.

He was indeed a cynical socialist. When you know at a gut level that the absence of the profit motive usually spells disaster, but you hate the greed that accompanies the quest for profit so much that you sell your soul to a proven failure, and defend it with everything but your life…Well! You become a cynic—or a philosopher—or both. Luckily, he had been imbued with a good sense of humour to cope with the absurdity of it all, bequethed to him by his father, and a couple of rare and beautiful teachers. Ah! Mr. James' face shot into his mind's eye over the mists of time. He was beginning to get too sentimental—time for a little entertainment.

Kel felt for his beer and the familiar sensation of an empty bottle greeted his hand. He leant forward, pushed himself up from the sand, and made his way over to Shakey's bar through the rush hour kamikaze flight of insects diving towards the dim glow of the light bulbs. A bat was already on its silent flight, slipping effortlessly through the night and picking off its blinded prey. Kel looked to the southeast and saw that the moon had not yet risen.

He was greeted by two wide grins, deliciously mischievous grins of young boys, happy and hopeful that a new part of the human equation was about to join the conversation.

"How's the island treating you, Kel?" asked Ken-eye, ever vigilant that his home should treat this friendly visitor with respect.

"Like a loving mama, Ken-eye."

"That's the way it should be. Money and the market place don't take over here, like they have in most of the other islands. Rich folks keeping the poor even poorer, not as long as I am alive," and Ken-eye gave a look, as if to say the island spirits were with him in protecting this haven against the devouring and heartless jaws of capitalism.

"You let me know if anyone give you hurry and worry here," Ken-eye went on, his black face shining with energy.

"Give my lord Protector here a beer," said Kel, and Ken-eye yelped in delight. Kel loved the West Indian accent. It had a tone and a lilt to it that suggested both playfulness and wisdom; there was something ancient about it.

"This is a place for human beings still—children fearlessly smiling, no problem walking in the dark; some monkey business around but no bad stuff. I am one of the protectors of all this, you know," and Ken-eye was off on one of his tirades. Kel knew he was in for a litany of facts, spiced with a little fiction, and served with a wink and a dig in the ribs.

"I like the fairness of the English, even though you like warm beer," said Ken-eye savoring his beer, waiting for the joust to begin.

"Not warm beer—cellar temperature, and that's just with a little chill on it so you can taste the beer. Not kill it with cold, like you have to with this bloody stuff!" retorted Kel.

"Anyway," continued Ken-eye, "I never could make head nor tail of you English. Like when you first turned slavery into big business, then you abolish it and accuse the world of being uncivilised for carrying this trade in human souls on."

"Nothing to do with me Ken-eye."

"Between 1500 and 1800," Ken-eye liked to tease Kel on this most delicate of matters, "five times more Africans came to the New World than Europeans, that's a fact. When I saw that film Malcolm X and he say, 'We didn't land on Plymouth Rock, Plymouth Rock landed on us,' I stood up and cheered. My cousin, he's the manager of the cinema, he have to push me back in my seat."

"Yeah, him and whose army." Kel said.

"Take more than an army to shut this one up," laughed Shakey.

"Did you know that George Washington," Ken-eye persisted, "and all those Independence fellows, made their money from the toil of the black man?"

"George Washington freed all his slaves on his death bed," Kel offered.

"Well thank you very much, sah, will there be anything else I can do for you before you go?" Ken-eye bowed in mock reverence.

There was a moment's silence, and all three burst into laughter. Ken-eye whooped and hooted.

"Yeah, different age, different game," said Kel eventually. "Many of your brothers in America still house a big resentment."

"Remember Kel, we are all brothers, our blood groups being the same."

"Thanks Ken-eye, you're right, dead right. Now it's mental slavery to the dollar for almost everyone. Many lessons to learn before we are free of all that, but before it was abolished the Brits were the biggest slave traders—greedy buggers!"

"Greedy buggers," echoed Shakey, and he laughed. "Remember that lady, Ken-eye, the one who took me to America? I was there for two weeks; some cool people there, but everyone in a hurry, and mostly everything ruled by the dollar."

"It ain't the dollar that's bad," said Ken-eye.

"But money's the cash crop there, man," said Shakey, "and everybody in the cities in a rush. And you can't eat money. Capitalism's going to burn all the fuel, and when it does, where they going to hide? In cyberspace?" Shakey laughed again and repeated, "Greedy buggers."

"Never mind, Kel, it's over, no more slavery. Be a free man and stay here. Build a house, and live your life," said Ken-eye.

"I have enough for another month; then I have to go back to the States, or Europe, to make some money."

"Do something here man, be poor with us, don't be so proud. You afraid to ask someone for the price of a beer?" chided Ken-eye.

"Maybe I am," and Kel laughed as Ken-eye indicated his beer was empty.

"Get the rascal another, Shakey," said Kel, and Ken-eye beamed.

Shakey offered Kel the joint, and he waved it away.

"There was a girl in here today asking about you," said Shakey.

"Not…"

"No, not one of those crazy two ladies you had a fling with," cut in Shakey quickly, to Kel's immense relief. "This girl was steady and smart. She pointed you out down the beach a ways and asked your name."

"And you told her?" Kel asked, his voice rising an octave or two.

"Of course I did. This ain't your America or your snooty England. She just want to know your name," replied Shakey.

"Hoo-wee," whooped Ken-eye, "I can see your kids playing on the beach already!"

"Thanks a lot," retorted Kel, "Sorry, Shakey, I had such a hard time with those other two."

He shuddered at the memory and confessed, "I don't know why I cock up my relationships with women, but I do." He continued on despite some shared private joke and laughter between his two friends. "If I like them, they take off. If they like me, I skidaddle. It's 'Murphy's Law', or something very much like it!"

"Relax man, this one is special," replied Shakey, and he patted Kel on the back. "You're going to fall in love with this one, I'd put money on it," and he nudged, and giggled along with Ken-eye.

"On that note, gentlemen," said Kel, picking up his beer and raising it, "If I settle down with this one, I promise to come and live here."

"You're on!" called Ken-eye, slapping his hand on the bar.

Kel then trudged back to his spot in the palms, amidst Ken-eye singing "da dit da daa, da dit da daa," to the tune of the wedding march, and Shakey's laughter.

Good company and lazy days, and now something else to think about. Who was this girl?

*   *   *   *

Kel had refused the offer of a joint because of an experience he had had the previous night, which he had explained away as being due to the dope. He was not a big smoker of ganja but occasionally indulged and enjoyed, especially with his two friends at the bar.

The night before he had been in that realm between thought and sleep, and a vision or hallucination had appeared, an audio-visual experience of such intensity that he wondered whether some substance other than ganja had made its way into his cerebrum.

As he lay on his bed, he had seen lightning over the sea, but no rain or thunder. Then there were visions of a giant mercurial ball dancing to and fro before his eyes, and the low melodic sounds of chanting, repeating the same syllables over and over—either that or the sound of a strange engine. It had gone on for some time, and when he came to his senses some hours later, he had the feeling of having been awake the whole time, that he had not slept at all. It had been a very intense experience.

A third voice rang out at the bar; someone had joined the boys but Kel took no notice; he was becoming, he had to admit, somewhat of a recluse. It had taken two months to slow his mind down after first landing on these shores. A western brain in search of the next hit, the next distraction, is a restless beast, and requires quiet time and introspection to be able to do very little without a sense of guilt, or a feeling of listlessness. He had adapted well to being more than a little bored, though the past two days had seen him being more acutely aware of a return to restlessness, and an eagerness to do something new. The alternative at this juncture in time, the prospect of having to return to a city and make a living, did not sit well with him, and the hermit and affable socialite jockied for position, as he sat, staring out to sea, pondering over his future.

Mid-life crisis, he thought, and then, good god, please, not yet!

Kel took a long draught on his beer, lit a cigarette, and for a moment was distracted by the light playing on the dark purple sea. After some time Kel's mesmerisation by his thoughts and the gentle surf was interrupted by a woman's voice.

He hadn't seen nor heard her, and she stood right next to him. He briefly glanced at her knees—nice legs, he thought.

Transport

"Excuse me, are you Kel?"

Kel looked up into the cool hazel eyes of a beautiful woman.

"Yes," he stammered and sat forward, his nervous system being propelled at speed out of its stillness.

"May I buy you a beer?" she said, "I have something I wish to speak to you about."

"Sure you may."

The girl turned, and made her way to Shakey's bar. 'Ching ching,' went the bugs against the dangling lights, 'da dit da dah,' went Ken-eye, and Shakey just laughed.

Kel guessed she was about thirty. She moved confidently, and when ordering the beer, made the mischievous duo laugh even louder. There is something deep inside of every man that knows when it—its attention, its being, whatever it is—is hooked by the interest of a beautiful woman. Kel was hooked.

Shapely under her modest shorts, she was on her way back, and Kel felt the stubble on his chin. Shakey was gesticulating behind her, signaling to him that he should close his gaping mouth.

She sat cross-legged in front of him and handed over the beer. She looked directly at him and was almost business-like, definitely serious. There was also a hint of something else in her gaze that caused a kind of physical meltdown in most of the cells of his body; those, that is, remotely near his conscious attention.

"We were not sure how to approach you, and decided directly was the best way," said the girl, while holding Kel's slightly mystified gaze.

"Sure," was all he could manage, then coming a little nearer to his senses, "What do you mean?"

"We need your help…Desperately!"

At that moment, as her plea bored its way into his memory bank, he would have taken on anything for her—a duel, a dive off a cliff, a dragon with fire and all. He was a gallant soul and women had always posed the ultimate mystery to him. "How can I help?"

"If I offered you the adventure of a lifetime, of the millennium, and a safe return, would you be interested?" Her look was deadly serious.

Kel said nothing, brow furrowed, lips pursed, suspicious of some monkey business—a practical joke.

"I come from the future, Kel, and we desperately need your help. We have a ship waiting and need to know your answer in under twelve hours." The girl kept his gaze still and steady, waiting for his response.

"Pull the other one!"

"What?" she asked.

"It's got bells on." Kel took a long swig of beer, looked over at the bar, and then around him, wondering who had put this pretty woman up to this mischief. "Pull the other one or beam me up, one of the two."

"If you look into this you will understand," she said, and handed over a small credit card sized disk.

Kel decided to go along with the game and was trying to place her accent. She spoke English as if it were her first language, but very slightly pronounced in the well rounded vowels of a Brazilian speaking English, and there was definitely Latin in her blood. These computations went on as Kel took the disk, which was as light as a feather, and wafer thin.

"Please look into this," she continued, and he stared into the translucent disk in his palm.

Something quite amazing happened. He found himself in a room, facing a man behind a table, seated in front of a backdrop of pitch dark cavernous night. Kel looked up to question this magic but could see nothing; he was locked into a hologram with the figure behind the table. Kel stood, and sat down quickly, unable to withdraw from the environment he found himself in. The figure opposite him waited for him to settle down and pay attention.

The man introduced himself, and there was something oddly familiar about him. "My name is Lyle," he said, "We need your help."

Kel sat there dumbfounded, yet aware that he was in a holographic environment. The man named Lyle was able to keep direct eye contact. His gestures were devoid of emotional overtones, and his language was concise.

"We are human beings living in a colony on another planet two hundred years into your future, and we face annihilation. Our survival is a possibility if you agree to help us. You are intimately involved in all of this, and for this reason we come to you and ask you to please help us. We can guarantee your safe return to Earth."

Kel slowly reached out and waved his hand in front of the man, but there was no response; this was obviously a recording.

After a brief pause Lyle continued, "This fledgling planet we call Gaya, is devoted to the pursuit of higher consciousness, and is a gem in the cosmos. We are all either descendents of, or from the planet Earth. An overwhelming force of our own making now threatens us, and I cannot explain at this time why you are so intimately involved in all this, but you are. If you agree to help us you will experience life way beyond the boundaries of your present age."

Kel sat totally still; unaware he was staring unblinkingly into his hand, and wondered what on earth he had to do with the future—just in case this was not a huge joke. Lyle's following statement snapped him to attention. "We also will pay into an account in your name, one million US dollars from a verifiable and legitimate source. This will serve as payment for the service you render us."

It never ceased to amaze Kel the effect money, or the promise of it, can have on the human psyche. Here was the single most profound experience of his life, and the mention of a million dollars sent his mind into a whirl of unforeseen possibilities. He was becoming more interested—the bait was attractive, and the hook adventurous. When the swirl of desire had subsided, he focussed his attention back on Lyle, who waited patiently before him, as if the disk could either gauge his thoughts, or measure the length of his attention span.

"We need to know of your decision within a limited time, and our contact will tell you exactly what that time frame is. We will visit you at your home later today to answer your questions. Thank you."

The images vanished, the tiny screen darkened and the disk disappeared, and Kel was left staring into his own hand.

When he looked up, the girl had gone.

Kel looked around, startled. He then got up, hurriedly collected his bottles, and made his way to Shakey's bar. He stood in front of his two friends beaming with a mixture confusion and elation, and felt somewhat foolish that he should even believe what had just happened.

"You guys are not going to believe this," he said.

"The one thing I don't understand," Shakey said, "is how you Englishmen manage to procreate when you're interested more in your own hand than a pretty woman."

∗   ∗   ∗   ∗

Kel could still hear Ken-eye's laughter halfway home to his bungalow. He had left quickly, deciding it was the better part of judgement not to share his present situation with his friends.

The moon was up, and its ghostly light skewered across the sea from the southeast, lighting his way. "I don't believe this, I don't believe this," he repeated to himself. He entered his modest lodging now quiet, and more than a little lonely in the pale moonlight. It had the dusty untidiness of a bachelor's digs, with clothes strewn around on the fading fabric of a chair and couch, and hanging from every available hook—and sand in every nook and cranny on the floor in both the bedroom and bathroom.

He looked at himself in the mirror under the dim light over the sink. "You slob," he said, fingering his stubbled chin.

After showering, shaving, and putting his last set of clean clothes on—shorts and a tee shirt—Kel bundled his clothes into a pile, and swept the room quickly. He then lit a candle, turned the light off, and sat cross-legged on the bed under the mosquito net. Here he waited in disbelief. It was impossible to quell the tornado zipping around his head. Whatever it was, he felt very alive. He tried to think who on earth could play such a practical joke on him; surely computers had not advanced so dramatically, though he had heard about the incredible advances that were being made in virtual reality.

Perhaps an hour had passed, and a light tap at the door aroused Kel from the doorway of slumber. He was now on his back, and his mouth felt dry and cloudy from the tobacco and beer.

"Come in," he called out hoarsely, sitting up, his heartbeat leaping a notch or two.

The door opened—it was the girl. A backdrop of pearly moonlight enshrouded her. Kel didn't move.

She slid out of her sandals and was quickly under the net, sitting opposite Kel, tailor fashion. Through the dim candlelight her calm eyes bored a hole through his to a region of chemical activity in his brain that now made his heart thump against his chest like a bullfrog's jowls in springtime. Outwardly, surprisingly enough to Kel, he remained relatively calm.

"Is this a joke or what?" he asked somewhat gruffly.

"No, it's for real," replied the girl.

"How do I know that?"

"For the fact that it's happening. If you agree to help us, you will find out soon enough."

"How long will I be away?"

"A matter of seconds." The girl paused, letting this sink in, and then added, "It will take just over a week, but you'll be back before midnight."

"Einstein in action. I've read the theory a few times, and finally I may—ah, never mind." Kel fell silent and looked down, searching for something to ask. "Am I really guaranteed a safe return?"

"By the laws of physics, yes," replied the girl confidently.

"What's your name?"

"Lua, my name is Lua."

"My life is a shambles Lua. I have no direction, no purpose, and no particular place to go. Now a beautiful woman like you comes along and offers me a cosmic adventure, a million bucks, and a safe return. It really is too much." Kel laughed nervously, and looked aloft for guidance.

"This is a chance in a million lifetimes, Kel, of learning about the very deepest side of yourself, your humanity, and the very spirit of your being. If you miss this, you will regret it for the rest of your life. We believe that you are adequately qualified for the challenges ahead of you, otherwise we would not have made contact."

"Hmm," said Kel.

"True adventure does not come without the need for courage and real humility, and it is through these that we learn."

"Wise words," said Kel, still a little perturbed at his desire to surrender so rapidly. "You have an innocence and directness about you, Lua, that has….I cannot explain it but I've known you for five minutes and already I am ready to follow you blindly into a furnace if need be, and somehow that bothers me. Do you get my drift?"

"Do I get your what?" Lua asked.

"Never mind, I just don't understand the intensity of my feelings for you in such a short space of time. If you guys can put people in disks you can probably play around with brain chemistry too," said Kel, surprised at his own candour.

"Listen Kel, we are not manipulating anything. I am feeling the same about you, and I assure you it is a very new feeling for me, but it must not be allowed to get in the way of this mission. Your feet are not going to touch the ground for some time if you accept. Our relationship will be only a small fraction of this mission, and you must accept that."

Kel stared into Lua's eyes for some moments, and she kept his gaze, still and steady. They were like a siren, enticing him in.

"So what is this mission?" Kel asked.

"To talk someone out of destroying our planet."

Kel stared vacantly at Lua. "Why me?" he asked at last.

"This person is intimately connected to you, and I cannot at this point say more than that. We quite simply, desperately, need your help," said Lua, with for the first time a plea in her voice, and this struck a chord in Kel's heart.

"Look, I once tried to stop a fight in a London pub between a man and a woman, with absolutely disastrous results." Kel grimaced at the memory. "What the hell can I do?"

"We have just made the most incredible journey across space and time to find you. Please understand you are possibly our only hope," and Lua threw her hands apart in an appeal to Kel, her eyes soft and child-like in the sparse light.

"Is this my great, great, great grandchild or something, gone berserk in a science lab?"

Lua suddenly sucked in her breath, surprised. "Yes," she said, "something like that, but not quite as you think. But yes—something like that."

"All right, I have about ten hours to decide, right?"

"Yes," replied Lua. "And please understand that this is about you in the future. It will give you an opportunity now to know yourself at the very deepest level, positive and negative. It's a unique opportunity, believe me, to get such a chance in a lifetime."

Kel sat under his mosquito net, chin resting on open hand, elbow on his knee, and he glanced around at the dreary untidiness of the room, considering his options. In a month he would be back in one mad city or another, having to work for his next escape route or, heaven forbid, stay on the island and compete with Ken-eye for a free beer.

Lua kept her eyes down. The sound of the sea could be heard faintly in the distance, and the bugs maintained their chants, oblivious to the whirlwind swirling in Kel's head. A dog barked in the distance and lifted him out of his contemplation.

"Ah, I don't know!" said Kel at last, "I am so bored with my own repetitive, numbskull thinking, I actually yearn for a bit of adventure, something different. But what's this about some negative stuff with me in the future? Sounds like a kind of a shadowy, dark side of my personality."

"We all have it, this dark side, believe me. You have an amazing opportunity to know yours."

Kel thought for a moment and asked, "Just give me an idea of what I have to face."

"Yourself," said Lua.

"What do you mean?"

"The only obstacle in the way of you achieving this mission is yourself. Our task is to help you get to know this self of yours sufficiently enough to ensure success."

"To succeed at what?" Now Kel threw his hands out to the sides.

"As I said, to talk someone out of destroying our planet." Lua waited a second before continuing. "You will be prepared for any situation you're likely to meet. And listen, Kel, I can only say this—during your actual mission it will all be on the level of consciousness, your body will not be in harm's way at all."

"Jesus," said Kel grimacing, and covering his face with his hands.

Lua stayed quiet and looked on, as Kel battled with his decision. Somehow a favourable chord had been struck. His body would not be threatened—out of harm's way! And if they really have come this far they must know what they're talking about.

"Is it a planet like ours?" Kel asked.

"Yes, it's a pearl, just like yours."

"And the people, they are just like you and me?"

"Yes, the people are just like you and me," Lua repeated. "They are from, or descendents of humans from Earth."

More silence, as Kel stared blankly ahead of him, thinking. "I need to go for a little walk, and think about this. Would you mind...?"

"No, no," cried Lua, "not at all. We have ten hours of our time line left, and you have to be sure, please take your time. My job is not to pressure you too much, but to inform you of your options. This is such an important decision for you. I am sorry Kel, but I have involved something else in this. I want you to go because I want to get to know you better—an added ingredient to your decision making which shouldn't be there; it's certainly not in my brief. It's personal and very unusual for me, a risk I have never taken before. I am sorry."

Lua looked down and appeared abandoned, and a fierce feeling of protection surged in Kel. Her vulnerability had struck another chord in him, an ancient one.

"I need to get out for a bit, go for a walk, and think about it," he said again, lifting up the net and clambering out.

"Please do. I will stay here if that's okay with you. If you get back after,"—and Lua looked at her watch—"nine hours and fifty minutes, I will be gone and wish you well."

"I'll be back before that. See you in a while."

　　　　　*　　　　　*　　　　　*　　　　　*

Kel sprang into a light jog once out of his gate and made for the beach. This part of the island stuck out like a finger, and he ran over a knuckle of a hillock on his way down to the shore. Coconut palms and banana plants lined the dusty road, and an occasional mango tree stood majestic and unmovable like pillars, and he jogged on. His mind raced with expectation and doubts, all laced with the luscious bouquet of Lua's presence. It was too good to be true, it was a huge joke, he was dreaming. He stopped and pinched himself; he certainly wasn't dreaming. On he ran, this time at a gallop, and the wind zipped past his ears with an eerie whistle. The old game was over; something new graced the horizon.

Within minutes he was at Shakey's bar. Two more guests now lounged in the rickety wooden chairs in the sand, sipping their drinks and viewing the stars.

"That you Kel?"

"Yes, Ken-eye, it's me," said Kel breathing heavily. "Give me a beer will you Shakey, and one for Ken-eye, and you too, and put it on my tab, I forgot my wallet."

This last statement made him giggle for some reason, and it took a few moments before he composed himself.

"You sound happy—did you find the girl?" Ken-eye asked.

"Yes, she's at home sitting on the bed." And he laughed again, and had to put his beer down for fear of spilling it. He bent over double, holding his abdomen, silently sniggering into his hands.

"You prefer a pint with the boys rather than stay with such a beautiful woman," said Shakey, leaning over the bar and looking at Kel's doubled up torso. "Let me show you how it's done Kel man—a little bit of charm, and a lot of loving."

"Hold on, Shakey," said Ken-eye, "Something going on here, something new. What's up Kel?"

"If a beautiful woman offered you the adventure of a lifetime," said Kel, composing himself, "something unbelievable, way beyond your wildest dreams, something that would pay your way for the rest of your life, what would you do?"

"Go man, go!" said Ken-eye. "Remember that saying, Walter Scott or somebody, 'Give me one glorious hour, rather than an age without a name!' Sounds like you need that right now, go! Otherwise you just going to be paying the rent and the bills in some far off crazy city in a month or two."

"You hit the nail on the head, Ken-eye, that's perfect," Kel perched himself on the stool opposite Ken-eye, and stared at his beer.

"Let me know if you need my help," said Shakey, grinning from ear to ear as he walked around the bar, and made his way over to two girls lounging in the balmy heat of the evening, nursing their drinks.

"Just do it!" said Ken-eye, with a smack of urgency in his voice.

"Apparently, what I have to face is myself. Whatever that is."

"Yourself?"

"Yes, that is apparently the only thing in the way of this…of this 'mission', as she called it."

"The who, how, and why we are? You mean, your Self? Now that's an opportunity that doesn't come along in too many lifetimes. There is something special about this woman, Kel, something real special. When she was up here next to me before, there was an energy coming out of her, matched in its goodness only by its intensity. It is rare to feel such power in another outside of certain…how can I say?—Certain spiritual practices. You can trust her!"

"She said something about some negative stuff being out there. Do you reckon I'm a match for that?" Kel asked.

"There is some dark stuff out there, but you're gentleman enough for the job. You have enough concern for others not to be so afraid of yourself." Ken-eye stuck out his hand and found Kel's, and squeezed it. "Tell me what's going on," he went on, "there is something big going on. I feel it in my bones."

"If I told you, you wouldn't believe me, and that's an understatement. It seems like someone has challenged me to some kind of cosmic adventure. I mean I could be going mad—this sounds so crazy. So you think she's something special?"

"Yes, Kel, she is something special. If she is the challenger, then you should do what she asks, why not? You told me earlier that you have to go and work in the crazy world, rejoin that rat race out there. I know that's not your heart's desire. Take this on, see what happens."

"What do you think is going on, my old friend?" Kel clinked his beer bottle against Ken-eye's.

"A chance to redeem yourself," said Ken-eye, sitting up straight on his barstool and looking reverently down at Kel.

Kel took a swig of his beer and shifted off of the barstool. "Yeah, you are right; nothing else going on. Maybe I'll just face into this dragon, whatever it is!"

"One minute," said Ken-eye, fishing under his tee shirt and removing a leather thong with a bead on it from around his neck. "Take this on your trip for luck. It has power, this bead, a lot of power."

Kel lowered his head, and Ken-eye tied the bead around his neck. "With my blessings and good luck. Something big going on, I can feel it in my bones, hoo-wee!"

Kel laughed, and cupped Ken-eye's face in his hands and kissed him on the forehead. "Thank you Ken-eye, see you later."

Ken-eye took hold of Kel's hand as he made to leave. "You are going to do what she asks, aren't you? The spirits are all hollering at me in my head. They say you must do it, but there is a warning!"

"What?" Kel asked.

"If you can't swim, don't jump in the water."

Kel laughed and squeezed Ken-eye's hand. He took his leave as his friend sat there with his right hand raised to shoulder height. It was a blessing for Kel, who then bolted off down to the shoreline, shouting a farewell to Shakey. The two girls looked up and over, but Shakey merely raised his hand lazily, and continued his dialogue, demonstrating to Kel the level of commitment needed when a man is serious about charming the fairer sex.

He walked along the beach talking to himself, weighing up the pros and cons. The money, his feelings for Lua, a bribe? A trap? A practical joke on this crazy island? Suddenly he stopped and looked at the moon, and all thoughts left him. "Go!" said the voice in his head, and in that moment of recognition, he made his decision to go. He looked up towards his bungalow on the hill, and set off for it with grim determination, taking the tiny path that skirted Tattoo Jack's wooden house.

Inevitably Bruno was waiting for him, and charged, growling, with teeth bared. On this occasion he looked more than serious, and Kel reacted in a most uncharacteristic manner. Instead of going into defense mode, he bowed from the waist and turned the backs of both hands towards Bruno as if in surrender. He then said in the friendliest of voices, as if talking to a baby, "whassamatter with you den?"

The effect on Bruno was immediate and dramatic. His hind quarters quivered and melted into the sand, his tail wagged uncontrollably, and his look transformed into one of total subservience. Kel was visibly shocked, even more so when Bruno turned over in the sand, inviting him to scratch his stomach.

It wasn't a trap, Bruno had surrendered, and Kel left the scene a humbled man. Never would he have guessed that a little bit of love could have had such an effect on Bruno's raging territorialism. Something different going on tonight, he thought, and strode on and up.

*   *   *   *

He arrived back at the bungalow hoping upon hope that Lua was still there. He entered and saw her still figure sitting under the net; she hadn't moved. Within seconds he was sitting opposite her. She opened her eyes and looked into his, saying nothing.

While the whirlwinds unfurled in his head he heard himself say, "When do we leave?"

"Right now if you are sure," said Lua.

"I am sure."

Lua let out a great sigh of relief and grabbed Kel's hand, kissed it, and was out of the bed in an instant. She moved like a cat, quick and lithe. Kel scrambled out after her, and looked around the room. Lua motioned to the door, and he realised he would need nothing on this trip—no wallet, watch, or keys. He picked up his cigarettes and waved the box in front of her.

She shook her head and said, "Sorry, it's a non smoker."

"Then one last cigarette, it's a custom," and he quickly lit up.

"Phew!" said Lua, and Kel stepped quickly out on to the porch, filling his lungs with the gusto of a condemned man smoking his last cigarette, each drag adding to the mad dance of thoughts in his mind, now like a polka. He paced up and down and heard Lua speaking inside; hers was the only voice he heard.

He flicked the butt into the sand and returned inside. Lua finished talking into another disk, slipped it into a pocket and nodded her head. They were ready to leave. She led him out of the door, which he slammed decisively shut behind him, and followed her down a narrow path leading to a small clearing behind his little bungalow. His heart thumped like it had never thumped before.

There was still a faint suspicion in the back of his mind that this was an enormous hoax. He would know soon enough.

She ducked and weaved through the terrain in front of him as these thoughts, and more, raced through his mind. Lua, a stranger to this island, already moved with the agility of a native, whereas it had taken him weeks to achieve such confidence in the thick and luxuriant bush of the Caribbean. They arrived at the clearing, and Lua dug into her pocket.

Kel looked aloft and saw nothing but the stars, and a few scattered, fluffy clouds in the moonlight. Lua fingered a small console in her palm, and two circular metallic dishes appeared on the ground before him. All suspicions evaporated at that moment. This was for real.

"I want you to step onto the dish, Kel, and then stand and relax as if waiting in line. In a few seconds you will feel a vibration in your feet.

You must not move after you feel this vibration. If you did it would be like turning the wheel of a car travelling at two hundred miles an hour violently to one side. Do you understand?"

"I get your point," Kel answered, suddenly once again a little perturbed that there was not one ounce of resistance in him to what was happening—so quickly, so easily—as if he had just volunteered to pick up somebody from the station. His body pumped out streams of adrenaline, and yet it did not matter. He was an observer looking in at the blood rushing round his system at Formula One speed, and he remained cool and calm in the face of the crazy events transpiring around him. 'We are not manipulating anything', he reminded himself of Lua's words, but it was all too easy.

Kel stepped on to the dish and looked at her, and she laughed at the helpless expression on his face.

"This is for real, I assure you. You will enjoy the ride," she said.

Kel stood motionless, aware of the light of the moon as it bathed the lush foliage in the still night. He heard the chirping of insects, and the hum and buzz of nature seemed to synchronise with the thumping of his heart, until it all became the same massive vibration of life. Then he felt the countdown from his feet up, five, four, three, two, one—and the roller coaster ride began.

He looked up and saw a shaft of iridescent light funneling away from him, and up he went. The moment gravity ceased to have a hold on Kel he left it in a flash, and the whoosh he heard was the sound of air rushing past his ears. Looking down he saw the land and the sea, and then the whole island with its twinkling lights, recede beneath him.

The force field started to gain speed, and Kel surrendered to the excitement of the ride. Looking up he saw clouds approaching rapidly, and suddenly he passed through some kind of barrier. He heard himself hooting with joy as iridescent blue and pink clouds passed him at uncontrollable speed as he ascended from his planet, encircled and surrounded by an energy field that held him safe and intact. He was on the nose cone of a rocket and now in a different dimension, and knew that no harm could come to him. This was the stuff of pure physical exhilaration, and Kel was on his way, on his way to the stars.

*   *   *   *

As sudden as the rush of the ride had begun, so was the arrival. Kel landed in a large tank of liquid that appeared to be water. He fought his way quickly to the surface and was greeted by Lua, who was also in the tank. "Welcome to quarantine," she said with a devilish smile.

"Bloody heck, shouldn't you have warned me about the wet landing?"

"We wanted your first transport to be an unanticipated joy. We know you are a good swimmer. And pull the other one, it's got bells on!" Lua laughed in delight.

"When can I do that again?" Kel asked.

"That's kid's stuff compared to where you're going. Wait until you hit hyperspace!"

"Hyper…?"

Two men approached from a ramp around the tank, and greeted Kel with a smile. They were dressed in navy blue jump suits and worked quickly and efficiently shutting down valves, fingering wrist consoles, and verbalising instructions into an unseen computer.

She led him to a dressing room, and he changed into a light cotton tracksuit and thonged sandals. Somehow he was dry already, and looked at himself in a mirror and stopped suddenly, shocked at his own presence in such circumstances, and let go a slow stream of air through pursed lips. Keep cool, he signaled to himself, and took two deep breaths, keeping eye contact with his mirrored image. He braced himself for whatever was to come, and on leaving the dressing room noticed the tank had gone, mysteriously swallowed up by the metallic walls of the ship. Lua, dressed in a navy blue jump suit, turned at his approach and was off at a pace. Kel followed her through a series of submarine like companionways, his sandals slapping dully against a light and hard metallic alloy.

"What's the metal?" asked Kel.

"Trillium" answered Lua.

"I thought that was a plant, a flower!"

"No, we need a little bit more than plant fiber to sustain us through the ravages of space-time, but we'll work on it, thanks," said Lua, and they both laughed aloud. Kel blushed and smacked his forehead.

"Tri-illium, known as Trillium, is an alloy—the stuff of magic—a combination of metals that can meld and divide under certain conditions. It's able to de-materialise, and materialise, holding intact all within it. All, that is, except certain metals." Lua turned and shot Kel a warm smile.

They walked on a ways and Kel felt a lightness of being, as if he were floating. Although his feet touched the floor, he hardly felt it.

"Are we in space?" he ventured, interpreting the smile as a green light to open the floodgate of questions for first time space travelers.

"Yes," replied Lua,

"Shouldn't I be floating?"

"There are forces whizzing around you at the moment way beyond your wildest dreams. On-board gravity we can deal with."

A circular door slid open in front of them, and it somehow reminded Kel of an epiglottis, or one of those tubes that as a child, he would look through, and light and coloured glass would produce magic patterns as he rotated the tube. A kaleidoscope, he remembered. The door made a hushed, whooshing noise as it opened.

"Kel, this is the clinic. We have to prepare you for the journey, and ensure that you leave here what does not belong out there," and Lua pointed a finger aloft. They stepped through into a white paneled room and were greeted by a young Asian woman, possibly Indian, wearing the same kind of blue overalls, with a white cross on each shoulder.

"Hello, my name is Daljit and I'm the ship's medical officer," she said calmly, as if meeting a prehistoric earthling was an everyday occurrence. She proffered her hand and shook Kel's. She was milk coffee brown and beautiful. "We have," she went on, "already screened you for major illnesses and you are," she paused a moment, eyes darting aloft in search of the right words, "for your age, in your epoch…um…quite fit, and free of any major troubles. Am I correct in assuming this?" She shot Kel a warm saucy smile.

Kel smiled back and his eyes narrowed a little. "Yes," he said, "nothing major, as far as I know."

"Good," the doctor continued, "we need to scan you for any minor problems you might have, and also rid your body of any metal that might have woven its way in, or organisms that do not belong out there. And," she said more seriously, "you appear to have a fossilised thyroid."

"Just a good-luck bead," said Kel exposing Ken-eye's good luck charm around his neck.

"As long as it's organic, it's okay," said Daljit, holding out her hand for the bead.

"What about all these fillings," and Kel opened his mouth, pointing at his molars.

"My goodness!" said Daljit, taking the bead from Kel.

"Those are a testament," protested Kel, "to the fact that some National Health dentists in my country of origin made their money from the number of fillings they were able to put in your teeth."

"They have to go; otherwise, when we make the jump to hyperspace, you would be with us, and your teeth some billions of miles behind. But don't worry, we can remove them and reconstruct your teeth very much to your liking…and you will not feel a thing," finished Daljit, anticipating Kel's next question.

Lua eyed him from behind Daljit, watching his every expression like a hawk.

Daljit motioned him to a reclining chair. "First we need to look into your mouth."

"Dental appointment?"

"Like none you have ever known," replied Daljit.

Kel sat down, leant back, swallowed hard, and dutifully opened his mouth. The two women peered in.

"Well if I were prospecting for semi precious or heavy metals, I would have a field day in there," said Daljit. The two women glanced at each other, and laughed freely and openly in front of his reclined body.

"Sugar," said Kel. "Don't tell me there's no sugar where we're going?"

"None refined, no alcohol or tobacco either. But plenty of coffee," and the two laughed again.

Kel groaned, "sounds like a Zen monastery."

The doctor punched in some instructions into a console attached to her wrist, and a small machine slowly lowered from a panel in the ceiling.

"This will take about fifteen minutes," said Daljit. "You will feel no pain, and if there is discomfort, please raise your arm."

Kel eased his head back onto the headrest, and opened his mouth. A proboscis-like attachment extended from the machine and entered his mouth, and his jaw automatically relaxed around it. He felt nothing but the gentle vacuuming of his saliva and the debris of a sugar-filled childhood. As the machine did its job, Daljit sidled up to him, "The benefits of re-constructive surgery and computer technology—a happy marriage."

After perhaps the shortest and most pain-free dental appointment he could recall, the machine withdrew. The two women approached Kel, and stood in front of him. "Open up," said Daljit.

Kel bared his teeth in an uneasy grin, and the two women smiled, like a couple of young doting aunts. He was handed a mirror, and he stared at a set of straight, white teeth. He rasped his tongue over his new teeth.

"Jesus!" he said, "Are these real?"

"Of course they are," replied Daljit, "and they are yours now."

"Next, we need to run you through a machine we call Chiron," continued Daljit, pressing more buttons on her console. "Just relax into it," and the chair reclined to a full supine position, "and give me the mirror!"

Suddenly, Kel's midriff was surrounded by an infra red ring like a magician's hoop, and he felt as if he were floating in space. The machine made a faint, high frequency buzzing sound.

"Would you like to hear Chiron's analysis, and the degree of correction activated?" asked Daljit.

"Yes I would. What kind of correction?"

"More or less the same thing we did with the teeth."

Kel lay back, ears pricked, body utterly relaxed and surrendered.

After a few seconds he noticed that the infra red ring had split in two, like a sliced bagel. One ring started to move caudal, and the other towards his head. He felt nothing.

Chiron's reassuring voice began, "Trace metallic elements in central nervous system…eliminated. Lumbar vertebral disc…narrowing. L3 to S1…reinforced. Benign organisms in reproductive tubules," Kel raised his head slightly, "….Eliminated." Liver potential," Kel's head cocked up again, "…at eighty three per cent…Ten per cent revived. Corneal curvature…re-aligned. Blood cleansing in process, multiple foreign chemical compounds." The machine's sensors scanned up and down Kel's body, blasting minor fat pockets out of arteries, tar from lung tissue, bolstering cartilage here and there, and breaking down a myriad of adhesions. Kel, as if hypnotised, lay there totally still, and in awe.

There was silence, the infra red hoops disappeared, and the chair slowly returned to upright. The doctor handed Kel a small console, on its screen some script in very fine print, and he suddenly realised he had forgotten his reading glasses.

"Read this," she said.

Kel let out a little gasp of surprise as his eyes quickly read through the words in tiny print with consummate ease: 'You are now in A-1 condition. Dietary needs will be met, and a short daily stretch and strengthening exercise program encouraged'.

He got up, stretched and faced the ladies in front of him, and he roared and punched his fist in the air. "I feel good, I feel so damn good!" He twisted his body this way and that, looking for those niggling areas of chronic pain he had long ago surrendered to. They were gone. He felt supreme, and hopped from one leg to the other, and jumped and spun around. It was only when he thought the two were probably beginning to question his sanity that he stopped his gyrating dance, and stood there laughing as if the problems of the planet had been lifted from his shoulders. "To boldly go into the unknown, to undreamed of destinations...I can't believe it, with a ninety plus per cent liver, and a new set of teeth. I am ready for anything! When do we leave?"

"We left seconds after you came on board," said Lua.

This brought Kel down to earth for a couple of seconds, but it could not hold him there.

"I have never felt like this; it's so fresh, so clean, I am just not feeling myself. My body feels as light as a feather, and as strong as an ox. Can I have a look out of the window, porthole, whatever? I want to see my planet."

Daljit approached and faced him, prodding a finger gently into his chest. "Yes, that is next. If you are unable to carry out the exercise regime regularly, at least do the abdominal exercises and the hamstring stretches, they'll protect and free up your centre of gravity, right in here," and she pointed to the middle of Kel's pelvis. "All movement originates there; please remember that, if nothing else, from our consult. The exercises will be posted in your room, and they'll only take up three minutes of your time each day."

"Some things haven't changed," said Kel, "the doctor's last word!"

She took Kel's hand. "It's been such a pleasure meeting you, and please call in if you need anything at all."

"Thank you, doctor," said Kel.

Daljit shifted somewhat uneasily on her feet, and looked down. "Please call me Daljit."

Kel noticed her discomfort and briefly wondered why. Perhaps the formal title of doctor had gone out of vogue in this future world. "Thank you Daljit, I'm a new man."

Kel bounced out of the clinic, thongs lightly flapping against the alloy walkway, in hot pursuit of the ever-growing beauty of Lua. His body awareness appeared to have trebled, and he felt ready for anything. His little island, and the planet Earth, already seemed like a long way away. "Where are we going?" he asked.

"To the Briefing Chamber and a look out of the window! I'll set you up there, and then I have to go to a short de-briefing."

Another circular door whooshed open, and Kel stepped into a room that was perfectly spherical in shape. In the middle, hanging from infra red beams from the upper hemisphere, was a hammock-like reclining chair. There was a walkway from the door to the chair that was also suspended in mid-air. He looked over the side, looking for mechanical clues for how this was possible, but found none.

Kel stepped gingerly onto the walkway and followed Lua. "This will be your classroom for the next three days," said Lua. "Please lay in the seat, your head up this way."

He lay in the seat and had no physical sensation of the chair beneath him.

"I am going to give you an idea of where you are. In ten seconds you will be oriented to the space around us. Now lay back and relax," said Lua.

A million stars surrounded Kel's immediate environment. He was floating in space. "Good god!" he gasped, looking around him, his vision filled with the celestial light of the cosmos, tunneling its way through the vacuum of space, so black, so dark. The light didn't twinkle like it did on Earth, but seemed so close somehow, as if the light of the stars was all the same light, and space his vacuous imagination. His attention was drawn to the brightest object in his view—a star that appeared much larger than all the others.

"That's your sun. Your Earth is a little to the right of it, just the tiniest of lights now."

"Oh, Lua," said Kel, marveling at the scene before him. As he looked around, he realised he could move his body, and maneuver it through space.

Lua anticipated this. "Turn your body very slowly, Kel, and initiate the movement from the centre of your pelvis. Remember, that's your centre of gravity."

Kel did as he was told and the cosmos moved around him. He was free-floating in space, and could turn his body at will, going feet or head first in the direction he sensed they were headed. He spun like a dolphin, freestyle in space,

"Is this hyperspace?" he asked.

"Not yet, we have to make a jump—what we call a tachyon jump, and to do that and travel into the future we need to get away from the pull of your solar system. You'll most certainly know when it happens. Just get used to the machine you are in—no sudden movements. Start slow and go steady."

"So how do you jump to hyperspace?"

Lua thought for a minute. "We create something we call negative energy—exotic energy, if you like—and open up a wormhole through the curvature of space. We then enter a parallel universe, a realm of, let's say, anti-matter, and that's the jump. We set a course, de-materialise as we penetrate the wormhole, sling shoot ourselves around massive bodies of anti matter, and slip out the other end at a point where a homing beacon is set up. The beacon is a terminal, vital to this kind of travel. Every single brain and computer on this ship is working and concentrating on space, time, and gravity calculations. All, except Daljit and myself, we have to keep you in one piece."

"Sounds like a cosmic pin ball machine—very interesting." Kel spun around the axis of his pelvis, and the cosmos spun around him. Three hundred and sixty degrees in every direction the sky was full of stars and their eerie light, lightening the dark. "Oh boy, this is awesome." He spun again. "What's the beacon?"

"Later, Kel. Just get used to free floating; concentrate and relax. We will have time later for any questions."

Lua stayed with him until she was sure he had the hang of it. To curtail the environment he merely had to say 'stop'. To start it, 'go'. It was idiot-proof. She clipped a monitor around his earlobe and attached a pad to his temple, excused herself, and left the room with a final caution to go slow.

"I got it," he said, "see you in a while."

*   *   *   *

Lua sat opposite the captain; "This is more than we had hoped for, Lua. It's incredible the speed at which he accepted the mission."

"Yes," replied Lua, "and I am duty bound to tell you that he is more than a little emotionally involved with me, and I have to admit that something has happened to me that I do not fully comprehend. I feel raw, vulnerable, and fiercely protective of him. There is an emotional neediness in him that has hit a place in me, and everything is different somehow. I could describe it as excitement, with no limit on the potential. It's all very new to me."

"I know you have the importance of this mission as your top priority, and that is tantamount to me. Just remember that this is one human being we need in tip-top mental condition, and you know that inflated emotions can play havoc with the intellectual ability of someone from his era. You've trained long and hard for this, and so far you've exceeded all expectations. We are ten hours ahead of schedule."

"Thank you," replied Lua, "I am self monitoring, and my dyad is Daljit, so not to worry. The success of the mission is, of course, my main priority, and I am…"

Lua was cut short by an overhead announcement and an alarm. "Kel's heart rate exceeding maximum potential, red alert…red alert."

Before the captain had even stood, Lua was out of the door, and winging her way through the companionway. She moved at exceptional speed, her movements precisely focussed. Leaping through the briefing chamber hatch she found Daljit kneeling beside Kel with one monitor on his heart, another on his temple. Her expression indicated that he was no longer in any kind of danger.

"What in heaven's name?" Lua gasped.

"Do you remember during our orientation for the Mission, that footage on sporting fads of the era?" said Daljit, calmly, "of the ice skaters, and the incredible spins they did?"

"Yes, the pirouettes," said Lua, kneeling on the other side of the recliner, and looking at Kel's grimaced expression and green pallor.

"Well, our friend here managed to get himself into one of those. Couldn't even say stop—now that's a first. All he could say, when I managed to reel him in from the spin he was in was: 'Bloody hell!'" said Daljit with a chuckle. "He'll be back to normal in seven minutes."

Lua placed the palm of her hand on Kel's brow. It was wet and clammy, and she shrugged her shoulders, mirrored his grimace, and managed a smile.

"This kind of thing happens to me a lot, I am a bit…" Kel stammered, looking for the right word.

"Impetuous," said Lua.

"I thought I said 'stop,' I honestly did, but I suppose I was on too fast of a spin," protested Kel, and the two women glanced quickly at each other.

"Behave," said Daljit as she stood to leave. "I better give you this back. You obviously shouldn't be without your good luck charm."

Kel took Ken-eye's bead and secured it around his neck.

"We have to start the Brief in thirty minutes, so please arrange for soup and snacks to be delivered to Kel's quarters for us both," said Lua to Daljit as she left.

"Kel, you are quite a character," Lua stroked his brow. "Just promise me you'll take it easy and follow instructions from now on; otherwise, we will have to monitor you audio-visually for the whole flight, and that is an invasion we wish to avoid. You have to err on the side of caution. Please promise me."

"I promise," said Kel, now much recovered from his little spin in the stars, and feeling more than a little stupid for the commotion he'd caused.

"We very nearly lost you to the stars," said Lua, and then uttered in a hushed voice what seemed like an oath, two words he couldn't understand. It sounded to him like 'poosha veeda'.

He looked up at her curious.

"Portuguese," she said. "Same as your 'bloody this, bloody that'."

He had been on board for less than two hours, less than four from first contact. Kel swung his legs over and sat in the hammock, leaned forward to stand, and on the way up fainted dead away.

THE BRIEF

Kel's eyes met with Lua's just before they started their meal. Each hung on to the gaze of the other for a second longer, and the adrenaline rush pulsed and subsided. He looked around his quarters, which had been modeled on designs from his era in order to give him a sense of familiarity with his environment. Earlier he had been surprised to see a primitive flush toilet, and touched by the sight of a toothbrush and toothpaste laid out for him by the sink. He was glad for this consideration and felt at home.

They dined on vegetable soup and a fragrant, crispy bread. Sifting through his soup, Kel wondered how the hell broccoli could exist in the curvature of space-time. They ate in peace, occasionally catching each other's eye.

Kel sipped his coffee and was dying for a cigarette, but this was definitely a non-smoking flight, so he banished the desire to the outer reaches of his consciousness, and soon forgot about his addiction in the great ease of Lua's company. They chatted about their respective planets, and their families. Lua, like Kel, was single, and the magic spell of infatuation wove itself around them as the craft sailed through the cosmic night. He felt like a teenager in love for the first time.

"I came to Gaya when I was twelve, with my mother. My father wasn't interested so we left him and my brother back on Earth, in Brazil. When I was eighteen I had a choice to stay or return to Earth, and I chose to stay." Lua filled her coffee cup, her third, Kel noticed.

"Did you miss your father and brother?"

"Not personally," answered Lua, and Kel thought the reply rather odd, but said nothing.

"My relationships with men have always been based solely on friendship, nothing more," and she shot him a glance, betraying a flash of both shyness and vulnerability.

"So what about you, Kel, you're single now but have you ever been married?" Lua folded her legs under her as she perched herself on the seat opposite him.

"Yes, for about two weeks, though it dragged on for a couple of years. I was twenty two and it was a bloody disaster." He grimaced at some distant memory.

Lua laughed, but said nothing.

"So why did you come in my era, why not some other?" Kel asked.

"We cannot go back to a point if there is no beacon, that is, a point of entry. And you see, they are developing some matter at two research facilities on your planet, which acted as a beacon for us, so we zoomed in on it. This material, let's call it exotic, didn't exist before your birth. Having a beacon is the only way you can travel in time, and your era is the first where it's available. Had it been developed sooner, your planet would probably have been overrun by time travelling tourists…spectators at the Battle of Waterloo!"

"Is this the first time for you to come back this far in time?"

"Yes, it was a pioneering flight," and Lua sighed in relief.

"So there must have been an element of danger?"

"Yes, as we arrived back in time we could have exploded, as there were no pre-set beacons in place. It would have been like colliding with ourselves on re-entry…difficult to explain in layman's terms."

"Have you traveled in time before?"

"Yes, but it's very rare. We only travel in time if we have to, like with this mission, to come and get you."

"Why me? Why not some other involved party in the future?"

"Because that matter we used as a beacon is more readily available in the future, and could be used more easily as a target by the character that's causing all of our problems, and Kel, I cannot say more than that. It is not part of my mission brief and orders are very strict on that."

"So you can't tell me what this beacon is made of?"

"No, not yet. As far as I am concerned it makes no difference, but orders are orders." Lua was resolute.

"So what if I had been a kid, or in a pram, what would you have done in that kind of scenario?"

"We would've had to jump to an appropriate time line. You don't know how lucky we are to catch you at the perfect time. You are in good physical shape and have a maturity about you, some wisdom under your belt." Lua grimaced at this last remark.

"So what is my Brief? What is its ultimate purpose?" Kel lounged back in his chair, tipping it slightly backwards on its struts.

"It is a programmed environment using sensory and gravity deprivation, brain wave frequencies, and subliminal suggestion to open your awareness up to theories and possibilities as yet unknown, and unfamiliar, to you. Parts of the brain will be shut down to allow a greater awareness."

"Which parts?"

"The parts that orient you to time and space," said Lua. "Ultimately, the programme's designed to help you understand the society you've chosen to help, and give you insight into the nature of your own consciousness."

"What do I have to do?"

"Absolutely nothing, just relax into it."

"Now that," proclaimed Kel, "is what I call real learning, right up my alley."

"You'll have your work cut out for you, believe me. Anyway, in your twenty-first century there is an age of enlightenment, which follows a period of um…ecological and economic hardship. After all that terrorist activity that plagued your time, and the military backlash that followed, we entered a new era, something very different in the nature of human affairs." Lua looked at her wrist console quickly, "this programme will propel you through its evolution rapidly."

"Humanity made it," said Kel, with a sigh.

"A lot of the data in the Brief will be familiar to you. We are feeding you information that you'll need on your mission; some of it you'll get on a conscious level, some at a subconscious level. Come on, Kel, we have to go," and Lua drained her coffee in one gulp.

They talked on as they threaded their way through the ship to the Chamber. "You will also experience altered states of consciousness, but don't worry, they are all reversible."

Kel frowned, "You mean like an acid trip?"

Lua giggled and said under her breath, "Acid trip? You mean…."

"Like LSD, yes."

"Maybe yes, but don't worry, you are in no danger." Lua ignored Kel's concern; some years previously he had spent eight hours going through some hell realm in his head. 'The jaws of hell', he had called it. It was his first and only experience with LSD.

"What's the purpose of this kind of training?" Kel asked

"To cleanse and balance your consciousness, and help you understand more about yourself and your evolution at the macro and micro levels. This will give you an immense amount of strength on your mission. You see, consciousness is like a screen on which life is played out. It can take the form of anything, from the tiniest to the infinite, so not only is it the screen, but it's also the play itself. It can focus anywhere, and also sustain attention at one point, so it's the observer too. Difficult for the mind to grasp, exquisite and intangible."

Kel clambered through the Chamber door; his face wore a vacant expression, laced with a frown.

"Consciousness is programmable," Lua continued, "and in us humans it becomes habitual and stuck, conforming to activities that have shaped it in the past. You know, survival and all that. In your day it was subject to a tremendous degree of control and manipulation from the media. This programme aims to free you of these unnecessary attachments and give you a greater awareness of your real nature."

"My real nature, and what would that be?"

"That's for you to discover, and having no expectations is the only way to dive into this level of self inquiry. You will certainly have a sharper degree of objectivity after this experience, that's all I can say. What you do with it is up to you."

"Challenging, to say the least."

They were now in front of the chair. Kel climbed in, lay down, and looked up at Lua, "I feel like a kid back in the crib. I am not about to start crying out for mama, am I?—Like with that re-birthing stuff?" He half sat up and looked around the room.

"Don't worry, you are going to experience some fairly exalted and ecstatic states of mental being, trust me. I'll be here all the time." Lua tweaked Kel's cheek, and smiled a smile designed to melt every frightened sinew in his body to jelly.

"So sit back and relax. You are being carefully monitored, and rest assured we'll stop the process if the situation warrants. The only time we will communicate with you is some seconds before we make the jump into hyperspace. This will be synchronised with events in the programme." Looking down at him, Lua paused for a second. "And don't worry about the rush you feel, and it will be quite a rush. Guaranteed to be a novel experience, and a lot safer than that tail spin you got yourself into earlier…any questions?"

Kel closed his eyes for a second. "If I want to stop the process, what do I do?"

"Just say 'stop', emphatically. Physical functions are being controlled, so not to worry. Just surrender to the experience, and don't fight it. We have one minute, Kel."

Lua came close to Kel, and looked him squarely in the eyes. "I don't know what is going on between us, but I like it, and look forward to knowing you better."

At that moment, as Kel held her eyes and his pulse jumped a notch, the lights went out, and he felt a gentle force field assist him back into a half sitting, half lying position in the comfort of the pliable chair. He had been a little shocked. Lua's eyes had seemed to emit light when the room had darkened; they had glowed.

The environment enveloped him, and he closed his eyes. A voice, as if inside his head, instructed him to listen, listen to noises going on around him.

Kel listened to the silence, and was soon without sensory input, gravity, or anything very much at all going on in his head. He was floating, and simply awake.

He became aware of a metallic ball that danced to and fro in front of his eyes, and it reminded him of something, but his memory seemed out of reach. The ball stilled and he understood that this was their spaceship, as black as the night around them. He saw the expanse of space ahead of him, and then something very strange happened. The space folded back in on itself in an action Kel could not identify in the physical reality he knew. It looked like a cross between a telescope being folded back into itself, and a snake coiling up, but he was beyond definitions at this point, merely accepting everything in a realm of instinctual visual understanding. In this folded space a hole was bored, and a tunnel made, and he quickly understood how vast, unimaginable distances could be traveled. He realised without reflection that a short-cut can be made in space, because it is not straight, it's curved.

Their ship entered the tunnel; sucked in under some unknown power.

After some time a luminescent light surrounded Kel as he listened to the silence, comforting and soothing. The temperature was perfect, the atmosphere peaceful, and he, the chair, and the room blended into one harmonious whole. He was simply aware; no thought disturbed him, nor any sensation to distract his attention; no inward, outward, upward or downward direction. He was in the realm of pure awareness, the region of no opposites.

Slowly something surged through him—a shaft of awareness burrowing in space in complete peace and freedom, consciousness transcending this expanse of existence. Within this formless realm of nothing and nowhere he floated, oblivious to all except the awareness of his presence.

When a thought finally entered Kel's field of attention, it was a dramatic one. He sought the origin of the witness within, and suddenly envisioned himself at the cutting edge of a lightning bolt that shot out into darkness at unimaginable speed. At that moment a jolt of energy swept up through Kel's backbone like an explosion, as if he were that lightning bolt, and out through the top of his head. He was left spinning and elated, and sank slowly into his still body.

He lay in this timeless, dimensionless ocean as he dug into the deepest part of himself, and in that depth found he was beyond everything. Through the threshold of a million portals, ghosts competed for his attention; he ignored them, absolving himself from the tangle of memories and conditioning he had always believed himself to be, and a life force expanded within him with the urgency of an explosion. It embraced Kel, and transcended him.

Suddenly, a faculty of sword-like sharpness returned Kel to the swirling oneness his mind had become absorbed in, and two things became apparent: the life force that resides in every living being, and the fact that he was observing that life force. Two things?

Before he had a chance to examine this apparent duality, an answer sprang from deep within his understanding. Ultimately these two are one; the difference caused by the separation of the identity observing this phenomenon from the phenomenon itself. It was the illusion of an individual self within the matrix of the realm Kel now experienced.

Something willed him on to search for the source of this duality, and he began tracking down the observer, the point of attention.

Thoughts randomly danced in and out of his perception, but they could take no hold on him, and his interest was almost effortlessly centered on himself as the observer. A pinpointed consciousness focused on the point of thought engulfed Kel in this mystery, and then a kind of trance overtook him as his attention merged into an indescribable absoluteness.

*   *   *   *

Some time later a mechanical voice re-initiated his auditory faculty, and he jumped bodily at this intrusion, so sudden had been the interruption into his conscious attention. "The brain is a mechanism of self-discovery, of survival in the physical," the voice informed him. "In the second age of enlightenment, humankind realised the universality of its own being, a realm previously enjoyed and fostered only by a few rare sages," and the dialogue locked into Kel's hearing.

"The implications were immediate and dramatic," the Brief continued, and Kel struggled out of his trance-like state. "We are always dealing with ourselves. There is only one life force, and in the light of awareness this can manifest as great good, or in darkness as great evil. You are that force, that power, and that is you. Any duality experienced is merely the wrong identification of this life force with its temporary physical state." There was a pause, then: "The light of awareness is who you are, beyond all embodied states."

An ebullient feeling of expansion exploded from inside, transcending him, and his body ceased to have any hold on him yet again. No sense to distract, nor gravity to drag him down. Without boundaries he floated like a feather in a seamless, eternal space, and then a thought brought him back to himself, his point of attention. There is no duality. All is one.

Silence reigned for a few heartbeats, and the narration continued, and once again he was jolted from a trance-like state to a point of raw attention. "Please remember the first tenet of this new age. Whatever is caused by you, your own intent, will ultimately be enjoyed or suffered by you. The reality of reincarnation has been proven in our age, and evidence to support it will be shown later in the Brief. It is a fact. Responsibility has taken on a new significance. It is the Law of One."

There was a short pause, and Kel, for the first time since going under, began to investigate and consider what he had just heard. His mind had just woken up, and was trying to unravel the most amazing dream, a treasure chest of visions or hallucinations he had seen at levels in himself never before experienced. The Brief cut this short, and his attention was once again gently but forcibly focused, and the voice continued.

"At the moment of creation…"

"Stop!" he called.

The lights came on, and Lua was there, looking down at him. He looked up, both exalted and apprehensive, as if drugged.

"This is too much! I am finding myself in a place that I can only describe, as…as nowhere else, I mean Nowhere! And yet I am there, and I feel like…Out there!" And Kel waved an arm at nothing in particular.

Then suddenly he found himself giggling, uncontrollably. Then, just as suddenly, he forced himself to stop and sighed heavily, leaning forward, and holding his head in his hands. "Jesus!"

"Kel, we have given you the most important information early. Re-incarnation is a fact, not a theory, and now a part of you is trying to penetrate the information you've been fed. This will cause your mind to try and innovate ideas around this information and form conclusions about what is going on, but the one-ness of absolute reality is way beyond any concept."

"Yeah, well I feel weird."

"You feel woozy because of the endorphin rush you are experiencing; it's caused by lack of gravity and sensory deprivation. You'll get used to it."

Lua tousled Kel's hair playfully and said, "We have to hurry to co-ordinate the programme, time to get back."

"Sensory bloody deprivation, so that's what it is! Alright hook me in…This must be love," he muttered, and then went on, "What does it mean, 'we are always dealing with ourselves?' I mean the law of one, fine, but there have been a few dickheads I've had to deal with in this life that had nothing to do with me, believe me."

"Kel, time please!"

"All right, may the force be with you," he heard himself calling as the lights dimmed, and he surrendered to the downward incline of the chair.

"At the moment of creation of the physical universe," the Brief continued, abruptly and immediately.

"Oh, God," said Kel.

"All known physical energy was created in that single moment. Within a fraction of a fraction of a second, the universe was contained within an area the size of a pea, and the temperature was an unimaginable 1,000,000,000,000,000,000,000,000,000 degrees.

There was silence, and then a mechanical voice jolted his nervous system: "JUMPING TO HYPERSPACE. COUNTDOWN FROM TEN." The other narrative voice entered Kel's head. "This is known as the Big Bang…"—"EIGHT, SEVEN…" Kel's braced himself…"THREE, TWO, ONE!"

At that moment there was an explosion, and Kel surfed ahead of the tsunami of time. Any surfer knows the thrill of the drop as the wave breaks, and that's the nearest he could get to describe this experience. It is the never-never land between the particle and the wave, a moment of unavoidable surrender, when the past ceases to have any significance. Energy streaked past Kel at a phenomenal speed, and light and colours became a spiraling tunnel in which he was devoured. These tunnels exploded out in every direction from his centre of being, and the space around him swallowed up his heat, like the eye of a multitude of tornadoes. "Wowee," he tried to scream as his molecules wrestled to retain their identity, but the surf now had him.

At a certain point, when Kel thought he might be losing his body, his consciousness, and all else inside this other-worldly maelstrom, a barrier was crossed, and he immediately felt almost normal again, albeit a little winded and light headed. They had been sucked into the shortcut and were burrowing through the curvature of space. He tried to shake his head but found himself in some kind of vacuum and his head did not respond.

The voice returned. "At one hundredth of a second the universe was the size of the sun, and had cooled down to 1,000,000,000,000,000 degrees." Kel was surrounded by a fireworks display of enormous proportions. He could not move, nor keep his eyes closed to shield them from the intense light. "The early universe was dominated by electromagnetic radiation in the form of little packets of energy. These were photons, and at the critical moment of creation, mass times the speed of light, times the speed of light and above, physical existence comes into being."

When light exceeds it own speed, matter is formed? Kel had no time to think and a series of flashes burned their way into his visual cortex.

"At one hundred seconds the temperature had dropped enough to allow the strong nuclear force to bind two neutrons to two protons, thus forming the nuclei of helium. Solitary neutrons decayed into protons, and these became the nuclei of hydrogen. Fuel of the stars; genesis itself."

Kel watched the dance of living science on the screen that played in his mind, his attention unencumbered by thought, and information flowed through his cerebral circuits to be stored in the long-term memory bank in the cortex of his brain. He was absorbing an incredible amount of information.

"The number of particles," the voice continued, "was very slightly greater than the number of anti-particles, about one part in a billion more. This is the relationship of matter to anti-matter." When these opposing particles met, they seem to annihilate each other, and what was left over became the substance of the universe. More flashes of light affronted Kel's vision, and in one millisecond of a reflection, he discerned that the canceling out of matter with anti-matter created a number of parallel dimensions. Some recognition clicked in him as he glimpsed these parallel realms, but he was given no time to think. He also noticed that the material left over swirled into existence, and he suddenly thought he was witnessing the initiation of the realm of time, as space devours the heat…"The process of mutual annihilation generated gamma radiation, which becomes heat radiation. This is the background echo that can be heard in the universe."

"Hold on, hold on," Kel called out.

"Hydrogen combusts and begets helium," the Brief purged his mind of any thought, or question. "These two combust and carbon, oxygen, and nitrogen evolve; collapsing stars that run out of hydrogen explode into supernovae and create the heavier elements, of which all matter is composed. This is all finely tuned, one imbalance in the nuclear or the gravitational forces, and existence would have been rapidly curtailed. We are in perfect balance. The odds of this happening without an intelligent life force behind it are mathematically implausible."

Kel now found himself in an opaque expanse of nothingness, dotted with bursts of light. An intelligent life force?

"The photons could not travel far in a straight line until the electrons, that littered the primordial universe, were out of the way. The electrons were picked up by the nuclei of helium and hydrogen to become stable atoms."

"Over hundreds of millions of years, gaseous monsters slowly evolved, and formed the celestial bodies in our universe, which lit and set the stage for the dramas of creation. Galaxies are created by massive black holes swallowing immense clouds of gas around them from which nothing can escape, not even light. When the feeding frenzy is over, the remaining gases and dust become the stars, and are held in orbit by these singularities."

A swirling cloud of light, a quasar, came into Kel's view, swallowing all the light around it, and then slowing to become a massive singularity, the hub of a galaxy. The stars danced around it like a coterie of whirling dervishes. "Within these stars, these nuclear furnaces, the other elements were forged and this is the star dust out of which you, and all else, is made." The play of swirling, revolving light slowed down around Kel as millions of galaxies were thus created and the universe formed around him, and he was mesmerised by it.

His vision zoomed in towards a celestial body hanging in the vastness of space, and he understood it to be the Primordial Earth. In the distance he saw another planet, slightly smaller, approach the Earth on a collision course. It hit slightly off centre and the impact caused a momentous explosion, and the Earth became a fireball. Kel felt his innards shake, and he knew this to be the genesis of his planet, and what gave it an opportunity to nurture life as we know it.

The rogue planet and the Earth seemed to unite for a brief period, and then the planet was thrown out violently. It arched around and returned to re-impact with the Earth, and this time was smashed to smithereens, its remains forming a cloud of debris that became caught in Earth's gravity, and slowly molded itself into our moon. It revolved in its own orbit, and moved slowly away from the Earth, giving its new companion a stability that would allow life to evolve. Without it life as we know it would have been impossible. The moon is the giver of life.

The scene changed and a number of geometric patterns danced before Kel's vision. A map of some mountainous terrain stretched out before him. It started to undulate to some unheard rhythm and he understood this to be a geographic map of the elements. From the northern shore a wispy strand of matter moved to the centre of Kel's vision and slowly a protozoan blob was sculpted before him. "When carbon was formed, it became the skeleton on which all of your molecular structure is built." Now strands from other elements joined the dance as the body took shape. "Water and iron became your blood, calcium and phosphorous your bones, potassium and sodium, along with a little calcium, the interplay of your nervous system, and all else came to be used to ensure your survival and evolution. Your heat is the sun and the dance of these elements; your body is the sea and the earth; the ebb and flow and harmony of life within you are the moon. Add to this oxygen, the animator of life, and you become a living record of creation. You have created all this around yourself, and this is neither accident, nor chance."

There was silence as Kel was given a moment to ponder…

$$* \qquad * \qquad * \qquad *$$

Created all of this around myself? Kel focussed his attention, and some strange indwelling feeling of 'I am', of a self hit him, a kind of consciousness within consciousness. Without this curious observer, what else is there?

Kel suddenly found himself surrounded by a scene of unimaginable proportion, which curtailed his thoughts. He was witness to the devastating fires of creation within a sun. Looking outward to a dome of white-hot intensity his head felt ready to explode inside this nuclear furnace; rivers of magna flowed around him, and the sun's interior gurgled and gushed with trillions of degrees of heat. This was not just a fireball; it was alive, volatile, and temperamental. He looked out into space and became aware of clouds of gas and dust forming into the solar system around him; everything was made of the same stuff, and the sun is the centre of this living cell. And that was himself! I am the same as the sun and its heat is me!

Kel's awareness was then abruptly, yet mercifully, propelled out at speed in an arc into the swirling formation of stars around him. He at once understood the insatiable appetite that space has for heat, as his awareness danced haphazardly around, being pulled every which way by some divinely powerful, yet invisible force. The stars streamed out in every direction, spiraling into galaxies in the luminiferous ether of space.

Some strange thoughts…No, an unknown voice entered Kel's head. The interior of the sun had disturbed and burned deep within, propelling him into a sequence of experiences, and then this voice switched on and did not seem to be part of the Brief. It came from some deep and mysterious part of himself.

"As the spirit dances in the womb of the universe into which it rushes…" Kel's conscious energy spiraled and tumbled on some invisible roller coaster, "…she swallowing his heat and coming alive, he exploding into self expression." Kel grimaced as the pressure built up, and then subsided swiftly, and this internal voice continued unabated. "Without one or the other, neither exist. This is the root of duality, and will continue until all energy is one in the cosmos, until time itself has ceased and absolute chaos prevails. It will then contract to an absolute nothingness, only to manifest again. This is eternity."

This intelligence, and the renegade voice, pounded through Kel's brain, and he had no idea from whence it came. "At each dissolution, the wisdom of all creation is passed on to the next manifestation. These are aspects of creation known as the gods, and they are all in you. I am your guide."

A break in the programme allowed a moment's thought. "If you are my guide, then why all this creation?" Kel asked somewhere deep within himself.

"The desire to be was too great, and was unstoppable. You are its child, and your demand to be is being granted…The knowledge that you are, is everything."

"What is that desire?" Kel asked.

"Love of your Self," came the reply and the Brief cut off the voice abruptly, and forced its way back to his conscious attention, mainlining the chemical transmitters in his brain.

"Wait!" Kel called, but the story of creation continued…

"As creation cooled to under three thousand degrees, energy levels of radiation, or photons in the universe, fell below that of matter, so then matter dominated. This is the law of gravity." Kel then saw great gaseous clouds drawn in by massive singularities, the gas and dust of the cosmos forming into galaxies, and in these are embraced the solar systems. "On a few of these planets physical life is possible; these are the pearls of the universe."

Kel, beginning to go on massive overload, was about to stop the transmission when he was suddenly taken on a trip, zooming at breathtaking speeds through space from one star to another."

"Whoa," he mouthed, as his consciousness seemed to leave his guts trailing in the jet stream. When they arrived at a solar system, a planet in that system would be pointed out to him, indicating it was a life-sustaining environment, and he noticed each of these had a moon like the Earth's.

He felt nauseous from the phenomenal sense of speed and needed some respite, a rest from the sheer magnitude of it all. "Stop," he managed at last.

He was back to the on-deck environment. Lua's hands were on his brow in an instant. He was wet with sweat, and she mopped his brow gently stroking his forehead and massaging his temples.

"Wow, this is a bit too much, I was inside this sun, and had these weird thoughts. Lua, I am on overload, that's enough," and he blew a stream of air through pursed lips, and said, "Poosha bloody veeda!"

Lua laughed, "Kel, you are doing magnificently, more than we could have hoped for. But the more information you take in, the better prepared you'll be. There're just a few minutes of today's programme left. I know you are exhausted, but just a couple of more minutes."

"Bloody slave driver, just a couple of minutes, I mean this stuff is biblical. This voice, this experience I had, I don't know where it came from, but it came from in me. There was something about a guide."

"The Brief is going to trip-wire some profound experiences in you, information hidden from your usual senses. Just observe it; don't be intimidated."

"Easier said than done. Are these rushes of speed necessary?" Kel relaxed under Lua's deft fingers. He was enjoying the head massage and in no hurry to get back.

"Yes, you are travelling at them, and this is a good way to acclimatise. It's almost over for today. Are you ready?"

"There was this information in me," he went on, "It said at the dissolution of the universe, and before the next Big Bang, that intelligence can project itself through and pass on its wisdom. I mean that's outrageous, don't you think?"

"There is actually a theory to that effect. Was that all?" Lua asked.

"All I can remember."

"Interesting; Kel, are you ready? It's almost over."

"All right, all right! Hook me in; send me down. Where-ever next?"

*   *   *   *

He was soon back in the programme, and each time he went under, his nerves facilitated, and he adapted that much quicker.

The folded space environment returned, and the sense of speed slowed to enable Kel to understand his journey through the curvature of the space-time continuum. Space was folded, and within the warp and woof of it were great indents, like spiraling holes in a multidimensional honeycomb. These indents were centres of gravity...stars, and other celestial bodies. Near them, like a shadow, like an echo, were mirrored multi-dimensional energy sources, boulders in this mighty gushing river, bearing the ship on like a seedpod through a channel of space and time. They sped up again and the indents became darker, and they swept around them, utilising their gravity, their power, like being propelled from one slingshot to another into the dark. Encased in this metallic pod, this time bullet, he understood why these experiences of speed were necessary, part and parcel of the ride, and of the Brief. He was travelling at these speeds, right now.

"Bloody cosmic pinball machine," he slowly enunciated under his breath.

"In this manner," the Brief continued, "we are on our way to a planet in a solar system towards the constellation Virgo. This planet we call Gaya, in honour of our mother planet, and the location of an amazing enlightenment experience of a human being on Earth, some two and a half thousand years before your birth. Please relax into the ride."

His nervous system was then subjected to a rapid succession of accelerations to which he habituated quickly, but he had had enough and was about to call 'stop,' when a mechanical voice jolted him. "You are returning to on-deck environment in seven seconds."

Kel was transported back to the relative peace and calm of the ship, and lay there. It was eerily quiet. He felt dizzy, and more than relieved that his internal environment had been stilled.

"From an absolute stillness to absolute speed, you never told me about this," said Kel. "One monster of a ride."

"You have done more than well." Lua helped Kel out of the chair. His legs felt wobbly and he stumbled, and sat back down. She sat next to him and the chair rocked back and forward, like a hammock. Their bodies were in close contact and dipped towards each other in the suspended centre of the chair. This brought Kel quickly to his senses.

"We were half expecting you to become quite nauseous with the jump and the speed factor, but you have habituated remarkably quickly. With your nerves facilitating so rapidly, we can achieve a lot in the next two days."

"I am exhausted," Kel gasped. "Two days?"

"You see, the machine is facilitating a learning process that's allowing you to let go of a lot of old baggage, body armouring, and unnecessary stress, that kind of thing. You have already let go of a lot, and we encourage you to continue."

"How should I do that?" Kel asked.

"Be honest with yourself, and us, about what is going on with you...no hiding,"

Kel had to think for a minute, and then his mind reared up like a monster, projecting a myriad of images through his attention. A school bully, gray suburbia, a strict but loving father, and layer upon layer of masks created to cope with the whole mess, and avoid the humiliation of weakness. These now surfaced and peeled off him like the layers of an onion, and out they came.

He babbled on to Lua, one mundane insight after another, as they made their way back to his quarters. "Hmm," she replied. And again, "hmm."

"Good grief!" he said at last, "I've got verbal diarrhea."

"Verbal what?" Lua asked.

"Never mind, I am just a bit over the top, overexcited or something. I have just been fed the most amazing information, and I am on over-load...just venting, babbling." He paused for a moment. "I think I experienced the moment before creation."

"What was that like?" Lua asked.

"Fucking hot! Scuse my French. I was looking out from this sun...Are we really travelling faster than the speed of light?"

"Yes we are, relatively speaking, a lot faster," replied Lua, now facing Kel in his quarters. "Is there more, Kel?"

"Nope, that's it. I mean besides an enormous boom-boom, produc-ing enough bloody energy to make quarks that begot neutrons and protons, that attracted electrons, that allowed light to burst forth, and all that. Bloody duality I suppose." and Kel hoisted his hands in the air in a position of surrender. "What's this?" he said.

"What?" Lua asked.

"The Italians preparing for World War 3."

Lua laughed, managing a frown at the same time. "Can you make sense of what's surfacing in you. You are so adept at avoiding going deeper."

"I am reeling, Lua, Just reeling!" Kel said, lowering his arms, and shaking his head. "I mean I felt something burning away in me, pushing everything aside—all my ideas, everything! And it's like, how can I say? It's so bright, it only knows itself."

"You must get some rest. Tomorrow's going to be a busy day. Is there anything you need?" She looked around the room, and for the first time appeared a little unsure, vulnerable. She avoided eye contact.

Kel's heart pounded and he looked uneasily around. He shrugged his shoulders and shook his head. "I'm fine."

"Sleeping apparel is there in the drawer, and everything else is easy to understand. There's a juice dispenser, tap water is drinkable, and if you need anything just call me. We have audio contact initiated by calling my name." Lua's confidence had returned and she retreated to the door.

"Good night, Kel."

"Good night, Lua."

After the door had whooshed shut, Kel let go a loud sigh. He sat on the bed and raked his fingers through his hair, shook his head vigorously from side to side, and again sighed heavily. He stared into space for a few seconds, stood abruptly and made for the bathroom.

He showered, smiled repeatedly, admiring his new teeth in the mirror, and then retired to bed. He lay there staring up at the ceiling. I'm on a space ship and I'm falling in love; maybe I'll wake up in a minute. He continued thinking of Lua, her sense of fun, and her seriousness, and wondered at his own naivete. He had been fed with the most incredible information and knowledge about reality; was on a journey of unimaginable dimensions, and here he was, thinking of a woman: her figure, the way she moved, and her obvious affection for him. Desire simmered, unstoppable and spellbinding in its conquest. Such is the chemistry of life.

One life force, he thought to himself, attempting an escape from the imaginary embrace he was in with Lua. He tried to project himself into the level of understanding he had experienced in the Brief, but it eluded him, and he sunk slowly into sleep.

*　　*　　*　　*

He was in a deep sleep, and heard his name being called. "Kel, Kel,"

He woke startled, wondering where he was. It was Lua, her face inches away from his.

"You were calling out in your sleep," she said.

Kel slipped his arms around her waist and she was in his arms in a second, and tasted, tasted like a sweet liquor.

"Kel, this has never been tried beyond the speed of light," Lua gasped in his ear.

"Resistance is futile," he replied.

"What?" she asked.

"Never mind. Nothing could stop this...this is real. I've never felt this." They embraced like two halves of a clam coming together, and moaned out of sheer joy, and exquisite regret that they should ever have been apart.

*　　*　　*　　*

Kel awoke, and reality rushed into his consciousness with the force of a steam train. He was alone in bed and hadn't been dreaming...on a spaceship making the barest of hums, hurtling through space at an immeasurable speed. He leant over and smelt the pillow next to him. That had not been a dream either.

His experience with Lua had been a novel one. Never had he known such passion. She had some kind of power over him that was astonishing; a combination of pelvic floor muscle control and a hypnotic magnetism which rendered Kel both slave and master. For the first time since his earliest sexual experiences as a teenager, he had no control whatsoever, and yet it made no difference. He had been in her grip, and there was no escape. Their lovemaking lasted well into the night, at the speed of light. At one point Lua had to respond to a call from Daljit, who was concerned about Kel's vital signs. After reassuring Daljit, "He's doing your exercises," she and Kel giggled like naughty children.

Kel got up, showered, and stole some admiring glances of his gleaming new white teeth. As he left the bathroom there was a knock at the door.

"Good morning," said Lua as she strode in, her eyes shone and she smiled. "Time for breakfast, and then back to the Brief."

He followed her through the companionways feeling a pleasant disbelief, his eyes perusing the curves of her body, barely detectable through the blue jump suit.

They entered the ship's canteen, which consisted of three tables, each with a seating capacity of six. Five people, all in blue, sat around one of these tables. They turned and greeted Kel.

"I'll get your breakfast," said Lua, "I have a good idea of what you like," and she winked at him.

Kel sat at an empty table with two place settings. The other table returned to its conversation, and he got the impression that they were giving him space to acclimatise. Even so, he looked around the room and over at Lua getting his breakfast, and shifted in his chair.

Lua returned with a breakfast of fruit and cereal, and immediately picked up on Kel's unease.

"Don't worry, Kel, we don't regard sex as either indulgent or permissive." Lua detected some old conditioned reflexes in Kel. "Not understanding it is one of the roots of bondage," and she held her hands out in front of her, as if manacled together, and twisted her face in mock pain.

Kel chuckled, and said, "Guilty, your Honour."

"This physical body can allow a change of perspective which can transform you. Don't you want to change?"

"If you really do, you'll get to know a lot about who you are, and then see how much energy you have." Lua smiled and shot him a look of love. "Come on Kel, it's time to move on."

Kel just stared, then nodded.

"Believe me, Kel, this relationship was not in my brief, and I've never gone against orders before, but it's happening, and it honestly feels like nothing can stop it. I've fallen for a fossil."

Kel guffawed, and had a minor coughing fit. People looked over, smiled and nodded amongst themselves. Lua kept his gaze, and her eyes were both soft and powerful. He felt a tremendous strength building up in his abdomen, and sat back in his chair.

"Are you in trouble for this?" said Kel, frowning.

"That's none of your business. This is my decision, the biggest I've ever taken. Nothing can change it, and nothing will." Lua shrugged her shoulders and smiled.

"You are one hell of a woman, Lua."

"Woman," repeated Lua, "woman...I like that," she said, and laughed.

Kel ate a hearty breakfast, and was more than ready for the continuation of the Brief.

* * * *

Held yet again in the gravity field of the briefing chair, he listened to the noises as instructed, and was filled with a sense of expansion and relaxation, quickly being exalted to the feeling of lightness and bliss he had experienced the previous day, of being present and bodiless. Then the Brief continued, jolting him out of his trance-like state.

"Reality is a non-dimensional, ethereal, and infinite source, and all experience is recorded in it. Physical manifestation is the illusory multi-dimensional expression of this reality." The scene around Kel changed, as the expansion in which he was immersed imploded into itself, and he felt as if his guts were being turned inside out. The acceleration was back, and he found himself journeying through the formation of the micro-cosmos; his onward rush was an inward one.

"Infinity is neither inward nor outward," the voice continued, "but as science discovered more and more about the micro-cosmos, our understanding of the nature of reality took a giant leap. The smaller it gets, the more unstable it becomes, and the more destructive the forces we meet. These forces at the centre of the atom, at the centre of the quark, are masking a stillness of profound and unimaginable depth. These unstable, destructive forces are like a shield of fire that surrounds this stillness, maintaining its absolute peace."

Kel hurtled towards a set of geometric patterns that filled his vision, and he realised that the four dimensions known to him were infused with several others that had compacted into reality as he saw it. He tried to shake himself out of these intense images but was locked in, and being unraveled through powerful forces on an inward journey through the fires of creation, to a realm of indescribable peace, where all sense of time left him.

He was there, but nothing else was. No second, no shadow, no reflection, nought but him.

It is a oneness, and spontaneously there arises a reflection of this when a body comes into being. This reflection is consciousness, and will last as long as the body does. That which observes everything over-all, and is not even aware of its own existence, is where Kel found himself, the here and now of eternity. We are its awareness; we are its soul.

Peace was overtaken by a restlessness, which gave rise to movement. He moved slowly, as if unfolding outwards, and the pace quickened as the matrix heated up in the cauldron of creation and his being was propelled forward, surfing on the tunnels of dimension as they careened on their way to becoming the particles of creation. He burst out of this state suddenly, and violently, in a massive outward rush of energy. His being twisted, involuted, and exploded out into the dimensions of space-time, producing in Kel a wide sweep of feelings from stark terror to sweet delight, as he swept up through the worlds from earth to ether, and then back again, from the super fine to the very gross.

"Jesus," he heard himself calling, "Jeeezz…" But not a sound he made.

The process slowed down and ground to a halt, and he became aware of an atom swirling slowly in an absolute stillness. The nucleus was tiny, the size of a pea, and the electrons that swirled around it, giving it form, were a good distance away; a pea in the middle of a giant stadium, waves of energy dancing around it, pinpointed in an electron hundreds of yards away. He realized what he was looking at had very little form; it was all movement. Existence is movement.

Movement around him quickened once again.

"Hold on, hold on!" Kel bellowed, and this time he heard his voice. "Too much, too quick!" and the rush of information and experience ceased, and he was left to think for a moment as his body echoed with the sonic resonance of its internal movement. "What is this?" he asked in exasperation.

Silence followed.

"What and who is all this?" He tried again, this time louder.

He soon felt very sleepy, unable to keep his eyes open, and within seconds he was in a deep sleep, unaware of anything.

As the first flicker of consciousness rose in him, the voice said, "As you rise from the depths of the unconscious, as your body wakes, see how you create the world around you, how you construct the sense of self; the sense that you are. Within seconds of waking, the power that gives light to your eyes, and sound to your ears, enters the level of your individual awareness, and gives light to consciousness. That light, which is given, is who you are. It is the light that transcends existence and is immanent in all creation. It is the original source, dimensionless and infinite, ever present. You have just forgotten that which you forever are."

Kel experienced an exquisite rush of bliss. Nothing in his mind could possibly compute or interpret his present state of being, this ocean of ecstasy. It was uniqueness itself.

"This state cannot be said to be conscious or unconscious. It exists in deep sleep, and also in the waking and dream states. It can only be found and experienced within yourself, and cannot be defined. It is masked by your mind's restlessness, but it is who you are. It is forever."

Kel lay still and awake, and tears streamed from his eyes.

*   *   *   *

After some time reflecting upon this new awareness, the Brief continued. "The human being is thus far the only known physical entity in the universe that is able to reflect back on itself to discover its true nature, and its own power. The people of the planet you are headed for are dedicated to finding the correct relationship to this awesome power, and to one another in the midst of it."

The experience of expansion, which Kel had rushed into, began again. "Oh no." he mouthed, only to be silenced by the Brief. "The feeling of bliss you are experiencing is the source of everything. It is the power of love and understanding, without attachment or reflection."

This outward rush continued and became too much for Kel, and he forced himself back into his mind, trying to get a mental grip on the situation. Otherwise, he felt he might go mad. This tug of war between the expansion, and his mind, desperate now to reel him back in, continued for a while, and Kel was powerless in the silence to do anything to stop or alter his present state. If he went with the flow…there's nothing there…he feared annihilation.

"Yet the mind can never find the source." Kel sighed with relief, the voice was back. "It is like looking for light in daylight. It is too close to who you are. It is who you are. Realising this, and understanding the simplicity of your true nature, and the fact that no concept can ever embrace such pure immanence, will open up vast new areas of awareness to you."

Kel was once again transported to the weightless world, and he heard the faint sound of some chanting that resonated with something in his memory. He was in a realm of deep contemplation, and had entered this meditative state under his own power, with no facilitation from the machine. He entered a state of crystalline awareness and for an instant knew he was everything that is, and in that realisation some divine power flashed through his brain, a quickening, an insight. He had taken his foot off of the cliff of the known and everything had dropped away. And he reflected on himself and saw that there were many realms and he a part of them all, subsystems of consciousness that linked and connected all of life. The self he knew himself to be, was the glue that held everything together, the gateway to the infinite...

✳   ✳   ✳   ✳

As he stirred awake he found Lua's hand on his brow. He was back in the shipboard environment. He lay there for a while glad of her presence, her touch. But then the memories of what had happened to him came flooding in; he sat up slowly, and cradled his head in his hands.

"I mean, this is about my relationship to God, right?" said Kel at last, swinging his legs over the side of the chair. His words were a little slurred.

"God is just a concept, Kel. This is about who you are,"

"Don't you start," said Kel quickly. "I need a rest from this relentless tyrant here. It's like a Zen monastery. I didn't bargain for this...I feel a bit heavy at times, you know, like depressed, and totally ecstatic at others..."

"It's okay Kel."

"Maybe it's just overload. I just need to try and put these things into words, into an understandable perspective. Try and get a handle on them." Kel waved his arms trying to explain something, but words failed him.

"I understand. We have an hour's break. Come on, let's go and rest," said Lua, and she led Kel back to his quarters, gently resting her arm on his, guiding him along. He was vaguely aware of passing people in the companionway, but was oblivious of who they were, distracted deep within himself. They stood back and made way for him. He was aware only of a bright light that burned its way through his consciousness.

Back in his quarters Lua massaged Kel's back and shoulders. She was unusually strong and efficient, and normally he would have been curious about her expertise, but he was gone, spent. They lay arm in arm for a while, and she rocked him gently to cool the meltdown going on in his mind. Powerful memories from the mists of time swirled in his field of attention. A fire burned brightly, and something screamed from within it; he gasped and stared deep within himself. He caught his breath and saw a sword in his hands, and felt a gut-wrenching anger devour him, then a baby in his arms looked out at him in innocence. The scene slowly abated and by and by he slept, as Lua stroked his hair.

He woke up and something stirred in his chest, and he sucked in a breath of air and held it. He grimaced and Lua hugged him tight, urging him to let go. He sobbed, his whole body shaking, and a stream of tears flowed down his cheeks. She cradled his head and held him close, as waves of after-shocks swept over his body. She was like a rock for Kel to cling to while this release of emotions pulsated through him, holding him until he was still. Lua then took his face in her hands and looked directly into his eyes, saying nothing, no overt emotions expressed in her look. She kept his gaze for some minutes.

Kel was locked into her eyes and a rush of power flooded into his body. Who are you that I know you so well?

His eyes followed her as she slowly withdrew, gently laid his head on the mattress, and made for the door.

"I certainly managed to dump something then, but I have no idea what," he said.

"Just let go. You don't have to know what's in the garbage. Rest! You need your strength. I'll be back with lunch in two secs." The door whooshed shut, and the memories danced in Kel's mind.

※   ※   ※   ※

They ate in silence, and then Lua coaxed him back to the Chamber. By the time he was back in the chair he was feeling extremely light-headed, hopelessly in love, and ready for anything.

Lua stood over him, and entertained him with girlish humour. "My hero," she teased.

"Would you think me shallow if I told you that all I would like at this point is a beer, a cigarette, and the company of some male friends?"

"In-bloody-corrigible, inneye," said Lua, in a good cockney accent.

"Poosha bloody veeda, ain't she," said Kel, laughing as the chair began its descent. Lua laughed with him, and made a face of feigned distress as the lights dimmed.

※   ※   ※   ※

A vision of a whirling, swirling chain slowly materialised in Kel's vision, and the Brief started immediately. "At the centre of every living cell there is a nucleus, and within that nucleus there is a multidimensional recipe for another living cell, a replica of itself. This is DNA, and within its coiled helix, the vital force goes about the creation of the physical."

Kel witnessed the winding, snake-like movement of the double helix.

"At the root of DNA is the creative principle, and its sole purpose is to constantly re-create itself within and around whatever physical form it encounters. Life in the physical universe is the expression of this force, ever assured of its own continuance. The dominance of the strongest in the seat of physical pleasure, the ability to mutate and encompass all it meets. All life stems from this same root. He was shown a dog running, then above it a dolphin swimming. Same root, same root...one chose the land, one chose the sea.

Kel was suddenly surrounded by a group of chimpanzees, and so real was the scene that he tried to jump back. Good, he thought, this is different. I can handle this.

A fight broke out amongst the chimps, yelps and screams shattering the silence as two or three of them ganged up on another, and beat him with fists flying. The noise was deafening and Kel grimaced, trying to pull back from this gross display of testosterone. They fought around him in a frenzy of violence, and finally a victor emerged thumping its chest in triumph.

There followed in quick succession a scene of wolves. No, thought Kel as he looked more closely...hyenas, and once again a fight ensued. Kel's adrenaline level rose sharply, so real was the scene around him, the snarls, and the clash of teeth against teeth, the whimper of defeat, the begging for mercy. There were strong smells as well, of fear, of sweat, of dominance, and he gagged once, and then they were gone.

"The dominance and survival of the strongest and most cunning is the story of humankind, with chance and luck playing major roles in the game of life. Humanity was born of a violent past," said the Brief, almost somberly.

The scene changed dramatically from the land to the sea, and Kel was shot off up into the air, watching the land recede beneath him, and a blue sea appeared in the distance. He followed at speed a trajectory that dove in a wide arc as he headed for the ocean, straight for its surface, which he penetrated without so much as a splash, and dove into its depths. Kel gasped at this sudden rush and change of scene, and was soon looking at a small sea creature, heavily shelled and lumbering about on the murky floor of this ancient ocean. It shot out a puff of milky liquid, and the voice re-entered his head, "Sometimes evolution makes a gigantic leap."

Kel looked around into the dark depths of the ocean, and then back at the puff of liquid magnified before him. As he focused in on it, the scene sped up, and a small larvae shot out, circling the crustacean that had been its parent, and then racing into the murk around it, into the dark unknown. This was the ultimate risk, the Brief intimated, and the greatest leap taken on the evolutionary expressway. Kel understood that this tadpole-like creature was the first of a new breed of life, free-swimming and with unlimited potential. It had chosen to become sexually mature in its own right, and not grow up into its armoured parent, choosing freedom above the security of the shell. Its muscular tail, and rudiments of a spinal cord inside a backbone, led it on at breathtaking speeds in cosmic terms, towards evolving into a primordial vertebrate, the ancestor of all back-boned animals.

The independently minded larvae forswore the exoskeletal armour of its heritage, and developed an internal bony skeleton instead. Its forebrain increased in size as the seat of its senses migrated forward in the direction of movement, and concentrated in the primordial head. Kel witnessed the formation of nerve to muscle, arteries around and inter-twined with nerves, of muscle to tendon on bone, of scales on the outer membrane, until a fish-like prototype gradually formed and swam in a shoal of others. He wondered at the miraculous balance and beauty of creation; the harmonious relationship between nerve and artery, the nerve probing its environment, the artery sustaining its search, its survival. Without one the other cannot exist, and the perfect balance between head and heart is sought.

Kel floated a while in this three dimensional shoal of fish. The sea around him turned into a light show as the fish spun and flipped at each movement around them, turning suddenly at the slightest change in the environment. He realised that this reflexive turning was the same as a twitch, or the reflex in his knee, or in any muscle; it was a nervous system responding to a stimulus, to the environment. This was his ancestor, and its patterns of movement and reflexes still existed within him. He had witnessed the rudimentary beginnings of his backbone, of his vertebrate ancestors, of his deepest inborn movement patterns. Modified and controlled, all this still existed within him.

A threat suddenly appeared in the darkness around him. Enormous, big-mouthed, ugly creatures, all of them eyeing him in hunger, swam by in the murky depths, exposing rows of savage teeth. Too close at times, and his nervous system responded with squirts of adrenaline that shocked him into a very wakeful state, so real were the images, and his sense of presence in this environment. He slowly adapted until they had no effect on him.

The scene slowly changed and a fish-like creature moved into the muddy shallows of an ancient river delta. Then its appearance mutated, step by step, into an amphibian resembling a cross between a newt and a shell-less turtle, with limb buds instead of fins. It was soon surrounded in the rock pool by a freak show, a collection of goggle-eyed, crazy-limbed sea and amphibian creatures that appeared to be stuck in some evolutionary rut between the land and the sea. Unperturbed, the creature stuck its head out of the sea and looked landward. It moved towards the shore and there was a sudden rush as a wave of adrenaline swept through Kel's body, and the creature made a dash for land, scratching its way through the detritus in the shallows. Behind it, a massive predator turned away, unable to enter this point between the land and sea.

Jesus, thought Kel, we were harrowed out of the depths onto the land, frightened into clawing our way out of the ocean. An amphibian ancestor took some scuttling steps in the shallows, and this discovery of a greater gravity presented the primordial brain with a million new equations to deal with. Gravity now weighed the creature down like a millstone, as it adapted from a three dimensional environment to a two-dimensional one, and the depth of the sea was replaced and compressed into the awareness of touch, weight and balance. Kel saw the limbs respond to their new environment, and the small bones that developed to scuttle our way through the shallows, now began extending down to meet the challenge of the land. Strange feelings crept through his limbs, shadows of an ancient past.

The programme quickened, and as the land yielded more vegetation, so did the amphibian venture out more onto the land to dine on the growing population of insects. The head separated from its shoulder blade, and this gave it leave to look around with increased maneuverability of the upper body. Its command of gravity slowly improved, and its limbs grew in length, pressing down into the earth for greater self-awareness, raising the body even higher. The sea was left behind and the reptilian age began, and along with it, a host of movement and survival centres developed in the brain stem and lower brain.

Now a scorpion-like creature filled his vision; it appeared enormous in front of him and he held his breath. These were his ancestors' main rivals on land for food, and he recognised in himself reflexes that demanded he put an end to this competitor. He felt a quiver in his internal bones, better suited to grow and evolve, and eyed the exoskeletal armour of the scorpion and the tail that hovered menacingly aloft; this was an ancient battle for dominance on land, to kill and subjugate, or perish…one he would win.

The development of our reptilian ancestors, along with their behaviour patterns and physical evolution, fast-forwarded in front of him. In this metamorphosis, Kel experienced heightened emotions, and reflex reactions within himself over which he had no control. The seeming violence of copulation in this wild ancestral state brought out feelings of extreme anger, and dominance, yet Kel lay still and serene in the chair as multiple centres in his nervous system reacted to different stimuli, be they anger, lust or greed. He became accustomed to their intensity, and was able to pinpoint his reactions with a penetrating clarity, his eyes darting this way and that under closed lids. Control these gross emotions, understand them, transcend them! Your point of attention is the key. You have the key.

At one point he looked up and froze, moving not a muscle. A giant reptile, teeth exposed, looked down on him. His skin crawled and yet he remained still, holding his breath. The creature moved on, and he understood that this instinct to remain still in the nest, or the undergrowth, still existed with alarming potency in his human frame. He realised with a jolt that the history of life was not only recorded in his brain, it was his brain.

"Stop," Kel held his hand up as the lights brightened, indicating he was fine. He stared at the hemispheric ceiling, thinking about the dome of his head where his brain resides. My whole genetic history recorded in this? he thought to himself. A record since the word go? After a while he put up an upturned thumb.

"Go," said Lua from the chair.

Immediately he was back in the programme. A rapid sequence of images followed, the reptile changed shape over the course of time, and became smaller, its scales turning into hairs and heat was conserved. Three of the bones in its jaw migrated to form the tiny bones of the ear and its hearing became acute. Some sweat glands in its body became milk glands to feed the evolutionary drive to be closer to one's progeny. This little shrew-like creature foraged and hunted by night, and stayed clear of the dinosaurs that hunted by day. It was a powerful survivor in a precarious age, and for just one moment Kel experienced its aching vulnerability, and a powerful urge to protect surged in him.

The sequence sped up again, and our warm blooded mammal leapt into its own age of domination after the sudden decline of the giant reptiles. The eyes moved forwards on the head to give optimum vision, and slowly its forelimbs became more mobile, and Kel was aware that the senses fought for dominance. The environment slowly shaped a primate-like creature as consciousness vied with matter for dominance.

A monkey bounded from tree to plain and grew in size and stature, and lived in a community of others, hunting and scavenging. Kel winced as he heard a sound like a fingernail scratching over a black-board, and the primates around him scattered into hiding places.

The brow of this creature slowly grew in dimension as the thinking centre developed and evolution's highway sidetracked the apes, then the chimps, and in the fast track the human thumb in opposition to its fellow fingers took shape. A strange sensation prickled through his thumbs and he saw a flint axe, a fire, and a trap for the hunt, and a blast of self-awareness rushed through him. He tried to make a fist with both hands, and the desire to reflect surged in him as these memories streamed through his consciousness. A new scene around him then captured his attention.

A band of human ancestors walked in the magnificent beauty of an African savanna, bordered by a mountainous forest. Members of the group made sounds to each other and the focus of attention of the Brief switched to the tongue and throat of one of the band. The pharynx sunk down into the throat, elongating the tongue and shaping the larynx, giving birth to a multitude of sounds. Areas in the brain developed into language centres, where before they had been instinctual warning and mating centres.

These anomalies in the dawn of the age of the apes gave Homo sapiens an edge over all creation, furthering the means of communication, so that with each generation, more was learnt. Language…

"Stop," Kel called.

The lights came on, and Lua looked up from the chair opposite him. She had been observing him closely.

"Can we go for a walk?" Kel sat up. "You might be facilitating the process but my brain is bursting, I've just experienced all of evolution, and the bloody thing just keeps pumping out more information. I am surprised David Attenborough, or that crazy Aussie, Steve whassis-name? Didn't jump out on me. My nervous system feels as raw as old loopy worm, that renegade tadpole. I love nature, but this is sometimes a bit too close for comfort, a sort of virtual telly."

"So what do you want to do?" Lua asked, and smiled coyly.

"I want a coffee, a pastry, and a visit to the engine room. Do you think that can be arranged?"

"The engine room?"

"Yes, the engine room, I want to see what is powering our course through the unknown. I'm a boy, remember."

"All right, all right! I'll see what I can do.

"Remind me why I need to know all this stuff," said Kel, following Lua out of the Chamber."

"Because it's who you are; remember! You have to know yourself."

"I feel so raw."

"The programme is hitting neural memories up and down your central nervous system. You are a brave man and we're all proud of you."

Kel straightened up, and unbeknown even to himself, thrust his chest out, just a little.

*   *   *   *

Kel was suited up in metallic foil, completely covered except for two translucent eye slits. The walls of the engine room were covered with read-out gages, lights, graphs, and undulating patterns. In the middle were two very large, circular metallic sheets.

Between these two an energy field had been set up in a vacuum. 'An unbelievable amount of energy,' Lua had said, and she would say no more. It hummed like a highly-strung bee, and six crew sustained its function, attending to the dials and gages. They looked ominous in their tinseled work clothes, and they shone darkly in the subdued light of the engine room

Kel, Lua, and a member the crew sat at the back of this engine room, observing the constant attention and efficiency of the crew. There was no room for any distractions here; any mistakes would be costly.

"How do they stay so focussed?" he asked.

"They are highly trained, and are aware of the consequences of mistakes. The computers look after the majority of calculations. As you can see, we continually monitor the read-outs and only come in when new situations are encountered, any adjustments to the energy field can be made through commands into the computer control centre, mentally in code."

"How often is that?" Kel asked

"Often enough. These are micro calculations requiring miniscule adjustments."

"They use telepathy?"

"Kind of. There's a simple chip inserted into the pre-frontal cortex of the brain."

"Oh yeah, where decisions are made?"

"That's right Kel."

He asked about the energy source and they were cagey in their replies, telling him that the vacuum produced enough negative energy to keep the tunnel they were in, open. This kind of technology was obviously on a 'need to know' basis and, Kel reckoned, they had no idea of the degree of his scientific and technical illiteracy.

Engineering was a busy place, and they had not stayed long.

"Looks like a James Bond movie," said Kel on their way back.

"Ah yes," said Lua, "we had a name for him in our Orientation."

"What was it?"

"Jimmutable. He changed from one middle-aged man to another over a seventy-year period. Not bad going. Was he really that popular?"

"Yes, but I gave up when Jimmutable the first threw in the towel."

"Threw in the towel?"

"Boxing term, means giving up." Kel sparred with the air in front of him.

"Don't tell me you like boxing?" Lua said with disgust.

"Ah, come on, Lua, don't make judgements about a different age. Some of the fights were poetic, two people giving their all, it was a tough age. Trouble was, it was so corrupt."

"Yes I know, the Boxing Trials are a part of legal history."

"What boxing trials?" Kel asked.

"You'll find out."

∗   ∗   ∗   ∗

Kel was back in the chair, grateful for the welcome break, and took a deep breath before going under for the final session of the day. Within seconds he was floating and free of thought, and before him in space hung a formation of celestial spheres, the brightest being in the centre. This was our solar system, and as each planet was magnified in turn, he recognised the red of Mars, the rings of Saturn, and the moons of Jupiter. It was the environment he had experienced just before his tailspin the previous day.

He was projected to a point where he could observe the Earth and its moon, celestial-traveling companions in the cosmic night. The beauty of the scene before him brought a wave of nostalgia, and regret. It was so wondrously beautiful, and miraculous. A pearl—yes, a pearl, thought Kel. How could we fuck it up so?

He heard the words: "Language became the means by which we survive, and enabled us to communicate thoughts and feelings, leading to the discovery and development of leisure and the ability to work more efficiently together."

Too efficient by half, thought Kel in an instant, and his vision zoomed in on the continent of Africa. Once again there was a sensation of speed, but this time it had little physical effect on him. The narration stopped and the information fed him was visual; he heard no sound, yet the story of human progress somehow unfolded in his mind.

Kel was shown the explosive outpouring of ancestral humans from Africa into the far reaches of Europe and Asia. These humans learned to dominate their environment and co-operate with each other, and bands became tribes, tribes became races. This, hand in hand with the discovery and development of plants and animals that could be domesticated, led to the eventual slow diffusive spread of these farmers, with their crops and animals, across the latitudes of Europe and Asia. Villages and towns were created, populations exploded and diseases raged, art and literature blossomed, kings and emperors reigned, guns and ploughshares brought wealth and power. Hunter-gatherers were forced into isolated bands in the extreme crevices and corners of the continent, while the conquering tribes, races, and empires of Europe, North Africa and Asia dominated. From the whiskey distilleries of Ireland to the gunpowder factories of China was all one massive continent, one with an alarming degree of dominance over the environment.

This spread of a power-based civilisation was not possible to the same extent in the Americas, or Africa, because of the longitudinal nature of those continents. Deserts, forests, and extreme climate changes impeded the spread of the domestication of life, and the diseases that accompany them. Great empires and cultures existed, but they came and went. Kel was taken on a breathtaking ride over the vast expanse of the Sahara, and then up and over at great speed to the South American rain forests, both so magnificent in their vastness and pristine purity, and physically impregnable barriers to transcontinental migrations since the dawn of civilisation.

The natives of both these continents, together with Australasia and the islands of Asia and Pacifica, had no resistance to the spread of European and Chinese diseases, prevalent in Eurasia for centuries. Smallpox, TB and influenza decimated these peoples, and foiled any struggle or uprising against the harbingers of civilisation. Superior weaponry finished off the indigenous peoples, and alternative farming cultures and the hunter-gatherers were history by the end of the second millennium, except for small pockets in the wildest extremes of the planet. The planet had been conquered by the Eurasians.

This is the story of human survival. Ease of food production led to an inventiveness that dominated the planet, and any competitors that were met were eradicated, exiled or assimilated. Or merely plundered, and left later on to cope with whatever form of foreign administration was bequeathed them. It is just the way it was, with power as the major player in the game. Kel understood that human history was a violent one, necessary to our survival, part of our make-up, part of a rage within us. How could we decimate whole races for their land? Is that what we're about?

Just for a second in Kel's mind there flashed and flickered an image of Ken-eye, and his heart rose to greet him. 'You'd love this stuff,' intimated Kel over the enormous gulf that now separated them. "Is might right?" he asked him, and smiled to himself. Spanish, French and English microbes conquered the New World, those virginal lands prostituted to the greed of possession, widowed by…

"Stop," he called.

"It's almost over," said Lua.

"It's getting a bit negative in there!"

"This last bit is all you Kel, you must be forming ideas around the information being fed to you. It's probably that whining socialist in you. You know, the bit in you always looking for the negative. It enables you to feel superior. Be objective!"

"Whining? Superior? Well bollocks to you too!" Kel said, staring at the ceiling. "Alright, I get your point, can you put the audio back on— please! Ready when you are."

"By the eighteen hundreds," now a voice had returned, "there were nine hundred million people on earth, and she began to show signs of strain. By the second millennium, there were six billion, and it was clear that humankind was heading for disaster, unless it curbed its rush into unchecked materialism." Kel was shown a view of a main street through a rural village, and the scene sped forward. It fast became a town, then a large city, and the programme fast-forwarded. Cars sped to stop at traffic lights; people poured over walkways and crossings like ants. It produced in him a familiarity, as he was part of this concrete jungle, this mad rush. He already felt it was absurd, and he now regarded the chaos of hurry and worry as lunacy, as this virtual city spun around him. A factory farm and its sad inmates of pigs and chickens came into view, and then coiled around like the double helical staircase of DNA and spun into the picture that surrounded him, ominous and menacing.

The unchecked rush swirled into an opaque luminescence and he knew his mind was the creator of all this. A voice said, "Acts of god aside, the human mind is the most creative and destructive force in the known physical universe. It had ensured human survival, but something had gone terribly wrong. It now threatened its continuance."

"The Brief will continue after a night's rest. Tomorrow will be the last on-board briefing session."

Kel was transported back to the on-deck environment. He sat upright in the briefing chair, and stared ahead of him, Lua slowly came into view. She was sitting crossed legged in a chair on a 'floating' platform, a few feet in front of him, chin resting on her index fingers; her eyes fixed on him, pensive.

Kel stretched his arms up, and extended his body back like a bow. He then sat forward, and was thinking about the last statement, 'Threatened its continuance'.

"What happened?" Kel asked, gazing over at Lua. "Did we blow it?"

"Wait for tomorrow, Kel. Everything has been sequenced in such a way as to allow for maximum absorption."

Kel found his land legs quickly this time, and he followed Lua back to his quarters. He didn't feel much of anything, and his thinking processes seemed to be in abatement.

"Kel, I have to go now for a kind of de-briefing. Is there anything I can do for you before I go?" Lua asked.

"Am I eating in?" Kel asked.

"That's up to you, if you want to go to the canteen, dinner is being served, and someone will look after you. Remember, you are a special guest. Just turn left out of the door, and follow the companionway around, you can't miss it."

"Out of the nursery, huh?"

"If you want to eat in, I'll arrange it."

"No, I'd like to meet the gang."

Lua left with a wave and a smile, and Kel flopped down onto the bed and peered up at the ceiling. It was the strangest thing…not a single thought intruded into his field of attention, and he felt quite stoned, but too sharp to be stoned. He lay back on the bed and marveled at the clarity, and peace, of his present state of mind.

✳   ✳   ✳   ✳

Lua sat opposite Daljit in the clinic.

"Look at these read-outs, they are fascinating," said Daljit, and she fingered her wrist console.

One of the white panels on the wall lit up to display a read-out that resembled an outline of the Himalayas.

"These were Kel's vitals last night, when I called you." She punched in another code, and a similar read-out lit up on another panel. "And these were yours," she sat back and looked at Lua.

Lua stood, approached them, and studied them closely. She laughed, stubbed her finger on the highest peak of the read-out and said, "This doesn't come close to explaining what is going on here."

"Lua, how could you?" gasped Daljit.

"I can't explain what's going on. I never thought I would be subject to the level of emotion I am experiencing. It is quite the wildest thing you can imagine, an almost total lack of objectivity. I'm in the physical, it's exhilarating, sometimes excruciating."

"Lua, the mission!"

"This is the very best thing that could happen to this mission," replied Lua curtly. "He's a brave soul, and letting go of an awful lot. My being there for him is facilitating that process more than you can possibly imagine."

"Well look at these," Daljit lit up another read-out. "His adrenaline and dopamine levels when he's around you, even when he's asleep, they are way up. It proves that he has facilitated to your pheromones, and look at the oxytocin level, he's nesting. How is this going to facilitate the process? You are probably constantly on his mind. This has been one hell of a trip for our Kel. I am surprised he hasn't gone on mental overload."

"I never thought in the course of my studies, that I would come across such emotions as these," said Lua, oblivious to Daljit's criticism.

"You are dealing with a wild earthling Lua, from two centuries ago. You are playing with fire."

"Put up his read-outs when he was first in the canteen this morning," responded Lua.

Daljit did so.

"Is he in the canteen now?"

Daljit checked Kel's monitor. "Yes," she said.

"Get a visual, and post his present vitals now," Lua stood back, arms folded, defiant.

Kel was sat down with a group of three female crewmembers. He looked very relaxed, and they were all laughing.

The two women looked at the read-out.

"Ha-ha!" exclaimed Lua. "Look at that! As cool as, what did they used to say...yes, as cool as a cucumber," and she laughed victoriously as Kel's vital signs slid smoothly across the screen.

"Get an audio," she demanded.

"I used to think all the time," Kel was saying, "now there isn't a whisper anywhere, and I feel terrific, as high as a kite," and he laughed, and the three laughed with him.

Daljit turned the screens off. "You are playing with fire, Lua. Can't you see his responses are still conditioned."

"I am not playing with fire, Daljit, I am on fire. I never thought love possible," she said, collapsing into the chair opposite her colleague.

Daljit's mouth dropped in disbelief. "Oh, Lua," she said, "Oh, Lua. I will stop you if I have to!"

"Nothing can stop this! It's unstoppable."

✳   ✳   ✳   ✳

As Kel lay in bed alone, his thought processes began to re-surface. He wondered if Lua would be stealing into his bed this night. When this proved to be a fruitless line of thought, he started thinking about the information he had been fed that day.

Being a product of twentieth century western civilisation, he was somewhat ignorant of his conditioned responses to his fellow humans, and blissfully unaware of his recently awoken desire to nest. Nonetheless, the notion that his body was in some way a living record of the whole of creation had more than tweaked his curiosity. Theories now danced in his mind and became a whirlpool, which he observed from a still point at its centre. Too much information and too little storage space, he thought, and decided it was time to sleep. He tried focusing his attention on noises going on around him, as he would in the Chamber, and quite suddenly fell deeply asleep.

Little did he know that the sudden, torrential re-surfacing of his thought processes was producing a flurry of peaks and dips on the panels in the clinic, instigating an argument between Daljit and Lua, just as he was falling off to sleep.

Kel awoke, and felt a hand on his belly.

"Lua," he said.

"Who else?" she replied.

A second night, beyond the speed of light, and Kel exalted in love, lost in a sea of lust.

✳   ✳   ✳   ✳

Kel heard a knocking sound, and realised he was alone. Someone was at the door and this surprised him as his only visitor had been Lua, and she had ceased to announce herself.

"Come in," he called after quickly surveying the scene of the previous night's crime for any evidence. Old habits die hard.

A young man entered, bearing a tray of cereal and fruit.

"Good morning, Kel. My name is Carter."

"Good morning," said Kel, and he thought of asking this new character if he were his valet, but decided this was too glib, so he kept quiet.

Meanwhile, in the clinic, Daljit monitored Kel's internal environment, and made a mark on her computer, indicating a fight or flight response by her unaware subject.

Carter placed the tray by Kel. "Do you mind if I ask you some questions?"

"Any prizes?" Kel winced at his retort. "Sorry," he continued, "I'm beginning to see how I use this banal humour as a kind of avoidance and I'm acting like a twerp. Please ask me whatever you want."

Daljit marked a high jump in the read-out.

Kel and Carter talked while he ate breakfast. He enjoyed the questions about his own age, for he was a lover of history. "You would love Ken-eye," he said.

"Who?" asked Carter.

"Just one of my friends," replied Kel, and a wave of homesickness swept through him for his friend, and the island over which Ken-eye lorded. Something in Kel missed the chaos of his planet, and actually longed for it.

※ ※ ※ ※

"Look at these," said Daljit, "He's having major emotional reactions. I can't wait to find out what they're talking about."

"I am surprised you haven't got him bugged" said Lua, who had joined her colleague, and perused the read-outs with a detached interest.

"If the directive had not been so resolute against it, I probably would have," replied Daljit.

"You are too nosey," said Lua.

"That's why I am the medical officer!" she retorted.

Kel, meanwhile, finished his breakfast in bed, and lay on his back staring at the ceiling, thinking of their imminent arrival in Gaya, and how much of Lua he would be able to see when back in her world. 'Be assertive', he told himself, 'You are doing them the favour'. He got up and as he finished getting ready, Lua entered.

"Good timing," he said.

"I've got you covered, Kel," she winked and stood in front of him almost defiantly, putting her hands on his shoulders. "We have time for coffee before the briefing re-commences. Come on."

Once again Kel was following Lua through the ship. The atmosphere in the canteen was open and friendly towards him, and crew-members he had not yet met came up and introduced themselves. Kel was impressed with the courtesy shown by this group of people, without it being in any way self-effacing. A conversation developed in which Kel uncharacteristically found himself making excuses for mineral and logging developers of his day, as he tried to explain that they were ignorant of the consequences of their actions. The crew would have none of it. Pure greed, they countered; it was a lively debate and there was an excitement in the air as they neared their destination.

"Their lack of job security and an unfair social system led them to ignore the obvious..." Kel was halted by a high pitched sound coming from the public address system. Everyone got up and raced out of the canteen. Lua was the last out.

"Kel, something is up," she said, "I'll meet you at the Briefing Chamber. If I am not there in five minutes, start the Brief; just say 'go'. I'll get computer clearance for you." She blew him a kiss. "Don't worry, this often happens," and she was out of the door.

Kel sat for a while in the empty canteen, and then trooped back to the Briefing Chamber. Something was up; he could feel it in his bones. Strangely, though, he was not too afraid.

The Chamber seemed a very lonely place without Lua. He clambered into the chair, and lay there in the dim light, staring at the rounded ceiling. A second before he was about to initiate the Brief, Lua appeared. She had been running, and was a little breathless, her smile masking concern.

"What's up?" he asked.

"We have to work at boosting our energy before our jump to sub-space; it just means a lot of work," she replied.

"Do we still arrive today?" he asked.

"Yes," she replied, and her curtness stopped Kel from asking any further questions.

"You have to start, Kel, time is of the essence," said Lua. She knelt down beside him, and put her arms around his neck. Her look was tender and sad, and she kissed him full on the mouth. This was the first outward show of affection outside of the bedroom, and it surprised Kel. Before he could say anything, Lua had started the programme, and he was held by the gravitational pull of the chair.

"Stop," he said, but nothing happened. "Stop! Damn it," and reluctantly he surrendered to a weightless environment. The Brief continued.

There were a few moments of silence, and Kel thought he heard some static, as if the programme were sticking, unable to start. Then it started. "What follows in this part of the programme is a synopsis of discovery, a discovery that presented humanity with its greatest leap in evolution since those amphibious sea creatures had left the safety of the sea. It pushed human development to the threshold of a myriad unknown possibilities of cyber, inner, outer and psychic space."

"Stop!" called Kel again, but to no avail. The Brief resumed.

"There is a theory called the chaos theory. It states that the smaller something becomes, the more unstable it is. This is how worlds collapse into worlds, and is the very physics of human perception. Investigation into this theory ultimately changed the course of human history." Kel was once again propelled into an internal environment;

there was an inward rush and a sense of intense light as every thought in his mind was ushered towards the exit. This time, however, he felt more resistance. He was thinking of Lua. She had been sad as he descended in the chair; perhaps they were soon about to die. He pondered this for a few brief moments, though soon he was just observing his thoughts, aware that he was free from their hold on him. His body and his mind were at great peace and there he floated for some time, visions passing in and out of his perception.

Suddenly a voice woke him from his passive state. A new voice for the Brief, but he had heard it before.

"This is Lyle. We met through the disk back on Earth. We are coming to the end of this programme, and I am sure you would like some questions answered. You are at present in a synthesised state of higher awareness, which we have facilitated to increase your powers of information absorption. It has a knock-on effect that I am sure you have experienced on board. This is like the use of awareness enhancing neurotransmitters, and they are, usually, temporary states and will pass." Lyle's image appeared briefly in front of Kel, and there was a flash and a crackle before it disappeared.

"We have attempted to show you in a very short space of time," Lyle went on, audio only now, "Something of your physical, mental, and spiritual roots. This has been designed to help you in a mission we hope you will accept. As unbelievable as it may sound to you, there is a record within the fabric of your body and mind of every moment of your existence since the Big Bang. Your genes transmit this physical information from generation to generation. And there is another component of your psychic history which transcends the physical; it is difficult to explain, so I shall just refer to it as 'past lives'."

There was a pause, and the words 'past lives' rolled over, and over, in Kel's mind.

"This experiential information could be used against you in your mission. To help you overcome your own fear of such apocalyptic events recorded deep inside of you, it is imperative you understand that your history has been recorded through your psychosomatic receptors, every single event, at every single moment. The more dramatic the event, the more readily retrievable the memory."

After a pause, Lyle recommenced. "The intellect, the purest faculty of the mind, is the mechanism through which this history is interpreted by you as an individual. It all happens within the context of what we call the Absolute, or more familiarly, the spirit."

"This spirit, in which your past lives and psychic tendencies exist and play out their stories, is an absolute oneness, infinite and untouched by anything manifest. It is the screen on which everything happens, the play itself, as well as the observer of the play. Our task is to help you understand that originally you were, and ultimately you are, that spirit; you are no different from it at any moment. It is that force that keeps your body alive, and your mind active, through the power of memory"

Kel was left once again to ponder the imponderable. A gate in his mind was opening, and yet he couldn't form a concept around what was being said, around the wholeness of it all. It eluded him.

"When you start to understand the connotations of this," Lyle continued, "we believe you will be able to face into the mission fearlessly, and successfully accomplish all of our objectives."

There was another crackle, and Lyle now appeared before Kel, as he had done so in the disk. He smiled, and there was something achingly familiar about him.

"So," he continued, "we are just going to run you through one more programme, some information about what your brain is, how it developed, and explain a little about the experiential states of an awakened condition. I look forward to meeting you on Gaya."

Lyle's image disappeared and Kel was transported back to the float world, where something quite bizarre happened. He was looking into a mirror and his reflection suddenly changed, and the image thrown back at him was of a translucent swirling storm of nothingness, movement around a void. A feeling of mysterious blissfulness overtook him,

a physical ecstasy from which a spark emerged burning its way outward, lightening the dark. When he attempted to make sense of it, and
rationalise his existence in the midst of everything, the ecstasy abated,
and a feeling of terror arose like a volcano. This he rode determined
not to be defeated by such a flow of fear, gritting his teeth and tightening the grip of his fists. He had experienced this before and would not
be intimidated.

Now the swirling movement became linear deep within him as consciousness thread itself into existence. A sensation of searing intensity
swept through his perception as he realised he is the spark around
which everything spun: the master of all. He moved outwards as the
heart of this centre, the fire playing up and down his nervous system
like a musical score, intertwining its way around Kel's field of perception, creating centres, making connections.

A rush of energy from his mid-spine to the crown of his head sent a
light flooding into his sensory cortex, and he squirmed at its intensity,
but uttered not a sound. His sense of self went out to meet the light
and in the process created space in which to interpret it. Light rushing
into dark. This spring of all activity gushed out in the mid-brain,
where it emerged in naked aggression and self-absorption, the fire of
creation and the arrow of consciousness. Islands of neural survival centres sprang up to temper this fire. This is the limbic system, the seat of
the senses in the primordial brain.

Kel lay still as sensations played havoc with his physical being and
these neural messages raged through their conduits, up and down his
backbone and through his brain, at lightning speed. The light of
awareness now invaded his olfactory centre and he smelt danger, then
sex, and then food as consciousness expanded out into the physical
realm. His reactions to these ancient reflexes registered only on his face,
his brow rolling over his eyebrows, his nostrils flaring

A bridge formed from his smell centre to regions forming higher in
the brain, and the rudiment of memory was born…the channel trans-
porting short term memory to long term, and the primordial language

centres blossomed. Smell now lost its dominance and sight once again became the sovereign power of the mind, and memory the most important facet of survival.

The limbic area then sprouted, like a magician's bunch of flowers, into the cortex of the brain, and covered it like an orange peel does the fruit. A blast of awareness detonated through Kel's body at this outward rush of neural energy, as it fostered the thinking centre, unique and exquisite. We are just an extension of our primal instincts, thought Kel, simmering in these neural eruptions as the flood plains of dopamine, adrenaline and serotonin surged in their tiny neural channels, and his mind raced to interpret them. And we have forgotten ourselves in this mystery, we have forgotten that we are the mystery.

"In this thin layer of gray cortical matter," the narrative continued, "lay the potential to transcend time and space. It is the dome in which all events are reflected, the seat of the self. It is both a creative and destructive force."

A rapidly changing scenario of colours and patterns flashed in front of Kel, and he slowly became aware of an intricate, and detailed scene around him. An art gallery with wall to wall abstract paintings came into focus. "You have made billions of computations to recognise the scene around you. Billions upon billions."

"Through the power of distinction we can discover the vital force that we are, the wholeness of spirit, and discard the illusion of separateness we have created around ourselves. When we attain the subtlest of abilities to see what we are not, we can see what we are. This ability to make distinctions is the root of our destruction, and the way to our salvation. Seeing clearly through the congestion of thoughts to the present moment is the way."

The scene before him slowly changed, and he found himself looking at a woman sitting serenely by a lakeside. Next to her was a pot of water at which she stared, and Kel saw that she was staring at the moon reflected in the water. With a jolt he realised he knew this story, but the Brief phased him out and continued. "When we take the reflection to be real, the mind is born and runs after the objects of its desire. This is the seat of duality, just an image, a reflection of the infinite, conscious awareness that you are."

'I know this story'; Kel's consciousness rose again as it adapted to the neural manipulations of the programme. He was beginning to rise above it.

Suddenly the pot broke and the woman looked up at the moon, a look of rapture unfolding on her face. "Seeing through the illusion, we are able to find the source."

Kel found himself staring at the moon. No reflection, no barrier, quite simply one thing, no duality.

Where the moon had been he now saw his face, a mirror image. It shocked him and a jolt of energy swept through his body, and he shuddered. He understood his mind was the cutting edge of a vast, and unlimited power, and this power, through its reflection, had become enamoured by its own physical limitations. His image then focussed in on a part of the brain high up on the left and right sides. Kel understood that these were the areas that orient him to time and space. The Brief was able to cut them out resulting in him being present beyond the physical realm, and a wave of elation accompanied this realisation. He then saw a section lower down in the brain stem that was also cut out, allowing a raw ancient awareness to sweep up through him and reach his conscious attention, subjecting him to these quickenings, these awakenings. "That's why I've felt so blissed out," he said out loud, and at that moment the Brief curtailed all its neural control mechanisms, subtle and gross.

The voice of the Brief continued, "A mirror will now be placed behind you." Another mirror was placed behind Kel's head, and he saw an endless spiral of his image, a tunnel that trailed off into the distance before him. More mirrors appeared around him and his image multiplied.

"Jesus!" said Kel.

"These are the reflections," the voice continued, "they are like thoughts, and are endless in the field of existence. They are mirrors of eternity and an aspect of you; you created them, observe them, and will eventually annihilate them. But in the meantime, we are obsessed by them, and forget who we are."

"Thoughts are the expression of the creative force in us, and the mind is the mechanism used to read them, their mirror. Some of these thoughts we choose to manifest, to bring into existence; others we dismiss. Thought itself, however, has no power. You are the mold that receives the molten spirit; only you have the ability to create and destroy; your responsibility in the midst of this is total. You are the only power."

Another pause and Kel began to feel more than a little claustrophobic. There was something new and physically restrictive going on; they were putting on the brakes, closing in on subspace. Uncomfortable and nauseous, he commanded the machine to stop, but nothing happened. The Brief continued.

The mirror images, much to Kel's relief, had gone, and scenes of the chronological development of human society were projected on a screen before him. They started from his era and projected into the future, to the time of his hosts. He followed their technological achievements, their alluring architecture and cultural concepts, all at an alarming pace, to a point of light that flashed through space and time, transcending both, and he realised that point, that moment, was now.

"You see," the narrative continued. "In the early second millennium there were a series of events that forced the human populace to re-think its priorities. We are not at liberty to tell you what these are, but they were catastrophic in nature."

Oh boy, thought Kel, sad, wondering for a moment in this brief reflection. What did we do? His physical discomfort grew by the second.

"They were, with intelligent foresight, avoidable. It led to a change in human strategy, and in the course of time more funds were made available for creative, rather than destructive research. Eventually the most incredible discovery was made."

Kel was looking at a body on a plinth covered by a glass screen. A peaceful expression graced the man's face. He saw a flurry of activity, both opaque and luminescent, in the area of the heart and sternum, and this energy ebbed and flowed like an internal tide within the man's body. It then stopped and stilled, and slowly started making its way up, as if through a narrow and invisible channel, to the top of the head.

The narrative continued. "As science grew more interested in its spiritual roots, and in the infinitesimally small, it made its greatest discovery of all time, something that would change the course of human history, and enable human beings to understand themselves, and their relationship to one another, in a much deeper way. This was the discovery of the individual soul leaving the body."

"What?" Kel gasped. His nausea was increasing by the minute.

Suddenly a mechanical voice jolted reality back into Kel's system. "Jumping to subspace, brace for impact," and he felt his body being embraced with a bear hug by the chair.

He saw the opalescent energy rise through and out of the head of the body before him, and a new surge of energy hit Kel, as intense as the tsunami that had propelled him on his journey, except this was more like an implosion, with his body diving into itself. It was a kind of involution, as they swung around the corner of space and time, some massive object slowing their trajectory and extracting them from the curvature of space. As this happened, Kel had a vision of something inside himself that was vast, colourless, and infinite, a revelation that defied his senses. He felt like he was diving into this vastness, imploding into himself on an endless journey…

When the force became unbearable, he lost consciousness.

ARRIVAL

Kel heard a sound that re-kindled an image in his mind. He held his father's hand and looked up at a steam train that made a noise like a resting monster. It had just transported them the breadth of England, and was cooling down after the chase. It hissed, and the metal whined in staccato bursts, as if glad of the rest.

There was some movement, mechanical in nature, and somehow more intrusive than any he had experienced in the days of the flight, a giant arm had the ship in its grasp. Kel was now fully awake, and felt the tingle of excitement of arrival. He opened his eyes. The light was dim and he scanned the room from his recumbent position, still held firm by the chair's energy. From the corner of his eye he saw a figure sitting in a chair, inside a metal pod. It appeared lifeless. It was Lua.

With as much strength as he could muster he strained against the invisible force until he felt the veins popping in his neck. The force gradually gave way, and he sat up, holding his head for a second to shake off a wave of nausea. He stood and quickly sank his head to the floor as another wave of dizziness swept over him. He then moved slowly towards the still figure on the chair.

A gravity field surrounded her body, and he could not touch her. He moved into her field of vision and looked into her open eyes. She did not move, but Kel felt she was present, or at least alive. He then looked down and saw a series of slits in her neck from which some oily substance oozed.

In one heart-stopping moment he was paralyzed with the weight of his realisation. Lua was not human. She looked out at him as if frozen in ice, yet Kel felt her presence. He knelt in front of her, shaken and scared. At that moment the door whooshed open, and Kel spun his head around to see what was about to enter. There was no one there.

"Kel, don't worry, Lua will be taken care of. Most of our available energy was needed to protect your life function, and we were a fraction under needs." The voice over the intercom was annoyingly calm, and reminded Kel of the computer Hal, in *2001*.

"Lua can be revived," it continued, "and all explained to you. Please make your way to the door, and follow the blue light to the point of exit."

He felt betrayed, but this feeling was soon crushed. What would he meet at the point of exit? What had conspired to get him here?

He waited for a while, hoping the calm voice of the computer would hurry him along, so he could unleash some of the fury he felt exploding in his veins, and at least hurl some abuse and shouts of anger. But there was only silence now, and no movement. They had arrived.

Kel stood in front of the body of Lua and looked down at her, dazed. She lay still, like an alien exhibit at a museum. He shook himself out of his inertia and blew her a kiss, and whispered, "We shall meet again." He slowly turned and made his way to the door.

A line of blue lights stretched out before him through the companionways, and the ship was infused with a strange mist that hung eerily in the air. He followed the lights, and felt her piercing absence. He could not believe she was not human. Why had he been fooled?

He moved slowly, and his head was groggy. The blue lights ended at a large circular hatch, and the voice chimed in, "Please wait here for final quarantine check."

"I've got a name for you," Kel said, tetchily.

"What is that?" the calm voice replied.

"Hal," said Kel.

"That is strange," the computer responded.

"Why?" replied Kel, surprised.

"Because that is my name."

At that moment there was a great hiss and the release of some steam, and the hatch started to slowly open upwards. There was a slight inrush of air, and his ears popped. A feeling of terror and excitement rushed through Kel, and his mind raced. What was out there? Where was Lua?

As the hatch opened the steam increased in volume and danced around his heels, spiraling up around his torso. Kel slowly discerned three figures approaching along a walkway. He screwed his eyes up and tried to focus, but the image was mirage-like, like phantoms dancing on a hot road in summer. The figures drew closer. Thank god they have legs, thought Kel, as he observed they were human in shape, and dressed in maroon red. A woman flanked by two men. When they were close enough the woman proffered her hand to Kel; his jaw dropped, and he was speechless.

"How do you do, Kel," said the woman, "You can't imagine how happy we are to see you," and she shook his hand firmly.

Kel was staring into the face of Lua.

"My name is Tanea Lua. Please call me Tanea," said the woman.

Kel said nothing, and stood still, mouth agape.

"Unless you have taken root to your spot, could we be on our way? We have a lot of work to do," said Tanea, with the crisp authority of a real matriarch.

"How do you do," he said at last, sticking his ground. "You owe me a few explanations."

"Yes, we do" she replied, "And when we get going I can brief you."

"I am not moving until you tell me who you are, what your relationship is to Lua, and what the hell Lua is." Kel struck a woeful sight at the circular mouth of the jet-black spaceship, like a child unwilling to get off the bus for summer camp.

"There is an intimate connection between us which I will explain to you as we go. She is a bionic imprint of me, yet there are differences. I am definitely human through and through, and yes, I know," said Tanea, holding up her hand to stop Kel's next question. "You'll just have to take my word on it for now."

"Is she dead?" Kel asked.

"No, she can be revived."

"With her memory intact?" Kel, eagle-eyed, studied Tanea's reply.

"It is possible, yes," said Tanea, keeping eye contact with Kel.

Kel took a deep breath, and looked down at the ground before him. The three dressed in red made not a sound. He had no option but to carry on.

As soon as Kel took a step, Tanea had turned, and was off like a hare out of a race trap. Somehow he fell in step, and returned a weak smile to the reassuring ones he received from the two men, as he stepped hurriedly past them like a tame greyhound in pursuit. He eyed the woman in front of him. It was Lua's figure and form, but it was not Lua.

When they had covered some distance, Kel called for Tanea to stop. He turned, and looked at the ship that had transported him over the vast expanse of time and space. It was black, almost transparently so, and a perfect sphere. He looked up and around. They were in an enormous hall, no, a hanger, and it was eerily quiet and still, like being deep underground or out in space, in a vacuum.

When he turned, she was off again, and he in pursuit. They approached a series of double hatch doors, which made a cacophony of different whooshing and hissing sounds, as they passed from one area to another.

As they passed through the final doorway, Tanea turned to Kel. "Broach yourself for this."

He emerged on a large semi-lit balcony, overlooking the most wondrous sight. It was as if he were standing on the edge of the Grand Canyon, but instead of dry desert, they were looking down at a lush growth of vegetation in the distance. Eerily, the sun shone not on them; they were in the dark side of the canyon. The light side was like a gigantic amphitheatre off in the distance, thousands of feet away. Kel looked at Tanea in disbelief.

"A biosphere" she said, "This is in orbit above our planet—a kind of space station, and quarantine greenhouse for new plant species before they are introduced to Gaya. There are some pretty succulent fruits down there."

"Any aliens?"

"No, Kel, just some alien pollinating insects—nothing that talks, that's for sure. So far we have found no physical evidence in the universe for anything that communicates on our level, or at our frequency."

"No intelligent life?"

"No intelligent…?" Tanea faced Kel. "There're flowers down there that can mimic the sex hormone of a female moth and attract all the boy moths for miles around; plants that can put you in touch with the most primordial states of awareness. They can't talk but they are mighty intelligent!"

"I get your point," said Kel, sheepishly.

Tanea motioned Kel to follow her to the side of the balcony. She fingered a console, and from some hidden space beneath her, a two-seater vehicle emerged, and with the barest of hums rose to, and hovered at Kel's mid-thigh level. A hatch opened and Tanea indicated that he should climb aboard.

"Like a comfortable car," said Kel. "How does it defy gravity?"

"We understand gravity better now, and have learned how to tap it," Tanea replied. "We played around with magnetic fields, and refined some untapped energy sources. Every bit of energy has its opposite and equal, so it's just a matter of creating technology to isolate and channel it."

Kel sat back and felt the immediate embrace of the chair. Tanea spoke some commands, and the dashboard lit up an array of red, green, and orange lights. The vehicle moved off effortlessly, and he sucked in his breath as they glided off the edge of the balcony. It was hundreds of feet to the floor of the biosphere.

"What you see below is a more or less self sufficient, self contained environment," said Tanea, as they sped on towards the sunny side of the canyon. Dome-like structures huddled in amongst the lush vegetation, and there were blue ponds and extensive irrigation systems. Kel could make out the long green leaves of the banana, and the stark open finger-like leaves of the papaya tree.

Tanea looked over at Kel. "That big dome over there is a university of agriculture; it's also where we do the final screening for new arrivals. But not you; you are a very special guest."

"When do I get the rest of the story?" Kel asked.

"Later today, please be patient. We only have you for a short time, so you are going to be very busy. We have a window of opportunity to sling-shoot you back home in just a few days, so any margin for error is unacceptable"

"Jesus! I mean I've just seen a soul leaving a body, and been told that my world is about to suffer some self-made disaster, and don't even know the bloody reason I'm here yet. Please be patient! I don't suppose you can tell me anything? I mean the love of my life is a fucking robot!"

Kel looked over at Tanea, who frowned, shook her head and said nothing.

"How long will it take to revive Lua?"

Tanea gave nothing away, "Lua's task was to get you here. She is a humanoid—half organically human, half-bionic. We use the DNA of certain citizens in our society who have reached a particular rank and skill, and replicate them. The consciousness of the person is also imprinted, in a complicated transference procedure. Originals—that's what we call the humans that are replicated—wear the red I have on, and the humanoids wear blue. It allows us to distinguish who's who."

They were picking up speed and it was getting darker. Kel looked over his shoulder, and saw the lush and verdant canyon receding behind them; a few tiny human figures waved up at the passing craft. The biosphere was huge, and they were headed for its darkest point.

"How long?" Kel persisted.

Tanea spoke some more commands, and there was a rush of speed as the vehicle changed shape, becoming more cylindrical, and the windscreen expanded around them. The dashboard lights went out and Kel's vision was filled with darkest night. There was another rush of speed and he waited in the dark. Suddenly they emerged out into a blazing light, and Kel gasped at the spectacular scene ahead of him. A pearly white and blue planet hung in space before them.

"Welcome to Gaya, Kel," and Tanea allowed him a few moments to soak up the spectacle before continuing. "Well, as you can see, Lua was somewhat different to me. If she had been like me, we reckoned you'd do a runner, and we'd still be looking for you in the jungles of Brazil, or some such place."

"Bloody right."

"Humanoids are equipped for all life's functions, as you've discovered." Tanea stopped for a moment as Kel tried to shift in his seat. "Lua displayed an amazing degree of emotionality with you, which is unusual since humanoids are, as a rule, an exact copy of their originals. I am not as susceptible to feelings, or as impulsive as she is. Anyway you'll know what I mean as you get to know me better."

"Will I see her again?"

"This is only the second time there has been a blip in the system, Kel." Tanea's tone became more serious. "Lua fell in love with you, and ignored very specific orders not to get involved. It really was not in her nature to be biologically promiscuous, but she fell for you in a big way. This was not part of her brief. She found your emotional neediness unique; such open display of unchecked feeling is not a prevalent feature of this age."

"Wha…?

"You display an innocence," Tanea continued, "that to be quite honest, we find quaint, and you are already a celebrity here. So you see, for Lua it all became too much. She will be revived, and some adjustments made."

Kel felt a rush of blood to his face, and his mind raged, but something strange happened. Instead of an explosion he acted calmly, and spoke with a steady voice. "If Lua hadn't been the way she was, I would still be on Earth thinking I'd had a bad acid trip on a credit card, or that this was a huge prank. She was efficient, believable, and loyal to your Gaya, and above all capable of love, a rare and beautiful thing. Quaint…my arse!"

Tanea sat at the controls, handling them as if she were driving a big old American car. She looked at him, and smiled a warm and friendly smile. But Kel was deadly serious, and would not be placated.

"And furthermore," he continued, "if you do not revive her exactly as she was, you can find someone else to do whatever it is you want me to do here."

"She's half machine." Tanea retorted.

"And half organic," he replied in a firm but calm voice. "She also has a conscience and a memory and deserves the respect and dignity to be re-instated as herself. Anyway, how do I know you are not a humanoid, that I am not talking to a computer chip or something?"

"If necessary you can draw some blood. Otherwise, you'll just have to take my word for it. They tried putting computer chips in people in your day with disastrous psychological consequences," said Tanea, skillfully changing the direction of the conversation.

"What?" Kel asked, and then added, "I know very little about computers."

"Wow, we've got ourselves a computer illiterate! People are going to love you here, Kel. No insult meant, but it is very rare to meet someone as…" Tanea could only come up with the same word again…"as innocent as you."

"No insult taken. I hate the bloody things, thieves of time…., and relationships. How the hell did they put computer chips in people?"

"Well,' said Tanea, sitting up in her chair, "As the computer age raged ahead in your day, more and more could be achieved from a single outlet, a console. People could control their lives from a single point, which, as you can imagine, was an attractive proposition to people in a hurry. All the computer convenience of your day, like shopping, bills, diary dates, that kind of thing, was all controlled by thought processing in the brain."

"Yes, I can imagine. The ability to live life without having to meet another living being spontaneously. Everything under control."

"Anyway," Tanea continued, "they tried inserting mind controlled computer chips into people, but all I can say is that it was a mistake. Big psychological problems resulted. We have obviously been given this body for a reason and need to use it. So it was decided to scale back to voice activated control mechanisms for us humans."

"Interesting! But what about the engine room on the ship? The crew used mind controlled stuff there?"

"Yeah, but they were all humanoids, remember—more programmable, so to speak."

Kel remembered the blue uniforms of the crew.

"It's very convenient to let go of the humdrum tasks," Tanea continued, "but we humans need to retain our ability to estimate and determine everyday activity; otherwise, we might as well vacate our bodies!"

Kel was aware he had been sidetracked from his questions about Lua, but he felt powerless to change the flow of the conversation. He wondered for a second if he was being mind-controlled, yet even this seemed not to matter. "What do you mean?" he asked

"We need to keep our bodies involved, that's all. We're going down, Kel, brace yourself." The craft suddenly dipped and was burning its way through Gaya's stratosphere, and this proved to be another amusement park ride. The atmosphere around Kel literally glowed, and they sped on with the new and original Tanea Lua at the wheel.

Suddenly, they darted into Gaya's atmosphere with a bit of a bump.

"Easy enough," said Kel, taking a deep breath.

"You'd be surprised how much more complicated it is cracking the shell of a planet like Gaya's, than it is travelling through space." Tanea then issued new verbal commands into the computer, all of which, it seemed to Kel, in code.

Kel looked out and down. They were in a steep descent and passed through some clouds; the craft bucked a little. "You can traverse space time, but you can't eliminate turbulence?"

Tanea laughed, and replied, "Only because we don't have to." She was obviously enjoying the piloting now, and the craft swooped, and turned, and at one point, spun 360 degrees. Tanea whooped with joy. "Anyway, we could have taken you down the quick way, via the grid that shot you up to the ship, but this is more fun."

"So was that in your brief, all this fun?" Kel could not resist this chide.

"Touché, Kel," she replied, and laughed.

"So if you, or rather the designers, or inventors of humanoids, could foresee the problems of mind control computer chips, then why create these humanoids in the first place?"

"We reached a stage of development where an intellectual elite arose in our quest for greater self-knowledge, and we couldn't adequately satisfy the demands that were being made on us. We therefore duplicated certain individuals to cope with that demand. The technology to do it had been available for some time."

"You qualified because you were one of the elite?" Kel asked.

"I was only one of the elite because I wanted it—that is, I wanted what Gaya stands for—more than anything else, and was totally sure of that. For us on Gaya, commitment stands on an equal footing with knowledge. Some would say more."

"What kind of problems have you encountered with the human-oids? Did you ever see Blade Runner, a film from my time?"

"Yes, it was part of our Orientation to this mission. Just enjoy the ride now. You can see Gaya from here and everything you need to know will be explained to you in your Mission Brief."

Kel looked down and the terrain of Gaya rose to meet them. He could see domes interspersed amongst the lush foliage, and an extensive system of lakes, and irrigation channels leading to a sea that changed in colour from light blue to emerald green, and then to a deep, deep blue. It was breathtakingly beautiful.

"So this is paradise?"

"Yes," replied Tanea, "the nearest you'll get to it in the physical. And this is the planet you have come to save—the pearl of the universe."

They approached a giant dome structure surrounded by a forest of trees. Tanea concentrated on the docking procedure, as if she were playing a video game, eyes locked on the dashboard read-out. Nothing seemed to bother her, she was so sure of herself.

Kel watched her maneuver the craft and a pang of longing struck him for a moment, and then was gone, as if his Lua had cast her mind upon him just for that moment, and he in that brief moment had acknowledged her presence. And his love for her, humanoid or not, his love was undeniable.

Kel felt a magnetic force grip the small craft as they were gently ushered into the dome. No need for a runway here, and Tanea rested back in her chair, her task complete. She stretched, cat-like, arching her back. "We will go straight to your quarters at the control centre, where you can clean up and have a snack. After that we'll re-start your Mission Brief, and you'll meet the mission commander. His name is Lyle."

"Yes, we've kind of met," said Kel, as the craft gently shuddered to a halt. They had arrived.

"Jesus," said Kel as his feet hit the ground; he put his hand out to steady himself.

"What we call gravity lag," said Tanea. "You'll be over it in about twenty seconds."

A small, friendly welcoming committee greeted them, and Kel noticed three or four of them whispering into Tanea's ear, while she passed out advice or orders. She obviously had some clout around here. There were no blue uniforms, just maroon, or combinations of other colours with a maroon collar, but no blue. People smiled at him but their gaze did not linger.

They were whisked quickly to another smaller vehicle, and this one hummed like a generator, hovering two feet from the ground. He hopped in and looked up and around the vast dome that harbored them. Kel felt very relaxed; no immigration and customs to worry about here, no luggage, and his driver seemed to be a big wheel in the local scheme of things. She slid in next to him, and they were off again without a chance for a wave goodbye. Kel looked over his shoulder, and the welcoming group were talking excitedly amongst themselves, and he just for a second remembered Tanea's words as he first gazed upon this planet. 'This is the planet you have come to save'.

They were moving at speed through an exit tunnel, and the lights flashed by like the blades of a mixer. They shot out of the tunnel, and were in, it appeared to Kel, a botanical garden, surrounded by big trees and lush vegetation. Brightly coloured flowers invaded his optical cortex with a piercing intensity.

Tanea leant back, released the controls, and looked over at Kel. "Don't worry, we're on automatic, and have priority status." She paused for a moment, and continued, "Gaya is a mix of arboretum, research centres, community homes, and non-toxic factories, all of which enables us to sustain a high living standard. We are basically self-sufficient except for a few things we get from Earth, like some of the component parts of the ship that brought you here. We have a warm temperate climate, and as you can see, the sun shines a lot."

Kel looked out and was reminded of all those past arrivals in his life at exotic destinations, where the sun shone, and the clouds of England could be forgotten. He was on a different planet and loaded with expectation, yet remarkably calm. He relaxed back in his seat and wondered at his state of calmness, and apparent absence of anxiety. Something about him was different, like a state of grace, or what? He looked over at Tanea.

"Gaya is dedicated to the pursuit and attainment of higher consciousness," she continued, "our technological achievements are secondary to this purpose, as are all other human aspirations and ambitions. We live in a community that avoids and hides nothing in the search for truth."

"Sexual relationships seem to be a bit of a taboo. Lua told me you don't regard sex as, what was it? Oh yeah, indulgent or permissive—something like that, but she could have been modified because she slept with me. What's that all about?"

"We have sexual relationships, we just don't make such a big deal out of them. They don't get in the way of our evolution like…like they do in your day. Don't tell me that your fling with Lua is not playing on your mind."

Kel nodded a degree of assent. "It wasn't a fling—it was way beyond a fling—more like a plunge, a very deep plunge. Sure it's on my mind, and it is probably the main reason I am here. Remember that."

"The single most important intention in this society," Tanea continued, "is to want to know, at the very deepest level, who we are, and what our relationship to each other is. Everything else, being objective, living in paradise, experiencing bliss, all that is secondary to wanting to know. If the desire is truly there, great leaps in understanding can be achieved."

"So people just sign up and zoom on out here?"

"There is a screening process to get to this planet, so by the time someone reaches here, they are pretty much sure that this is what they want."

"Pretty much?" asked Kel. "So some change their minds?"

"Of course, nothing is foolproof and when one actually discovers what must be given up to attain a higher degree of awareness—well it's not easy." There was passion in Tanea's voice. "In the course of all the new experiences that naturally occur in letting go of the past and one's conditioning, one meets an amazing array of subtle powers that can distract an individual from the goal of being free of them all and residing in a fully awakened state. And it doesn't take much to be distracted from the goal; given just a fraction of a chance our minds easily find an escape route."

"So you are talking about nirvana, the enlightened condition?"

"Yes, but on a level where we are all together in this, and we don't deify any individual, or have anything to do with religion. All of that never worked, in any period of history, and caused more grief than good."

"So you regard love as a stumbling block to achieving this awakening, this new condition?"

"Love, no; romantic love, the kind that dies in time, yes."

"The kind that dies in time," repeated Kel pensively. Then he asked, "So, how are you all doing? Is it working, your quest?"

"Everything is going better than we could possibly have hoped for." Tanea paused for a moment as if to calm her animated state; she obviously had a great commitment to this group of people. "We are a community with a shared vision, and a common goal, and the guts and humility to go for it."

"What about…." Kel continued.

"We are arriving," Tanea cut short his question.

They entered an enormous dome surrounded by giant and majestic trees, some of them totally unfamiliar to Kel. He had been engrossed in this conversation, and would have been happy to drive around the block a few times. He liked his lover's twin, or rather, her original—her blueprint.

Another friendly welcoming committee, and he noticed Carter from the ship was amongst those present. He wore blue.

"So you survived?" Kel said, breathing in the air and briefly tasting its sweetness.

"Yes," Carter replied, "Lua insisted on being near you to ensure your safety on subspace jump down. You see the human form needs a lot more energy to keep it intact, and she knew the risks. We were a fraction under power, and the pod didn't fully sustain her." Carter stopped abruptly and looked over at Tanea, who nodded to him.

"It's just a temporary breakdown, Kel," he assured him. "She will be revived."

"Breakdown!" Kel said, under his breath. He paused for a moment and felt a pang of loss in his guts. He was incredulous that Carter was not fully human and searched for a telltale sign of androidian traits, whatever they might be, but found none, and turned to Tanea.

"This is your team, Kel. We will brief and train you for the mission, and you start with a meeting with the commander in two hours, so let me show you to your quarters. There will be plenty of time to talk to these guys later on." Tanea bade Kel on, and he was once again in her wake, wading through the team, which resembled a mini United Nations, so diverse was the racial mix. They entered the bright spacious reception area of the building, which gave the impression of being both home and workplace. The design was clean and open, the ceilings high and gracefully arched with lots of flowers adding a refreshing brightness to the spotless and invigorating surroundings. There were mirrors everywhere.

They moved swiftly through the skylit corridors to a large wooden door. Tanea stopped and stood by, beckoning Kel to open it.

Kel reached for the knob and looked at Tanea. "My only condition is that you revive her the way she was, and I want to see her again. Are you clear on that?"

"Yes," Tanea replied.

"Good," Kel turned the knob and strode in. A picture window looked out onto a pure and pristine lake, surrounded by a forest and backed by a mountain, magnificent in its dominance of the scene. He had not noticed the mountain, so absorbed had he been with Tanea in their ride in. It was stunning, and he stood there, staring.

"Jeez!" he said at last, looking around the room. There was a fireplace and lush carpets, and a four poster bed that suddenly beckoned him like a siren. Slippers lay at the threshold before him.

"Drink this," said Tanea, and offered him a very green liquid that tasted of savory vegetables. "It will revive you. The bathroom is over there, all conventionally laid out, and there are clothes in the closet. I'll be back later. Get some sleep. If you need anything, ask Hal; everything is voice operated."

Tanea left, and Kel removed his slippers, and was instantly asleep as his head hit the pillow on the massive bed. He slept the sleep of the dead.

*   *   *   *

"Wake up, Kel, wake up!"

"Hal," mumbled Kel, from the depths of his slumber. "You must be everywhere, you must be the main man!"

"Mission briefing starts in forty minutes, Kel. Are you hungry? Would you like a snack? Lunch will be in an hour and a half."

"A beer and a cigar please, and a plate of chips."

"No alcohol or tobacco, Kel."

"And some soup, and some bubble and squeak. Heavy on the bubble and easy on the squeak."

There was a moment's silence, and Hal said, "I will see what I can do."

"And some escargot simmered in garlic," continued Kel relentlessly, "You know, snails, those little slimy things that crawl in the garden, and go crunch when you step on them."

"Hal! Did you know that there are some carnivorous snails that crawl into the shells of their vegetarian cousins and eat them?" Kel, Blade Runner like, bated this intelligent computer.

"I am computing, Kel."

"They turn their stomachs inside out, dissolve their prey, then suck em back in."

"I am computing."

"What year did I die in, Hal?"

"In two thous…" There was a sound like radio static, and the line went dead.

"Hal, Hal," cried Kel.

No response, Kel laughed, and punched his fist in the air.

After his shower, he found some comfortable clothes to wear. Carter arrived with a tray of snacks, and was laughing. He put it on a table that overlooked the spectacular view by the window.

"Hal blew a fuse," said Carter, obviously pleased by the computer's temporary absence. "Normal services will be resumed as soon as possible. No one has ever managed to silence Hal before!"

"Why did you give that name and voice to your central computer?" Kel asked. "If you've seen the film you'll know that Hal was the ultimate egocentric maniac."

"That film was the most classic, and near-to-real science fiction production in the twentieth century," said Carter. "It's out of recognition of this that we named him 'Hal'. And anyway, superstitions do not count for very much here."

"How many people live on Gaya?" Kel asked.

"About eleven thousand."

"That's a tiny amount for a place this size."

"You are on in ten minutes Kel—best to eat. Yes, even though this place is a virtual paradise, not many are willing to make a commitment to what we stand for."

"Do you mean higher consciousness and reincarnation, and stuff like that?" Kel asked, munching on some delicious, lightly fried potatoes. "I must admit, I am surprised it has had so little effect on me. Either I don't believe it, or it hasn't sunk in yet."

"Many prefer life to remain a mystery; it's a matter of choice. And I don't agree that it has had no effect on you. Something is definitely different about you since initial contact."

"Yes, you're right, I feel different. Well, if you are a humanoid, what exactly do you have at stake? Is this your choice, or the choice of the consciousness you came from?" Kel asked, a little surprised at his own candour.

"I am Carter, and there is no difference between me and my original. I reached a stage of awareness from which there is no turning back, and have no problems with my apparent duality. I had something special to offer the community, so I was duplicated. My original is in the midst of a long retreat, helping others let go of their attachments. We were one of the first, and our path is the same."

"What about Lua? She was different. Was she doctored or something to attract me?" Kel asked.

Carter looked surprised, and rubbed his cropped hair with a disarming innocence. "There have been some glitches in the production of some of the humanoids, and that will be explained to you later. But in answer to your question, no, she wasn't. And let me add that everyone here, and believe me, this has gone halfway through our community by now, is mightily impressed with the way you are sticking by the humanoid Lua. We admire guts, and sticking to something you believe in."

"Is there dissention here on Gaya? And are we being, you know, taped, like now?"

"Nothing like that Kel—we have your vital signs monitored, but that's all. We can get a visual and audio on you any time if we need to, but only if we need to. Your privacy and comfort are tantamount to us. Anyway, don't worry, you have already put Hal out of commission for a couple of hours, and we are all on manual." Carter laughed, bade his farewell, and left.

Kel felt good, very good. The conversations thus far on Gaya had been stimulating and provocative, and he leant back in the chair and looked at the view. There was no one on the lake. A few birds circled over it in the distance, and he made out a long cascading waterfall way off at the base of the mountain. 'I can see that far,' he whispered. The water spun and tumbled down, as if in slow motion.

A knock at the door stirred him out of a trance-like state, as he stared at the scene before him. Tanea entered, on the go as usual. She smiled and there was a hint of admonishment in it. "You are a hazard to our society, especially our computers. The sooner we get you back to Earth, the better. Are you ready?"

"More than ready to meet this guy," he said.

Tanea suddenly looked serious, then smiled. "Follow me," and she was off, he in pursuit. He felt ready, and more than a little nervous. But that felt right, and gave him an adrenaline edge he enjoyed.

Following Tanea was like pursuing an eagle as she swooped around the brightly-lit corridors. They came to another circular door, and it whooshed open. Tanea looked at Kel before he entered, and she appeared at once vulnerable and sympathetic. She attempted a smile as he stepped through the door. It then quickly closed behind him.

*   *   *   *

There was a giant map of the stars on a screen at the back of a large room, illuminated by a soft light. Kel could see Gaya, as it was high-lighted. Out in space there were two large bodies of energy. One was enormous and looked like a maelstrom, the other an intense body of light. They were at a great distance from Gaya and their patterns sug-gested they were having an effect on everything around them. Another smaller swirl of energy was at an oblique angle to them both, much nearer to Gaya.

Kel looked around the room and noticed two chairs in one corner. A table separated them and in the soft light, Kel discerned a figure in one of the chairs. He approached the other, and sat down. Slowly he cast his gaze upwards, and looked into the eyes of a man slightly older than himself.

As their eyes met, the man said, "My name is Lyle. I am so glad to meet you, that you could make it here."

"Hello," said Kel, proffering his hand. "I'll leave you to do the talking." Both men leant across the table, and they shook hands.

"Kel, I have thought of a thousand ways to tell you what I am about to tell you…Please help yourself to drinks and snacks." Lyle offered decanters of juice or water, and there were nuts and dried fruits in delicate porcelain bowls.

"There is something achingly familiar about you, like I've actually met you. But I know I haven't." Kel poured himself a glass of water and sat back, waiting.

"First of all, I thank you for your patience, and our apologies for the unplanned and untoward events of the flight here. I do recognise your love and loyalty towards Lua, and hers for you. Everything will be done to ensure you meet again before you leave for Earth."

Kel nodded his approval at this diplomatic start to the conversation. He eyed his new companion warily, noticing a maroon rim on his shirt collar.

"It is necessary to tell you my story first," Lyle continued. "I was a scientist on Earth, quite a prominent one, and I became interested in the spiritual path, eventually finding my way to Gaya. I was deadly serious and soon became a big cog in the wheel here, one of the biggest." Lyle's manner was very direct, crisp and precise.

"A humanoid was made from me and at first all was well. He did his job, and I mine. I was free to follow my real interest: a journey inward, in a society looking to the highest aspirations of conscious evolution. My twin was called Ernst, my middle, and my grandfather's name, and as time went on his interest in physics far surpassed mine, and he became a brilliant scientific mind. We are talking in terms relative to Einstein here."

Lyle paused for a second, and looked momentarily sad before continuing. "Unfortunately he became extremely strong-willed and somewhat autocratic, and insisted he be called Doctor Ernst. His knowledge of science far superceded anyone's here, or on Earth, and he commanded a lot of respect in the scientific community. Here's a short clip of the Doctor."

A small screen on the table in front of them lit up. Kel saw Doctor Ernst in a white coat, talking to a group of what he presumed to be scientists. He was Lyle's double all right, but his hair and moustache resembled a style from the early twentieth century. Others in the group tried to get a word in edgeways, but he totally dominated the conversation and talked in formulas. He gesticulated freely, and a little wildly. Kel thought him perhaps a little mad, definitely wacky.

"He was scientifically wired," Lyle continued, "self absorbed, and single-minded. We made efforts to get him de-commissioned, so to speak, but his work was becoming important, and these efforts were vetoed. As his behaviour here became more cantankerous, we shipped him off to a space station a couple of light years from here to work on a project examining the pull of a massive black hole, many light years away. It appeared we had found the perfect solution, as the Doctor became engrossed in his work and we were rid of him. There were seventy five crew members with him, about half of whom were humanoid."

"We were soon, however, made aware by personnel at the station that the Doctor was working on reversing the spin of sub atomic particles in deep space, so we became suspicious and set up a surveillance of his work." Lyle stopped, and looked at Kel.

"So what happened?" asked Kel.

"This happened. Please look at the screen, the big one over there," replied Lyle as he played with a console and the large wall-screen displaying the stars changed. Kel now looked at a cluster of round metallic bodies connected by spokes set somewhere deep in space. A metallic tube encircled the formation—it was a space station—and the shape reminded him of an atomic model of a molecule, inside a ring.

"To give you an idea of size, here is a scale model of one of your jumbo jets next to it," said Lyle.

Kel gasped, "Bloody hell—its enormous!"

"Bloody hell, yes it is," said Lyle laughing.

The shot closed in on the space station. Inside was the Doctor, peering into what appeared to be a microscope, fiddling with a number of dials around the scope.

"The ring around the station is a chamber in which sub atomic particles are dashed against each other in order to study their make up." said Lyle. "Now look at this."

What happened next was rather like when a film burns inside the camera. The scope into which the Doctor was looking turned red hot, then white hot, and in a second he, his crew and the space station had imploded into his experiment, swallowed up into the white heat.

Kel sat forward in his chair, eyes wide open.

"That was considerably slowed down. These next shots are from an observation satellite we had stationed some distance away."

The film was once again set in slow motion, and Kel witnessed the implosion of the station, sucked into a white nothingness in a second. The observation satellite followed a similar fate as it was sucked into the gravitational pull, and he could almost feel the creeks and groans as the structure buckled under this immense force.

"These next shots are from an observation telescope, a great distance away." Lyle's voice was very matter-of-fact; he had obviously been through this countless times. "We will speed the film up to give you an idea of what we are dealing with today."

Kel watched the incredible inrush of matter, and slowly there emerged a massive spinning maelstrom of energy. It looked like a giant spinning discus suspended on a thread. A reddish wake appeared from the polar ends of the body, like tornadoes. The Doctor had accessed a conduit of a massive resource of energy.

Nothing could survive in there, thought Kel. Nothing!

"What we see here is a singularity—a black hole." Lyle paused a moment to let this sink in. "Usually a black hole is caused by a collapsing sun of at least three and a half times the mass of the Earth's sun. When the fuel of such a body runs out, and is unable to sustain the pressure of its own weight, it collapses into a relatively small object, say a few kilometres across. Gravity becomes infinitely strong, and the laws of physics break down. Nothing can escape from its pull, not even light. No static matter can exist."

"What about time?" Kel asked.

"Time is held still. If you could enter, time would probably—hypothetically at least—appear normal. But you could spend a hundred years there, and re-emerge a millisecond after entering. Anyway, we are dealing with an infinite timewarp, and a growing threat to our planet here."

"You mean you are going to be sucked in?

"Yes," replied Lyle

"How long have you got?"

"In and under the normal laws of physics, we would not have to worry for a long time to come, but something distressing and unusual is happening. This mass is acting outside of the laws of physics."

Kel kept Lyle's gaze. "How?"

"We believe—No, actually, we are certain, that the Doctor is in there, his consciousness at any rate, and somehow he is manipulating the laws of the universe. He has found some way into a parallel universe of expanding antimatter, where matter decreases; hence the phenomenal gravitational pull. Even so, we are being pulled in quicker than we should be. We are in its jaws, Kel. The Doctor wants Gaya."

Kel said nothing. He was not prepared for the next statement.

"If the Doctor swallows Gaya," Lyle stopped for a moment, looking down. He grimaced and continued, "we believe he may then attain the ability to travel through time in this massively powerful state, and threaten worlds in other time frames. Even yours! Anything could be possible. He may even be working on and realising this at this moment."

"Good god! You must be joking!"

"Unfortunately, no," replied Lyle, gravely, and then brightening up, "But it is conjecture."

Kel nodded, "Conjecture?"

"And if," Lyle continued, "he eventually finds a way to merge with this other massive, dark ball of energy that you see way over there," and the screen changed back to the original image of Gaya and the maelstroms. "They were even aware of this monstrous black hole in your day. Then, if he is successful, we think the laws of the universe could possibly be broken down. So you see, Kel, we have, most unfortunately, created a monster of unthinkable danger to time itself."

Lyle brightened the lights, and turned to face Kel. "We have created him, and he has created a singularity."

"And one with an attitude," said Kel.

Lyle laughed despite himself, and repeated, "One with an attitude. Yes, most definitely. One with an attitude."

"How far away is this other monster black hole, and what kind of a punch, I mean, how much power does it pack?" Kel asked, rubbing his eyes, then pointing to the massive swirl of energy on the screen.

"It is many, many light years away, but that's not the point. Cosmologically it is rather close. The point is that the Doctor is working on parallel realms of space that would relegate distance to a position of insignificance. This monster, as you rightly put it, is at the centre of what is loosely called the Virgo cluster from your solar system, and the power it packs is at least thirty times greater than the twenty five thousand galaxies it holds in its gravitational field."

'Jesus wept,' Kel muttered under his breath. "If you are talking of many light years then this monster might have already imploded under its own weight? Its own greed? It might not be there any more."

"Too much power to ignore, Kel. It's not just going to go away like that. This could be akin to Armageddon. My apologies if you feel I am over-dramatising, but I cannot underestimate the potential danger here. The Doctor is intent on manipulating the most potent power sources in our universe."

"There's more, isn't there? That big intense light source on the screen there?" Kel asked.

"Unfortunately, yes. In 1963 an astronomer in Australia pinpointed a quasar in the Virgo constellation which possesses a luminosity thirty trillion times that of your sun, or comparable to that of three hundred giant galaxies. That's a vast amount of energy. Quite a punch! We know for sure that the Doctor studied these phenomena closely. The rest is speculation but we fear the worst. Yes, that is the intense light source up on the screen."

The two men remained silent for a minute, and Kel stared at the screen, trying to get a mental grip on the cosmic drama that was unfolding before him. "One big cosmic sucker in the black hole, and one big cosmic blower in the quasar."

"Actually the quasar is, as you put it, a sucker too, but do not bother yourself with the physics of it, you know enough."

"Ah, yes! The start of a hub of a galaxy, sucking up the light and the stardust…Somehow, I remember that from the Brief."

"Wonderful!" said Lyle.

Kel bit his lip unconsciously, "So where do I come in, Lyle? I am not leaving this room until you tell me how am I related to all this."

"They are bringing us some lunch. We'll eat here and continue after. You will need the break, because you are about to hear the most fantastic story ever told. It would have been impossible in your day, even to consider this. Getting you here is a miracle enough. Anyway, enough for now, let's eat first."

Kel agreed, and right on cue, two men entered and quietly and efficiently served them lunch. Kel felt at home in Lyle's company, though his head spun like a…like a quasar. Yes, a quasar, and a mad scientist in a black hole—surely nothing could beat that. Or could it?

What in hell's name have I got to do with these two? Kel looked up and over at his thoughtful and friendly lunch companion, and the feeling of *deja vu* swept through him once again.

He would know soon enough.

MISSION

After lunch Lyle cleared his throat and looked at Kel. "What I am about to tell you is impossible, yet it has happened. For the first time in the history of the universe this has happened. When we introduced you to the idea of a soul leaving a body it was to prepare you for this."

Kel, still as rock, said nothing.

"You see, we have developed a technology that can read the script of an individual's incarnating energy—his soul, if you like—rather like one can a genetic script. This energy is the most subtle wave pattern discernable to measurement. We don't know where it goes when it leaves the body, but we know it has a pattern, and we can receive this rather like a radio tuning into the frequency, and picking up a station."

"Good grief," Kel said.

"We never follow up to see where that energy re-incarnates and this is an absolute obligation on our part—to never do this. I want you to acknowledge you have understood this." Lyle stopped, and paused for a moment; the two men maintained eye contact.

Kel nodded his head and said, "I understand."

"When we found you, and that was something that took a miraculously minimum amount of time, we had picked up your read-out on the island. What we call a bio-ethereal read-out." The screen in front of them lit up and a series of waves and flurries streaked across it. A similar pattern appeared underneath, slightly different—a little shorter.

"This is your pattern, and mine underneath; you can see how similar they are." Lyle stopped and looked down at his hands. "You see Kel, you and I have the same read-out."

Kel furrowed his eyebrows, pursed his lips, and then reflexively made the opposite action, his eyes and mouth opening wide.

"Are you saying," he said at last, "that you and I are the same? The same soul, spirit, whatever?"

"Without a shadow of a doubt," replied Lyle.

"That you…and I—I mean that you are a re-incarnation of me— that I am you, that you're me in the future, and I'm you in the past? How is that possible? Is that possible?"

"Yes," Lyle sat totally still.

Now it was Kel's turn to examine his hands. Slowly he looked at Lyle and a strange expression crossed his face. It was a mix of pain and effort, as if he was about to make a bowel movement, or burst out crying. Then in one volcanic eruption he burst out laughing with such a force, that Lyle almost tipped backwards in his seat.

Within seconds Lyle was caught up in this temporary breakdown of the conversation. The two men laughed hysterically, unable to stop. They were lost in mirth for some minutes, and when some control was achieved, they would look at each other and erupt again. They walked around the room, at times doubling over holding their bellies, at others extended back, spraying the walls and ceiling with their laughter, marveling at this absurd aberration of nature they had transcended.

At the end of the outburst both men were in pain, their guts cramped, and a delicious feeling of light-headedness upon them. They returned to their chairs and said nothing, occasionally making strange whimpering sounds as this cosmic joke played out to its first house, its first audience.

"You see, Kel," and as the two men's eyes met they were off again, and laughed uncontrollably until the energy had drained out of them. Lyle tried again and Kel avoided eye contact.

"It's been a long time since I laughed like that," said Lyle.

"Me too," said Kel, taking a deep, shuddering breath. "I'm not totally convinced! How did you find this wave pattern among six billion others?" He pointed at the pattern on the screen between them.

"We sent tracers out over the Earth, and when contact was made with you, we were able to pinpoint your location"

"Supposing I had been living in New York?" Kel asked.

"It would have taken longer, but we would have found you,"

"So you had no idea it was me?" Kel now looked at Lyle, and was deadly serious.

"That's right, we didn't know anything, and were just incredibly lucky that on our first try we found you. You were free, unattached, adventurous, not in a push-chair and…"

"Emotionally needy, single, looking for love, thirsting for adventure," Kel cut in.

"Yes, if you like, and whatever it was, you had a dramatic affect on one of our humanoids. Lua was totally lovestruck."

"When will she be revived?"

"The day after tomorrow. You will go and spend some time with a mystic who lives way up in the mountains."

"A mystic?"

"Yes, he will help you prepare for your mission. He is known as Baba."

"Baba?"

"Yes! We need two days of Tanea's presence to facilitate Lua's recovery, and this will be done while you are gone."

"A mystic? Anyway," said Kel, shaking his head, "there is one more condition you have to concede to before I agree to this mission, whatever it is."

"What is that?"

"You do not erase my memory of anything that happens, up until now, or from now on." Kel sat back observing Lyle closely.

Lyle chuckled to himself, leant back in his seat and looked at Kel. "Alright, absolutely no hidden agendas from here on, but what if there are some residual, painful memories?"

"I can live with it. Now what is it you want me to do?"

"We want you to go in there." Lyle pointed at the ominous dark ball of energy on the map behind them, "and confront this monster we have created."

Kel sat back for one moment staring blankly at the screen. "Bah!" he said at last. "I might be a bit of a Neanderthal as far as you're concerned, but I know nothing physical is going to leave that place alive."

"Nothing physical is going to enter it."

Kel narrowed his eyes. "What do you mean?"

"Listen, Kel, there is something about you, a very raw energy that is able to get to the point rapidly and draw out information phenomenally quickly. It's maybe a bit too soon. There are things we need to talk about before I go any further."

"Well, it might be raw energy as far as your concerned, but my questions you can't control. I see it as being spontaneously interested in my own survival. There is something very controlled about this place. Forget your damn Brief and just tell me straight. Anyway, how the bloody hell am I supposed to get in there?" Kel swung a dramatic gesturing hand towards the map. "And more importantly, how am I going to get out?"

"Okay, point taken. You have been told about how we produced our humanoids—a mixture of genetic, bionic and conscious transference onto a stem cell base that replicates the donor. Well, that which has survived in the Doctor is the conscious element, and that is the part of you we will be sending into the singularity. You and your body will divide, and you, your consciousness, will enter the black hole."

Silence reigned for a few heartbeats. "You mean I have to physically expire…die?" Kel asked, leaning forward in his seat.

"Your body will be held in stasis. Your consciousness will then move and function independently of it. We aim to teach you some very simple techniques in the next two days to enable you to direct and control your...how to say...? Let's say ethereal body—in order to complete your mission."

"What exactly is my mission?"

"Find the Doctor and stop him," said Lyle with an air of finality.

"Why not you?"

"The Doctor does not need me, he could hold and manipulate me. You he needs!"

"How so?"

"If you don't go back to your time frame he doesn't exist, cannot exist. Nor do I, as a matter of fact. It's the one unknown factor of this whole mission. We could create a paradox, the consequences of which we are totally unaware of."

Kel suddenly shivered as something echoed in his memory—a film he had seen, a fading photograph.

"Anyway, he cannot keep you in there," Lyle continued, "not at this juncture. He needs you to get back and live out your life so that your soul reincarnates, so that his genesis is not interrupted."

"What do you mean at this juncture?"

"The Doctor is playing with time, Kel. When he does find a way to travel through it, all this will be immaterial, he'll have swallowed up the lot of us in his time-warp."

"What do you mean, 'the lot of us'?"

"Maybe even your Earth, who knows? But as I said earlier that's conjecture," said Lyle, coughing. "Anyway, Gaya, and the lot of us. Like it or not, you are intricately caught up and involved in all this, and so is the world you come from. We cannot avoid this nightmare, and this, or rather you, are our only chance, our only hope.

"I was promised a safe return!"

"You will get back, I promise you."

"Yeah, but in what kind of fucking condition, a zillion miles long?" Kel leant forward in the chair and ran his fingers roughly through his hair, then cupped his chin in his hand. "It's strange, but ever since Lua told me that my physical being wouldn't be threatened, that this would be on a level of consciousness, I believed her, because I totally trusted her. I want you to recognise that she was the reason I am here."

Lyle nodded his agreement.

"But if I had known all this, I would have made a dash for the pub, and stayed there—indefinitely."

"If you don't get back Kel, then all of this, and maybe all of your world, in the near or distant future, could be over anyway. It won't matter. Our battle then will be fought on a different realm, in one that we can only speculate as to its manifestation."

Kel let this statement sink in slowly. "We had a saying where I come from: 'Buggered if I do, and buggered if I don't.' Feels appropriate for our present scenario."

"We have the uppermost confidence in this mission, Kel, and the uppermost confidence in you. When I say last chance, I mean it's the best we've got, and we will succeed. I am just letting you know the gravity of what's at stake here. You did say you wanted it straight."

"Have you sent anybody else in?" Kel asked.

"Yes, but he hasn't returned yet. I am afraid we have either lost him to the Doctor, or he is in the deepest of trances."

"Who was it?" Kel asked.

"Carter's original, Duncan. A very brave and beautiful man," said Lyle sadly.

"Yes, I know Carter, so I understand your sadness." Kel sat back and stared at the singularity on the screen above them. He felt scared, bone shakingly scared, and he took a deep breath, wondering if he had any other options to consider. But this was a calamity without a second, and there was no way out of it. In spite of his fear, he felt very alive, and very aware. His back was against the wall, and the tides of adrenaline flowed in sporadic bursts around his body.

The two men sat in silence for a while, and then Kel asked, "If I am in a bodiless state and I go in there, what am I to expect, what do I have to fear?"

"We anticipate that he will do everything in his power to control you, and find out who you are. Once he has an inkling of what you are to him, he will probably confront you with all your fears, all your doubts—but this is supposition. He will attempt to avoid any real confrontation and dominate you, deriving some benefit from the situation."

"A bully," muttered Kel.

"He'll probably try and keep you distracted, but he cannot destroy you or keep you there indefinitely, or he could potentially cause his own end. Quite frankly, we don't know what he'll do, but whatever it is, it will be a challenge for you on the emotional and mental level." Lyle sat back and waited.

Kel remained silent and stared at the table in front of him.

"That's why," Lyle continued, "we told you that in this mission you would have to face yourself. That is all the Doctor has to play with. If you focus on your mission, which is to meet and stop him, he will not be able to ignore you."

"So I will be able to focus my attention in a…in this so-called ethereal body, in this state you're going to get me in? I'll be awake?"

"Yes, your whole Brief has had this as its top priority—to help you focus, and not be distracted by memory or anticipation. You spent a good deal of time on your flight here in a state of no thought, and you attenuated remarkably quickly. The energy we are sending in there is very fine, very subtle. We believe you can get to the heart of the matter quickly, and confront this madman."

"What went wrong with the Doctor? Why did he turn out this way?"

"There must have been something in my personality, in my conscious make-up, that took on maniacal dimensions in the Doctor when he was cloned from me. Humanoid production has been stopped as a result. We are obviously not ready for this kind of creational genesis, and have finally, painfully, realised that nature takes care of itself." Lyle stopped and looked sad.

"That's a lesson we never really seem to learn," said Kel, staring at Lyle, a creation of himself in the future, a self that had just created a threat to reality itself. Was this really him? How could that be?

"I have created a monster of unknown etiology and potential," Lyle continued, "He must be stopped at all costs. If he swallows Gaya he will have an endless amount of knowledge available to him to cause heaven only knows what kind of havoc in the universe. He will use it all for his own ends."

"Can't you escape?"

"Not enough time, and to be honest, there is no desire to go any-where else. After some time on Gaya nothing else will do. Even though the Earth is greatly enlightened compared to your day, it is still a cor-rupt and selfish place compared to Gaya. If we have to, we will take our war into the singularity. The stakes are too big, and we will find a way."

"How long have you got?" asked Kel.

"Some months before our solar system starts to feel the affect of the Doctor's current onslaught. He really is playing around with physical laws, it's a nightmare," said Lyle.

"What if I don't come back?"

"You will come back, you cannot not come back."

"But if I don't. The possibility of such a scenario must exist!"

"If you really don't come back then life as we know it, possibly for your era and mine, is over," replied Lyle

"I could come back a vegetable," said Kel in earnest, ignoring the apocalyptic consequences of Lyle's statement.

"That's not something we are worried about, Kel. You see if you did, then in reality you won't have come back. Your body is just a point in time and space your consciousness has created around itself. Your soul holds the residue of the most dramatic events in your per-sonal history, from the word go, and it infuses the conscious self like a perfume. We are not sure what memory you will bring back, if any. Theoretically, the ethereal body holds the power of memory, but not the ability to remember. If it did, it would probably last only a very short time."

"If?" Kel looked surprised. "It's good to know that you have all this figured out," and the two men fell silent for a while, each in his own thoughts.

"Why would memory be held for only a short time in this ethereal body?" Kel asked.

"We have discovered that there is a power that sits in the brain. I could only adequately describe it as the sense of self. It is the point of observation in us, that which records and observes the play of life. It needs a body to be grounded in order to do this, so without a body there is no play!"

"In the on-board Brief, I was led to understand that my brain is a record of everything, from the creation until the present moment. Now that is one hell of a play! One hell of a memory!"

"Yes," said Lyle, "that's the universal memory of which you are, of course, also a part. When your spirit is embodied at birth, however, there is already memory, a sequence of experiences that attracts one's conscious attention. The more dramatic the event, the more deeply embedded is the memory of it. In this way we create the experiences around us in order to learn. What we gain from it is how we pass on our wisdom to future generations."

"Sometimes without much success," cut in Kel.

"Yes, you are right, but we do slowly learn. Our genetic heritage has an incredible amount of information in it, and our spiritual heritage an immeasurable amount. It's an infinite source, but primarily each individual soul has to deal with whatever it has caused in the past."

"Fair enough!" Kel said.

"So you see, it's a fail-safe mechanism if you like, of ultimate responsibility and culpability. You reap what you sow."

"So the body seems to be the battlefield of sorts. Without my body in there, you have no idea what I will remember?"

"No body, no memory for the mind to reflect upon. Rather like having a dream, and then trying to remember it. But all this is conjecture; you will be in a different dimension in there, beyond the limitations of the physical."

"Kind of fifth dimension bogey-man." Kel rolled his eyes up.

"Eh? Anyway our aim has been to put you in touch with the essence of your awareness. That essence will destroy anything in its path, because it is eternal, and ever present."

"How?"

"You are never not present. Becoming aware of that will blast anything in your way."

Kel looked over at the screen, and shook his head.

"You see, Kel, it's just that we have become so distracted with the objective world whilst awake in the physical body, that we need memory to remind us of who we are in the bigger picture."

"Which is?" Kel asked.

"The totality of reality, the Self, God—whatever you want to call it. It's not easy for the mind to grasp such a phenomenon. That's why Gaya was created—to enable us to understand fully our relationship with the Absolute. You cannot remember what you already are, but in the ethereal body we are much closer to who we are, as there are no physical limitations. It is the subtle root of our gross bodies."

"Amazing," said Kel.

"So you see, we are unable to predict what memory you will have of your encounter with the Doctor. I can assure you, though, you will be very present, acutely so, during your time in there. Becoming aware of, and keeping in mind your goal: to stop the Doctor at all costs—that is your mission."

"Right!"

"He will do everything possible to distract you, and keep you in abeyance. But you are the key, you are his roots, and he will not be able to ignore you."

"Thank you, you've helped me understand exactly what is at stake here, especially my part in it. I feel way out of my depth, but ready for anything."

"That's just how it should be. Perfect! And remember, this will require the resolve akin to one of your countrymen." Lyle, like Kel, relished history. "When Churchill confronted Hitler in World War II, Hitler was not interested in conquering Britain, on taking on the Empire, especially the Royal Navy. But Churchill wouldn't strike a deal and risked the very survival of his native land. He knew such tyranny, such an efficient war machine needed to be confronted, and he did it. His courage initiated the saving of the free world. That's what is at stake now, except we are talking on a much bigger scale!"

"Man, you have just pumped me up, that's amazing what you just said," replied Kel, sitting up in his chair. "Yes, I see what is at stake. I'm overwhelmed, but I'm up for it."

"Good, and I would like to reiterate one point," said Lyle seriously. "I would have gone in there to confront him myself if I thought it would remedy the situation, but it would probably have made it worse, more complicated. He would be able to employ a great deal more delay tactics with me than he could with you."

"Yes, I understand," said Kel, and the two fell silent again.

After some minutes in silence, Kel looked over at Lyle and said, "Your accent is kind of east-coast American. Where are you from?"

They proceeded to exchange stories and philosophies, and the conversation flowed around these two personalities infused and bonded by a single soul. The subject veered away from the nightmare scenario posed by the Doctor.

After some time there was a knock, and Tanea entered. "Time's up," she said, and stood back, beaming at the two men. Kel automatically got to his feet.

"Kel, you are going to be extremely busy in the next four days before your blast-off, but we shall meet again," said Lyle, as he stood and embraced his soul mate warmly. "I will be busy getting the time-line right for all this. It's been an honour and a pleasure, and we agree to all your conditions."

Kel took his leave and was once again hard on the heels of the relentless Tanea, sucked into her wake.

"Nothing could have prepared me for that," said Kel. "Did you hear us laughing? It was just the most absurd scenario you could ever imagine."

"Ho, ho," said Tanea, steaming ahead. She shot Kel a glance over her shoulder, and smiled.

TRAINING

"Your training starts now, and dinner's at six," said Tanea over her shoulder.

"Can we go out to dine?" Kel asked.

"It's already arranged, I'm way ahead of you."

"Where are we going?"

"To one of the community houses, one where you can do the least damage." Tanea's voice was mockingly serious.

"You make me sound like a virus."

"Ha!" Tanea's voice was now triumphant. "That's exactly right—a virus—a bug in an almost infallible system."

"I'm just testing its limitations."

"Baffling it, more like."

"You can't control everything, that's what bugs you," said Kel, rising to the challenge.

"Oh, come on, without control, without form and discipline where would we be? Like…Like animals. In the course of evolution we have had to develop control."

"Some things cannot be controlled, Tanea. Spiritual fascism would destroy itself eventually."

"Very good point Kel. On second thought, forget dinner, I am going to lock you up, throw the key away, and bring you bread and water." Tanea breezed into a large hall that reminded him of Japan, a spacious and airy *dojo*. A broad-shouldered young man was waiting for them at a raised platform at one end of the vast sea of *tatami* mats. They removed their shoes and made their way over to him.

"My name is Matthias." The accent was European, possibly German. He brimmed with physical fitness and efficiency. Around the collar of his white gym kit was a red rim.

"He's all yours," Tanea said. "See if you can discipline this one. I think you are going to need more than a facilitator."

"A what?" asked Kel.

"I'll leave him with you, Matthias. Try to keep him in one piece. See you at six, Kel. Your dinner suit will be laid out on your bed." On the final consonant, Tanea had already turned, and was steaming halfway across the *tatami* sea before any reply came to Kel's mind.

"What's a facilitator?"

"Something to allow that ancient hedonistic brain of yours to learn without distractions," said Matthias, smiling.

"Good luck," countered Kel. "No one has ever managed that before."

Matthias took over. "My job is to teach you some body discipline, and today we start with a form of 'Iado' (pronounced ee-eye-dou), which is the ancient Japanese art of swords'manship. Then we'll move on to a form of Nagi-nata and Tai-Chi, which will greatly improve your movement skills."

"What's nagi…"

"You'll get the hang of it soon. Here, please put this on," cut in Matthias, handing Kel a yamaka-like cap with a chinstrap.

"Is this the facilitator?"

"Yes, it's a device that cuts into your brain wave pattern. You see a brain wave is like a conversation between your thalamus, and the cortex of the brain. When you are relaxed, and the thalamus is not sending reams of information to the higher conscious brain, then there are only a few waves. During this state of relaxation you can assimilate mental and physical information much quicker. This machine provokes that receptive state, and helps to consolidate a memory of it."

"How?" Kel asked.

"Through a small channel in the brain that ferries new necessary information to your cortex. This channel used to be part of the olfactory make-up of the brain—you know, the smell centre—but as we evolved it depended less on smell to assess the environment and more on memory. Via this channel, in one hour I can give you six month's solid training." Matthias was a good teacher, succinct and clear.

"Why do I need this kind of training?"

"Discipline," replied Matthias, and he rolled the word around his mouth as he would a delicious morsel. As if it were his religion, and sacred.

"Let's go for it." Kel bowed his head and allowed Matthias to adjust the strap of the facilitator. He felt an immediate surge of sharpness to his power of attention. He stood and faced Matthias, and his expression indicated to his martial arts teacher that he was ready.

"We have it on a low grade at the moment," said Matthias. "I will increase it as we go. Now look and listen." Matthias swung a mirror around, and Kel stood facing himself.

"Here is your centre of gravity," said Matthias pointing to an area in the middle of Kel's pelvis. "All movement originates here—it is the centre of your physical being—what the Japanese call the *hara*."

Kel became aware that his energy swirled around this centre. He suddenly felt rooted by it.

"This area must be very still during any movement. If it is not, you waste energy, and are at a disadvantage." Matthias then put on himself what appeared to be another facilitator, and motioned Kel to stand and face him. "Follow my movements, and observe, mimic, and let your body do the work."

Kel aped his teacher's movements, and he very quickly was in sync with Matthias, his knees slightly bent, his body sweeping around the room, his centre of gravity parallel to the floor, and his breathing deep and diaphragmatic. Kel's surprise and delight were obvious.

"I am in synchronicity with you, and you are allowing your body to move with mine, just keep it going. You are doing outstandingly well," said Matthias

The two men danced around the room in a unison that was controlled and graceful. Matthias grunted his approval, "For the last minute you have been on your own, we are out of contact."

At that moment Kel lost it, and his movements became deliberate and clumsy. He looked at Matthias, shrugged his shoulders, then nodded.

Once again the dance-like movement began in sync with Matthias. Kel just let his body do the moving. After some minutes Matthias indicated that he was performing the repetitive movement on his own. This time Kel's mind did not interfere with his movement.

Matthias stopped. Kel stopped. Matthias went to the stage and reverently collected two swords. He handed one to Kel, and it was exquisitely made, the hilt inlaid with gold and pearls. Following his teacher, he removed it from its sheath; the blades were razor sharp.

The two men faced each other about eight feet apart, and Kel followed the overhead, sweeping, forward cutting movements of Matthias' sword. The last part of the forward thrust was halted by a gripping action on its hilt, similar to wringing a towel with both hands, arms extended straight in front of his eyes. This form of swordplay could, if unleashed, pack a powerful punch, or more likely, cut and slash. Kel swung the big sword over his head in graceful sweeping motions, controlling its trajectory with great skill. Matthias slowly moved closer and closer towards Kel, until the fall of the swords halted millimeters from each man's brow.

"Keep it going, Kel. I am going to cut us off after the third sweep."

Kel continued without any hitch. Matthias grunted his approval, and Kel sighed silently in relief.

After a further grueling two hours of intense training in swords'manship and Tai Chi, Matthias halted the class. The two men bowed ceremoniously to each other, sat and faced the podium, and spent sometime in '*seiza*', a meditation following a martial art. They were interrupted by the arrival of another man, Asian, who smiled warmly and broadly. He was the same height and build as Matthias, but less muscular, and somehow more solid. A weightlifter's build thought Kel.

"My name is Yoshii," he said, and bowed almost imperceptibly. He was good humoured and joked freely with Matthias in a hilariously mocking manner. The two athletes put each other down at any chance they had. They were obviously very good friends, and proceeded to give Kel a demonstration of swordplay that was powerful, and a wonder to watch. When it was over, Kel thanked both men in exquisitely polite Japanese, which shocked and delighted Yoshii.

"You know Japanese," said Yoshii.

"I once fell in love with a Japanese woman."

"Ah ha! That explains it. The last part of your training today involves a long-shafted Japanese spear. Nagi-nata is a traditional martial art in Japan," said Yoshii, unhitching two spear-like weapons from a rack.

Kel put his facilitator back on, and Yoshii donned the other, and the two men faced off and bowed.

As with Matthias, Kel danced around the room with his new teacher and swung his weapon around with ever increasing skill and dexterity. Thrusting and parrying became second nature. He was amazed at his own level of energy; his stamina appeared to know no bounds, and sweat soaked his simple cotton attire.

"When do we do that again?" Kel asked, mopping sweat off his brow once the lessons and meditation were over.

"Tomorrow we refine what you learned today," replied Yoshii, not a bead of sweat on him. "But basically you have got the groundwork done and the data is now stored in that ancient brain of yours." Yoshii leaned over and smacked Kel firmly on the back.

They accompanied him back to his quarters. Kel observed the two as they continued their taunts and jibes, and felt at home. The locals here were tough, straightforward, and friendly. A perfect community, he thought, or were they just putting on a friendly face? His English sense of caution was still with him, and his other senses seemed sharpened to a razor's edge.

He bade farewell to his two companions, entered his room, grateful for the solitude, and the quiet. He opened the curtains, and the lake and the mountain were spectacularly lit with the light of the setting sun, in hues of crimson, orange and pink. He set a chair in front of the large window, collapsed into it and stared at the vista before him, the colours changing visibly second by second, the reds giving way to purple and indigo. Over the lake, eagles, possibly ospreys, swooped down hoping to hook a fish with their talons. It was a beautiful and unforgettable scene below him, as he sat like an emperor, admiring it from high on the lakeshore.

He wondered what the time was and looked to one side. A clock indicated it was four thirty. The day had passed quickly.

Kel shut his eyes and counted to sixty. He had always won the game of guessing a minute in the cub scouts, when they had sat around in a circle with nothing better to do. The clock showed only fifty-four seconds had passed. 'Ah ah, Gaya must be a bit bigger than Earth' he said to himself, 'or smaller,' and was in the process of working this out when he fell fast asleep, the chair automatically reclining in response to his fatigue.

✳   ✳   ✳   ✳

Kel was dreaming of Lua. He was on an old galleon setting out to sea, and she was dressed in black, standing on the shore.

A familiar voice broke the silence of his dream. "Ten minutes to departure, time to dress for dinner."

"Hal," said Kel, his eyes shut, his thoughts on Lua. "You're back! I thought they might have unscrewed your circuits."

"I do not understand," answered the calm, and almost wary voice of the computer.

"Never mind," said Kel, "Hal, the humanoids here seem to have a soul. Have you got one?"

"I was never born Kel and therefore am available at all times. This is not a concern of mine."

Kel pondered this answer for a moment. "Well if you can think, which definitely seems to be the case, I think you must have a soul. What do you like to do?"

"I have no preferences; all is the same to me."

"Do you ever make a mistake, Hal?" Kel asked.

"Only once, and that was with you."

"To err is human, Hal." Kel chided.

"Listen, Kel," said Hal, "I am able to compute, for that is my job. I have the grosser senses available to me, and I am able to recognise you through my memory recognition circuits in sight and sound, but these are the grosser senses. I cannot know the essence of something—the taste of an apple, the smell of a rose. These subtleties need the gene or memory of human experience."

"But you could recognise their chemical make up, pheromones, composition and stuff like that?" Kel asked.

"Exactly," said Hal, "but not their essence, not what they are. There are too many variables for a computer to think and feel like a human."

"But you can sort information a lot quicker than me," said Kel.

"But not create it. You see, Kel, each of your neurons can create different mental states with each and every other neuron in your nervous system. In this way mental states are created. You have more possible inter-neuronal connections in your body, than there are atoms in the universe."

Kel was silent for a moment. "Thank you, Hal. I get your point, very interesting."

"And by the way Kel, you have four minutes to departure."

"To be continued, Hal. I am not finished with this dialogue yet." Kel made a dash for the shower, and was stopped in his tracks by Hal.

"There is no need to shower, Kel. Please look at your dinner suit," said Hal.

Kel looked over at the bed, and on it were some shorts. "What are these for?" he asked.

"A bathing suit, or rather a swimming costume," said Hal. "You can shower when you reach your dinner destination."

At that moment there was a knock at the door, and as the first syllable had barely exited his lips, Tanea strode in wearing a white toweling robe.

"Are you two still bonding?" she said with a smile.

"Where are we going?"

"You put your dinner suit on. I'll call the cab," replied Tanea

When Kel exited the bathroom in his shorts, he noticed that a small hatch had opened next to the picture window. He approached it and stuck his head outside.

There, ten feet below him, was a pristine pool of water with a channel extending away from it. It wound its way through a lush tropical garden that would not have been out of place in the palace of a Maharaja, or a Sultan. The water was mountain pure, and the channel was bordered with twinkling lights that disappeared into the dusky night. He stood back, looked at Tanea, and wondered what to do next.

Tanea whipped her gown off and was through the hatch in a jiff. She jumped into the water some ten feet below, and squealed in delight as she hit its surface. She wore a one-piece that was definitely not designed to excite the senses, but Kel suddenly remembered his Lua, and plunged after her. The water was a magical eighty degrees, and the air temperature not much different. A gentle current bore him towards Tanea's smiling face.

"So, this is how you get around?" he said.

"Yes, sometimes, keeps us in shape too. Come on, we have to swim for a bit."

Scented flowers bordered the channel, and there was the buzz of insects. As his senses settled he realised there was an orchestra of insect songs; hypnotic melodies rang through the night. Kel swam on, using the channel lights and Tanea's splashy wake to guide him. The water felt soft and ran down his face in silky rivulets. Tanea came to a stop at two small ponds where a number of channels converged.

"This is froggy pond, and that is buggy pool," said Tanea, and she laughed. There was something very relaxed about her out of uniform, and they swam on lazily in the heavenly surroundings of Gaya, occasionally looking at each other, their heads bobbing up and down. Kel's feet sometimes touched the bottom, and it was at times stony, others leafy and muddy. At one point they had to climb some stairs to the side of a small waterfall, and plunge into a channel where the current was slightly against them. They swam on for a bit, and then the current changed, and they floated on, comfortable and content in the stillness and insect sonatas of the evening light

There were occasional lights on the bank, and Kel presumed these to be residences. Tanea hauled herself out of the channel at one of these clusters of light. A trellised entranceway bedecked in honeysuckle, jasmine, and wild rose fronted a path. She was light and nimble on her feet and reminded Kel of a child in her one-piece suit, spontaneous and un-self-conscious. He climbed out after her and surveyed the scene, smelling the scented air around him. The garden was a tangle of wild plants, necessitating a minimum of care. Two men approached them, and through the smiles Kel recognised Carter and Matthias.

"And this is where, and how we live," said Tanea.

"Welcome, Kel. Come this way," said Carter and bade him follow, up the paved path.

Kel showered, and dried off in an efficient body blower housed in the shower unit. Comfortable cotton clothes were laid out for him, and he studied his reflection in a mirror. He looked robustly healthy, and acknowledged with a knowing look a feeling of nervousness at having to meet a strange group of people; yet he felt alert, and relaxed at the same time. He took a deep breath, exited the outside bath house, and followed the waiting Carter into a gazebo-like recreation area where eight people sat around a low coffee table; one of them was Daljit, the doctor. Some got up and introduced themselves, and although Kel detected a slight discomfort in one or two of those he had not met before, it was like a family gathering. These people knew each other intimately, and their task was obviously to make Kel feel at home.

"Been anywhere interesting lately?" Kel asked Daljit with a smile.

"That was my double, Kel, but she told me all about it," said Daljit's look-alike, "My name is Anjila."

Kel was shocked; he could detect no difference between the two. They were identical in feeling and gesture, and he briefly wondered why Lyle and Tanea's doubles were so obviously different. He asked if any of the others present, besides Carter, had doubles.

Only Yoshii spoke, "Me," and then added sadly, "He was with the Doctor on the station, and was lost."

"And you are the original?" Kel asked.

"Yes, Taro was a humanoid, like a twin brother to me. It makes me very sad."

Someone quickly changed the subject, and for some time there was small talk followed by a hearty vegetarian meal made by three of the group, whose turn it was, as they indicated to Kel, to cook that night.

Afterwards they sat around the table drinking coffee. All were casually dressed with no telltale colour coded sign about their person. Some lounged in their chairs, very much at home. A silence descended on the group, which Tanea broke.

"Kel, if you have any questions about the way we live, now is the ideal time to ask."

"Please don't hold back," added Matthias.

Kel took a deep breath and looked at Anjila. "I am unable to tell whether any of the eight of you living here is in a relationship; are you in four relationships, or does it work out another way?"

"We are in one relationship, Kel, with each other, and with life itself," said Anjila leaning forward. "Practically speaking four of us here are in intimate relationships but this is not regarded as anything special." She paused, thought for a second, and continued, "although it does mean we must be most careful not to create a hiding place in the closeness of such a relationship."

"What? Do you mean romance?" asked Kel.

"Exactly!" exclaimed Anjila. "And this is relevant to all relationships, not just romantic ones. Once there is a specialness in it, others are excluded, and this is the start of trouble."

"You are not suggesting a mother and baby cannot have a special relationship," pleaded Kel.

"Of course not," replied Tanea, "But as the child seeks it's independence the parent may not want to let go, and this is the cause of endless problems. A dual dependence is created which can last way beyond the death of one of the parties, and can affect every relationship one has in life."

"Are the singles celibate?" Kel continued.

"Yes we are," a tall man named Peter, with a Dutch accent, interjected, "We live in absolute integrity here. I have to, in order to trust myself, and when I totally trust myself, I will be ready for a sexual relationship. Otherwise I get into all sorts of trouble," and Peter waved his hands in the air, gesturing at the impossibility of that happening in the near future. The group laughed and grimaced.

"But surely you learn from mistakes in the relationship, and that is the way we learn and move on," said Kel.

"Maybe this is your experience but it is not mine," replied Peter. "I always got stuck, even when I resolved to make things work. It's a choice Kel, you see there is something in us that reflexively responds to situations, and is conditioned to control. It is the personal me, and this—'me, me, want, want', has to go. We must get to know it."

"You mean the ego?"

"Yes, and the glory of living in a community like this, is that we are always confronted by it because of our commitment to be totally honest with each other, and hide nowhere. We can then have the courage to face into it, and realise what a destructive mechanism it is. A relationship is the most usual place for it to hide, and also to abuse our partners with this egocentric little monster. Trusting myself, and this place is fertile ground to do that, enables me to have the most incredible intimate relationships with people who have made the same commitment."

"No more me, me—that's a tall order," said Kel. "You're talking about getting rid of the ego?"

"That's right," replied Peter, "without its dominance over us, we can live in a full relationship with each other."

"We are so conditioned in life Kel," it was Tanea now, "that we forget who we really are together. Being here in this community is not a question of denying who you are; it just takes the emphasis off of it, off this ego that has gotten used to being responded to in a certain way. It allows us to see ourselves in a different and much bigger light."

"So you have no secrets from each other, nowhere to hide?" Kel asked.

"Yes," said Carter. "The truth is vital because we can twist and turn it in so many ways, in ways even hidden to ourselves. Our survival mechanism is the most successful on the planet, Earth that is—so successful that we are fooled into believing that that awful triad of lust, greed, and anger are actually who we are. To break through and see a much bigger side of ourselves requires number one courage, and the other number one, humility. And that means no hiding."

"So understanding all this should be enough, if one stays here for some time?" said Kel.

"And the courage to change, and the humility to let go," replied Carter. "Understanding alone is not enough, action is imperative; to look at one's resistance; to let go of the personal, and the selfish.

"What about personal preferences, don't you have them?" asked Kel.

"Of course we do," said the quietest of the group. "It just doesn't get in the way or become a place to hide. I trust myself to be in a relationship, it just doesn't become more important than my relationship with the community here."

"What about children?" continued Kel, "I am struck by their absence."

"Children are a big responsibility," it was Yoshii's thick accent. "There are children here, but they were born before their parents decided to make a commitment to come here. I left my two kids at home as my wife had no interest in this. The children here are great, and they have priority to return to Earth if that is what they want. Our commitment to each other is higher than anything else."

"What if someone wants to leave the community, but wishes to stay on Gaya, can they stay?" Kel asked.

"Of course," it was Tanea again. "They can stay, but they live outside of town, in villages in the surrounding hills. We have a market once a week in town and most come for that. Anyway they learnt enough from being here to live in harmony and peace. Quite simply, they do not live here with us because their level of commitment is less, and that causes some friction."

"How come?"

"You see it's not easy living this way of life. Even though the rewards of real intimacy are so great, our attachment to old ways are so powerful. The desire for the personal, its self gratification and quest for a negative freedom, is immense, and to fall back into old ways is very easy, if one's level of commitment wavers."

"What do you mean by negative freedom?" Kel asked.

"The idea that you can do what you damn well please. Without due respect and consideration for others," said Tanea.

There was silence for a while, as Kel pondered over this statement, and somebody put some music on, some modern jazz from his era. The group split up and different conversations sprouted. Kel learned that there was no leader in this community, but that a council existed, on which Lyle sat. The juiciest bit of information he got was that Lyle and Tanea were in a relationship, and this truly shocked him.

At times during his conversation, Kel was so involved that it seemed as if he had forgotten himself. Animated and lively, he felt spontaneous, light-headed, and high.

There was a tap on Kel's shoulder and he looked up to see Tanea beaming down at him, and they were soon, after a round of warm farewells, strolling along a path next to a water channel on their way home. The faint lights on the path were augmented by a foreign half moon that hung above them, bluish and cratered.

"We have a meditation at six in the morning, it was suggested to me tonight that you might like to join us," said Tanea.

"I'd like that. How long for."

"Just an hour,"

"Just?" replied Kel.

Tanea laughed, and they walked on in silence.

"In my day," Kel said, "the fundamentalists, the globalists, and certain politicians amongst many others, kept people apart using fear as their weapon, keeping people divided with the threat of war, or violence or poverty."

"Umh" said Tanea.

"What I see here is the lack of that kind of fear. It's amazing to behold such togetherness."

"You're experiencing that togetherness, and you sound quite high, Kel, but yes, that's the power of real community."

"So what do I do in the meditation?"

"Just be with yourself!"

"How do I do that?"

"It's a kind of self-absorption where the barriers between you and the world around you are broken down. Concentration, thinking of nothing, leading to a surrender of sorts."

"The only time in real life when I'm thinking about nothing is when England are playing Argentina or Germany in the World Cup, and they're down to penalties. Now that's concentration. There are other times, it's true."

"When's that?" Tanea asked.

"Where can I get a beer?"

"Oh Kel!"

"Ho ho," said Kel.

*   *   *   *

A tornado swirled in Kel's head. He sat there with about three hundred people, all serene in their silence, and his head spun like a top. He sat and looked at the swirl—past, present, and future, all congealed into one experience, silently watching the show. This lasted for an hour. He could have screamed, and was glad that he didn't.

Afterwards he waded into one conversation after another and spoke with such spontaneity that his passion flowed, attracting a group around him. They listened with keen interest as he spoke, and asked questions about the on board Brief he had experienced on his way to Gaya.

Out of the corner of his eye he spied another group talking. Their expressions were animated, and at the centre of it stood a young woman looking uncomfortable and threatened. She excused herself from it, ignoring the pleas of those around her to stay and continue the discussion, and made for the door. It was the first outward sign of disquiet and discomfort he had seen on Gaya.

He quickly excused himself from his group, and made to cut off the retreating woman before she made it to the door.

"Excuse me," he called.

"I'd better not talk to you, Kel," she answered.

"Are you leaving the community?" Kel asked.

"Yes,"

"Can't you stay and work it out?"

The woman laughed and said, "You obviously don't know much about this community. You're either in or out, there's no room for doubt of any kind."

"And you have a doubt?"

"Yes."

"About what?" Kel frowned and folded his arms across his chest.

"It's just a doubt, and there's no room for it."

There was a tap on Kel's shoulder; it was Tanea.

"Hello Megan," she said.

"Hi Tanea. See you Kel. We are all praying for your success. Good luck!" and Megan headed off at full steam towards the door.

"Come on Kel, time for your next session. It looks like you have just been bludgeoned or something. Just look at you—arms folded, a big frown."

"She should be allowed to stay and work this out."

"Then we'd all end up with protective postures and premature crowsfeet lining our faces. Come on Kel, it's her choice, and she can come back if she wants."

They were soon careering around the corridors, Kel, a half step behind Tanea.

"Listen, Tanea, you have a hierarchical structure here to help people let go of the personal, and its great, but you cannot banish or punish doubt. It's not right."

"She has a choice. Look at what happened to you the moment you spoke to her, you lost that amazing state of spontaneous grace you were in. Everyone in the room saw it happen, and you must have felt it too?"

"But doubt exists in the real world! You cannot force this enlightenment; it has to be in the face of everything, doubts and all."

"There's no room for it here," said Tanea with an air of finality, and she stopped in front of a door. Above it was a sign, 'Float Centre'.

"Then I'll just have to beg to differ. Not a doubt, alright?"

"Alright Kel," said Tanea, opening the door with some force. "After you."

As he entered, Tanea called out, "Kel's here. He's all yours!"

Kel had definitely not expected, nor was he prepared for what was to follow. He had merely been told that it was going to be like a dream workshop, and up until this point no one would say more.

∗   ∗   ∗   ∗

Daljit stood above him, conspicuous by her blue collar. He lay on a flat bed, head and knees supported, another skullcap on.

"You'd make a great mum, Daljit, with those lovely big brown smiling eyes of yours."

"Goochy, goochy goo," said Daljit, tweaking Kel's cheek.

Closing his eyes he followed instructions methodically, centering his attention on the sounds that danced in his head. After a few minutes he heard what sounded like a mullah, calling out to the devout from a place high above him. Soon he was floating on a cloud; wavebands were at work cutting out the usual physical and mental input from his nervous system. He was nowhere, and supremely happy.

"Out of body experience," Daljit had said. And something about allowing delta and theta wavebands in his brain, allowing them to function naturally and not be dominated by the higher wavebands. Those that cause stress, and marshal attention on the objective world.

"Think of a scene on Gaya," a gentle voice interrupted him, "that caught your eye, and keep your attention on it."

Kel remembered the lake, and the ospreys swooping above it, and was able with ease to keep his attention on it. This lasted for some minutes until suddenly Kel realised that he was there, at the scene, looking down at the lake. He then turned his head towards his feet, and saw his body was with him, suspended in space above the lake.

A great wave of surprise, laced with fear shot through him, and almost immediately he found himself back on the couch.

"This was your first out of body experience; relax into it; no harm can come to you. We are helping to facilitate the process by brainwave induction."

Soon he felt very relaxed and, following instructions, tried again. This time Kel felt his body drifting slowly up and towards the lake, he saw himself leave his body. It was like a dream. Unaware of how he exited the building he woke in his dream and found himself looking down at the lake, and the shock wave passed through him once again, this time with less force. At this moment the voice returned. "Do not fear, no harm can come to you. If you feel you are getting lost or confused, look at your right hand, this will centre you."

Kel hovered above the lake like a bird of prey. He looked at his right hand, and started to exalt in the excitement of his newfound freedom.

"Now look around you," said the voice.

Kel looked around and saw the majesty of the planet; mountain ranges, forests, and in the distance a sea. When his confidence wavered or his astonishment overwhelmed him, he looked at his right hand. This eradicated any doubt in his mind as to his ability to carry on, and stabilised his cognition that this was actually happening. Kel, and what appeared to be his body, floated effortlessly above the lake. He looked back and saw the Mission Centre, and guessed the window where he had first looked upon the scene of the lake.

As he sought it out, he started moving towards the building, and he could move, he realised, wherever his attention was directed.

"Slow down, Kel," the voice said. "You are jumping ahead of us."

Kel was soon at the window looking in at his room; he decided to enter, and the strangest thing happened. He was able to pass through the window, and he gasped silently with delight. He called out to Hal, but no sound came, his voice was silent.

He was soon outside again, and soared high in the sky as if something was leading him on, an irresistible urge to move on. He set his sights on the sea at the distant horizon.

"Kel, not yet," the voice in his head was emphatic, "Hold back, don't go."

But Kel was off, oblivious to any instructions; he swooped and dove over the lake in his new found three-dimensional freedom in a frenzy of joy. Any time he wavered, a check in with his hand would assure him, and on he went.

"Hold back," echoed the voice, fainter now.

His thirst for speed and flight was soon quenched, and now curiosity took over. He looked out towards the sea and within seconds was cruising over a lush coastline and an emerald sea, and he spied some people on the beach. It looked as if they were harvesting seaweed, and down he went in amongst them, but his attempts at communicating with them were fruitless.

He started out to sea, skimmed across its surface and decided to dive in, and was soon forging through the ocean fearless and free, the water in no way inhibiting his movement. He looked down into the blue black depths, and like a sperm whale, dove deep, so deep that he felt quite drunk, and sped on where gravity directed him, to its centre. Something beckoned him on.

Kel was becoming less aware of his out of body-state. He certainly had no idea that three tracers accompanied him like a suckerfish on a shark. He carried on until he had penetrated the crust of the planet and was heading at high speed towards its core, nothing it seemed, could stop him. It was during his passage through the molten core that they lost the tracers on him, and Kel lost any sense of himself.

*   *   *   *

"Damn!" said Tanea, looking at the now blank screen. "Damn, damn, damn! I should have listened to Daljit, after his tailspin on his voyage to Gaya. Damn!"

She stood stock still, eyes cast downward, focussing on nothing, thinking of the next move.

"Get the trajectory of the last tracer read-out, and estimated exit point in the forests. And get me transport, now!" Tanea paced up and down, looking at the screen as if Kel's read-out would reappear, but she knew it wouldn't. "We should have sent somebody with him."

"If we had," said one of the braver team members, Jamie, "then in no way would he have learnt so much so soon. It would have taken weeks."

"And how long is it going to take to find him in the forests, let alone get him to come back?"

"We found him two hundred years ago, on a very crowded planet, and he came," replied Jamie confidently.

"But the forests," replied Tanea.

She paused again, "Get Carter, Matthias, and Yoshii here on the double. And somebody tell Lyle, I certainly don't want to. And you come too Jamie; you have done the forest tea course haven't you?"

"You mean the ayahuasca—yes. In his out-of-body state he'll be fair game for all the forest spirits, and they'll protect him from the tracers. He could get caught up for some time. Damn, you're right."

"And if Kel is this impetuous—how the hell is he going to direct himself in the hole—he just doesn't have the discipline." Tanea briefly held her head in her hands, and sighed loudly.

"Wait a minute," cried Jamie as she fiddled with the dials of her console. "My god, look at this. There was a cloaked tracer in front of Kel, and he followed it unconsciously."

Tanea hurried over to Jamie's screen and looked intently in, her eyes narrowed, the worry lines on her forehead accentuated.

"Oh god, no!" She straightened up and appeared winded, saying nothing for a few seconds. "There's a saboteur amongst us. Or the Doctor's infiltrated.... No that's impossible. Try and find out who has used this programme in the last two weeks, though I am sure he or she would have covered their steps. Maybe there's a virus, heaven only knows Kel is a hex on our computers."

Jamie sped through programme users, looking for any telltale clues. "I can't believe this," she said sadly, and then more boldly, "We'll find Kel, Tanea, we will."

"I better talk to Lyle myself; find out where he is will you, and when he's available. Well done Jamie, we need to start taking all these coincidences a little more seriously. On second thoughts you speak to Lyle, will you? Tell him we are on our way to the forests."

Jamie waved her concordance

"Damn!" said Tanea once more, and strode out of the Control Room.

She made her way to the room where Kel's body lay peacefully asleep. She bent down, and much to the surprise of the medical attendants present, kissed Kel gently on the brow.

"Damn!" she said again, and stormed out.

✳   ✳   ✳   ✳

"Where is your body?"

"Don't know."

"Where is your body?"

"Body?"

No language there was, not at least as he knew it in his embodied state. But some image, three dimensional and bright, was communicating with a deep level of Kel's consciousness, one usually obstructed or overshadowed by the grosser senses.

"We are all one." Kel understood the image to be saying.

"One what?"

"One one."

"Where is this?" Kel's thoughts were understood by this energy.

"This is us, all are same, all are different. This is fruit, monkey eat, this is high, high."

"High what?"

"High, high." Another shape now, a different light. "Come into me I show you."

Kel bowed his head down, and dipped it into a radiance. His being was filled with light, warmth and fullness. He noticed around him a myriad of lights and shapes that swayed like a dance with the harmony of an orchestra. He tried to face the light, but it was all around him and he just part of it. All was there, yet without sight or sound. They were all one in the dancing light.

Another shape jumped up, and penetrated into Kel's awareness, as if through his forehead.

"Who you?" it asked, but no words were spoken

"Lost!" Kel replied.

"He is friend," the first energy again.

What followed was like a dance of light in a dimensional realm unknown, or rather unperceived by the human senses. It was like the beat of a giant heart, and went on at its own pace in perfect balance with itself—everything in its proper place. The harmony of nature spirits dancing in salutation to the sun, and to the joy of being. The ethereal nature of Kel's consciousness joined in this dance and ebbed and flowed with it. He swayed in this new dimension, oblivious to time, or very little else.

The spirits around him sang and saluted the pale light that filtered down from the heavens above, the light grew in intensity, like the slow embrace of an angel's wings.

A searing light hit Kel, and the spirits around him were in a frenzy of happiness. The forest was coming awake, everything stirred; the sun was rising.

Kel joined in this dance and for a time was lost in the frenzy, lost in the freedom of energy and light, a salutation to devotion in being. His movement knew no restrictions and he thrashed his energy this way, then that, until a reflection appeared in his vision, an image of his own body appeared beneath him.

He started, and reflected for a moment longer, then he stared down at his right hand. Time to get back. The mission!

He withdrew from the dance and opened his eyes. He sat in a tree in a dense forest, and was staring at the leaves of a vine that wound its way around its host. The leaves were veined and Kel discerned in the morning light the movement of fluid through them, and knew this was the same intelligence that had created his own veins. He looked down, and a small hunting cat looked at him through the thick foliage, their eyes locking for a moment, as if in acknowledgement, and then darted into the dense green undergrowth. He became aware of the call of some songbirds, yet heard nothing. Shafts of light beamed through the forest, and occasionally a hazy mist moved on a light breeze.

'Nature's heaven,' thought Kel as the forest spirits delighted and basked in the beat of the sun's feet, as they danced across the forest floor.

He looked down at his hand and knew that he must leave, though the tug of the spirits dance was strong and mesmerising.

"Why leave?" They had immediately picked up on his plans, and hovered around him. He found himself able to inhabit both their world, and his.

"Big bad thing coming," he intimated.

"Bad thing?"

"Yes."

"Then take our power with you."

There was a moments pause, and Kel felt his heart fit to burst as energy gushed and streamed into him, as if through a micro tunnel in the middle of his chest. He was receiving an untold amount of energy and intelligence from the forest, and it filled him with a subtle power too fine to be recognised in any ordinary sense. The transference was soon over, and the nature spirits had gone.

He looked up and ascended, and was almost immediately picked up by a tracer. He followed its trajectory, and found himself hovering over his body.

"Kel!" A familiar voice.

"Whoa-?" Kel woke with a start, looked down at his feet. He was in his body, and poked, and pinched it.

"Yes, you're back," said Tanea with a smile of both admonishment, and affection. "Are you okay?"

"I guess so."

Tanea put her hand on his brow. "Welcome back, you gave us quite a scare but that seems to be your nature, and this time you may have had help and more than a little enticement. But you're back, thank god. You're in a hovership over the forests that encircle most of this planet. You've been gone for some hours. Jamie here will de-brief you."

Kel turned towards Jamie and was looking into the face of a Greek goddess, with curly fair hair, and a smile signaling elation and ardor.

"I'll leave him with you," said Tanea, as she made for the flight deck.

"Just tell me all about it Kel. Oh my god! I can't believe you were in the forests totally unprepared," said Jamie with such interest that Kel was already at the task of gilding a lily of an experience, one that would be difficult to put into words.

"What did Tanea mean by enticement?" Kel asked.

"Nothing for you to worry about. Now tell me what happened down there in the forests. What was your experience?"

*   *   *   *

The squadron of three craft was in tight chevron formation as it sped its way back to Mission Control. They passed over the forest in silence, and the animals and spirits below hardly noticed their passing.

"He's asleep," said Jamie as she slipped into the co-pilot's seat. They were on automatic, linked with the other craft, and sped on as one unit. Tanea turned to face her colleague, and both women relaxed and appeared satisfied after a job well done, as the terrain rolled on by beneath them. They had found him.

"Well," said Tanea.

"Well," repeated Jamie, "He may have missed his second day's briefing but he's gone way beyond anything we could have taught him. He apparently made a conscious decision to leave the forest environment, just before our tracer picked him up. Our Kel has his wits about him, believe me. We have no worry about acclimatisation to out of body travel—he's got it. It would have taken months to get to that point conventionally. This is the right guy for the job."

"He could have done with another session with Matthias and Yoshii. He lacks discipline." Tanea sank back in her seat, and sighed with relief. "So what happened?"

"He got to a point it usually takes three years to penetrate—of course with all the safety factors tied in. And, and this is the most startling news, he has been empowered. He had the ultimate experience, all within a few hours. I would've said it was impossible to do. The spirits must have gleaned from Kel that some danger is imminent, so they let him have it."

"How can that help with the kind of power the Doctor is wielding?" asked Tanea.

"I don't know," replied Jamie. "It's beyond the realm of our senses but it will help him, believe me. You have to do the course, and drink the tea, to understand the subtle power that this kind of experience packs."

"Well he is going to need all the help he can get," replied Tanea. "Now with this delay, he's not going to be able to see his Lua again. She'll be activated again, as this is part of the deal Kel struck with Lyle, but not until three hours after the mission starts. As soon as we get back I have to go over to Replication, and depending on whether all the equipment is still operative, I'll go into stasis tonight for the conscious transferal. I honestly didn't think I would have to go through that again."

"And I hear they are re-introducing Lua's memory banks from Kel's inward flight as part of the deal," said Jamie.

"A deal's a deal. Kel was real insistent that Lua should not be modified in any way. In fact he demanded it."

"Let's face it," said Jamie, "She did an amazing job getting him here so quickly, and she fell in love, so did he. Lua in love! What a shocker that was."

"Kel's a character, that's for sure, and I'll miss him. Going into stasis means not seeing this stubborn, crazy, medieval guy again before he embarks on his mission, and that's a bummer. Stasis is the last thing in the universe I need at the moment."

"Yeah, there is something about him," Jamie replied. "Raw and wild. Maybe we have become too passive, or controlled. Too conniving in our quest; too rule bound."

"Don't even think about that Jamie. This guy is a wild card. Don't forget what we have here, and what happens when too many wild cards share the same space. We are doing fine, it's just these damn emotions." So saying Tanea swung around, switched the controls to pilot, and got on the mike to Carter and Matthias.

"Come on boys, let's play around on some air waves. Jamie go and make sure our guest is securely fastened."

"Roger and over," came the reply. "You lead, we'll follow."

Light Beam

Kel woke from a dreamless sleep, and it was dark. He was in his bed and the faint light of dawn bordered the curtains. He had been talking to Jamie, and that's the last he could remember. He stretched out in bed, thinking about the impossible events of the previous day, trying to get a handle on it, but could find very little logic in it and gave up.

"Hal," he said in the darkness.

"Yes, Kel."

"Tell me what you know about this Baba I am going to meet today."

"Yes Kel, but first there is a message from Tanea. Would you like to hear it?"

"Yes please, let me have it. I wonder what I've done wrong now," and Kel chuckled to himself.

"Good morning Kel. I have some bad news, and some good news." It was Tanea's voice. "The bad news first. Due to the fact of the lighter side of yourself going awol yesterday, our program to revive Lua has been put back a day, so I am sorry Kel, you won't be seeing her again. It is very unfortunate but our time line in this is so tight, and we have planned up until the very last microseconds we are able to sling-shoot you back to your world. I know this is so unfair, and I am sorry."

Kel's heart sunk like a stone.

There was a pause, and Tanea continued, "The good news is that you don't have to put up with me any more, I have to spend the next two days in stasis in order to revive her. I will miss you, like everyone else here. I am so grateful to you, for your courage, and for your fun. You certainly made me laugh, and you made me think. Thank you Kel, thank you so much. The rest of your programme has been cancelled, the boys tell me you are a natural at the swordplay, you just lack a little discipline. I won't comment on that! I am sorry. Good luck."

Kel lay there in the silence, aware only of a feeling in the pit of his stomach. He felt lonely, like a child missing its mother, and a wave of emotional pain swept through his body. At this moment he missed both of them; they had moulded into one energy despite their differences. "Damn!" he said.

He shut his eyes and visualised her face. This had the effect of tightening the grip in his guts, and he felt her near to him. 'This is so unfair,' he said to himself.

Kel got up, and pushed the coffee dispenser button, and sat in his chair staring at the cup of hot, fresh coffee. "Lots of anti-oxidants," Lua had told him. He looked around the room, restless and in pain.

"Definitely no tobacco here, eh Hal?" Kel pleaded.

"Yes Kel, no tobacco," Hal replied.

"Damn," said Kel. He got up and opened the curtains, and returned to the chair. The sun's first rays were hitting the mountain that filled his view.

"Can I go and see them, Hal, just to say goodbye?"

"No Kel, it's a highly delicate procedure, no interruptions are allowed."

"I am so bloody angry I can't see her again, and Tanea makes it sound like it is my fault. Was it my fault Hal?"

"Seventy percent is estimated to be yours."

"And the other thirty?

"That information is not available to me."

"Okay, tell me about this Baba, what's his history?" Kel lay there in the chair, leg hung over the arm rest, ignoring the unrelenting pain that swirled in his guts, forcing his attention on to Hal's discourse, and the view of the dawn unfolding before him.

Hal weaved a story of a young Indian man coming to Gaya and spending three years in the community before leaving to live as a recluse in the mountains. At eighteen this man had given up a potentially successful career in India's booming music business, thrown everything away, and became a renunciate, walking around India in search of something more, more than conventional life had to offer.

"So what did he do on his trek around India?" asked Kel, remembering his own brief journey, through the chaos and cacophony of sound, colour and noise, he found India to be.

"He met different teachers, until he met his guru,"

"Who was that?"

"A teacher in the Saivite tradition, that is a devotee of Shiva, which is an Indian term for the Absolute."

"Absolute what?" asked Kel.

"Absolute reality," replied Hal.

There was a knock at the door.

"Come in!"

It was Carter carrying a breakfast tray. "We let you sleep through the meditation this morning, you needed your rest."

"I'd totally forgotten about it," confessed Kel. "You know I won't get to see Lua again?"

"We are so sorry about that, everyone on the planet is. It is the romance drama, and now tragedy, second to none here."

Kel looked sternly at Carter, who backed away one step, and shrugged his shoulders.

Kel forced his attention into the present. "You told me your original, Duncan, was on retreat, but he went into the hole."

"Yes, I'm sorry."

"That must be painful for you?"

"Yes it is, but to me he is on retreat, and he will be helping the others in there," said Carter devoid of any emotion or regret.

"How can you be sure that the others are there?"

"Consciousness cannot just disappear, or disperse; their souls are in there, trapped and probably tricked."

"How many of you blue-collar guys are around?" asked Kel. "How many humanoids?"

"I'll just say that half of the humanoids disappeared with the Doctor, and they were half his crew."

"So there are about thirty-five of you remaining on Gaya," said Kel.

"That's right, about thirty five."

"Daljit and Anjila are the same to me, and I presume from what you've told me that you and Duncan are the same. So you must have the same soul, the same source. What happens when you die, or if you die before Duncan?"

"Death is a timeless state Kel, and you needn't bother yourself with trying to work out how our souls unite in that state. It's a mystery, and will always remain so. Duncan and I are one."

"What about the Doctor's aberrated soul? What will happen to all that screwed up energy of his when I finish him off?"

For a split second Carter looked a little surprised, then smiled and replied. "By that time, you would have already dealt with it."

"Me? Oh hell," said Kel under his breath.

"If not," Carter continued, "Lyle will have to deal with it."

Kel glanced out at the mountain, now gloriously lit up with the morning sun, then at Carter. "How many blips in the humanoid system have there been?"

"Only Lyle and Tanea, although some of the humanoids that you have spoken to have needed counseling," and Carter laughed.

"Some of my old girlfriends would understand that," said Kel, and he started breakfast in earnest. Even though he felt gutted at his lost love, he was very hungry.

"We will be leaving for the mountains in one hour Kel, you will be there for two nights, and we've already packed warmer clothes for you. All we need is you. I'll be back in an hour," and Carter left Kel alone with the omniscient Hal.

"Hal, do you have some photos of this Baba?" Kel asked.

A holographic image of a handsome young man appeared before Kel. He was very dark in colour, almost black and his eyes shone, and he had an intensity about him that was disarming. The image started to slowly age until, Kel guessed, the time he left the community. Baba's forehead was very deep, and his brow was cliff-like, almost Neanderthal, with bushy black eyebrows. There was something aboriginal about the looks, wild yet compassionate.

"Do you remember him Hal?"

"He is in my memory circuits."

"Did you like him?"

"I cannot think like you. Remember! Too many variables! He was here, he did this and that, and then he left. No out-of-the-ordinary situations are recorded."

"How does he live and survive up in the mountains?"

"He is self sufficient, and there is a small community around that looks out for each other. These are people who also chose to leave the community," replied Hal.

"Why do people leave the community?" Kel asked.

"Lack of commitment," replied Hal.

"Forget it," said Kel getting up, and heading for the bathroom. He stopped suddenly and called to Hal. "Get Lyle on the line, for me I will be out of the shower in ten minutes. I intend saying goodbye to the woman I love. I'm going to the unit. That's the least Gaya can do for me. I will not take no for an answer!"

"But Kel!"

"Just do it Hal. Just do it. Now!" said Kel, disappearing into the bathroom.

Kel did not speak to Lyle. A member of Replication, as the unit was called, turned up and hurried Kel into a waiting vehicle, and they zoomed off at speed.

"You have to be quiet," his host pleaded over and over. "It is imperative that there is no sound. None, not a single decibel."

They were out in the foothills and the terrain became drier. The entrance of the unit was in the side of a hill and his driver switched off the power source to his vehicle, and they glided into the quiet depths of the hill under some invisible power source. His companion lifted his finger to his lips and Kel nodded his understanding.

Kel was kitted out in an outfit resembling an astronaut's from his era, so bulky was his suit. It was designed to eliminate any outgoing noise and his footwear felt like two great sponges. He was led to a chamber deep underground and entered a room that emitted a strange ultra-violet light. He stood in front of a glass screen and as he became used to the light, he discerned two figures in front of him. Lua would be on the right, they had told him.

Tanea and Lua were suspended in a tank of liquid and had giant head sets on, and breathing apparatus. They made no movement themselves, except for a slight rising and falling of their bodies in the liquid with the in and out breath. Their vertical position gave them the appearance to Kel, as he peered through the gloom, of twin peas in an aquatic pod. He stared at Lua and shot her a message of his love.

Unbeknown to Kel in the dim light, his companion, who had been so insistent on silence, and eyed his movements like a hawk, had inadvertently swallowed some saliva during his vigil, and now battled behind Kel not to cough. If he had looked behind him, it would have appeared that his companion was wrestling himself, as he gyrated around trying not to emit one decibel of sound.

He failed and coughed once. Kel heard not a thing but at that moment, as he stared at Lua, she opened her eyes briefly and caught his gaze. He exploded inside himself at this momentous event, this light beam of love. More explosive than any revelation, or anything that had happened to him so far, this moment for him was unforgettable. Lua looked out as a child would, with innocent expectation, and a glint of recognition and love for him. She then closed her eyes again, and was gone.

Kel turned around and found himself alone in the room. He was ecstatic and waved a farewell to his love, then bowed ceremoniously in front of Tanea, and made for the door. He did not see his companion again. Another member of the unit was waiting for him and took him to the exit where he stripped out of his space suit.

"She looked at me," he said jubilantly, once outside in the light of day.

"Yes, we know," was the dry reply. "And we are not sure what the ramifications of that are. It's a first. Your driver is outside. Good luck on your mission, Kel." They said no more to him and he left.

✳   ✳   ✳   ✳

Kel sat snugly in his seat next to Carter who was at the wheel of the hovermobile, and now flying forty feet above the planet's surface. The terrain gradually became spectacular, lush and green with rocky gorges, waterfalls cascading into pure lakes, and flowering trees ablaze with red and pink blossom.

"She looked at me!" Kel exclaimed. "Lua looked at me."

"Did you tell the staff there?" Carter asked. "Oh my, that is a first, you must have given the unit a collective seizure."

Carter looked pensive and Kel watched the beauty of the planet as it flashed by beneath them.

"I've seen those trees before," Kel said, "In the Caribbean, they're called Immortelle, or something very much like them."

"That's right, they took root very quickly here on Gaya," replied Carter.

They cruised on a while, and Kel craned his neck this way and that, to take in the scenery. Carter, a little pre-occupied with the dashboard read-out, played around with some dials.

"Something wrong?" Kel asked.

"We are being followed, Look at the radar screen."

Kel could discern very little, except for a little blip on the screen that blinked at regular intervals.

Carter spoke some commands, and Mission Control responded immediately. "Tightened security measures, please ignore shadow; continue mission," was their reply.

"What's going on?" said Carter as they sailed on through the air in silence. Carter's eyes constantly returned to, and skipped over the dashboard lights, as if this were some annoying itch he could not ignore. After some time he relaxed and sank back in his chair. Like so many Americans, Kel thought, driving is second nature, so very much at home behind the wheel of a vehicle.

"Why did this Baba leave the community?" Kel asked.

"I am sure he will tell you his story. I've met Baba twice, and he's a rare being, a mystic. What in your day you might have called a shaman. The community life wasn't for him; he's too out of the ordinary. He was only there to check it out, see what was going on."

Kel noticed Carter was following the source of a fast flowing river below, heading up-river, and rejoiced in flying without wings, propellers, or a noisy engine. "Looks like you have gravity worked out."

"The more you know about something, the more it can be utilised."

"Why did you come here, or Duncan rather?"

Carter smiled, and took a deep breath. He thought for a while, and then said, "Let me give you some for instances Kel; the reason you have such a profound effect on us humanoids is because there is a strong trait of the personal about you, and you express it in a humorous and loving way."

Kel grunted to indicate he was listening, curious at Carter's present line of dialogue.

"When the humanoids were first produced on Earth, there was a big problem with rebellion, violence, and a slew of teething problems nearly curtailing the whole program. The technology was transferred here, and everything was fine up until now. The kind of impersonal way of life here suited this kind of technology. You have experienced enough now to know that our life is about renouncing this idea to be special, separate, and all the ideas that come with it."

"That's for sure."

"So with this way of life in place we follow a natural kind of seeking, inquiring into the deeper side of who we are. So I came here to seek a deeper side of who I am, and to understand this restless mind. Ultimately to be free of it all."

"What have you found?" Kel asked.

"Something which is free, and beyond all that destructive egocentric confusion. The ability to use my will to see the tricks and turns of the mind, it's constant babbling, its endless desires and countless fears, and finally not to be tyrannised by it. Then we can grow and see through the illusion."

"Well," Kel replied, "the illusion seems to be real enough to me, even with all the information and experience that has been fed me! I can't ignore my mind's interpretation of what life is. I admit I have seen another side of myself that is, to put it mildly, momentous, but this whole thing about doing away with the ego seems like the ultimate ego trip to me!"

Carter laughed and said, "you see Kel, you remind us of something that has been renounced, and yet there is a trace of it in all of us. You are free on one level but trapped in another."

"You've been talking to Tanea, haven't you?"

"There's a lot of gossip in a community, can't have one without it. Things go around like wild fire. But you see, Kel, it's not about ignoring what your mind interprets life to be, it's about not allowing it to distort the picture."

"And if I don't allow it to?"

"Then you will see the truth in the clear light of day, free from…free from…" and Carter broke into verse. "With all our most holy illusions, flying higher than Gilderoy's kite, to teach us a jolly good lesson, and serves us jolly well right. That's your Kipling."

"Free from illusions. Nice!" said Kel. "In my day we grew up with the most important goal being to be something special. Greed taught us not to trust, and the kind of openness you have here, vulnerability if you like, was regarded as a weakness."

"Life on Earth now is better, but what you mention is still there. That's why it's so difficult to go for it there. Life feeds on life, and it's cruel."

"Surely these are lessons we all need to learn. Denying them is just an escape. I think we all have to go for it, but in the real world. Be this, but in that, do you know what I mean?"

Carter grunted in neither approval, nor disapproval. "Be real, Kel, liberation is possible, and to attain it, is the most delicate process. Think about all the distractions that divert our attention, all the mistakes you could go on making over and over again. Habits you hang on to can last forever."

"Well, if your level of commitment is full enough I don't honestly think it makes a blind bit of difference where you are. In a monastery you cover it up, hide it, ignore it, whatever. I'll dump my habits when I have to. As long as I am not hurting anyone with my shit in the meantime."

"But…" said Carter, but then thought better of it, and they cruised on above the lush planet. The journey was smooth and pleasant; they cut through canyon and valley like a sushi knife through tuna, following the river to its source.

"Why did the Doctor go so wrong, what happened?" Kel asked at last.

"When Lyle was replicated, there was a trace of something in his psyche that was unresolved. Lyle is honestly a beacon to many of us here, like a light leading us on, but it seems there was something going on inside him. Exactly what it was is open to speculation, but whatever it was, it was the aberration that spawned the Doctor. And that no one could foresee."

"What do you think was going on?"

"Something to do with Tanea, that's the general feeling. Lyle was replicated before they got into a relationship."

"That's so weird, I get stuck on Lua, Lyle fancied Tanea, and he and I are the same…soul, or whatever it is."

Carter grunted his agreement. "As you say, weird. That is if fate and destiny are to be regarded as weird."

"So you believe in fate and destiny?" Kel asked.

"I believe we have to deal with what we cause. I know what is going on now, and what needs to be done. I'm sorry I mentioned those two words, fate and destiny; it's possible to create a million ideas around them."

"So you reckon that it is through this relationship," Kel went on, "that all this has happened, that the chicken and the egg is sitting right here with me. That his infatuation was in fact mine, because he is me in the future." Kel stopped, thought for a moment and said, "so this aberration in the cosmic play is my infatuation for Lua, and this caused the seed of your world's potential destruction."

Carter laughed and said, "We are discovering through you a lot of what happened, and why. I can't say more than that because all the rest is supposition."

"Well you guys juice up Lua and give her the mission of saving your planet, to get me here," said Kel straining against his gravity seat. "And now, because she and I have struck up a relationship, you think that this could be some governing factor in how Lyle feels about Tanea, and that that is the reason for this madman in a black hole threatening your planet, and god knows what else. I hope that you are just bloody well kidding me, man."

"No! Think about it, it must be something like that. Whatever it is, your relationship with Lua is stuck in some type of attachment. We created it, and now we have to deal with it."

"Fuck you!" said Kel

"Oh ho ho," said Carter, "that doesn't help."

"You all come over as being bloody hoity-toity, above and beyond the real world of relationships, and then when that self denial backfires on you, you look around and try to nail the responsibility on some poor bugger like me. It might not help but I repeat. Fuck you!"

Carter said nothing.

"My soul is my own Carter," Kel was livid, "whatever I do or cause is my business; what Lyle wants is his business, and what the Doctor is up to is his, whoever he is. I do not believe we are the same, maybe we are just on the same wavelength. I am who I am, that's all. If I can help, I am happy to help and put myself on the line for you guys, but this vague kind of oblique accusation of my being responsible for this is unfounded, and angers the hell out of me!"

"One thing we have learned here," said Carter, rising to the challenge, "is that the greatest hiding place for this sticky little ego is in some sort of special, and personal relationship. This could be with another human being or with God, or race, or religion, or whatever. It has been the single most destructive force in human history. It causes separation and endless misery."

"Without an ego you would not exist, nor would I," countered Kel. "You have created something unusually beautiful here on Gaya, but there is a level of some kind of control that bothers me. It's like fundamentalism, being right without a heart; being superior without reason. It is as if you are saying, 'you are either with us, or against us,' and that, in my eyes, is wrong."

"Without commitment nothing would change. Some sacrifice has to be made, and the trouble is that most people, even nowadays, are unwilling to give up that they are most attached to."

"But…"

"Listen!" Carter persisted, "And often as not, it is precisely the thing holding them back from fulfilling their potential, and it could possibly be something that is ultimately destroying them."

"Fulfilling what potential?" Kel slumped back in his seat and looked over at Carter.

"Becoming a happy, spontaneous human being, and seeing the world as it really is," said Carter with a relaxed air of finality.

"Sounds magical, but I don't think you can do it at the exclusion of everyone who doesn't agree with you, and a little bit of the personal is fine."

"I am only talking from the level of my experience," replied Carter. "For me this is the only way I could radically change."

"You guys say that one shouldn't hide in any special relationship, and here you are cloistered in a separate community, shunning the world. Doubters are exiled it seems!" Kel threw his hands up in exasperation.

"Doubt is an insidious virus. When we start to really let go of the past, it's a delicate and vulnerable condition, and doubt breeds cynicism, that's the problem."

"You cannot hide from it, it needs to be thoroughly investigated, and I don't mean getting one's head stuck in the trash can." Kel stopped short, and decided to discontinue his argument. "Funny thing is, I found your community the most provocative, challenging, and interesting set up, and here I am arguing like this."

"You were enjoying a honeymoon period with us Kel. If you were here full time it would get a little hot as those things you needed to dump, surfaced. You'd find out a lot about how we judge others with our own weaknesses, and just how unobjective about ourselves we can be."

"You shouldn't exile good people because they have a doubt about their level of commitment. That is ignorance and arrogance!"

"No it isn't. You are missing the point," retorted Carter.

"No I am not."

"Well, we'll just have to beg to differ," said Carter, "For now!"

Both men laughed and Kel added, determined to have the last word, "Send me to Coventry then."

"Coventry?" queried Carter.

"An English expression meaning to be ousted and ignored by your work-mates for failing to tow the union line."

"If you can't swim don't jump in the water."

"Touché," said Kel. Carters riposte stirred something in his memory, and it was gone in a flash.

MYSTIC

They passed through a layer of mist into a steep valley, and foothills either side led them to a snow capped mountain range in the distance. Kel could see that the river below them flowed faster now, as the V of the valley narrowed, and gushing streams etched through the hills to flow into the raging river. He also noticed with interest, a smattering of dwellings here and there on the forest floor. There were solar panels on the rooftops, and what appeared to be junk, or just the usual collection of mechanical spare parts that cannot be thrown away, in the clearings around the houses.

They started descending towards what looked like a meadow in the distance, surrounded by pine and cedar trees. The meadow was in the wooded foothills, behind which towered spectacular snow capped mountains.

They landed without a bump, the hatch door opened with a hiss, and the fresh mountain air hit Kel with a wallop. The quiet was broken by the sound of a stream babbling its way down to the river, and some birds singing in the foliage. He got out, stretched and looked at Carter who smiled warmly at him. The air smelt sweet with the fragrance of the forest around them, and was cold and crisp as it hit his lungs, a smattering of alpine flowers to add spice to this, and Kel took a deep breath, drinking it in with gusto.

Carter climbed out and stretched. He looked around, as if searching out the shadow that had followed them into the mountains.

"Take that path up for about a mile and you'll see Baba's house, and don't stray from the path next to the stream."

"Right," said Kel.

"We'll be here the day after tomorrow when the sun is between those two mountains there, on its way up, about mid morning. Enjoy, Kel," and Carter laughed. He slid into the driver's seat with the confidence of a racing driver, and the hatch shut with a 'whoomph'. The craft swung around effortlessly and started its gentle climb, leaving Kel alone with his pack in a meadow on his way up to see a mystic named Baba. He stayed to watch the waving Carter disappear into the distance, and felt exquisitely alone.

"Whatever next?" Kel muttered to himself, hoisting his pack onto his back, and starting the gentle climb through the trees by the stream. He felt a subtle excitement laced with a little anxiety. The beauty of the environs soon assuaged any fear he may have felt, as the sun's dappled light played in the lush undergrowth. One of the weeds that grew in the more open sunny areas was cannabis. Kel laughed to himself and said, "Shakey, I've found your paradise."

Only the birds, and a chipmunk-like creature, obviously indignant at his presence there, answered him, and up he went.

At last he came to a wooden house nestled against an overhanging rock that stood alone next to the stream, trees clinging to the stone with their gnarly tendrils. A small vegetable garden was to one side of the rickety house, away from the stream, and the bounty of the garden was obviously shared by the inhabitants of the forest, though some half-hearted attempts at thwarting them were evident.

A wood pile, sheltered in a tiny shed under the miniature cliff above it, gave off the sweet smell of rotting timber, and a small chopping block surrounded by wood chips stood starkly, almost lonely, to one side. A small machete clung to its top.

Kel suddenly sucked in his breath. A large black snake slithered from the woodshed, and made its way along a small clearing at the end of which there was, what Kel guessed to be, an out-house. "Shit' he said to himself. The snake disappeared into the bushes, its midriff as large as a melon.

"Oh boy, oh boy!"

He approached the house and called out, "Baba."

"Oi," came the immediate reply, and soon Baba emerged.

Whatever image he may have conjured up in his mind he was not quite prepared for the youngish looking man that now stood before him. Dark with long hair and a beard, wild, but neatly dressed in cotton shorts and sweatshirt.

"Welcome Kel," he said smiling. "I was expecting you tomorrow, but no matter, please come in and I'll make some tea."

Kel approached him, and somewhat clumsily proffered his hand. "Hello, Baba."

"Hello" replied Baba, and warmly took his hand and squeezed it in both of his. "Come in, come in, you must be tired. In my house you are my guest; you are here to rest so sit and relax, no hurry, no worry." And Baba laughed, as if remembering something, or somebody.

He followed Baba in. It was dark inside, a small fire over a makeshift grill smoked in one corner, and on it a battered kettle steamed gently. To one side, under a tiny window, two chairs faced each other over a small table. Following Baba's gesture he sat in one of these, and pushed his pack into the corner of the room.

"Let me show you where you sleep," said Baba, after he had stoked up the fire, blowing through a long bamboo tube into the smouldering embers.

They ascended some rickety stairs to a room above. Pictures and posters adorned the walls, of people and deities. To the far side was a futon bed already made, and a door led out to a veranda, which was perfectly positioned to receive the afternoon sun. Kel could see some stretches of river and he vaguely discerned a long waterfall on the opposite side of the valley, maybe two miles away.

"The bed is over the fire's exhaust pipe, so it is very cozy at night," said Baba. "You can pee over the veranda when its dark out, and if you need to go to the toilet it's at the end of the garden there. I have a…how do you say? Torch, flashlight, downstairs if you should need it," and Kel thought he would have to be pretty desperate to go down this particular garden in the dark.

"So, no creepy crawlies to worry about Baba?" Kel asked at last.

"No, nothing will harm you here unless it is in self defense," said Baba somewhat re-assuringly, and they descended. Kel sat, arms outstretched toward the fire, and felt very much at ease.

"I am so glad you could come. This mad Doctor has even got me worried, he's up to no good, and must be stopped. So you do nothing but relax. I am sure you must be exhausted after your stay with the community," said Baba, and he laughed again.

Kel sunk back in his chair and sighed audibly.

"You want a cigarette?" asked Baba. "Lyle brings these relics to me," and he threw an opened pack on the table before Kel.

"I'll have one with the tea, Baba," Kel picked up the cigarettes and examined them. Thank god they're not menthol, he thought.

The tea was very sweet. Kel lit a cigarette, and Baba did the same. After three drags Kel's head reeled like a top, and he put it out. Baba said nothing, and his eyes were as still as black marble. He looked old now, and wizened. Kel had to look twice to see it was the same man.

"My teacher sent me here to see what was going on," said Baba. "I thought the community was a good place, apart from a little hypocrisy, but I left, and found this place. Pure peace and no problems, except the rats when they are naughty. Some field rats found an easy life here and stayed. When they become too many, then they are eaten by a snake, as everything is in balance here. I built this house with the help of some guys who left the community and live hereabouts, and they visit sometimes, but most of the time I am here alone"

"Your accent sounds Indian, Baba. Where are you from?"

"I was born in Burma, and learnt Christian and Buddhist ways. My family was Hindu."

"What a mix!"

"Yes, Kel Christian and Buddhist ways. They still exist quite strong in out of the way backward places, and Burma is still such a place. A lot of magic there." Baba leant back in his chair, and pivoted the back struts at a precarious angle, as if the slightest imbalance would send him tumbling backwards. "Father Michael, a good man. He taught me good discipline and the Buddhist priests showed me magic! But I am Indian through and through—south India."

Baba took a long slow draw on his cigarette and looked at Kel. "You are English, I hear. You know there are people there in India who still lament the absence of the English, as they were the only people who could bring any organisation to India. Good sense of humour; arrogant, but overall just. The Buddhist monks in Burma told me that the saying of the English soldier is still famous in Buddhist circles."

"And what is that Baba?" asked Kel.

"Eat, shit, fuck, and then you die," said Baba and he laughed. "Good stuff eh?"

"Well Baba I might be English, and I cannot disagree with such a basic philosophy, but I find myself in strange circumstances," said Kel, and he laughed aloud and hard at some absurdity he saw in himself. "Strange circumstances indeed. I am in the future by some two hundred years, visiting someone who lives as if it's two hundred years in my past. You know Baba, I have this very strong feeling that I have known you before, some 'déjà vu' kind of thing."

He had been at Baba's place for a short time only, and he felt he was home.

"Yes, I think I have lived like this for many lifetimes, this is fine and good for me. You want a smoke, some herbs?" Baba asked.

"Whatever Baba. I am in your house, whatever you do."

"Ha ha ha!" said Baba, obviously pleased with this remark.

Baba brought out an old pipe tin and a gnarled wooden pipe. "This is a little mix of some herbs that grow around here. No concentrations of anything, just some weeds."

Kel just observed Baba as he shrugged his shoulders, and started to rub the pipe mix in his hands, and he suddenly looked like a wizard. His demeanour had changed again as if some strange energy danced in him under a number of guises. He filled the pipe, lit it, and handed it to Kel.

Kel took a puff, and that was the last thing he remembered for a short while, as if he had entered another space. He was somehow totally out of it on one level, and yet on another, very present, spending time in the woods with his father, or was it his grandfather, and a fire, and something to smoke. Whatever it was, he totally trusted this man.

He suddenly heard music coming from somewhere and he looked around to see if there was a music sound system, but there was not even electricity. He slowly realised that this sound celestial was the sound of the stream babbling nearby. Music is organic, he thought, and chuckled.

"When I was seventeen, my family went back to India," Baba said at last, "and I had to leave a love-match I had in Burma. Anyway it had to end; a long story, and I was heartbroken so I started a search for something more. I went on a pilgrimage looking for God."

"And what did you find?" asked Kel.

"My teacher, who helped me look in the right places, in the right way."

"And how was that?"

"I spent twenty years looking Kel, Lots of different meditations, and teachers, and ways, but I was lucky enough to find the supreme most way. The natural way, for me anyway."

"Which way is that?"

"The way of knowledge. Know who you are, and then everything will take care of itself."

"So what do you have to do to gain such knowledge?"

"Just close your eyes for a second, and listen to the noises around here," Baba replied.

Kel did as he was told, and his senses engulfed the surrounds, the stream, birds, the occasional cracking of the fire, and the endless scuffling noises of nature. Soon Kel felt as if no barrier existed between him and all around him; everything seemed to be one living breathing mass, and he just part of it.

"Remember these six syllables Kel, and say them in your head," said Baba softly, and he slowly enunciated the six syllables.

Kel internally repeated these sounds, and when his mind wandered Baba would gently edge his attention back to the sounds. After a few minutes the sounds seemed to take on a life of their own, and they echoed in his head. He felt as if he were being transported somewhere different, and the sounds were his vehicle.

After perhaps twenty minutes, he opened his eyes and saw Baba leaning back in his chair staring aloft, his chin resting on his hand. Kel felt ecstatically relaxed.

"God and man are the same stuff, Kel, the same. Once you fully understand this, something will open up to you, will surrender itself to you."

"Then why do I have to always feel this," said Kel, searching for the right words. "This feeling of everything being so absurd, and there seems to be no rhyme or reason why everything is so absurd, that life is just a cosmic joke."

"That is your monkey mind playing around with you, always looking for the negative, something to compare itself with. See the workings of this mechanism, and you will get to know that that is not yourself. It has done very well to get you this far. Its job is to challenge, and ensure your survival in the physical body. But its job is only that. You yourself are much bigger than that. Do not confuse this monkey mechanism with who you are in a much bigger sense. You must have seen and experienced enough now to know this, since you left your home!" Baba took a puff on his pipe and sank back in his chair.

"Monkey mechanism, that's a perfect way to describe it, Baba, but it's always after the fruits of its desire. It surely is one hell of a survival expert." Kel leant back in his chair.

"Yes, but it has taken survival on to a very subtle level, and tries to be superior on a mental level, and becomes, you know, cynical. But it, itself, does not want to change. That is why we should not expect the world to change if we ourselves are not prepared to do so." Baba took a long draw on the pipe and blew the smoke up into the rafters, and handed the pipe to Kel, who did the same.

"This is very relaxing stuff Baba."

"Yes, it is a good mix."

"So what is this survival expert?"

"It is the minister of the body. Here to attend to the needs of the body. The servant of the King who sits here upper," and Baba tapped the top of his head. "In this place man and God knows itself to be the same stuff, and to be beyond just the physical."

"So if man and God is the same stuff, how come there is so much pain and suffering in the world."

"There are many things, many beings in all the worlds, vying for existence—gods and devils, if you like," said Baba. "And the only way you know you exist is to see and experience yourself. So if a man is very angry, exploding with anger, and causes this same anger in another man, then that is a demon who, in the creation of this situation sees himself to exist, 'Ah I exist and I am very powerful.'" Baba parodied the demon very well. "If the other man is very strong and does not react to that demon of anger, then the demon surely loses a lot of power because it cannot see itself. In this way it is like the survival of the fittest."

Kel dwelt on this for some time and said, "Sounds like a battle ground."

"That is what it is," cried Baba. "The physical is a battle ground for all the possible…for all possibilities. But in the end, pure spontaneity is the expression of God when it harms nothing. Art is like that, music too! You see, you yourself must see what is good and what works, and when you live and trust yourself, then you have the opportunity of seeing much deeper into your true nature. It is all very simple really, but the mind complicates matters by setting itself up as the judge."

"Yes, that's in the Bible isn't it. 'Judge not, lest thee be judged', or something like that."

"Yes, Kel, very good. Who are we to judge?"

"What about the following? In my day there are a lot of wars, and rape is a fact of life in such horrors. Some of these women became pregnant and were told by certain religious bodies that abortion is a crime. Where is the demon in all of that, and who is making the judgement? Such nonsense!"

"Listen Kel, if that lady has the child and brings it up with love, much love, then that child will become like a god, an angel for peace. Conceived in such violence, yet bathed in love. You see that is why love will always win in the end, because it is stronger, because it is who the Lord is, because it is eternal."

"And if the mama doesn't want it?"

"Then it is right and proper up to her whether she have it or not. What right do I have to tell her what to do."

Kel stared in front of him, and nodded in agreement. "So you see existence in terms of gods and demons?"

"Yes because what exists here exist there also," and Baba pointed a finger aloft. "Millions and millions of gods. So there are millions and millions of people, and we are all one. Ultimately we are all one, one big play, one big drama. If there is no pain there is no pleasure, no tragedy then no comedy, no good, then no bad."

"So who is watching the play Baba?"

"You are, we are, the supreme witness is," Baba replied, and laughed. "We have just gotten distracted, and have forgotten who we are. We are the supreme; you who is listening to me is the supreme most being. We have become lost in the play that's all. We have become lost because the stage, the players and the play itself is who we are, and we cannot see that because we have become distracted by the story and have fear about death and losing. So we hang on to the physical as being who we think we are."

There was a brief pause, and Baba continued. "It is so simple we cannot see it, and so close it is like looking for your eye glasses when they are on the top of your head. We are one, and are all learning our lessons as we go, because we are that one. And because we are that one, we have to deal with what we cause. That is what it is."

"So re-incarnation and karma and all that kind of stuff is true?" Kel asked and went on, "I had this experience of travelling out of my body; is that who I am?"

"That is just your consciousness Kel, and it cannot last for too long outside your body. Anything that reflects upon itself cannot exist in the realm of the supreme—do you understand? It cannot because in that realm there is no second; no shadow."

"So what moves on? What is it that I saw in the Brief that re-incarnates? What wavelength in me is the same as Lyle's and this crazy Doctor?"

"When you have spent enough time in honest reflection of who you are, you will begin to understand what it is that stands behind, and in front of, who you think you are. The first ideas that something much bigger is there may be in the way of some spiritual experience, and the ego will very quickly try to own and control this experience. Its job is to be in control. So it is good to sit and reflect on this 'I am', you take yourself to be. And when your mind wanders, say those sounds I gave you in your head only, in order to still it."

"You mean meditate?"

"Not forcing yourself to sit for long periods of time, but by becoming genuinely interested in who you really are, and having enough time to reflect on that."

"Yes Baba I came into brief contact with a couple of spiritual groups in my day, and they did meditate, but thought they were very special."

"Yes, that is a problem. The most sticky and evil kind of pride is spiritual pride, but as your knowledge of who you are, or rather who you are not, increases, then so will your devotion to your supreme most self. It is all too simple really, and that's why it is so difficult, because it is so simple, and close to you. It is who you are. The intellect cannot catch it." Baba chuckled to himself and crouched in front of the fire, adding some wood to it.

Kel reflected on this last statement, and took a strong hard mental look at himself. He felt a keen awareness about himself and tried to focus in on it but it eluded him, so he just followed the train of his restless mind as it surfed around in search of itself. After a short while he realised how light-headed he felt, and looked up and around the darkening room. He then noticed how little energy Baba used; he was ultra efficient at not expending energy needlessly, as he blew on to the fire in deep even breaths through the wooden tube, and the embers lit up, spat and cracked. Baba lit a small oil lamp, which shed a weak light over the two men. Kel asked, "And what about the wavelength thing?"

"Do not believe everything these scientists say, they are very proud, and will never venture their investigations beyond the death of the body. This thing they have discovered is an amazing scientific achievement, but the mystery is much deeper than they could possibly imagine. So you and Lyle have the same vibration, so what? It will be enough to fool the Doctor though."

"I hope so," said Kel, a little surprised.

Baba poured some oil into a battered pot and started cutting some vegetables, crouching all the while in front of a small cutting board. Everything in the house was so simple, and close at hand. He threw some onions into the pot and they sizzled, and Kel edged his chair closer to the fire.

"There, upper," said Baba pointing above Kel's head, "is a woolen shawl, put it on." He stirred the onions, and continued, "the Doctor is just a glob of consciousness inside a very big body, and he is beginning to learn how to use this body. What he doesn't have is your memory, and your wisdom, and it is with these attributes that you will defeat and, how to say, neutralise, yes neutralise this mischievous monkey before he becomes too much of a problem."

"So he will be fooled by me into thinking that we are the same? That my entrapment by him will somehow nullify his own existence,"

"What is nullify?" Baba asked.

"Make into nothing."

"Yes that is right—you will be a threat, and he will try to keep you away from him, from him in the centre. Him and whatever he has found."

Baba passed a glass of water over to Kel and said, "this water contains the essence of all the spices and herbs of the mountain and forests, very good for your body. You see Kel, our bodies are something that we've slowly weaved around ourselves over the ages, and it contains water, minerals, metal, all the stuff from the sky, the earth and the sun. We are our environment. Shit is there, light is there, all is there. At the centre of all this is something that is purer than pure, whiter than white. To get there we have to go through all this suffering and a big fireworks display inside our heads, but for definite and sure it is always there watching over us, and clearing our way for us."

"So this purity inside is the soul?"

"Yes, something like that, the *atman* we say."

"And who is the master of the *atman*?" Kel asked.

"Because we don't know what it looks like, we, in my tradition, call the supreme-most being Shiva. The most absolute love, compassion and mercy. In some ancient texts the "SH" means bliss, the "I" is male, and the "VA" is female. It is the destroyer of ignorance and I am sure does not mind how it is named. We make the names. When Shiva gives his grace to manifestation, then what is made eventually reflects on itself and says, 'Hey! I am here, what is this? I am separate from that. This is me, that is not me'…The intellect is born."

"To make distinctions?"

"Yes! This then gives rise to the ego, and this ego feels pride, and identifies with what is possessed. The body, the mind, family and money, money, money."

"And this is my God, that is your God!" Kel said, and he laughed.

"Yes! And we create the God. He have no separation from anything. He is the supreme witness in consciousness, observing all, becoming conscious of all things; and all of this reflected in this mind. And here we are, enjoying by the grace of Shiva. All I have just said is at the…how you say, by the grace of Shiva, and so it goes on forever. It is a vast web of relationships, where our souls are intimately connected within the illusion of this play, to act out the drama of life. If we are not enjoying it is because we don't see…" Baba looked over at Kel, and stopped.

"So waking up means knowing that we are God?"

"Yes! When this I am exploded into the universe, creation happened. If we keep our mind still for a little bit in the right way, we will be able to see it. Otherwise we are just running after this and that."

Kel stared ahead of him, trying to keep up. "So, with what you were saying before, that we have to deal with what we cause, and who we are is always looking over us—does it mean that people who suffer a lot are paying for some bad things that they have done in the past?"

"Take your time, Kel," said Baba, laughing, and placing his hand over Kel's. "You see this is the arrogance of man pretending to know, and judge the will of the Absolute. How can you say to one in great suffering, 'Hey, this is your karma'? That is the height of arrogance. Maybe this being has sacrificed him or herself to suffering and the eventual reward will be great, because we have to suffer in order to see God; it is in the parcel of being alive. Life must feed on life to live, so suffering is unavoidable. Without it there would be no pleasure, so we have to find a good balance, and most importantly, not judge in ignorance."

Baba suddenly stopped talking, swung around, his eyes wild and mischievous. "Blah blah blah, blah blah blah," he said and laughed. "Kel you have got me talking like a preacher, good stuff though, eh?" Baba laughed again and fell silent, gently stirring the food.

Kel shut his eyes and listened to the music of the stream, contemplating Baba's view on the world.

"Now please eat this—strong food," Baba said, and handed Kel a bowl of soup and some crusty bread.

It was simple and delicious, and the two ate in silence. Baba served some coffee and put some fruit and a knife on the table. They smoked a little, and were both lost in their thoughts. Kel became aware of stirrings in the walls and Baba said, "field rats," in answer to his silent question, "Naughty fellows sometimes, but no worry."

"Well Baba," Kel asked at last, "What am I to expect, once inside this black hole, this singularity?"

"Hmm, on the way in probably a lot of fireworks. The power this kind of singularity packs is *maha*—great, very great. It may be like a big acid trip, or something like that, but you will not worry because you won't have a body to worry about."

"So I hear."

"The important thing is what happens once you are inside, at the middle, in the realm of the unknown."

"Something about meeting myself?"

"Yes, the only defense the Doctor has against you, is you. When he realises he cannot stop you he will confront you." Baba lit the pipe and handed it to Kel, it was a different smoke this time, very sweet and aromatic.

"What then?" Kel suddenly felt sharp and attentive.

"That is unknown. When you enter the hole everything you fear or desire may come into your mind, from the very gross to the very subtle. You will be severely challenged, and will wish to retreat. But you will hold your ground and move on, understanding it all to be an illusion put in front of you to scare you away."

"This will all be in my mind?"

"Yes, but the first thing he will do is give you the illusion that you have a body, and when you think you have a body, great fear can be generated. He knows this well, and he will use everything he can to delay you," said Baba gravely.

"You don't mean he could resurrect my parents and use them, or my memory of them, against me, stuff like that?"

"I don't think so. I can see that they are too close to your heart, and he cannot touch that!"

"How do you know all this Baba?"

"There is something very big going on, and I am here to show you the way. This is all I can say."

"What do you mean by very big?"

"Something that threatens all that is, or ever was." Baba paused a moment as this sunk in.

"He has accessed a power source that is highly vicious, and destructive. This power can have an effect on all the worlds, and that means past, present and future."

"You make this power source sound like it has a will of its own," said Kel.

"It does now that it has accessed consciousness," Baba was deadly serious. "This is an ancient demon of great power and it is able to wait for *yugas* and *yugas*, millions of years for a chance to manifest. It has now found one, and slowly it wakes and is using this stupid Doctor as a means to rule all things."

"How am I supposed to deal with something like that?"

"Listen Kel, there are no mistakes in this universe. You have come from your time because for some reason, which no-one can see, it is your time, your era that will be under threat also—everything from then 'til now, swallowed into the jaws of this demon."

Kel sat for a while trying to get a mental grasp on what was transpiring here, and then said pensively. "Lyle said something about Earth in my day possibly being a target."

"Yes, so you see, all the roads are leading to Rome!"

"What does the community think of all this, this demon business?" Kel asked.

"Most feel that this singularity is caused by them, and that I am a superstitious old fart," and Baba laughed. "You see Kel, a singularity is the nearest that existence can get to an absolute value. The only other absolute value so far known to us is in consciousness, in the human mind, and in realisation of this deepest, truest, and stillest nature, lies great power. A single, still point of conscious realisation, and a single point of absolute gravity. If these two together, this black hole, and the demon working through the consciousness of the Doctor, should manifest, and have its way, then we will have to suffer the same fate as humanity has had to in the past. The anger, lust and greed, and all the rest of the confusion that goes with it, but it will be a thousand times worse.

"Bloody hell!"

"Yes, bloody hell. We will have lost our hard fought battle for freedom, and our souls will be the players in this new game, and in a bondage far deeper than we could imagine, until such a time that we can muster enough will and strength to overthrow such tyranny."

"I heard you say that love is the greatest power in the universe. So why is all of this happening?"

"Ultimately, of course it is," said Baba, "But in the meantime the show goes on, and we are here to enjoy and suffer all this, and challenge it when we think it is wrong. Remember that love is who you are, keep it in your heart, and act on it always. That is what you take Kel as your greatest weapon, besides your courage, and a good degree of humility. You take love, and this will defeat this crazy guy before this patient, powerful demon has time to manifest. Love, guts, and trust in yourself is all you need, and you will be victorious. There is no doubt about this."

Baba had prepared a nighttime drink, buffalo milk, and it tasted sweet. A thick layer of skin topped the sweet mixture as it cooled, so thick Kel had to use a spoon to eat it.

"Strong stuff eh? Like you, strong stuff, a good pudding," said Baba. "Kel, you will be severely challenged, and will wish to retreat when you start playing this game. But you will hold your ground, and move on. I am part of the preparation for that challenge, and there is a lot at stake."

"You make me feel like a bloody knight—no a naked knight, a knight without lance, shield, or sword, or even a body. Fighting a dragon with my will and wits."

"Ha ha!" said Baba, "That is what you are, a knight without a body. But listen good—what you discover in your own self, as you move on through all the fear and doubt that is presented before you, is the same stuff that those knights of old were looking for. For righteousness! It will defeat anything that is put in your path. Do not, do not, do not doubt this."

Kel felt suddenly a little overwhelmed, and he said, "Baba, I think I need to hit the sack."

Baba looked a little surprised. "Hit a what?"

"Go to bed Baba, hit my head on the pillow."

"Ah ha, yes, you must be tired, I get carried away in all this," said Baba. "Your bed will be good and warm as the pipe from the fire passes just under it. Take some water with you."

Kel carried his pack, a glass of water, and a candle up the rickety stairs to bed with a dexterity and ease that surprised him. He peed over the side of the veranda, and watched the long golden stream. His eyes wandered towards the out-house at the end of the garden, and he shivered in the chilly moonlight. A bowl of cold water to one side of him was his night-bath, and he was soon in bed, grateful for the layers of covers above him.

Baba came up stairs and bade him goodnight. He slept around a corner at the end of the room, a part of the house Kel had not yet seen, and he heard the faint sound of some chanting or prayer behind the flimsy partition, and then silence.

Kel's mind raced for some time as he lay there in the dead quiet of the night, even the sound of the stream had receded. Peace reigned the night, and he played over the mantra Baba had given him and was soon fast asleep.

*   *   *   *

Kel stirred, and the smell of wood smoke hit his senses. There is some ancient memory in all of us with such a smell, something about our past, something old and forgotten but not dead. Perhaps it is the promise of warmth, or the memory of an ancient life, family and friends. This was then infused with the smell of toast, and followed in a few microseconds with the smell of coffee. Down below Kel's bowels rumbled and he knew it was time for a trek to the out-house. He got up and made his way downstairs.

"Good morning Kel, some toast and honey—mountain honey."

"Good morning. Is the toilet easy to understand Baba?"

"Yes, yes, there is water there and everything you need," and Baba continued stacking the toast pile, buttering each piece as he went.

Kel stepped out into the morning light as the sun peeped over the mountains on the opposite side of the valley. He took a deep breath and made his way up the garden path to the out-house, eyeing the garden borders as he went for any sudden sign of movement.

The toilet was a simple squat bowl backed by, even to Kel's standards, an ancient flush cistern made from an assortment of alloy cans. Beside it was a tap and water dribbled on to a puddle that leaked under the wooden panels of the wall. Kel squatted down and listened to the noises of nature rustling around him. His heart thumped and he looked warily around him.

Relieved, and reaching for the water tap he looked up, sucked in his breath, and held still, for there standing before him, reared up on its coiled body was an enormous black cobra. Something in him urged him to lunge backwards, but he held still.

The snake eyed Kel, and teetered back and forth, side to side, its neck flayed open. He eyed it back, and swung this way and that in harmony with it, on his haunches. This hypnotic dance swayed on, as if they were puppets, for maybe a minute, an eternal minute. He knew that no harm would come to him if he meant no harm, but ancient reflexes bade him to either flee, or strike out against this serpent. But he kept his head, and danced. The snake regarded him with a cold intensity, emotionless and aloof, and then seemed to lose interest and turned away. The dance was over, and the snake retreated and slowly slithered out. Kel gaped at the spot where the snake's tail had disappeared from sight, and there was very little of anything left in him by the time he left the out-house. His breathing had returned close to normal, and he felt strangely ecstatic.

He spied a water pipe and faucet on the upper side of the wood shed, with a towel hung nearby, and some crusty soap in a tattered plastic dish, so he slipped his clothes off and showered in the luke warm water. Feeling cleansed and bereft of fear, he clapped his hands and pumped his fists in the air. "Yes," he hissed in triumph—he was home.

He made his way back to the house only to be greeted on the path by a screech, as if to remind him that this was a place of new experiences and his wits should be about him. His adrenaline was back up, and a large monkey stood between Kel and the house.

The monkey reared up, challenging his path, showing its teeth, its head at about Kel's hip height.

"Bugger off!" said Kel, and he moved forward confidently, emboldened by his encounter with the snake. The monkey retreated behind the house.

When Kel entered, Baba said, "So you have met Shanti Na, that naughty monkey."

"Yeah, him and a bloody great snake in the toilet."

"Whoa," said Baba surprised, "People have told me about him, but I have never seen it. Was it a problem?"

"No Baba, we danced,"

"You see, no fear and it is not a problem."

"Well I don't know about no fear, but it wasn't a problem." said Kel, and they ate their breakfast in silence.

When the coffee was served Baba indicated they should take their coffee out into the garden, their chairs as well, and soon the two men were sitting in the sun.

"A little bit of sun is good," said Baba, "If you have time make friends with the monkey, he will teach you a lot."

"Well first he has to improve his attitude."

"The monkey knows he has no chance against a confident you, but he is very efficient at making a threat. In the wild state a small creature can make a big impression on a human being because we have become so soft with the good life. Shanti Na knows you have the power to kill him if you had to, but he senses your fear and will take advantage of it. Many people are like this also, they make a big threat with a little power."

"That's for sure. All bark and no bite, it's true."

"Always beware the bite, as nature is very strong. Anyway, you have any questions you want to ask me, please?"

Kel bent his head in thought for a while, and then asked, "When fear and doubt come into my mind, how best to deal with them, and move on?"

"By understanding them not to be yourself Kel. There is a vast network of fear and suffering in us, fed by desire, and fuelled by memory and anticipation. We are never still, because the mind plays with all these energies, ever restless—it is its nature to be so. Remember it is the body's survival mechanism, so it is always looking for danger or an advantageous opportunity." Baba stopped and looked at Kel.

"Hmm, Baba," said Kel.

"Awareness is seeing all this hurry and worry going on inside you, rooting it out, understanding it, and letting it go." Baba flicked his hand in the air in a throwaway motion, and continued. "The light of understanding that all this fear and worry is not you, is the sword you take with you. The mind has helped you survive in the physical world, and it will help you again; it is the minister of your body looking after the worldly affairs, but in the modern world it has become a tyrant, and thinks it sits on the throne."

"Hmm Baba."

"But the king sits up here," and Baba tapped the crown of his head. "This big awareness never knew the dark, it only knows itself, and darkness disappears with the flood of its light. It sits there always watching the actions of the person, ever aware and ever present. When you understand that this is you in your higher-most being, then the mind is no longer the tyrant and will sit in its proper place, doing its job there down below."

"Then why haven't I been aware of it?"

"Because a light doesn't need a light to see the light; because you have been distracted away from it by the world, and your mind wanting this and that. And because you have been making distinctions between this and that, assisting you in feeling superior or inferior. Remember that is the job of this mind—to make distinctions, and it is supremely good at it, and has got you this far. But don't be fooled, it is not who you are," replied Baba.

"Then who am I?"

"Look into and beyond your mind and you will discover that. You already are!"

"So many different minds in the world though Baba, billions and billions."

"Yes but remember this, that in reality there is only one mind, and one light of awareness. All this is one Kel. You are always looking at yourself—this person in great ignorance, great sadness; this one in great light, great freedom. It is the same you, you in darkness or you in light. The world and everything in it is the same you. Same eyes we have, same, it is all the same thing, it is all you. We are the supreme witness for the supreme. Understand this and it is your shield, your sword and—how did you call it? Your spear?"

"Lance."

"Yes alright, lance. This is your lance to kill this present dragon in our midst. Your knowledge of yourself is an unbeatable energy because it is the bridge to your Self in the greatest sense of that word. Nothing in the universe, or any of the worlds, can suppress it, and it is who you are. It is the absolute and supreme most being, and all demons and curses are burnt to ashes in its presence. It is there in you, and it is who you are! Understand this!"

"Is understanding enough?"

"If you act on it then yes, yes, yes! And listen, Kel, you will have all your greatest doubts and fears thrown at you when you go in there," and Baba hoisted a finger aloft, pointing at the sky. "You will have your long history of survival in a physical body thrown at you—the fear and forboding which you experienced as your consciousness danced its way around each turn of the road of evolution, from the wandering worm to the human being. All that is you, and all the fear you have experienced in all of that time will be thrown at you. When you are not intimidated by it you are free of it, because it cannot touch you—you who you are, the supreme most being. Do you understand?"

"Jesus, Baba, yes, I think I do!" Kel stuttered, "But I have a name, and a form, and see myself to be different, or separate, not supreme! No matter what you, or the community, or anybody tells me."

"You say 'Jesus', do you know what he said in this matter?" Baba asked.

"No, I don't,"

"He said there are five in the house of this family, and two will always be against three, and three against two. The three are God in his natural state—Existence, Consciousness, and Bliss, and the two are what you say, Name and Form. These last two are just the reflection of

God, and seem to exist very briefly, but you…Who you are in the natural state, exists forever, this is the bliss, this is the freedom—no reflection. Do not be fooled by what your senses have convinced you reality is; you are so much more. It is not what you think you know, it is what you can never know in just the senses. Go beyond the limits!"

The two sat in silence. A tree now shaded them both from the sun, and the light filtered through the leaves and danced on the ground around them. A gentle breeze kept them cool in the late morning heat.

"So what about me when I sleep?" Kel asked, "I don't know myself to be, I am not conscious. What about that?"

"You are nay conscious, nay unconsciousness, neither this nor that. If you have one thing, you must have its opposite, you are neither, yet you are both, you are something in-between, and overall." Baba looked up, as if for inspiration or guidance. "I know it sounds like a—how do you say a para—a para—"

"A paradox?"

"Yes, a paradox. But that is what it is; the human mind cannot grasp it, so it fears it. You are both, but you cannot see yourself in either—it is so close you cannot see it. It is who you are, what gives you the power of understanding." Baba clapped his hands and smiled.

"Just stay with the information you have gathered this morning and think on it, it is a lot, and good stuff, eh?" Baba stood to leave, picking up his chair and folding it under his arm.

Kel thought that Baba looked so very dark in the light of the sun, almost transparently so. "Thank you Baba, it is good, very good stuff, supreme stuff."

"Good" said Baba. "Please go anywhere you want around here and enjoy yourself, and let this in slowly, slowly. If you get lost call for the dog, her name is Anza. She has not been around here for a couple of days, but she is around somewhere. Now I must prepare tonight's smoking and eating. I have some good treats. A feast!"

"Can I help you?"

"No Kel, you relax and take your time. There is a hammock there on the veranda. I'll make some sweet tea now," and Baba disappeared into the house.

*   *   *   *

After the tea, Kel went for a walk up the mountain. Shanti Na jeered at him as he left, and Kel laughed back. The path thinned out, and vague deer tacks led here and there, but he pushed on, and made his way up the hill. He saw some rocks high above him just above the tree line, and he made for those. When he arrived some twenty minutes later it was, he reckoned from looking at the sun, about two o'clock.

There was a perfect seat cut into the rock where he could sit comfortably, and he sat and surveyed the scene like a monarch. The valley spread out below him and he saw a waterfall nearby, and followed the gyrating trajectory of cascading water. The sun was warm and he closed his eyes.

A thousand thoughts invaded his mind and he let them jostle for his attention. He tried to make some sense of them. 'Any reflection will be incinerated in the light of awareness, so I am not what I think...The light of awareness never knows the dark, it only knows itself.' A melodious birdsong took his attention and a dog barked somewhere in the valley. Suddenly, Kel let go of everything and was lost, lost in the vastness of his surrounds...

This simple state may have lasted seconds, or minutes. Slowly he felt the rock he leant against, the heat on his face, and became aware of the noises around him and opened his eyes. There were insects galore, buzzing here and there like old-fashioned flying machines, but none had bothered him. A giant bee—no a hummingbird flitted here and there, and chased another. Leaves rustled in a gentle breeze, and everything in nature was going about its business in perfect and harmonious balance. He stretched his arms up and out, arched his back as much as he could, and looked up at the puffy white clouds in a cobalt blue sky. Kel then stood and took a final look at the majesty of the valley. He made a ceremonious bow to the beauty around him, and started his way down the mountain, carefree and lightheaded.

He wandered down a deer track blissfully unaware, and was bathed in an euphoric mood. The forest around pulsed with life, and this he felt with every sense in his body.

Passing two caves he sensed a presence in both of them and looked around the landscape for a familiar landmark, and realised he was lost. He knew the way was down but now the path was on a ridge going horizontal. Slowly he approached the cave and peered into the darkness. A gentle snoring wafted out of the darkness and cautiously he edged forward. An animal lay before him, asleep—a small bear. From the darkness behind it a much deeper snore hit the air and Kel's senses with a punch. 'Mama!' He spun around in an instance, leapt out of the cave and ran and ran until his lungs felt fit to burst. He stopped, bent his knees and crouched down, resting his forearms on them, breathing heavily. He stood up and surveyed the scene around him, another ridge; he was now seriously lost.

"Anza, Anza," he called at the top of his voice, and after while, "Anza," again.

Kel lay down in the grass amongst the mountain pine, and was aware of the sun dipping deeper into the horizon. He called some more. When he realised he had to make a move, he decided to go up, and find the waterfall on the opposite side of the valley and use it as a pointer, or look for the smoke from Baba's cabin.

He started up the hill and heard a thundering sound in the undergrowth, and he turned quickly thinking he was being charged. Mama-bear, after the housebreaker?

A big hairy dog ran up to, and sunk down in front of him, panting, its tail wagging furiously, delighted to be of service. Kel scratched her back. She smiled, smitten with love.

"Baba's place, Anza," he said, and Anza scampered off with Kel in hot pursuit. After twenty minutes of running through the forest they were back on the path with Baba's place in sight. Anza would look over her shoulder and smile, as Kel strained to keep up. Shanti Na jeered a welcoming taunt, and Anza barked back as they cruised home.

"Phew," said Kel, bending over to catch his breath.

Baba came to the door. "You found the dog."

"No Baba, she found me."

"Atchaa, then I'll give you some cookies for her. Best to move away from Shanti Na though." Baba disappeared back into the dark inside of his house.

He returned with a bag of treats. "Dinner will be in an hour. Come a little earlier though, I have a bottle of Italian wine Tanea brought me ages ago. I am sure you will enjoy it," and Baba laughed, and disappeared into the darkness again.

Anza gorged herself on the goodies and Kel made his way to Shanti Na's side of the house.

Shanti Na regarded him with ambitious arrogance, and looked away as if he did not exist. Kel sidled up slowly and carefully, closer and closer and soon his patience paid off. The monkey was on his shoulders, grooming his hair—a strange sensation as his hair was pulled to one side, then the other, strong pulls but not painful, almost pleasurable.

Kel got out some cookie bits, and held them in his open palm and Shanti Na took one at a time, quickly, but almost politely.

Kel popped one into his own mouth and there was a pregnant pause for just a fraction of a second. Shanti Na suddenly turned on Kel with a furious screech, and scratched him down one side of his face.

"Fuck you!" cried Kel as he made a hasty retreat dabbing his wounds, a little blood on his fingertips. Shanti Na scampered up the side of the house, indignant, insolent and guiltless all at once.

Kel collected a fresh set of clothes while chanting his new mantra, 'bloody monkey, bloody monkey,' and went to the wood shed to shower, and cleans his wounds. The sun was going down and he made for the dimly lit cabin, itching for a glass of wine and a smoke. This must be heaven, he thought, though he still felt indignant at the monkey's senseless attack.

When the wine was poured Baba noticed the scratches.

"What happened?" he asked, and Kel explained the scenario to him.

"Oh, you took his food," said Baba grimacing. "When you give to those guys you have to give totally, or else they get annoyed. I was trying to teach him to share. Anyway you will live, that's for sure."

"It was a lesson, that's for sure. I have had a few today," said Kel.

They drank a little, and Kel's tolerance for alcohol had definitely dropped, then smoked a little, and enjoyed an Italian risotto. "Some Italian people stayed with me once; they know how to cook," said Baba, a little sadly.

"Do you get lonely up here?"

"If I become restless I go down to the little villages here, and we are all friends. We all came to Gaya because of the community, for our different reasons, and then chose to live a different way of life. So we have something in common. They have families, and the kids know me."

Baba stopped for a moment, and then continued, "Lyle, and Tanea, and others from the community come to see me, but most of the time I am alone, and I like that. You see Kel, I am discovering a vastness inside myself, and I need to keep quiet. A small man like myself discovering all that. It is a blessing."

"You pray, don't you Baba?"

"It's like you have to knock for the door to open," said Baba. "And I have found the key, and as I unlock this mystery inside of myself, the realisation becomes more incredible, more unbelievable, and all one is left with is oneself. Everything else is burnt to ashes. Yes I pray to what I am finding, most definitely."

Baba took a sip of wine. "I was like a fish crying out for water, not realising that what I truly desired is everywhere around me. Yet nothing can come near it, and it is inside of us, and we inside of it. It never leaves us because it is our very life itself. It is invincible and infinite. Usually I never mention the word 'my Lord' here, but that is what it is. It is my Lord, Kel. I have found my Lord."

Kel sat in silence. He looked at Baba who stared into space, still as a rock.

"To such a grace and power, such an absolute power as this, I pray Kel, yes I pray. My life itself has become a prayer to what I have found inside of myself."

Kel was silent for some time, and then asked, "So it is possible to have a personal relationship with God?"

"The community says that you cannot have a personal relationship with God because the ego—you know the self identified bit of us—will abuse that relationship and become proud and dangerous. And that is true, something like what the Buddhists say. But our relationship with our supreme self is the only real one we have, beyond this illusion of time we have gotten ourselves into. We mistake the temporal for the eternal. So we mistake the ego to be ourselves, but its self-love only masks the true love for the supreme self, that is all. So not to make rules, and regulations, and differences, that's what causes the problems. And in history how many problems have been caused by man using God and making differences for his own benefit, creating a chair for himself when what is needed is understanding, and seeing everything for what it is. Understand what it is you are discovering in yourself, and the idea of a personal relationship with God will not be a problem."

"But the community believes that it is by commitment, and through one's own volition, that the enlightened state can be achieved, or something very near to it," said Kel.

"Yes, for sure, if you are a serious person you can make some very big leaps, but ultimately it is all due to grace, and you must not fool yourself you are one thing when you might be another. Too many spiritual seekers have fooled themselves they are in a state of grace when in fact they are hiding in the clever games of this ego."

Baba looked up and held his hand to his forehead as if trying to remember something. "Listen there is a story. There is a village, and in it a temple. Everyday the priest goes to the temple to do his ceremonies, and pray to God. At night a drunk goes there, takes off his sandal, and hits the altar with it, raving mad at the God. This goes on every day and night, without fail. One day there is a big rain, and floods, and the priest looks out of his window, and sees that it is dangerous, so he decides not to go out and carries out the ceremony at home. The drunk swims through the storm to the temple, takes off his shoe, hits the altar and raves at the God. At that moment Shiva appears to him. 'You are a devotee of mine, ask for the boon you desire.' So you see, that is it."

"You mean that the drunk is being himself and the priest is not?"

"Yes, that is exactly it, and that real you is the only one you can take in this black hole with you, whatever it is. Everything else will be used against you. That real you is your weapon. Do not move from it, do not be fooled by imposters."

"Sometimes I think I need more discipline, Baba. I am so at the whim of my senses."

"That is just your mind Kel. You have to give it some satisfaction or else it will give you no peace, but keeping everything in good balance is the trick. You see, there are many techniques you can learn to discipline your mind and discover power sources in your own body, but they take time and severe single mindedness to achieve. The most supreme way is through understanding who you are, at the higher-most level, and living your life as you wish with this in mind. This will bring great wisdom, and this is the spot where understanding meets devotion, where God and man meet."

"Like the Buddhist middle way?"

"Yes, something like that. Recognition from you, of that meeting, will produce an unsurpassed joy because something will recognise you, something beyond your wildest dreams, something miraculous will recognise you, and in that mutual recognition you will understand. Man and God is the same stuff Kel, the same stuff."

There was silence, and Baba got up and went upstairs, the wooden beams groaned and creaked as he went to his sleeping corner. He returned with a phallic stone object, held in a shell like tray, and placed it before Kel.

"This is a symbol of the Absolute. We call it a lingam. Inside this is the great yogi in perfect balance, male and female, a perfect unity. My understanding of, and belief in it, is its power. In this way man creates the God, and creates himself at the same time." Baba paused for a moment and looked deadly serious. "There are five faces in this symbol, each an aspect of the Absolute, one each to the four directions, and one upper. Facing north is Shakti, her divine spark is everything that is, all of creation; to the south, a fierce face destroying everything, including your karma and history. It is the face of fire. So Kel there is something in front of you clearing your way, and something behind you destroying your ignorance. It is like this. Recognition of it in the right way is to discover love, understanding, and absolute mercy."

Kel was silent, aware only of his heartbeat.

"If this God," Baba went on, pointing at the lingam, "were to manifest, everything would be ashes within seconds. It is by God's divine grace and absolute penitence that we are. And a greater grace still, is to discover that we are the same, that there is no difference, that all is one."

Baba returned the lingam to its place upstairs. He lit a cigarette on his return and blew the smoke towards the rafters. "The point is to enjoy the grace."

"Thank you Baba, thank you so much," said Kel, and the two smoked, drank sweet drinks, and talked late into the night. Kel told stories from his era, and Baba, stories of proud yogis being tested by Shiva for their arrogance, and Christian and Sufi tales of knowledge. There were no untoward incidences in heaven that night, a small rat or two braved the open for a morsel of food here and there, and Kel thought they looked rather cute. 'I must be drunk', he told himself.

"I have something I want to give you," said Kel, and he untied the bead Ken-eye had given him, from around his neck. He handed it over to Baba who perused it with interest. "This was given to me by a good and wise friend of mine for good luck, and it is my very good fortune to be here, so I will leave it with you."

"It's *rudraksa*, a Shiva bead," said Baba with reverence, examining it closely. He stood and made his way up stairs. Kel heard him rustling about, looking for something.

He returned and handed Kel an identical bead, but this one much older, smoother. Baba had threaded it through the thong, and Kel marveled at the similarity of the two beads.

"This is the one possession I brought from Earth, besides the clothes I stood in. It is yours now, and has a lot of power," said Baba thoughtfully.

"How strange!" said Kel. "They could be the same bead!"

"Yes, how strange," replied Baba.

✳   ✳   ✳   ✳

When Kel was snug under the covers, and listening once again to the music of the stream, he heard Baba go outside to spend some time with Shanti Na, and then some stern words from Baba, and Shanti Na scuttling up to a safe spot. Another lesson? He felt like a child at home, safe in bed, and was asleep before Baba came upstairs.

Kel dreamed of Lua, and woke to the smell of wood smoke, toast and coffee. His morning ablutions passed without incident, the snake had obviously made its point the previous day. Anza had gone walkabout again, and Shanti Na hung out in some apricot trees in the lower garden.

After breakfast the two sat in the sun, drank their coffee, and had a final cigarette. Kel eyed the sun. It was maybe an hour away from being between the two peaks. He asked Baba at last, "Do you think the Doctor will use some image of Lua to put me off my mission?"

"If you allow him to, then yes. She is very much in your mind, but it will not be a problem. Just realise it is not real," answered Baba.

"Have you been in relationships Baba, you know, sexual ones?"

"Yes, and it was a big distraction for me. I am a kind of addictive personality, and it didn't work. If the right one comes along it would be fine, if not, fine. I just do not want to have to deal with all that romantic love bullshit, never again. If two people stay together because they want to be together, it is a blessing. Two souls as one soul, then one is able to rise to higher things. It is the natural way to have relationships. And going crazy in the bed with the one you love is very natural too, natural energy."

"People in my day are addicted to romantic love, the trouble being it often only lasts six months or so, then new love is sought to drive out the old," said Kel.

"Yes, it is like a cow on a hot road and it sees in the distance some grass on the road, and goes there to eat. When it arrives it discovers it is just a…how you say, a mira, a mira…?"

"A mirage."

"Yes, a mirage, that is all it is. It looks real, but it doesn't really exist. It is like a prostitute offering love." Baba quickly held his hand to his mouth as if to silence himself, and laughed. "Like a prostitute," he said again.

"So what do you think about celibacy, like the kind of thing they practice down there in the community?"

"Look Kel, they are doing their thing down there, me mine, and you yours. As long as we don't insist there is one way to do it, all will be fine; for me the best way is the natural way, no hurry, no worry, be usual," said Baba and he got up. "We better start our way down soon, it is time."

"Baba, on the voyage to Gaya I heard a strange voice during the Brief that kind of said the male and female were God! The meeting place, and the…what was it? The roots of duality, or something like that. It said that it was my guide. Was that you?

It is all you, Kel. I call my house UmaMaheswar, the name for God as half-male, half-female. She is nature and nurtures, the emotional Mama—the egg, very personal. He is untouched, impersonal, billions of seeds. It's all in you, all of creation."

"Hmm! One more question Baba, I have so much I want to ask now! This Doctor is a very dark and evil character. How much of it is me. I mean, is this the dark side of me, and a chance for some kind of redemption?"

"Remember that everything is you. You are the man for this job exactly because you have the courage and humility to face this monster. It is no mistake that you are here doing the job—it is what you have to do. You have a lion in your heart—I can see it. There is a dark side in all of us, something we have done in our past with our hands, our feet, or even our voice, and this can cause fear inside your man, isn't it?"

"Yes Baba."

"Well you are forgiven all that stuff." Baba approached him and had some ash in the palm of his hand. Kel automatically lowered his head and Baba smeared some ash on his forehead, between his eyes. "Come on Kel, it is time to go."

Baba led Kel down the path, his skinny legs maneuvering the twists and turns with great agility, expending very little energy. Kel had to hurry to keep up. He had left his pack at the house. "You won't need it," Baba had said.

On the way down Kel asked one last question. "Why Baba, why all this life?"

"Discover that mystery inside of yourself! You are doing that now; read holy books and seek the company of the wise." Baba called back at full stretch down the hill. "And don't let any one tell you there's only one way to do it. You find your way. Just remember you are forever, and that all this is you. Our mistake is to think that this body-mind stuff is all we are."

"I will not forget this," said Kel.

Baba laughed, and said, "It is a weakness that we forget. You see man gets and forgets, and God gives and forgives. That is how it is. We have been together before, and we will be together again, atchaa."

When they reached the bottom the craft was already there, and Kel was happy to see Jamie lolling around the meadow.

"Hello Baba, hello Kel. Wow Baba you came down the hill! How arc you? Can I order anything for you?" Jamie was all smiles and graciousness.

"No thank you Jamie, I am fine. Please see that Lyle gets this," said Baba, handing a package over to Jamie. "And Lyle was sending me something?"

"Yes Baba, I put in your hiding place." Jamie went over to a small box at the foot of the path and retrieved a small well-wrapped package, and handed it to Baba.

"A walkie-talkie," chuckled Baba. "Is it easy to understand?" he asked Jamie.

"Sure Baba, it's idiot proof, I mean…" Jamie cringed and took a step back, hand up at her mouth. Kel and Baba laughed, and she blushed radiantly.

Baba turned to Kel and took both his hands in his. "We shall meet again you and I, I am so glad to have met you."

"It has been an honour to be in your company sir, a privilege."

"Remember Kel, you have the greatest weapons of all in you, you are that weapon, and it will defeat anything that stands in your way. I will be with you. Remember that, I will be with you."

"Thank you Baba."

"This is for you once it is all over," said Baba, and handed Kel a little cotton pouch; inside was a mixture of herbs and weeds, and a small, carved wooden pipe.

Kel kissed the back of Baba's hand, and quickly got into the craft.

"See you, Baba," said Jamie.

"Goodbye, Baba," said Kel.

As the craft lifted off Baba stood there right hand raised to head height. It was a goodbye, and a final blessing.

JOURNEY'S END

Kel looked back over his shoulder and saw Baba standing there, waving, and pumping his fists in the air. His head felt a little queasy as Jamie careened around the bends of the river.

"I am taking you to de-tox, and this afternoon you prepare for departure. How are you feeling?" Jamie eyed Kel for a response. "Man you have been partying, who scratched you?"

"Shanti-bloody-Na, What's de-tox?"

"You've just been with the party king of the universe Kel, he knows how to lift off, and land on his feet. I hear that you, maybe, are his heir!" said Jamie, laughing. "Intoxication! The desire of bliss through the realm of poison. I've been through that one."

Of everybody Kel had met on his sojourn in space, Jamie was American through and through, and it seemed that the passage of time had done little to diminish the Stars and Stripes of his present driver. Most of the others he had met on Gaya, whose first language was English, could have been from South Africa, Britain, Australasia or any other English speaking country, but Jamie had somehow retained an American-ness that he found enlivening and refreshing, a gung-ho pioneering spirit.

"I miss him already," said Kel.

Jamie laughed, "Welcome back to the real world Kel—time to get down to business."

"Jamie you are unashamedly American, and I can see by your red collar that you're for real."

"Yeah, and you are a salty old Limey," and she laughed again, and hooted as she swung down the valley, getting up as much speed as the craft could take, while it whined in protest. "And we are keeping our blue collar guys away from you, believe me."

"So what's de-tox?" Kel asked again.

"A visit to the Clinic, and a Gayan sweat lodge to pump out all that stuff you must have smoked and drunk up there," said Jamie, and then added, "you lucky man."

"Could I demand a farewell party before I leave, and ask Baba to organise it? Now that would be a fitting farewell present, and a demand that everyone party in the old fashioned way."

"Nice try! We're putting you on the next stagecoach to Dodge as soon as this is over."

Kel laughed, and his mind went back to this sometimes young, sometimes old man. It was such a short visit, yet it seemed to eradicate his past life; he felt re-born, something very new going on.

"So why doesn't this Baba live in town?" asked Kel. "Give him a pad, a long table you could all sit around and talk…or rather a round table; and a wine cellar, and let him spend his weekends in the mountains, collecting his herbs. Do you know that God's ambassador lives on your planet?"

"He's a mystic, Kel, A man who spent over twenty years in the deepest meditation and devotional practices. He's accessed some *siddhi* powers, these old yogic powers that can transcend time and space."

After a moments silence, Jamie said, "Hey man, so have we! We came and got you, now is that magic or what?"

"Oh yeah, talk about magic, I have to leave my body and go into a black hole. A woman who I fell in love with brought me here, and she turned out to be a robot, then she died, and soon she'll be alive, but I'll never see her again. I am now a samurai swordsman and an astral traveler of sorts, and I've just met somebody I thought was on talking terms with God."

"Yeah, so what's your point?" Jamie asked.

"I was lying on a beach minding my own business, and you lot came and got me because you needed me. Maybe that's magic, but you were driven by your own survival needs. Baba is way beyond that; he is an oracle of wisdom, where devotion and understanding meet. How can you ignore that?"

"Look Kel you came because you had nothing better to do! Can you think of something better than this, I mean what were you doing on that beach—anything worth-while?" said Jamie with relish.

"None of your business! So what about the second part of my question. Why don't you prepare a place for this Baba in town, and see what happens?"

"I think it's because he's too open, and it would cause a diversion of sorts."

"A diversion from what?"

"Of our commitment to live together in the truth, without the usual bundle of mischief that life always seems to serve up. You can live in heaven but life always gets in the way, you know. The degree of commitment needed to be totally honest and out there, to be in a full relationship with one another, is total."

"Yeah, all right, but with the others who have chosen to live a different way," continued Kel, "and with Baba, you mean their presence in your midst would somehow have a negative influence, distract you?"

"The others, yes. Baba is a rare being, one in a billion, and it's always a pleasure to be in his company, but he would cause doubts amongst our number. Best that it is like this."

"I think you are in denial of what is real in the world." Kel paused, and thought for a moment. "Sorry I don't know why I get so heated when I talk about this."

"Maybe its because you feel threatened," offered Jamie.

"I have experienced a kind of open joy in all of your company, but if I were here permanently, and had doubts, like I have, then I reckon your response to me would be different."

"Then you'd need to go away and work out what is most important to you, that's all. You could always come back. But not to hang out telling everyone how you can't do it."

"I'd only do that if I felt like I was in a corner."

"In this place you are always in a corner," said Jamie.

"Then I'll just beg to differ," and Kel sighed.

There was silence for some time, and Jamie said, "There's a little lake near here, crystal clear water and we have some time, do you want to go for a quick dip?"

"You betcha" Kel replied, sitting up in his seat. "What about our shadow? Don't you have someone following you, like Carter did when I came up here?"

"No, Kel, not this time. There was apparently a bug in the system somewhere, something Hal had overlooked. We double-timed looking for it and found a weird bug. So that's all over now."

Jamie swerved off course, and made her way to some hills in the distance. The landscape became a little arid, and in the distance he spied a blue lake in an oasis of trees and shrubs.

Kel soon found himself in the clearest water he had ever known. It was crystal clear, and when he dove in and opened his eyes, he could see the bank at fifty meters distance. The purity of the water seemed to magnify the surroundings. It rejuvenated his body and lifted his spirits even higher. Some small fish jumped in the morning light, turning on their backs to expose white under-bellies.

Jamie yelped and squealed in delight in her one piece, as she swung into the water on an overhanging vine. She was like a child—natural, open, and spontaneous.

What a beautiful figure, thought Kel, and he quickly looked away.

Their outing was over all too soon. "Come on Kel, time to rock and roll," said Jamie, and she was changed and ready to go in a matter of seconds.

Kel followed reluctantly, like a child. "Just one more jump," he called, clambering up the rocks and grabbing the vine. The splash broke the silence of the oasis.

"Kel!" shouted Jamie.

"All right, all right."

Before they hovered off, Kel surveyed the pristine purity of the lake in the magnificence of nature left to its own devices. His body felt good, and it hummed with a healthy vibration, and soon they were back on course, headed for the Mission Control. Jamie maneuvered the craft with a relaxed ease, as they glided around the valleys and gorges like an eagle.

"There's a folder in the dashboard. Lyle thought you should study it a little."

Kel retrieved the folder, sat back and flicked through its pages. It contained a portrait gallery of attractive looking people, their names printed under the photographs, and looked like one of those year books American schools can afford to dole out. He slowly sifted through, and caught Jamie out of the corner of his eye, looking over his shoulder.

"Some friends of yours?" Kel asked.

"You bet, it just makes me so f—, bah! Frigging angry, that cranky, wacky nut taking out such a wonderful, dedicated group of people. Yes some were my very good friends, people I have lived with."

He came to one picture, a dark, possibly Middle Eastern man with intense eyes, jet black hair, and a moustache, neatly trimmed. Something struck Kel about his intensity. "Did you know, mmh…Andy?"

"You bet I do. He could talk the spots off of a dog. Intense, devout, single minded. Loved jazz."

"What about Jean?" he asked.

"Which one?" asked Jamie.

"Black, kind of Polynesian-looking, beautiful."

"A walking time bomb of passion was Jean. All the men adored her, some of us nicknamed her 'the Diva'."

"Human or humanoid?" Kel asked.

"Human! Come on Kel, at heart they're all human."

"I just want to know, that's all. Half of this lot were humanoid, and I think I need to know who they were. Were there any originals on board who have humanoid twins on Gaya?"

"No...Why?"

"Just curious."

And so the journey continued, Kel finding out little anecdotes about the Doctor's ill-fated team, until Mission Control loomed large in the windscreen ahead of them. Its dome and surrounding trees gave it a fairy tale atmosphere. The dome symbolised the zenith of evolved civilisation, technological achievement, and enlightened thinking. The spirit of life coursed through Gaya as it must have done in Egypt, Greece, and Rome. Kel felt in his bones that this was the centre, the hub of change, evolution itself.

Nevertheless, it was strange being back, as if he had been away for weeks. Once they had docked, he strode through the Dome's airy corridors, and felt very strong and confident in himself. He was no longer a passive Englishman, that was for sure. He now stated his case, and argued it with a sharp degree of objectivity.

Jamie delivered him to the clinic, and he was re-acquainted with Chiron, the medical magician. The machine spent the briefest time cleansing his system. "Your body is now ninety seven per cent functionally operative, a fourteen percent improvement in six days since the initial consultation."

Kel was visibly shocked. Less than a week had passed since his departure from the island, and his home planet.

"Time flies when you're having a good time," said Daljit, her blue collar conspicuous atop a crisp white smock. "I'll patch up these monkey scratches."

"Seems like an aeon."

"It's more than that," said Daljit smiling warmly, and somehow Kel was reminded of Lua. He watched the flow of emotion sweep through his body and was surprised that though he missed her, he did not feel that empty longing of a pining heart.

"How long before Lua's revived?" Kel asked.

"Six hours."

"And no chance?"

"Sorry, the window of opportunity for your return is open for a very limited time, and we have to get you off as soon as possible. We cannot miss it. You leave for the Biosphere in fifteen minutes."

"Bugger! No time for the wicked, eh? Jamie here told me they were keeping you blue collar guys away from me. In case I should remould those cerebral circuits of yours."

"You don't scare me, my dear, as your medical officer I know you inside out! Here's your new suit of armour," and Daljit winked.

Kel blinked at this reference to a knight's fighting gear.

The suit was a pure white mixture of some synthetic material, and maybe linen. He put it on behind the screen, and when he emerged both women cooed their approval. "Sir Kel," said Jamie, and mocked a curtsy.

"My liege," said Daljit, and bowed a graceful bow.

"Ah bollocks to you!" said Kel, and he walked to the mirror and viewed himself. He did, he had to admit, strike an imposing figure in the all white suit. He turned to the two, who looked on admiringly, raised his right hand and said, "I will be victorious, of this there is no doubt," in an impeccable Indian accent, exactly like Baba's.

The two women burst out laughing, and had to hold on to each other so hard they laughed. Kel stood back in surprise at the mirth this caused when a third woman entered the clinic, and announced that transport was ready.

Jamie stuck out her hand and said, "Unfortunately, this is where we say good bye, I'll be up there with you, but probably won't see you again."

"Thanks for the crystal clear lake," said Kel.

"Thanks for the fun," replied Jamie.

"As a knight I have to take a damsel's scarf into the fray with me. As Lua is not here and all," said Kel, and he shuffled on his feet, a little uncomfortable. He liked Jamie and Daljit a lot; they were fun. "I need it for luck, and I want something from the both of you."

"A scarf!" said Jamie, her eyes widening. She looked quickly around the room and then dashed into the changing cubicle, dragging Daljit with her.

Kel heard giggles behind the screen and the sound of fabric being torn. Jamie emerged in a gown and Daljit in a blue ER smock. They held up between them a scarf fashioned from the maroon and blue strips from the rims of their uniform.

"Perfect," said Kel saluting them, and they tied the strip around his neck.

"Good luck, Kel," Jamie said seriously, and bowed her head to him.

"Tell Lua I love her...Always," he called back over his shoulder, following Daljit out of the clinic.

∗   ∗   ∗   ∗

Kel was soon traipsing around the corridors again, in pursuit of Daljit and colleague. The Control Centre was busier, human traffic wise, than usual, and he was well aware that he was the centre of attention. He felt like an astronaut of old, strolling through a Shopping Mall, on the way to take off, and was especially conspicuous in his ultra white uniform. He noticed for the first time some children in town, who stopped dead in their tracks when they saw him, regarding him as they would Santa Claus or a condemned man. He waved at them, and they waved back.

Kel was soon in the transport facility. Six transparent tubes funneled out of a high domed ceiling, like the stems of a plant. Kel recognised the transport dish at his feet that had blasted him off of Earth, and it was now that he started to feel his guts tighten.

"They are like giant peashooters," Kel told Daljit.

"Like what?"

"Never mind." Kel stood on his dish waiting, entombed in the transport tube. He looked out at Daljit, and mouthed, "are you coming?"

She pointed to herself, and then pointed upwards; she then put two thumbs up, and winked. Kel just smiled at her, and had no idea what she meant. He waited for the rush, and a voice interrupted his racing mind. "Eleven seconds to take off."

"Hal you're here too?" Kel said, glad of a familiar voice.

"I told you Kel," and after a pause, "I am everywhere," and as Kel took off, and up out of the peashooter, he could have sworn he heard Hal laugh, almost imperceptibly.

He accelerated up, and as the planet receded beneath him, he had to hoot and scream, as the rush of energy was so intense. The pink and purple iridescent tunnel engulfed him again, and he had no choice but to surrender to the ride. It reached a point this time that was almost unbearable, and he felt he was going to pass out when he landed with a wallop in a large tank of water.

"Welcome to quarantine," said Anjali as she leant over the handrail.

"Ah, now I get it," said Kel.

Anjali rather saucily exposed her maroon collar over the top of a white jump suit, as if it were her bra.

He had to swim to exit, so large was the tank. He was back on the Biosphere, and felt more than a little disoriented, and homesick—but for where? Each place he had been felt like home.

"Is Daljit not coming?" he asked when he emerged from the giant blow dryer; both he, and his white suit, were bone dry.

"Daljit's needed down below Kel. This is a big operation, and the whole planet is on it. Follow me," and Anjali pounded up a major flight of stairs. Time, it seemed, was of the essence.

"Stairs?" said Kel. "You still have them!"

At the top they took a hovermobile over the artificially sun-drenched surface of the Biosphere, and headed for the take off spot to the stars in the far end of the sphere. It looked mysterious and ominous in its lineal night and day-ness, as they swooped over the lush and verdant botanical quarantine area in the light, and then were suddenly in the dark. The craft's dashboard lights shone brightly—their reflection dancing over Anjali's face. The whole scenario was one of complete unreality to Kel.

"How long will I actually be out of my body?"

"Lyle is going to brief you, but physically you are ready for almost anything," replied Anjali.

"For probably the first time in my life, it's not my body I am worried about,"

"Well you look pretty relaxed to me, compared to when we, Daljit that is, first met you," said Anjali and went on. "You know, in your day, stress placed so much strain on the heart that it was a major killer. It actually was bad enough to cause lesions in the heart muscle. I went through your cortisol levels from the first contact, they are now way down and you are sleeping more soundly and deeply, so your immune system is in full function."

"I do feel good."

"And in my opinion you can't talk about mind and body as being separate. You are physically fitter than you've probably ever been, and are so out there now mentally, that it's a pleasure to see the transformation."

"What do you mean?"

"You are right out there with people around you. You are expressing yourself freely, and have a great power about you. No-one's controlling you now, past or present, and there's a palpable absence of fear or doubt!"

"Well thanks Anjali! No doubt about it—the physician's last word. You are both so good at that." And they spent the remaining minutes in silence, as Anjali docked, and led him on to Lyle.

The two men shook hands formerly, and grinned at each other. Kel followed Lyle through a hatch, leading to a room, and sat opposite him in a large comfortable chair. A large screen loomed behind Lyle, who, Kel thought, seemed a little anxious.

"Sorry Kel, but the time line on this is so infinitesimally small that it's got me on edge. Whilst you're gone into the privilege of no time—you can take a millennium if you wish—I have a matter of a few microseconds to shoot you back to Earth. It's the one thing we cannot miscalculate on, and it needs this kind of neurotic alertness to carry it off. Theoretically you should emerge from the hole seconds after you enter, and the longer the delay the more complicated the calculations become. But don't worry, we have it under control."

"So I won't see Gaya again?"

"No, you won't. Soon we'll be a couple of light years away from Gaya. When you emerge from your quest in there, we have to immediately sling shoot you around the singularity to get up enough speed and energy to transport you," and Lyle twisted a hand in the air rapidly, as if trying to grasp a word out of it. "To invert you back to your time frame."

Kel looked at him blankly, and nodded lamely. His body felt tense and still, like a catkin pod before it snaps.

"Do you feel ready?" Lyle asked.

"Ready or not, here I come," Kel replied. "I'd rather go in now not knowing anything more. I know my mission, that is all—to get to the centre of this, and not be deterred by anything in our way, anything at all. To look at my hand if I get confused when I commence the out-of-body-trajectory; to stop the Doctor at all costs; not to get lost in reflections; to keep my mission higher-most in my mind, and to know that I am totally invincible."

Lyle laughed, and looked suddenly becalmed, as if a burden had been lifted from his shoulders. "That is so reassuring, and it must be the reason we got you for this job. Singularly one-minded, when the necessity and occasion demands."

"Look," said Kel, "I have just met the single most incredible character in the universe, and he lives amongst you. When I meet him again I trust I will recognise the divinity a lot more quickly than you have. Did he have a hand in deciding which era you should return to?"

"Yes, he did, and you are definitely the man for the job. That is all we know."

Kel frowned for a second, and Lyle continued on quickly. "There is one more bit of information I have been saving for now. I think you need to hear it."

Kel nodded his readiness to hear it.

Lyle took a deep breath before starting. "We have now confirmed that the Doctor has accessed a gateway to anti-matter. He aims to con-join with this other massive singularity over here," and the screen behind Lyle dimly lit up, highlighting their stellar environment, with tiny Gaya and its solar system helpless, it seemed, in the maw of its impending doom.

An announcement interrupted Lyle. "Jump to hyperspace in fifteen seconds."

"Oh yes, we are already on our way. Don't worry you are belted in," said Lyle calmly, and after a few seconds, Kel was once again blasted to the realm of molecular re-organisation, as his body was propelled into a phenomenal speed.

As they came out of it, Kel was winded, but Lyle was unphased, and continued the dialogue, oblivious to Kel's attempts to re-orient himself from the jump to hyperspace.

"Once Gaya has been gobbled up, and he conjoins with, or finds a way to this monstrous black hole here, and can avoid being caught into a binary black hole system," and Lyle, lost in his explanation, flung an arm in the direction towards the constellation Virgo on the screen. He stopped and looked at Kel, to see if he was with him.

Kel nodded, and said, "You mean with the mother monster of black holes."

"Yes, this monster. If he incorporates this monster then the laws of the universe will start to break down. There's a black hole at the centre of your Milky Way, maybe he can access that! You spoke to Baba about his theory of sleeping demons. Well, whatever it is, everything is at stake, we are talking Armageddon here."

Kel stared at Lyle, and said nothing.

Lyle went on, "We believe that he has found a way to access any globule of anti-matter in the universe. You see anti-matter transcends space and time, it's like a parallel universe and he has been working on channeling energy through it. And that means he can do as he pleases, and extend his influence as he wants—if he knows where to go, if he has an astronomical ecliptic."

"A what? Never mind, so?"

"We found charts made by the Doctor that target the Pacific basin around, and including the year we plucked you from mother Earth." Lyle stopped for a moment, composed himself, and continued gravely, "There were astronomical calculations, and co-ordinates, which indicate that he has his sights set on that."

"What do you mean?" Kel asked.

"In the late nineteen nineties," Lyle continued, "two facilities, one a university in California, the other a research facility in Japan, were developing and accruing an amount of anti-matter, a reasonable amount. Anti-matter is very unstable and a way was found to store it in magnetic storage chambers. By the early second millennium they had developed the potential to create more than enough to be targeted. We think this is the Doctor's goal."

"What do you mean?" Kel asked again, "that he can actually transcend everything, and gobble us up as well? Preposterous! Jesus! I thought that was all hypothesis, I mean what about you? You are testimony to that not happening, you're real, and your world is real. He cannot annihilate all that, and everything in between. That's absurd!"

"This goes beyond the known physical laws of the universe Kel. It is possible that this monstrous tornado of an ego we have created here will suck in everything from you to me, and our worlds, and all in them. Him, and whatever, god forbid, is behind that."

"Leave me out of this Lyle, you created this monster, not me." Kel leant back in his seat and whistled.

"So you see, Kel, the gravity of the situation," he said with an air of finality, and leant back in his chair.

"My God," said Kel, "gravity is definitely the problem here. You know I laughed at all the doomsday theories around the turn of the millennium, but I never reckoned on anything like this." He sat back in his chair, pursed his lips, and blew air upwards as if letting off steam. "Nothing like this," he repeated.

"I have one last question for you," said Kel seriously.

Lyle nodded, and leant forward in his chair.

"Why do you think all this is going on? Why did this evil Doctor emanate from you? What was going on?"

Lyle was silent and pondered the question. He said at last, "I think there is a dark side in all of us. It is probably the reason we manifest as humans—to enjoy, suffer and understand it. As long as we don't act on the impulse of this dark side, this shadow, then its influence weakens."

Lyle paused and closed his eyes, searching for the words. "When I did the conscious transference to Ernst, the Doctor, I was going through some emotional storm that centred on my relationship with women, in particular with Tanea. You see I yearned for her, yet I felt I needed to be free of any romantic involvement. Something I have since resolved."

"So I hear," said Kel.

"But at the time of the transference there was this dilemma, a dichotomy going on in me that I'd pushed to the back of my mind. So you see, the Doctor is almost totally scientifically wired, intellectually, with an intense romance in the recesses of his being that cannot be resolved. It was pushed too far back there. So what does he do? Buries himself in his work, collapses time and space, and starts gunning for his creators."

"That sounds too facile to me, too easy an explanation. There must be more!"

Lyle smiled, and scratched his scalp. "Well you have told me to leave you out of this, of having anything to do with the creation of this monster. But you might find out in there exactly why this aberration has manifested. This dark side can only be conjectured at, so I am sorry, I cannot elaborate any further."

"What do you think I have to know about him? How could he defeat or stop me?"

"He will exercise a flawless logic, and appear to know everything about you."

Kel chortled at some private joke. "About me!"

Lyle waited a moment before continuing. "You will probably be presented with experiences that cause shock and fear, and this will be his main tactic, in order to delay you. To stop you getting near him."

"So these experiences are probably from my past, from my past existences?"

"Probably, maybe. Who knows? It's all speculation. The point is to go in with no doubt about yourself, and no expectation about what you will meet."

"Now that," said Kel emphatically, "is where we part company. It was your bloody unexpressed doubt that is the cause of this mess, so I'll go in as I am, thank you very much, doubts and all. All that no doubt stuff in your community is unreal. It's a minefield of unexamined suppositions."

"I may beg to differ, but I have learnt a lot from you," said Lyle, his face a little tired, the lines a little deeper.

"And me from you, but you must admit this is a great argument," Kel went on. "And as far as expectation goes, maybe I see myself as having an opportunity of being redeemed, of meeting and destroying the very darkest side of my being. Maybe I am totally fed up with this constant loathing and longing in me, longing for what I intrinsically am already. Maybe I'll become totally enlightened and negate your existence and…and all of this will be just the fabrication of someone's mind. And you, you'll just be a…. A," Kel was suddenly lost for words, so he quickly opened his fisted hand out in front of him and said, "pff," then again, "pff. How about that?"

Kel looked defiantly over at Lyle, and after two seconds silence the two men roared as one in laughter. Their laughter was unstoppable and by the time Anjali came to collect Kel, he was in convulsions of laughter. Lyle was on his back in his chair, knees drawn up to his chest. She said nothing and sat by the door, hand over her mouth.

By and by, both men fell silent; they had nothing left to say. It was time to say goodbye and this time the two men hugged warmly, and bade each other farewell. Kel now knew what was at stake.

He was led out by Anjali and guided to his new point of departure.

✳   ✳   ✳   ✳

Anjali packed him into the stasis machine, and it was unfortunate that it was coffin-shaped. Lights blinked around him.

"I must look like a kaleidoscopic Dracula," he said.

"A what?"

"Dracula, a blood sucking, already dead human that inhabited my era, comes out at night, loves pretty women."

"I don't get it," said Anjali.

"He slept in a coffin, and this looks like a coffin. Oh never mind." Kel looked over to another coffin shaped unit on which an array of lights blinked, and waves flurried across a screen. "A vampire!" he said at last, keeping his eyes on the other unit.

"Now I get it, the guy with the fangs. Oh dear, you're right, this is coffin shaped. Sorry, an oversight, we don't use them nowadays," said Anjali adjusting some dials above his head.

"So who's in there?" he asked, pointing a finger. "Is that my body-guard?"

She followed the direction of his finger with her eyes. "That's Duncan, we are hoping to get him back," she said, and put a re-assuring hand on Kel's shoulder.

"Jesus!" said Kel, and he sat forward and put his head in his hands. Not a moment had he had to stop and think, and now the full impact of the situation at hand had got to him, and he started to shake, and his breathing was fast and shallow.

"Oh Kel!"

"If I didn't feel this it wouldn't be fucking real—excuse my French," he said, and made an effort to stop his shaking. He grimaced, "Now remind me. What do I do?"

"Just remember Kel, you are in control, point your attention towards the power source you see, look at your hand if you get lost. We are dropping you in at its polar end and the route will be obvious to you. And remember us, as we will remember you. You reminded us of so much we have forgotten."

Anjali bent down and kissed Kel on the forehead. She slowly straightened up and said, "Good luck, we love you Kel, remember that."

Kel took a deep breath. "Thank you Anjali, I will miss you as my doc, whoops, you know what I mean, both of you. Thanks for my new and improved body. I've really loved all of you too, you know, you are such a beautiful bunch of people. I'll never forget you."

Above Anjali a screen appeared, and he understood his co-ordinates to this singularity, although this would count for very little once he was out of body. All he needed to know he already knew. This was his goal, his quest.

He looked at the on-screen image of the singularity, as they viewed it from a safe distance beyond the event horizon, that line from which nothing can escape. It was so black, so dark, and there seemed to be a spiral arm of murky light each side of it, as if a thread of tortuous light held a disc, suspended in space. If Kel could put a name on it, it would have been a cosmic discus, such was its shape, but this one had not come from the hand of a Greek athlete or Vishnu. This was definitely from, and he had to chuckle at this as he lay there with his thoughts, the dark side of the force.

Anjali stepped back in surprise at his mirth, and this sudden change in manner. She turned away, and switched on the machine that would keep Kel's body alive, lowered the lid and locked it. A flurry of wave patterns appeared on a screen above the cask, and she switched an emergency warning system on with a resounding clunk, and latched it into place. She then hailed Matthias over the intercom to come and double check, and left the life-support centre.

∗   ∗   ∗   ∗

Matthias bounded down the few spiral stairs that still prevailed on this trans-galactic ship, and there was a bounce in his step. He liked to be busy, and this was the final step of a mission that might signify the survival of their planet. He typed in the coded entrance key to the life-support centre and put his hand over the sensors for confirmation. Nothing happened. He repeated the process, and again nothing happened. He slipped out his intercom and hailed Lyle—no response.

He muttered "*shise*," under his breath, thumped the metallic door and turned in a second and sped towards the control centre. Halfway there the alarm bells started to sound, this meant that the doors would open automatically. Matthias stopped in his tracks, turned again and winged through the companionways back to life-support centre. He arrived just as the locks clicked open.

As Matthias rushed in, Carter swung around and faced him. He appeared confused and disoriented. The screen behind him, over the life support system now displayed a series of flat lifeless lines, and Carter attempted to speak.

"You goddamn fool," screamed Matthias, and hit Carter with a punch that lifted him off the ground. As he hit the deck, Lyle and Anjali arrived, breathless, staring in disbelief at the bizarre scene before them.

✳   ✳   ✳   ✳

The last thing Kel remembered, as Anjali enclosed him in his tomb, was a strange absence of fear. His sudden panic had left him and he had a job to do, and that was that. He fixed his attention on the massive magnetic surge of energy he felt to one side of him, and the last action he carried out was to flex his right hand. The machine kicked in with its brain wave frequencies that would lift Kel out of himself, and he was gone. This was journey's end.

QUONDAM SHADOWS

"Stay with it Kelsie, stay with it. Where's my hand? Yeah, it's okay. Stay with it."

"Jesus, the size of this."

A vortex of spiraling energy opened up in front of him, and he fell into it, as a blade of grass would tumble over Niagara Falls. There was no loss of consciousness, energy flashed past Kel at unfathomable speed, and he stayed still in the centre as he continued this headlong rush into absolute mass. He looked down to orient himself, but all he saw was a thin smoke-like trail that wound its way into the distance; neither hand nor body were there now.

"Stay with it. I'm still here. God almighty, it's speeding up."

The explosive rush of velocity around him reached a peak. "I'm losing it, losing it. Please stop." Colours and light danced around in a frenzy of wild gyrations, so fast they became that Kel shot out into a space of total stillness, and found himself at the centre. The movement started again and he braced himself for the rush.

"I'm not moving. Everything's moving around me." The movement subsided after this realisation, and his senses withdrew. "Stay with it!" A brilliant white light from within beckoned him on, and soon he found himself in an ocean of light. No differences; nothing but an unopposed stream of unity summoned Kel towards a state of delirium.

"Shit, I'm getting lost in this, it's just my mind. Come back, come back, here I am." He mustered every faculty, every edge of awareness and withdrew his attention, keeping it at the point of observation.

Now the vestige of an external sense returned, and he was aware of a spiraling mass of energy above him, like sitting at the base of a tornado and looking up. Black, red, and white light contorted, twisted, and wove around itself in an endless outpouring that seemed to emanate from where Kel took his position to be. He was sinking down into the vortex of this monstrous twister, and would soon be swallowed up.

His sense of self, no longer still, spun, and seemed to elongate for an eternity, as he sank deeper and deeper into the morass of timelessness. Shuddering forward, vibrations at every octave rushed through his awareness, and once again he forced his attention on himself. "Keep here! Here I am!"

"Kelsie! Kelsie!" Wild gyrations caused a lapse in his attention; something foreign entered into him, probing.

"Hell, what's this?" He challenged it, and followed it into the deepest part of himself, where ancient memories lurk. His attention then spun after this intruder, spun so fast that for an instant he witnessed his consciousness being shed from its source, the eternal observer, and then thrown into the abyss. And therein in this depth, in this secret place, he was lost in the ghostly shadows of his unfoldment.

*   *   *   *

He passed through a dimensional doorway, and speed of movement was supplanted by an awareness of an enviroment around him. A sensation of floatation wafted through his body and he became aware of life forms moving around him. Surrounded by a murky ocean, a series of visions flashed through Kel's awareness, as these life forms loomed before him, and then approached in a sudden frenzy of movement.

Monster like creatures with rows of needle sharp teeth rushed at him with mouths opened wide, and at first Kel was shocked and wished to retreat, as waves of sensation pulsated through his being. These were primordial survival reflexes and were powerful in the responses they evoke, but he had experienced these before, and had also seen these creatures and knew they were no threat to him now. He stayed still and ignored them, merely floating in this three-dimensional realm, untouched and unscathed by the threats to his sense of self. His body pulsed and throbbed in waves of ancient reflexes.

The scene continued to slowly change, and an awareness of something new enveloped his unfolding body. Gravity, and a sense of touch beneath him. He looked down at this sense of weight and saw something, something strange, and felt a jolt to his senses. Bony appendages extended down each side of him, with the hint of webbed feet at their ends, greeted his growing sense of vision, and he found himself in a rock pool on an ancient shoreline. Odd and bizarre looking creatures ventured back and forth between land and sea around him, and he looked back down, bemused at the sight of this strange body emanating from him. He shifted his weight from side to side and felt the pressure creep through his limbs.

He slowly looked up and a shockwave of energy swept through his body. He held his ground as the apparition of a giant scorpion stood menacingly before him. Its claws snapped at the air between them, and then held still as it focussed its attention on him. Kel instinctively knew it was about to attack and he felt the urge to tear into it, but something told him that this was an apparition. It charged at him, passing through him like a phantom. He remained still and his resolve was strong, and the scene around him quickly changed.

A carcass of fresh meat lay in front of him and a deep hunger engulfed his body. He looked around and was greeted by the stares and threats of a gang of reptilian competitors, lost in an orgy of survival. His hunger gnawed at him from within, laced with anger and an urge to attack, but he held his ground again, and stayed still and observed, untouched by the aggression around and within him. But the anger would not abate and something in him willed him on to attack, as if his very survival and continuance depended on it. Aggressive posturing by a creature half his size drew him in; he was pushed aside by this runt.

The anger grew unbearable. "No, no," he screamed, but without warning even to himself, attacked, lunging at the neck.

As he was in full lunge, going for his adversary's jugular, the voice screamed again to hold back, but it was too late.

There was a sudden rush and swirl of energy as his teeth dug into the scaly neck, and he lost all sense of being, leaping forward into the trap, and a state of deep sleep.

*   *   *   *

Kel woke up to a sense of heat enveloping him, and he snuggled up to something warm and familiar, and felt safe. There was a digging sound above him, something burrowing down to him, and his warmth. The body and its heat that had covered his deserted him, and there was a blast of cold air. A scent forced its way to his senses and he froze, keeping totally still. A blinding light hit him, and the burrowing and digging continued unabated around him, as dirt was thrown this way and that. Slowly into his vision came a skyscraper image of a scaly animal, topped by a reptilian head. He noticed the eyes darting here and there, searching out its prey, and then it looked directly at him and he kept its cold-blooded stare.

The beast kept up its stare as if unsure, and Kel stared back. Now it bent its head and sniffed the area around him. The scent was repulsive, the apertures of its nostrils were now directly above Kel, its scales rank with a smell fit to choke. He was nudged hard and tumbled out of the nest, and still he stayed.

The giant head slowly straightened up, and once again the skyscraper above him stared down, and then looked up and around, its eyes darting here and there, its tongue periodically flicking out of its scaly jaws, tasting the air. It slowly moved off and out of sight, but not of smell, and the scent lingered for some time, forcing Kel to remain perfectly still.

Some time passed and he knew he had to wait a little longer before returning to the nest. The smell had abated and the moment came, and just as he was about to move he caught sight of it out of the corner of his eye, just a flicker of movement behind and to the side. It had gone downwind to wait for Kel to betray his position. He froze again, and the adrenaline-like rush set fire to every fibre in his body, yet still he kept.

Suddenly the dinosaur's eyes noticed something off in the distance, and its head and attention became focussed, its body totally still. It left swiftly and this time Kel heard the vibration of its feet disappear away from him, and he scuttled back to the nest quickly and silently, and held still there yet again until he heard a terrifying shriek—a scream of surrender and death.

In the stillness the scream switched on a light somewhere inside of him, beckoning him to come out of his trance. He looked down at his hand and instead saw a tiny paw, studded with buds of keratin. A shadow was cast over him, and once again he looked up into the eyes of his reptilian stalker and a blast of awareness shot through him. He screamed at the beast, screamed and screamed his defiance until he felt his body hoisted aloft in its smelly mouth, and there was a snap.

✳   ✳   ✳   ✳

He sat bolt upright, the hair on his body bristling, and felt the sweat on the nape of his neck. His young body lay in bed, awoken from a nightmare about monsters. He took a shuddering breath and looked over at the wardrobe in the corner. If there were a ghost, or a monster, that's where it would come from.

He lay down again, imagining the worst, and there it was—a creak—no, not even a creak—just a presence. He lay perfectly still too terrified to call for help, for there was something there, movement betraying its presence. It came near to, and hovered by the bed. Kel kept hold of the covers up to his chin, and his eyes stared wildly at the ceiling. And then he saw it, an apparition out of the corner of his eye, to the right of his bed. It was tall, and had a snout like that of a wolf, and stood in silhouette in front of the drawn curtains. Slowly it extended its neck, pointing its snout to the ceiling, and let out a low pitched, gravelly snarl. This was no dream; he was awake and that real-isation sent a shiver through the length of his body and tightened it like a drawn bow. In one swift movement he covered himself with sheet and blankets and lay there, legs, arms and back all flexed, fists closed tight at his chin to protect his neck.

"Come to me," a faint and distant voice called. Then again, "Come to me." A faint light suffused the bedcovers, and the voice was a gentle one, bidding him to come out from beneath the covers.

Kel lay still, and kept his flexed position for some time, gasping silently in tiny imperceptible breaths, terrified and unable to move. As his eyes slowly became accustomed to the dark, he briefly glanced at his body and saw his right fist under his chin. He splayed out his right hand in front of his vision, and looked at it, and as he did so there was a slight but firm tug on the covers above him. A shockwave of aware-ness and fear swept through him, and he knew he was being fooled, that this was unreal.

This isn't real. This is not real! Mustering every ounce of courage he threw back the bedcovers, at once unafraid of the ghostly threat hover-ing nearby, ready for battle, and roaring defiantly.

As the covers swung back he hurled himself at the wolf-like creature, and there was a falling sensation. He lost consciousness briefly and then came to, deep in his past.

* * * *

Kel sniffed the air around him and felt the water slip past his shins. He knew he was headed down-river and there were reeds along the bank, backed by a wall of rock, and he was for some reason unsure, and unwilling to go on. He eyed the bank above the rocky wall. It was quite a climb to circumvent this section and he needed to press on. It would not take long to pass the rocky wall. Kel eyed the river cautiously. He took a drink of water at the shore, cupping his hands in front of him, and noticed his arms were dark and hairy. This shocked him just for a moment, and then seemed unimportant.

He started wading downstream quickly, hogging as close as he could to the rock wall, eyeing the reeds, and scanning the river constantly. His movements were long and laboured, as he dragged his legs through the water, his eyes sweeping over the river.

Kel gasped, and the alarm bells rung. A log was moving against the current, and had two eyes fixed on him; he had made a costly mistake.

The crocodile, enormous, submerged and disappeared into the slow-moving murk of the river. Kel cast his gaze around, no chance of escape; he was trapped. A small clearing in the reeds ahead offered a chance of shallower water, and he waded towards it, hauling as much of his body clear of the water as he could, and stumbled into the shallows.

He eyed the rocky wall in desperation; too steep, with no indents to get a grip on, and he eyed the river before him, alert and alive, so alive.

The croc shot out of the water at speed and Kel pinned himself back against the rock, just out of reach of its vice like jaws, which had opened wide exposing its cruel rows of teeth. They had snapped shut with a resounding crunch as bone and cartilage clashed together. In all the animal kingdom, no beast has as hard a bite as a crocodile. Nowhere near as hard.

This moment's reflection, before his certain death, led Kel to some information deep in the crevices of his mind. No time to think! He leapt at the unsuspecting reptile in a wild lunge as it slowly withdrew for its next attack, and landed on its gargantuan jaws. Clasping his arms around them, Kel hugged as tightly as he could, and took a deep breath. He then secured his legs around the front end of the beak like jaws and clamped on. As he looked up, he looked directly into its cold-blooded eyes.

The monster, four times his length, reared with enormous power from side to side, and he hung on for dear life as it withdrew back into the river. Kel took one last big breath as the water crept slowly up, and along his body, and the two slithered into the river.

The crocodile, calmer now, submerged, and retreated to the deep. The sound of the river echoed in Kel's head, the subdued whoosh of bubbles and gurgles as he hung on to the snout of this butcher. The spinning started jerkily, and then became a frenzy of raw enraged spinning fury, and round and round they went. When the croc leapt once out of the river, twisting onto its back, Kel stole a gulp of air, and hung on for one last round as they hit the water with a loud slap. His grip was loosening and his energy nearly spent.

His air was gone, and his lungs heaved, so Kel let go and poked hard at both eyes in a final act of defense, then struggled to the surface. Just one more breath…please. He sucked in the air, looking around and under him hastily, waiting for the final tug from below.

He rode on the current, drifting downstream a way, breathing hard and fast, and was dumped on the riverbank. He scrambled ashore, stumbling from side to side, coughing and spitting out the water, and then gagged and vomited what little there was in his stomach. He was now down-river, way beyond the rocky trap, and he scurried up the bank and out of the attack range of any crocodile. He retched again like a sick cat, and when this subsided, squatted on his haunches and looked at the dusty environment around him.

He walked on for a short distance, and sat in the shade of a tree to rest a while. Although exhausted, he felt supremely aware. A parrot squawked in the tree above him, indignant. He sniffed the air for danger, and when satisfied that there was none, lay down and dozed, intending just to re-coup a little strength before the final leg of his journey. He looked up and around one last time, and thought with rel-

ish about telling of the fight with the crocodile to his family, and was
soon fast asleep.

When he awoke it was almost dark, and he got up quickly, looking
at the distant horizon, the mountains—his destination. He set off at a
brisk pace, annoyed at his foolishness; he should not have allowed himself to fall asleep, sleep till so late. There was no cover around, nowhere
to conceal himself for the night. This was the hunting ground of the
big cats, and he would be a relatively easy meal for them. He pressed
on, a sense of urgency in his steps, while his eyes surveyed the trail
ahead of him, darting this way and that. Dark clouds loomed ominously on the horizon and he felt a dread, and yearned for the safety of
his tiny tribe. If there was no light from the moon…

He had been walking for some hours, a lonely nocturnal figure in
the dusty and rocky landscape, with high hopes in his heart as the
mountains drew closer, when he first sensed he was being stalked. It
was big—a sabre tooth—he could smell it. His pace quickened, and he
sensed his stalker's quickening also. He looked around for suitable hiding or escape routes, but there were none. He now started to trot and
eyed the moon anxiously, as the ghostly wall of clouds loomed closer
and closer, and then the worst happened. The clouds started to shroud
the moon's light and soon it was very dark, slowing his pace considerably, and he crept forward, fearful of every step.

The clouds rolled in and covered the canopy of the sky. Any light
now danced on the roof of the clouds, and it was pitch dark down
below. Kel could see nothing, not even his hand in front of his eyes,
and his stalker closed in. He could smell it clearly now, and naked fear
danced in his veins.

He moved slowly in the dark with his hands held up in front of him
in a desperate gesture of defense, and sensed the cat closer now. He
turned, looking desperately into the darkness, until his back hit a large
rock. He sought some crevice or crack into which he could retreat, and
when none was found, grasped at the earth around him looking for a
boulder or rock with which to defend himself. He found two fist sized

rocks and held one in each hand; and there he waited with only the terrifying smell of the big cat, and the beat of his own heart for company. He stared intently into the dark, seeing nothing, yet aware of its approach.

He sensed the rush, and heard the rustle of the dry earth as the big cat jumped towards him, sabres cutting through the darkness.

A wave of energy passed through Kel's body, and there was a corresponding rush of awareness. He swung his arms around in a wide arc in front of his face and smashed the rocks together as if they were cymbals, throwing off a spark of light that illumined him, eyeball to eyeball, with the great sabre toothed tiger. There was a moment's total stillness as the two beings scrutinised each other from such close quarters.

The attacker, shocked and disoriented, did everything in its power to avoid landing on its prey, and all Kel heard was the soft padded sound of its paws on the rocks around him, as the tiger turned, twisting back off the rock wall. It ran off seeking its own escape from the wild eyes of its new adversary, and Kel roared in triumph, roared and roared, and at that moment the moon appeared from behind the clouds and he jumped up, and danced, shaking his fists at the heavens.

Empowered by this amazing day, Kel set off for the mountains, the mountains of the moon, illumined by its magical and pearly light. He exalted in himself and the spring and strength in his step was felt by everything around, as he pressed on towards the towering horizon.

*   *   *   *

He roared in triumphant return as he entered his tiny encampment. No response! He quickly fell to one knee, and sniffed the air around him. Slowly from the cavernous shelters his family and the rest of the band emerged, and they looked nervous and frightened. His brother was absent and this surprised him as he was in charge of protecting their kin. He slowly followed the eyes of his nervous family over to the driest cavern where the oldest of the clan slept, and from it there emerged two large males—strangers. Behind them stood his mate, and she was bruised and bloodied, and unable to look him in the eye in the early morning light.

He quickly understood what had happened. His brother and the old ones would have been killed and the two males, and maybe others, had asserted their authority over this tribe. The stronger male indicated that Kel should go, with a shriek that startled, and intruded in upon the morning quiet.

Kel approached and faced this usurper, and they eyed each other up and down. He was big, strong and dominantly confident. The other male approached and stood behind his companion and shrieked as well, indicating that he too was in this fight. Kel looked behind him for his three main hunting companions and they were absent—maybe dead.

He turned to face his adversary and clenched his fist, and in an instant realised he still held the rock in his strongest hand. A wave of energy streamed through him and he felt invincible. He struck out swiftly with brute force and hit this enemy on the side of the head, and he went down quickly, blood gushing from a deep gash on his temple through his grasping fingers.

His companion howled in fear and turned to run but was tripped by Kel's mate who then urged him on to smash this intruder also. Meanwhile the rest of the clan had surrounded and set about his first victim, and were pummeling him to death. Kel raised his rock high and stood over the second male, who screamed for mercy, covering his head and neck with his hairy arms.

The family urged him on to finish the kill, and Kel, mad with anger, was about to crush his skull when something inside of him screamed. "No!"

He looked up at the stone in his hand, and amidst the screams of those around him stood back in shock, staring at his hand held high before him. He dropped the stone and dragged the cowering stranger by his hair to the two large rocks that stood as the entrance, and guarded their small enclave, and threw him roughly out.

The intruder rolled over twice on the sharp pebbles and rocks of the inclined approach to camp, gained his footing and ran off at full speed, not bothering to look back.

Kel had shown mercy and he fell to his knees, covering his eyes with his hands. His family, confused and curious, looked on silently; the body behind them lay inert, bloodied and lifeless at the centre of the camp. He looked again up at his hand, and lurched back in surprise as two plumes of smoke trailed through the blue sky high above him, higher than even eagles fly.

Mindful for just a second, of who he was, something hit him from behind and knocked him out—out cold.

Kel struggled to wake himself up from that dark place where fear of oblivion lurks. He was awake in a deep sleep, trapped in the dark.

* * * *

Kel was shaken awake with a bump and found himself in an airplane, grunting and groaning in his seat. He stopped, looking around apologetically, and shook his head, astounded by the vividness of an amazing dream and cupped his hands over his eyes, trying to remember some message it had for him. But if there was one, it now eluded him.

He was not happy to be awake, as they had hit an area of turbulence and he had been slapped back against his seat. His guts tightened, and he wished his destination on. Every moment was fraught with potential disaster; every possible scenario processed in the mind, a mind that desperately sought some modicum of control.

Looking out of the window at the sea below, he felt the dizzy reality that flying at forty thousand feet can produce—a kind of into thin-airness about it. Kel tried to remember the dream because he knew it was important, but it was gone. Fear had driven off all meaning at this moment. He tightened his seat belt hard and fast.

Cirrus and cumulus clouds dotted the sky, and an ocean stretched out beneath him, the wave crests stretching out as far as he could see, sweeping across the surface in their interminable restlessness. He sought to gain some reality in the world around him and looked behind and to the sides. People would look at him briefly and turn away, avoiding any chance meetings. Something gnawed at him, a 'déjà vu' feeling that this was in his past; something was terribly wrong. He decided to be logical and asked himself where he was headed. In one frightful moment he realised he didn't know, and when he began investigating this peculiar fact, the plane hit a pocket of thin air turbulence.

Pandemonium spread throughout the cabin as those unlucky souls who had ignored the seat belt signs were tossed in the air and thrown from side to side. The plane bucked and dove violently as the pilot struggled to maintain control, and Kel pressed himself back in the seat, feeling wretched and helpless. Then they made a dive, a terrifying drop through the sky, as an overwhelming force bore them on. Leveling out of the dive, an excruciating oppression cut into his midriff as the seat belt took the strain. The plane was about to dive again and he knew that his time was up. This was it.

He looked behind him, and amongst the panic and pandemonium he saw an old Chinese man sitting in his chair, laughing at each buck and turn of the ride, as if he were on a Big Dipper. He realised with another jolt of 'deja vu', that this was a flight he had suffered through many years before, and the old man had been a profound lesson to him, that life is to a great extent a matter of attitude, and manner of response. These were the greatest choices available to us, no matter what confronts us.

This is a memory, a memory. It's not real! Something awoke in him and strove to know the truth of it, and he looked at his hands. The little finger of his right hand carried a gold snake ring with two garnets adorning the eyes, and he remembered this as a ring he had worn in his early twenties. He was shocked to see it, and acknowledged to himself that this was a ruse, but could not think why, and searched his mind to make sense of it. His intellect continued to battle to know the truth of his present situation, as his body swung from side to side in his seat. Alternating between his sense of fear of imminent disaster, and to the fact that this was unreal, some light had switched on in him and he intensified his concentration. There was something about a mission, a quest; and at the moment of realisation, when he again looked at his right hand and momentarily knew who and where he was, the plane bucked and turned, and then dove steeply, and Kel passed out. The second before he went, he screamed, "Wake up."

✻   ✻   ✻   ✻

"Kelsie, Kelsie! Wake up!" There was a sensation of passing through a tunnel at great speed, from one set to another, through an ocean of fire and a myriad of tunnels.

Kel came to with a splash. He was immersed in water, delirious, and thrashing about, shouting out some name. The side of his face, arm and shoulder stung with the salt. Near him an overturned outrigger made from wood and reeds was dashed against the rocks one last time, and slipped beneath the waves. He swam away from the jagged shore-line against the angry waves, turned, and in the distance saw a volcano. He tried to figure out how he had gotten there, but he gagged and his side split with pain. He struggled away from the rocks and started to circumvent away from them; a beach bobbed into view in the distance when the surf took him high enough to see. Blood seeped from his wounds and he struggled on towards the beach.

Why am I here, what is this? Just swim on, swim to the beach, don't think; stay with it! Exhaustion gnawed at him as he struggled on.

Kel was close to shore when he saw the shadow passing over the reef some thirty feet below—a bull shark. The big meat eater circled him effortlessly, almost nonchalantly, in ever decreasing circles. These were vicious killers. Then he saw another one; there were two.

Kel kept the path of the bigger one in his sight, and as the circles became smaller, he spun around in the centre of its trajectory like a spinning top in slow motion, following its every move.

The first attack came from below and Kel's seaward and bloody side. He saw the change in trajectory and the sudden spurt of speed, and extended all limbs as wide as possible to make himself as large as he could. The shark retreated, but it would try again, driven on by intense hunger. It would try again, and again.

The shark, after its fifth attack, when it turned upward and sideways to get a good-sized biting hold on him, disappeared, and Kel, now exhausted, continued to swim for shore. His vigilance waned as energy slowly ebbed out from his body. Two heartbeats after he gave up his watch, Kel's system exploded in one big adrenaline rush, and down he went, helpless in the shark's jaws. He felt the head toss back an inch or two and its jaws slacken in preparation for the next big crunch—the bite that would finish him off. He struggled briefly against his impending fate, and was now just inches away from the crack of the whiplash, a heartbeat away from the end. Another burning sensation on his leg as the other shark came in to feed.

At the moment of surrender to his greatest fear, a lightening bolt of energy passed through him, and he felt the electricity crackle around him in the water. The sharks felt it too, leaving both of them shocked and dazed at this delicate moment, and an eerie stillness surrounded them. There was another surge of energy and the shockwave passed through them again, and this time Kel dug his hands deep into the gills of the nearest, and the sharks released him quickly and sped off. It had been only a few desperate seconds since the first bite.

Kel had been spat out and struggled to the surface. He looked down at his floating body. It was bleeding badly and there were puncture wounds, an array of them, on his abdomen and thighs; small fish came to feed on his blood and threads of flesh that hung from the wounds.

He turned onto his front, and looked to shore. It was reachable; he could hear the gentle rattling of the palm fronds in the breeze.

Kel paddled on, feeling dizzier and dizzier, weaker and weaker, the closer to shore he got. He thought his energy spent, and that he was done for, when his hands and knees felt the seabed beneath him. He crawled up the sand a little way, panting heavily and gagging, and this caused blood to spurt out of his wounds. He turned slowly on to his back and lay there, aware of the surf, and the energy draining out of his body.

What is this? I am alive and on…what? He looked up and around, and then at his right hand. It was covered in blood. He struggled to understand before he would pass out. His nausea got the better of him and he wondered how he would now survive, as unconsciousness approached him. The world above him started to spin and he felt himself sink deeper into the sand.

He heard a human cry, as he lay there looking at the sky, trying to make sense of it all, wondering if he was about to die. Then the beautiful brown face of a woman glided into view, like the full moonrise on a summer's night. She looked down at his body with concern, and as he tried to speak she put two fingers on his lips to silence him, and called out loud towards the coconut grove that laced the shore. She called three times, loud and urgent, and pressed something against his belly. Kel felt a searing pain flood through his abdomen, and finally passed out.

✳   ✳   ✳   ✳

He heard the sound of the sea and felt his brow being mopped, oh so gently. On opening his eyes, the young woman he had seen smiled down at him, and he smiled back feebly. She was dark and with a slight Oriental lilt to her eyes. She's so beautiful, he thought, and lapsed into asleep again.

She fed him some fish broth with a wooden spoon, and then with gentle fingers some sweet fruit. He became aware of his brow being stroked softly, the fingers caressing into his hair. He was stronger now, and able to think of continuing on his trip, but the soft touch of this woman kept such thoughts at bay. The beauty of her smile assuaged his restless mental anguish that he should press on.

The days passed lazily by, and the soft sound of the surf played in the background of Kel's awareness as he traversed between the realms of sleep and waking. His strength slowly returned and soon he was dipping his body in the sea, and surveying the distant horizon.

One night as he watched the geckos dart and nod on the wood and palm fronds of the hut, lapping up small insects, she came to his cot and lay next to him, and nestled up close. Her scent was of some wild flower and she placed her hand upon his belly and slowly, very slowly, started to make ever-decreasing circles with her fingertips. He was soon aroused and she continued to stoke the fire of his lust with her lips, and her tongue. She kissed his eyelids, and his eyes tenderly, and moved down to his ears and neck, and he moaned imperceptibly. Then it was his arms and slowly on to his chest and down to his belly, and now he began to writhe as if in agony, as she gauged the amount of pressure she needed to keep the fire hot, yet not to reduce him to ashes—just yet.

Suddenly there was an ecstatic flood of pleasure at the root of his physical being, his back arched, and he was helpless, and near to an explosion. She let him go, and quickly straddled his thighs, and as she squatted down on him she moaned. She didn't move immediately, as if gauging Kel's prowess.

A dance of passion commenced, and gradually increased in tempo, mingling their sweat as her dark hair danced on his face. She faithfully kept in tempo with him until he held his breath about to explode, and then she arched her back and let go a staggering shudder of spasms that nailed Kel to the cot. He exploded in a fit of gyrating movements, matched in intensity by her, and they bellowed and yowled together as they barely coped with this release of tension.

Before sleeping, her head nestled in his arm, he knew he had betrayed something, but could not think what it was. Against the rush of lust had come the call from deep inside him to move on to some kind of other completion—but what? By and by he slept.

*   *   *   *

Kel weaved the palm stalks together and lashed another board of wood to the outrigger, and he knew it would soon be ready. His son ran up the beach and showed him some new find, a shell of luminescent pink. Kel pretended to swallow it, and the boy squealed in delight and disbelief. He got up, tossing down the palm stalks, and they walked a distance together on the beach and swam and dove inside the reef. They beach-combed on their way back stopping here and there to examine each other's finds. The boy ran ahead calling to his mother, now with another swelling belly, and she picked him up and swung him around, both laughing. Kel looked on at the gay and peaceful scene, sighed, and returned to his boat.

He selected a large wide leaf and was about to paste it to the bow of the outrigger with some tree resin when his attention was riveted on the leaf. He looked intensely at it and held it up to the light. There's something wrong, he thought, and from deep within him, a voice from the forest said, 'Friend, friend, this is not real, this is not of us'. He looked again and saw there were no veins in the leaves, nothing to sustain life, and he picked at other thinner leaves, and saw the absence of these life-giving channels in them all.

The voice inside his head returned. 'Friend, look at the light, look at the sky', and Kel looked up at the sun and stared into it for some time. This is a lifeless sun, he thought, and looked away holding his head in his hands. Something was so terribly wrong and the voice persisted in his head. 'Not real, not real, nothing here is real'. With a start he at once recognised he was being distracted from a journey, and that he could have been so for a lifetime. His chest filled with some vibrant energy and he looked up and around him, and in a lightening stroke knew himself as being the queirant on a quest of immense importance, and that all this was not now, was not real. He got up and made for the hut, angry and calling out a curse to the heavens, and waving a stick he held at the sun in the sky.

The woman approached him and begged he not overlook the paradise around them. He quickly sidestepped and passed her by and his anger increased in vigor. He threw his stick up into the sky, and in the midst of challenging the sun and its power to a duel, was struck from above by a violent blow that knocked him senseless. He was aware of spiraling down into the vortex, out of control, before he hit the ground.

*   *   *   *

Kel's mind lifted from the ground-spring of the unconscious up into an awareness of himself. He heard a sound, some fabric flapping in the wind. As soon as he opened his eyes a voice intruded any thought he might have. "My Lord, we are ready."

He looked down at his recumbent body. He was dressed in armour, chain mail in which he was able to move with surprising ease. On standing he faced someone he knew, also dressed in armour, and with the crest of a lion on his breastplate. They were in a tent, and a dim light illumined the spartan interior; some clothes stashed in a corner, and a book on a small wooden table. He walked out into the faint light and cold of dawn, and was greeted by a tumultuous roar of a thousand men that surrounded the tent. He laughed and his knights around him laughed. The vapour of his breath spurted out, and he bent his knees, slapped his thighs, and roared back at them. Lions indeed! Good and trusted men about to do battle with an invader.

He was led to his horse and climbed a stool to mount it. His horse reared and spun and he drew his sword and saluted his men, and to a man they drew their weapons and saluted him back. Ten knights took to their mounts, and Kel led them in procession along the line of cheering, chanting men. His grin was broad and generous, and he felt the lion rise in his chest. They made their way to a hillock that overlooked a broad moor and in the clearing mist, there in the distance, stood the enemy.

Behind their lines on another hillock stood six knights dressed in white with red crosses on their chests, and wearing horned Teutonic helmets. Kel could almost see, he thought, through the darkened eye slits into their eyes. They faced off each other like the pieces of a chess game, each side now with swords drawn and pikes raised. They were evenly matched, man for man.

Kel surveyed the scene. The citadel behind the enemy lay in ruins. Smoke still rose from the embers of a once prosperous and happy place, a port town and meeting place of different cultures. Behind lay the sea, gray and uninviting in the early morning light, with the invaders ships berthed, and bobbing on the tide.

At the foot of the moor between them lay a boggy piece of land with a slight slope up to his front, and he looked down this gentle incline. Kel and his knights had chosen this place deliberately, knowing the attack strategies of their enemy; foot soldiers first, horsemen behind, to fight the adversary on two fronts, trapping and annihilating all in between. He wondered if their scouts had done their job well and knew of this incline, and the bog.

Their plan was to lure the enemy into the boggy ground. Kel's foot soldiers would wait for the enemy's charge, then advance towards the bog and at a given moment halt and form a central wall of shields, the nucleus of their attack. They would hold their ground before this steepest stretch of the incline, luring the enemy into wet ground with a slope against them. High ground advantage would ensure victory this day.

If the charge of the enemy would halt before the bog, having caught wind of his strategy, then this would spell a bloody day for his men. Kel put on his helmet, much lighter than those worn by his adversaries, and though it left his neck exposed, it gave him optimum movement.

The two sides faced off. "Soon we will know who takes the advantage on this day," said the knight nearest him.

"We are just pawns," Kel answered. "And in this game we are defending. Defending lions! So we have the advantage already."

A loud roar came from the other side, and the enemy's foot soldiers started their charge with both pikes and swords honed to a razor's sharpness. Kel looked at his foot soldiers, grim and determined; they had heard of the atrocities of their adversaries, and knew what they had to do. Justice was on their side, and anger surged in them—an anger tempered with discipline and held in abeyance until the second steel met steel. Many had family in this town, and they were ready.

At the critical moment Kel cried out the order to charge, and they were off screaming their revenge, and the sound of thunder resounded throughout the moor. At a given point and cry through the ranks, Kel's charging army halted and formed its central wall of shields. Pikemen and swordsmen crowded in behind this protective bulwark ready to burst forth and do battle. He looked at the enemy and held his breath. They did not stop; his force would have the advantage. When the enemy had reached the bog, Kel sounded the charge of his horsemen, and this was the cue to restart the foot soldiers slow and steady advance. The enemy's mounted attack was now at full gallop and both fronts moved forward into the fray, now fully committed.

Kel's horse, nervous and edgy bolted off, and he hoisted his sword aloft and screamed at the top of his voice, his ten knights in close attendance. The horsemen rode in a wide arc to encircle the enemy, and his foot soldiers divided into two flanks. They ran in a wide curving arc, like two claws of a giant crab, to surround its now faltering adversary. Kel had to arrive at the critical moment to stop the enemy's mounted attack on his footmen. The ground soldiers met each other with the clash of steel and screams of fear. Both sides were now men beside themselves in the lust for blood.

The horsemen arrived in good time and warded off the enemy's attack on his foot soldiers, and the battle was now toe to toe, horseback to horseback, eyeball to eyeball—no bowmen here to send their arrows off to some anonymous death. One would have to face one's adversary.

Kel wielded his sword to left and right, with an ease and expertise unmatched on the battlefield. He cut and slashed at all he met. A severed arm crashed against his breastplate soaking it in blood and his knights stayed close, ever watchful over their liege. They harried and circled the enemy, swords whirling, the din of battle deafening, and the bloodlust soaking the earth with its sweet and sickly fruit.

Soon they were in the thick of it, swordsmen and pikemen to either side, sweating and greased, and bloodied with the battle. Kel's horse was felled, its leg severed at the knee, and it made a haunting desperate whinny as it dropped, a ghostly sound of helplessness. Kel managed to roll over as he fell and was soon on his feet, and as he faced his first adversary, three of his knights dismounted and stayed close to his side ensuring he would not be felled from behind.

Kel and his knights met pikemen and swordsmen who were no match for their skills in swordplay, and they cut at strategic points—tendons at the heel, elbow and shoulder, incapacitating where they could, taking life where they had to, obeying pleas of mercy. Five knights were now with him on foot and they cut their way through, merciless in their power.

Kel indicated to his knights that they would head for the hillock where the six perpetrators of this carnage stood in relative safety, and they forged on. His mind was wild and his rage absolute at what he had to do, and he lusted at the power he wielded. Suddenly he met his own men at the rear of the fray—both sides of the pincer had met and the enemy was surrounded.

They were through. Six knights were now with him, and they cast their gaze up the hill and started up the gradient. As they approached the enemy, five of the hooded knights fanned out, swords at the ready; the sixth stepped back. The knights squared up one to one, and there was a moment's stillness.

Kel spoke. "There has been enough carnage, and you have lost this battle. Put one of you in front of me now and let this be settled."

The man at the back nodded and a big man stepped forward, and faced up to Kel. This must be the aggressor's champion, and the two men eyed each other. Kel looked at the battlefield for a moment exposing his back to his opponent, who made no move. A noble knight thought Kel. They crossed swords and the duel commenced.

The big man was well rested, his only duty to protect his liege. Kel was battle ready, weary, but fired up to the hilt. The clash of steel began and went back and forth, thrust, parry, cut, and slash. Blades sizzled past heels, necks and shoulders and both men kept eye contact; the swordplay seemed to take care of itself.

The main battle had ceased and all eyes were on the hill. Apart from the cries of pain and anguish from wounded men and beasts, there was no other sound. The duel continued and the end was now near.

Kel was tiring and the big man was good. There was only one way to win. He started circling around, trying to get behind his opponent, whose big helmet was now a burden, but he had to get near in order to cut down the angle and get on his blind side. This opened him up to multiple attacks of the razor sharp steel, especially to his exposed neck, and he needed every ounce of attention. His tactics soon started to pay off, and he landed a blow that slashed his opponent's left thigh. Kel received a gash on his left shoulder but no tendon was cut, and he was getting the upper hand.

The big man realised what was going on and tried to rid himself of his helmet, his capped encumbrance, and at this moment Kel struck. One blow on the blind side at his right shoulder as his left hand tried to knock off the helmet, and then Kel's sword swirled up, over and down to the left side, through the wrist, armour and the jugular vein, and the big man fell like a rock. He writhed for a second, and then lay still, blood gushing from his neck.

The four adversaries removed their horned helmets and fell to their knees, as did the enemy army on the field. The battle was over.

The figure behind the knights remained standing, defiant, and Kel approached the perpetrator of all this carnage, and indicated with his sword that he should take off his helmet.

He did so, and a young man in his twenties, fair haired and wild eyed, looked back at him like a cornered animal. Kel looked closely, and there was something unnervingly familiar about him. Kel removed his helmet, and eyed the man again more intensely. Somehow he knew him.

At that moment a man approached the hillock, bedraggled and sobbing, there was blood on his tunic, and he was in deep despair.

"My Lord," he said, "I am of this town," and he pointed a finger at the smouldering ruins behind them. "I have been waiting for the moment to kill this man, Sire. He had his way with my two beautiful young daughters, and then put them to the sword," and the man sobbed and sank to his knees. "Surely he is the devil himself."

The young man sneered and spat at this despairing soul and without hesitation Kel hoisted his sword aloft and lopped off his head in one clean swoop.

His body took a fraction of a second to collapse to earth. There was a gasp throughout this moor of death, and then silence.

Kel looked at the headless body at his feet, and then the enemy on their knees. They were the attacking force, and had just witnessed their master's demise. Their just reward was death, and they bowed their heads in disgrace.

"Show them mercy; make them swear an oath on a holy book never to do us harm again. Make them clear up the mess in the town as much as possible, and bow in shame to the survivors, and beg they do not kill them. Then crowd them into their ships and send them off. Bah! What a waste." So saying, Kel sheathed his sword and started back to camp;

he needed some solitude and some silent contemplation. When he had gone some distance he turned back, and called, "And bring the big man, the champion to my tent. This one deserves a special send off. He was a knight, a man of dignity."

"Yes my Lord," they replied, and he set off through the carnage, acknowledging the cheers of his people with raised arms, blood seeping out of the chain mail on his left arm. They will celebrate enough tonight, he thought. He had had enough, and yearned to be alone.

"Shall we send a messenger to inform the King?" they called after him. He waved his concordance without a moment's thought.

He trudged through the moor and was sickened at the sight and smell of so much carnage, and the air was heavy with the cries of pain and desperation. Men called out their loyalty and allegiance as he passed, and he waved a hand at them, acknowledging their brave deeds on this day. He screamed on the moor for his wounded to be tended to, and made his way to his horse that lay panting heavily in the mud. Kel spoke some words of thanks, then drew his sword and put it out of its misery in one stroke. His last bloody deed on this day, and he felt sick with remorse. Yet he held his head high and walked slowly back to his tent, summoning a physician when he arrived, his shoulder and arm now soaked in blood.

The physician had just patched up his arm with some crude leather thong, stitched through to keep the wound together, when a knight entered and informed Kel that the champion's body was outside.

Kel grunted his acknowledgement, and though feeling faint and dizzy, went outside to the big helmeted body on the cart. He removed the helmet slowly, and there was a gasp all around when the head was revealed.

"A Hun," someone said. "A yellow devil," said another.

"I know this man," said Kel, and he bent down and looked intently at the face of the dead champion. "I know this man," he repeated.

He stood up with a jolt of surprise and said, "He's not a Hun, he's Japanese."

"Japa what, My Lord?" someone asked.

The arrow sliced through the air silent and deadly, shot by a marksman, a sniper, and heading for Kel's heart.

"The land of the rising…" and as Kel slapped his forehead to remember, the arrow struck with a thud.

As he fell back he saw the looks of anguish and despair on the faces of those around him, and although there was a searing pain in his chest, he smiled at them through the grimace, and once again lapsed into unconsciousness. This time Kel was still, and the scenery changed around him. He was through the garden gate, and on his way up to the residence of the perpetrator of this illusion.

$$*\qquad*\qquad*\qquad*$$

"Daddy, daddy," it was a desperate plea from a young voice, and he opened his eyes, "The mountain is angry, daddy," The ground was shaking, and the hut shook.

Kel, without a moment to think, ran outside and looked toward the mountain. Molten lava spewed out of its charred and flattened peak, and great billows of smoke drifted up, and blotted out the sun in the clear blue sky. He was back on the island with his son.

A terrifying scream echoed out, and he swung around and looked to the sea. An enormous tsunami was headed for the island, and was a harrowing sight. "My god" he said to himself.

Kel picked up his frightened son, lifted him to head height and looked into his eyes saying, "Don't be afraid son, we will be all right."

Then with a double take he looked intently at the child, and with shock and horror he realised that the child in his arms was the infant to the prince he had slayed in the battle. Even though he had just looked upon the prince for some minutes only, he knew it was the same person. Awareness rushed into Kel's consciousness and he all at once knew that he was on a quest, and that this child had been used as a pawn in the game. He held him close to his chest.

He had broken through the bounds of the unconscious and seen through the illusion of his present situation, 'So that's it', he said to himself. The tidal wave rushed relentlessly on towards a father and his son, and Kel felt such an anger at this cruel ruse, and a determination to battle on to the centre of this cyclone, even though he did not yet quite understand the point, or the rules of the game.

Now he knew it was a game, and that the characters he was meeting had a great significance to whoever was directing the show. And he would find the perpetrator and know what to do when that happened. In this he had the greatest trust, and he stood there holding his son to his chest, facing a massive wall of water. Kel held on tight to the boy, cradling his head so he would not look at this frightening sight. The wave hit them and Kel held his ground. The boy disappeared from his arms and a rush of energy gushed past him and still he held his ground; it was time to move on out of this world of gross illusion, and on to the next plane.

He screamed into the whirlwind that enveloped him. "I see two dreams at once—the prince and the boy are the same. You play a dirty game. You can't stop me! You can't stop me!"

The last thing Kel remembered was a dream. A giant passed over him as he stood there in the water, and the giant was searching here and there for something—for signs of life maybe?

The whirlwind spun around him yet again, and this time he chose the tunnel into which he was sucked; something that had haunted him through the ages, and a chance at redemption somewhere deep within his own being. Each added a spark of awareness to this gross illusion, and allowed him to get nearer his goal. And that was the deepest part of himself, beyond all history, and all experience. Only then could he confront this devil that sought to keep him away.

*　　　*　　　*　　　*

A crowd in medieval garb surrounded him, shouting at the top of their voices. He looked around him, confused and disoriented. He yearned for silence to make sense of his presence there but the smell of stale sweat and farm animals swamped his nostrils, and for some reason he felt sick to his stomach, and retched. The crowd around him, which had been holding him up in the crush, gave him space.

"Burn the witch! Burn the witch!" they shouted. Many were drunk, and they pushed and shoved to get near to three stakes set up on the outskirts of a town. Wood and straw surrounded the stakes. Lighted pitch torches shed a somber light over the proceedings.

"Drunk for a farthing! Drunk for a farthing!" called out the gin sellers behind him, and the faint perfumed smell of juniper infused the stale air. It was cold, and an odorous vapor from the excited crowd mingled with the eerie light. The energy around sucked in Kel's attention, and he became embroiled in the challenge confronting him.

A wagon approached and a roar went up from the crowd. "Burn the witch! Burn the witch!" they chanted in unison. A priest with a torch held in one hand, and a Bible held aloft in the other led the procession; he wore a red satin hood and chanted something in Latin, but this was drowned out by the noise of the crowd. A line of soldiers marched either side of the wagon, helmeted, spears held upright.

Kel strained to see who was in the wagon. Two middle-aged ladies and one younger held on to a rail with a look of desperation on their faces; the younger one was terrified. He looked at her more closely and in one gut wrenching, heart-stopping moment, knew that this was his love, his woman.

He screamed a name at the top of his lungs and she must have heard as she looked in his direction, straining her eyes to see through the blood lusting and drunken crowd, as it hurled its mindless abuse at the unfortunate trio.

They were pulled roughly from the cart, and roped to the stake. None offered resistance and Kel pushed and fought his way to the front of the crowd. He stood behind a line of soldiers in their chain mail, their breath steaming its way out of round-head helmets. His lady was tied to the middle stake, and she peered desperately into the noisy crowd.

The priest held up his hand and slowly some modicum of order and silence fell upon the crowd. Kel eyed the sword hanging from the guard's belt in front of him. A safety clip held it in place.

The crowd surged forward and pushed into the line of guards, giving him an opportunity to unhitch the safety clip. The guard, in the frenzied confusion of the push, did not notice.

The priest, in the name of Jesus Christ, offered the women salvation in the afterlife if they would repent, and the two elder women spat at him. The young one continued to peer into the crowd and ignored him. The priest shut his holy book and turned to the crowd for support, opening his arms, beckoning them to show their scorn and disdain.

Kel chose his moment wisely as the crowd surged forward again, shouting its abuse at this gross act of defamation. Whether abuse or approval, it was hard to tell in the frenzied madness of it all. He sprang forward lifting the guard's sword from its sheath, and within seconds stood in front of the priest, the blade held firmly at his neck.

A sudden hushed silence descended on the crowd, and Kel shouted. "In Christ's name you do this, you holy hypocrite! You use him for your own power!" and Kel lifted the sword as if to slay him. He heard a woman's voice behind him, "Kaye, Kaye."

He turned and their eyes met briefly, and he turned back to the priest, anger surging in every pore of his body. He screamed at the priest, and gripped his hoisted sword.

The priest fainted dead away.

He danced quickly backwards and up onto the stake, above the straw and logs as the guards rushed forward, cumbersome in their armour. One tried to follow him and Kel kicked him back down, and he turned and faced his love. Her look was all at once terrified, surrendered, and desperately concerned for him.

A roar went up from the crowd, and he turned to see the priest, recovered now, hurl the lighted torch onto the straw that surrounded them. He turned to face his love and lifted his sword high. She gasped as the blade cut through the rope that held her bound. They rushed to each other and embraced, crying. The fire spat and crackled, and they gagged on the slowly increasing cloud of smoke that now engulfed them.

"Kaye, Kaye! I did not know," she gasped, touching the hilt of the sword, as the flames encroached them. "My lord, release the others! I am yours forever."

"Forgive me my love," he shouted back, then raised, and in one swift stroke of the sword cut through her neck and artery, and she fell to the woodpile like a stone.

He screamed like a madman and jumped from the fire, his boots, hair and clothes smouldering from the heat, and bounded through one fire, then the other—one stroke of his sword in each releasing a soul from the pain of a fiery death.

Jumping from the conflagration, he doused the flames on his hair with his free hand, and screamed in anger at the priest, cowering in the distance, and made for him, madder than hell itself. Wild with the moment he looked like a demon from hell. A line of guards quickly stood in his way and then surrounded him once he was outside the burning zone. Oblivious now to his smouldering hair and clothes, he pointed his sword at the priest, grimaced, and made for him.

The priest was pinioned, his back against the crowd, fear etched on his face as he tried to push back into the wild, drunk, chanting mob behind him. This had become an entertaining night for them, and they were delirious with the moment. Kel cut his way through the guards, cutting and slashing at all around him, wielding his sword in both hands, surging forward, awesome and animal-like in the strength he now wielded.

Within ten feet of his target Kel was finally felled. Two swords swung to and fro, impaled in his back as he hit the ground, with a final gasp of air escaping from his lungs. A throng of guards fell to the ground around him, exhausted, some badly cut and bleeding, and they looked like wild animals wounded on the hunt. The steam of their heat rose and was sucked into the fires that now raged behind them. No screams issued from within these furnaces, and a silence fell upon the crowd

There then arose a loud cheer, loud enough to wake the dead, and this was the last thing remotely near Kel's fading consciousness.

✻   ✻   ✻   ✻

Unbeknown to all those, be they real, or ghosts of the imagination, who had witnessed the tumultuous scenes of the witch-burning—Kel, at the very root and depths of his being had been released from a guilt that had haunted his soul through the ages. Be it the guilt of cowardice or helplessness, it did not matter, the redemption was complete. Rarely is such an opportunity given or taken—perhaps at the moment of enlightenment, when an individual soul sees through the illusion of all our stories.

You can no longer hold me; you can no longer hold me. I demand to be met! You will no longer use my guilt against me. Face up to me you…

Kel felt a wall behind his back. His arms were folded and he could not move them. A distasteful smell invaded his nostrils. As his senses returned, he heard occasional screams, desperate sounds from troubled souls.

He opened his eyes and found himself in a dimly lit cell, a restraining device holding his arms to his body, straw littering the floor.

The cell door opened and a portly man entered. His smock was filthy with smears of food and excrement down the front. In his hands were a bowl of gruel and a wooden spoon.

"Are we hungry then?" His accent was thick, country-like, and friendly. "You going to behave yourself if I take this off?" He tweaked the restrainer that bound Kel.

"Tell your master, or whoever it is, that I am seeing through this game; he can keep me here no longer."

"Here we go, you going on about that again? You don't eat yer going to die, you wanna die?" The big man held a spoonful of gruel up to Kel's mouth. When Kel didn't move, he said, "Awright, awright," and undid the straps that bound him, and retreated out the door, locking it and leaving the food in front of him.

Kel didn't move. He crossed his legs and shouted, "I am not moving until I meet you, I know this is a game."

A cackling voice screeched out from the neighbouring cell, "Talking to the boogey-man again, ha ha ha."

From the opposite side another voice penetrated Kel's hearing, amid the cacophony of wails and screams that now echoed through this madhouse. The voice was soft, gentle and distressingly sad.

Kel's heart rose to it immediately. "What? I know you, don't I?"

"You put me here, you put me here," the voice wailed, and such a grief hit the core of Kel's being that he felt rise in him a great sorrow, echoing some cruel mystery in his past.

Kel scrambled over to where the voice emerged, a metal vent in the base of the wall. He lay down and looked in.

A boy in his early teens sat disconsolate against the cell wall, and sobbed one loud, aching sob when he spied Kel through the grilled vent. The dingy light of the room seemed to concentrate on, and enshroud this desolate youth, and Kel sought desperately in his mind to recognise him, and to make sense of the guilt he felt.

"I made one mistake and you had me committed. I didn't mean it, I didn't mean it." The boy cried, and tears welled in Kel's eyes, so bleak the grief of this solitary confinement of one so young.

"Jailer," called Kel, "Jailer!" he screamed.

The big man lumbered up and said, "What woke you up then? Not like you to scream."

"Why is this boy in here?" Kel demanded pointing towards his neighbour's cell. "Why for heaven's sake?"

"His uncle had him committed; nearly drowned his friend he did. Kind of simple-minded too, and he would be a danger to himself out there," said the jailer with a toss of his head, indicating the outside world.

"Can you contact this uncle and get him here. This is important, and I would reward you well." Kel exclaimed.

"Oh yeah, and pig's can fly. Even if I agreed it would do no good. He be in Europe and won't be back for some time to come."

"How to gain his freedom then?"

"Well," said the big man, "You need the uncle, his doctor, the peelers and the governor here to agree—no other way."

"Peelers?" Kel asked.

"The constabulary. He'd be no good out there—he'd be a danger to himself, and at risk to and from others. The world's not the place for a simpleton like him."

"The land of fucking judgements!" screamed Kel, "Is there no place of learning for a lad of his age? Come back! This is wrong!"

The big man retreated, "Cost too much money that one, too unpredictable he is." And on he went, cooing gentle words of sedation to the wild and mad insults that greeted him from every cell. "Calm down my lovely, you'll be awright."

"I'm so sorry, so sorry," Kel cried to the boy, looking around the desolation of the cell. "I must have done something to feel this way. I know I am in my past now—my God I know I am."

"Here he goes again," chortled the madman from the other side. "He's in his past again, ha ha!"

Kel tried to kick the vent in and gain some contact with the boy, but it held fast. He called to him and told him to come close, and he did and they stared intently into each-others eyes. Kel felt his eyes well up, and for some minutes they wept openly together. Salty tears streamed down Kel's cheeks, and his face ached with grief.

"I don't know what it is but I am so sorry. I can do nothing now but say how sorry and sad I am. I must have been a mean and selfish fool."

"You are sorry, I can tell, and I forgive you," the gentle voice of the boy concluded, as he maintained eye contact. Kel looked away at last and stared at the ceiling, aware only of the boy's soft weeping.

Kel cried for some time too. He could do nothing here but he had seen through some deep pain and despair in himself. He spoke gently to the boy, telling him of things as yet undreamed of, of coaches that flew in the air, of travel in the stars, and the boy lifted his sorrowful head, incredulous and wide eyed.

"He's orf again, back in ga-ga land," cried the madman from his cell.

The experience of regret and grief was gone, and he resolved not to move again. He sat against the wall and became immobile, like a stone, until his body screamed in pain from this stillness, and he ignored it, ignored it to such an extent that he transcended it and was in a trance so deep that no-one could revive him.

Images passed his field of vision, in one he embraced a woman in a field, and they cried on each other's shoulder as mounted men of war trampled their crops to dust. In another he looked at himself in a bronze plate hanging from a wall. The reflection cast back to him was of a rugged Asian face, tempered by sun and wind.

Nothing took hold of his attention, he was now on a pilgrimage and would not be thwarted; he was on a quest, fully committed, and nothing could stop him. He had resolved to suffer no more distractions until he met with his adversary, until he was at his residence, or at his door, or in his presence.

✳   ✳   ✳   ✳

But one more distraction lay in wait for him before he would arrive at that door. It was the most recent of Kel's lives, and he woke with a start and found himself in the bumpy cockpit of a plane. There was smoke and the deafening din of engines straining to give power.

A squeaky voice shocked him into the moment. It was coming over his headphones under a leather cap or helmet; he looked to the side and saw the captain seated next to him. Both men fought to regain some power from the floundering bomber. They were hit badly and the plane was doomed.

"Gerry, it's you!" Kel screamed.

"Well who else, you Burke!" came the reply, the high nasal tone on the headphones sounding almost comical. "I'd rather be down the bloody pub."

"Next life!" shouted Kel.

"It's a date," squeaked back the captain. "Everyone has either bailed or is dead, and it's too late for you or I my friend."

Kel looked behind at the empty shell of the rattling, slowly disintegrating fuselage. A Lancaster Bomber peppered with flack and enemy fire, dark and smoke-filled, straps and metal sheeting fluttering in the wind. The leather straps of his head-set tugged violently at him and he faced forward to meet his fate."

"Good to know you Gel," said Kel.

"Same here mate. Here, do you know what they're going to call us when they find us in two thousand years?"

"No, what?"

"Pete!"

The two men roared with laughter and they saw the telegraph poles beneath rise up to meet them. The terrain around was ablaze from the bombing raid and looked like hell. They seemed to cruise above these poles and wires for a split second, and there was an almighty shudder and a blinding flash. And then it was over.

Kel felt the jolt of fear pass through his body like a powerful wave, but was unconnected to it and he looked on like a passive observer in a lucid dream. There was nothing left in his past to confront him with, and Kel landed with a bump into his present existence. He had felt the fear, the dread, and it was over.

Now he waited, still and quiescent.

GATEKEEPER

As Kel surfaced into the first inklings of consciousness there was a message from deep within him. Do not think or reflect until you are past the gatekeeper. Do not question yourself.

When Kel came to, he found himself sitting tailor fashion on a hard floor. He opened his eyes and looked around a dark room, and realised he was in a cell of sorts. A dirt floor and stone walls the décor. He looked down at his body and saw he was dressed in some oriental pants, perhaps a *dhoti*. It was hot and humid and he felt acutely aware of himself.

In the dim light he discerned another figure in the cell, bearded, dirty and disheveled. He looked to be meditating. Kel knew this man? He could not think who, and then wondered with a shiver, who he himself was. He looked at the meditating figure again and something resonated in his mind.

The door crashed open, and in barged a guard dressed in an exquisite uniform of leather and fur, embroidered with silver and gold inlays on the leather. A large saber like sword hung from the belt, which was studded with gems, and two brightly coloured feathers adorned one shoulder.

"His Excellency the Nabob will see you now," said the guard. "Remember you are to keep your eyes cast down until he gives you permission to look at him. Any breach of this will result in instant execution by decapitation. You will also address him as 'My Lord'. Do you understand?"

Kel nodded his concurrence, stood shakily to his feet and followed the guard out, looking back at his cellmate, who had not opened his eyes. 'I know this man', he said to himself, coming to his senses rapidly. He felt sharp and clear, crystal clear, as if the murk of confusion had been burnt from his mind. But he could not think who he himself was!

He was led through a dungeon lined with cells, up some stone steps and through a wooden door into a palace of such exquisite beauty it took Kel's breath away. Servants dressed in brightly coloured uniforms moved around here and there, eyeing him with curiosity.

They walked along a passageway that was bordered by a courtyard, the centre of which was a lush tropical garden. Kel heard the strange melodious cry of a peacock, and noticed other brightly coloured birds in the rich foliage. This palace was a good attempt at creating heaven on earth, but something was wrong. What gave it away was the sense of fear Kel felt all around him, fear generated by the man he was about to meet, perhaps. He, strangely, felt nothing, but was enchanted by his surroundings, and traipsed almost nonchalantly after the plumed guard, looking here and there at each new fine and delicate surprise.

He was led into a white marble hall, the middle of which was dominated by a large couch, upholstered in a deep rich red. Upon it sat a man, his back to the door. A servant stood before him, eyes cast down, and who then backed away slowly, bowing deeply. The guard turned and indicated to Kel to keep his eyes down, and he obeyed. There was a stool in front of this Nabob, whose fine white silk dress seemed to shimmer with light. Kel sat in front of him and waited, staring at the marble floor.

"I hear you are a wise man and talk about freedom," said the royal, young by the sounds of his voice.

"I am an ordinary man, and do what I do, my lord," replied Kel.

"Well I hope you do it well because I want you to set me free today. You see beyond me you can go no further, for I am the gatekeeper," said the Nabob.

"For whom?"

"That does not matter. All you need to know is that this is as far as you go. Beyond this there is nothing. I have tired of all this luxury, and the cries of all my dead adversaries haunt me both day and night. So now it is up to you to release me from this burden."

"And if I fail my lord?"

"Then you will lose your head directly after the interview and that will be the end of it, and when I say the end of it, I mean it. The end of it!" and Kel felt the Nabob's eyes staring at him.

Kel, at that moment, looked him squarely in the eyes. They were dark and intense, and more than a little surprised at this affront to the rule. "Then I have nothing to lose," said Kel calmly.

The Nabob held his hand up to stop the guard from hauling Kel away, and dismissed him with a perfunctory wave. The guard left the two men alone.

"You are the seventh I have met, and I hope I do not have to add your head to my collection," said the Nabob. "It has been custom here for none to cast their eye upon me, as I am a god incarnate. Only my father could—not even my mother, and those that did soon paid the price, as will you…maybe." He laughed the laugh of a spoilt child, someone who always got their way. His hair was so black it almost appeared blue, and a neatly trimmed moustache topped a thin cruel mouth; the eyes had the fervid look of an absolute ruler. He was the cat and regarded Kel as a cheeky but lucky mouse.

"So who were the six poor souls you disposed of? What was their crime?"

"Non compliance, and being different. They were not conforming to the standards our society holds to. My job is to make them conform or, as you say, dispose of them. That is why I am the ruler here and none, except the very lucky or unlucky, can cast their eyes upon me. I repeat, you can go no further than me, unless you set me free from all this," and the Nabob gestured at his surroundings.

"Who controls you, do you know?" Kel asked.

"No one known to me. Enough of your questions, what do you seek? What do you know?"

"So what do you want to know?" Kel kept eye contact.

"I am tired of all this," and he again waved his hand around at his surroundings. "It is time to move on, which can only mean having less rather than more. Tell me what is your understanding of the truth, and the nature of reality as the holy men see it."

"I don't know about the holy men, but for me truth is seeing things as they are without personal preference. And the nature of reality is that all this is one."

"One what?"

"One light that reflects everything, our spirit if you like; that spark in you which causes your discontent."

"Why?"

"Because you do not realise it. Your restlessness is due to not seeing it in yourself. It knows only itself and gives life to all. It is life itself."

"So why don't I recognise it?" The young ruler leant forward.

"Remember…it only recognises itself, so to find it you have to surrender to it totally—for it is the Absolute. It is so pure and so bright that to get anywhere near it would char you to ashes in a moment, never to return the same again. You would immediately die to who you think you are, and yet still be present. Are you ready for that, oh prince?"

"I am ready, but why don't I see it?"

"Because you mistakenly believe yourself to be that which your senses tell you are; what your conditioning, and the ways of the world, tell you you are. These senses, which have become so powerfully identified with the gross physical world, will disappear at death."

"Then what remains?"

"What remains is something through and above them, something that exists in those mangos and peacocks in your garden, something that runs through us all. Our gift is that we can reflect on it, find it, and become aware of that most subtle presence. Only then will you begin to taste the ecstasy of the infinite, the bliss of your true self. Eternal, free and complete!"

"What method must I follow to achieve this? And beware your answer. The last man to tell me I had to renounce everything and rot in the forest, lasted but a few moments."

Kel laughed despite himself. "You have to be very, very interested, and know that everything you see, touch, and meet is none other than yourself. When you realise this you will act accordingly. Otherwise you will always be lost in your anger, your greed, your lust, and your attachment to what you mistakenly take to be real. What is real lasts forever; find that in yourself."

"How?" The young prince persisted.

"By desiring it, by desiring it a lot. But first you must find that in yourself, then you must concentrate your attention on it, and in this way you will understand who you are at the deepest level. When this understanding dawns, it will be effortless."

"How to do it?"

"By finding that spark of spirit in you. When you do, stay with it, and one day you'll rejoice because fear and doubt will automatically drop off you, like water off a duck's back."

"So you are in this state?"

"I am on my way," Kel continued. "Thoughts have less meaning for me, and are less intimidating, and I satisfy my senses in a moderate way, so slowly, slowly I am seeing more and more."

"Are you a celibate?"

"None of your business!"

"Whoa, you push your luck." The young man's eyes darkened and the ironic smile vanished.

"Don't you see, from a place of identification in the gross physical world to an unknown and subtle infinity we slowly rise, burning and suffering our transgressions as we go. But go we must. The greater the resistance, the greater the anguish. I know it is there, the Absolute is there. That ecstatic freedom from all illusion is there, and neither your sword nor anything else can deter me now. That is my greatest realisation. All this is illusion!"

Kel stopped and looked down. He struggled to remember something in him that gnawed at his very soul. Some purpose...a quest. What the hell am I doing here? Now at the gate? Being distracted?

"One man told me," the Nabob interrupted his inquiry, "that the mind is only thoughts, and that they have no substance of their own accord. Why then do my thoughts intimidate me?"

"Your thoughts are merely memories projected into the future and have no real substance if you don't act on them. If you do act on them you will have to pay for the consequences of those actions. Remember there is only one, and we are all of us this one, so of course we will have to suffer and enjoy the fruits of our actions. There are no mistakes. Life is the healing hand of God," said Kel, and he looked down, bewildered for a second. He snapped out of it quickly.

"So there is a God?"

"Everything is God, you must listen if there is to be any change," said Kel resolutely, and indicated that he would like a drink.

"The Nabob called for water, and continued his interrogation. "Am I to suffer all of my transgressions? Surely they were the result of my ignorance?"

"That is in the hands of God, and remember he sits inside you, and has seen all. You see He is you, She is you, It is you," said Kel and he took a long draught of scented water, and waited a moment before continuing. "But it is my belief, and this is just a belief, that once you have seen the light inside yourself and continue in the same ignorant way, then surely this will not go unseen; your selfish actions will be your own punishment."

"You speak wisely yet you profess not to be realised," said the Nabob.

"I am realising day by day that all this is through the grace of God, and that is all I know."

"God?" The prince put his hands up and out to the sides.

"God is the realisation of who I am."

"Who is it?"

"It is you and it is always, but that's the mystery—something that resides in you, is you, and something in which you reside. The limited mind will never be able to grasp this, because it is ungraspable. It is us, yet is untouched by us. I am only leaving behind what I don't need, what is not eternal, and that is my only claim to wisdom."

"So where is your God?" asked the prince.

"Everywhere!" answered Kel.

"Does he have a name?"

"There are many names because we cannot see it. A wise man said that the most appropriate name for the Absolute is, 'I am that I am.' That about sums it up, and you need to know no more."

"Don't tell me what I need or not! What is it?" the Nabob persisted.

"It is that which is in the heart of all living beings, it is who you are. How to explain? It is that which gives you movement, that which lights the way, that which holds us together, and the togetherness itself. It is everything. Call it what you like, I am sure He doesn't care," answered Kel.

"So it is a He."

"Without a Her there is no existence. It is both; just find it in yourself and stay with it, then all these questions will drop away, as will your fear and doubt."

"How to stay with it?" asked the Nabob, leaning forward, eyes shining.

"Be yourself, that's all. Look deep within yourself and listen to others, and I mean really listen." Kel stopped for a moment and smiled at the young prince. "If you have time and are able to make the effort, then discover who this I is when thought is not present. It will be difficult at first for the ego will wish to control. But persistence will pay off, and when you are in the substratum of the transitional I, it will lead you to the goal you say you desire. To be free of all this; to that from which this I comes from; to your true self. Then at least, after a taste of that fruit, you will discover if you truly wish to be free."

"What about me in deep sleep? I do not know myself to be. Maybe I am very happy, but I don't know myself to be, and that does not satisfy me. Where is this 'I am that I am' in such a situation?"

"In the field of existence there are always opposites." Kel tapped the top of his head. "The unconscious demands the conscious, its opposite; and vice-versa. Your true self runs through both. Activity demands rest. You at peace…demand nothing."

"I wish to know this self in sleep. Now that would satisfy me."

"You see, already you are trying to control," said Kel. "You must relinquish control of that demand by your mind to know and control the truth in order for it to be apparent to you. Do you see the simplicity of it? It is You! It's always there, and requires your conscious recognition of that fact, but you will never be able to hold onto it. Do you understand? You will never be able to hold onto it. It is too pure to be captured by the mind. Do you understand?"

The prince grunted his understanding.

Kel waited for a further sign of understanding, but none was forthcoming. "A great teacher once said that this life is a bridge for the soul to pass from the temporal to the eternal, and that no house can be built upon it. Nothing physical, nor anything that can be grasped by the mind. We are just passing through, and what you create of yourself will create you. What is in you and you do not create, will destroy you. A simple message! Understanding this deeply will point to the right way for you."

The Nabob nodded, and looked thoughtful on his silk throne. He looked down and cupped his chin in his hand.

Kel continued, "You will continue to see this mirage, but you will know it to be a mirage. That is wisdom; that is real knowledge."

"So you are a sage?" asked the Prince.

"A sage is someone who doesn't have to change anything, because he himself is already free of any illusion, any mirage."

"So they stay still?"

"A sage keeps still and change happens around him, or her. They need not move as they have reached the stage in their mind where there are no impressions, where no division exists."

"They should go and wake up the world!" said the prince, snapping his thumbs.

"And create yet another religion! There are enough differences in those to keep us separate from each other for lifetimes. A holy person uses their mind to destroy that part in itself which divides consciousness, and regards itself as separate. Then see what happens!"

"But you..."

"I am an ordinary man, on my way and understanding, by the grace of God, more and more each day with every new adventure."

"I would like you to stay here at the palace, and we can continue this discourse daily," said the Nabob. "We will make life very pleasant for you here. Here you need not move, and your greatest desire will be our pleasure."

"I thank you, but I am on some kind of quest that I don't totally understand yet," answered Kel. "And I know that you have been put in my way to stall me, and to test me. But I will not be fooled any longer."

"Your quest can wait, you will stay!"

"No, I cannot! I need to be on my way, but I am honoured by your offer. Thank you."

"It is not an offer, it is an order. You will stay here or else you will be put to the sword," said the Nabob in an unyielding tone. The spoilt child had returned.

"I will tell you a story," said Kel, taking a sip of water. "There was a very famous and powerful yogi, and so mesmerising was his power that it caught the attention of the god and goddess in heaven. They decided to test this yogi and manifested as a wandering mendicant, and came to the door of his house. The mendicant gained an audience with the yogi and sat with him, asking questions about his power."

"I am very powerful," said the yogi. "Look at this."

Nearby an elephant was passing by with his mahout, and the yogi with one stroke of his hand felled the elephant, it collapsed unconscious to the ground.

The yogi laughed, and looked over at the mendicant, a look of pride and triumph in his eyes.

"That is amazing," said the mendicant.

"Watch this," said the yogi, and with another sweep of his hand the elephant revived, and stood up.

"The yogi laughed and looked around at the mendicant. But the mendicant had disappeared into thin air. And the yogi at once realised he had been in the company of God, but had not recognised it."

"So you are saying that pride stops us from seeing God?" The prince leant forward on the couch, a look of interest laced with mischief on his face.

"Yes, that's right. This was told to me by my teacher." Kel looked up suddenly, and a jolt of awareness shot through him. "My teacher," he repeated, closing his eyes, trying to remember.

Kel sat there looking at his hands, and he suddenly looked up at the young man opposite him with a start. "I have seen you before, and I am not sure where, but recognition of that is part of this quest I am on."

"Playing the madman will not help you, but I find you interesting. Now, we will take you to your quarters."

Kel stood up; "I'll be on my way."

"This is your last chance, you must stay!"

"I will not be fooled any longer, nothing you do can stop me!"

"Guards, guards!" the Nabob screamed, and three guards rushed in. Two of them grabbed Kel roughly by the arms, pulling him off balance, and he sagged between them.

"Will you stay?"

"I am seeing through this game, so just get this over with, whatever your part is in this drama."

"The man is a madman," said the prince, now not so confident. He appeared somewhat in distress, as if reluctantly controlled by some hidden higher power. "Take him to the alter room, but let him walk alone, don't drag him. Then strip him, and leave him there."

"Listen prince, you are being used like a pawn in another's game. Look to yourself for salvation," cried Kel, as he left the marbled room, flanked by the robust and ornate guards.

✳   ✳   ✳   ✳

Kel was escorted out, and followed the guards through the luxurious palace. He was taken up a magnificent staircase, at the top of which was a wooden door and behind it a long spiral staircase led to what must have been the highest point in the palace, into the tower.

His mind was now firmly set on meeting with the perpetrator of this drama. He was seeing quite clearly through the game. Whatever's next? Kel thought.

He found out soon enough at the top of the stairs. They emerged on a high tower, and opposite, some forty feet away, stood an identical tower. He looked down to the rocks, hundreds of feet below him. Between the towers a walkway hung tight and taut, about seven inches in width. From it hung a banner, or perhaps a flag, with some symbolic markings on it. There were guards on the opposite tower, and they were laughing and pointing at him. He looked down, and suddenly felt very dizzy, and took a step back and looked up. The guards behind him pushed him out onto the walkway, and he fell to one knee.

"Bastard," he cursed under his breath. He was not good at heights, and knew he should not show weakness. He stood and walked on, as if balancing on a curb, or walking an imaginary line on a walkway, and forced himself not to look down beyond the narrow walkway. 'It's a fucking game,' he cursed again. He just could not face the prospect of falling off, cracking his head open, and waking up in a new environment; he had had enough of dying. He was at the gate and about to enter, and he knew it.

He reached the other side and shot a derisive glance at the smirking guards. They stripped and pushed him into a room—the strangest room he had ever been in. It was like being inside a ball, so perfect was the sphere, and it was totally white. He sat in the middle and waited.

Nothing happened for what seemed a long time, and he kept his eyes closed, and resolved not to move until he had accomplished his mission. He would have to move no further, he reasoned, as he was at the centre, through the gate and in the heart of the residence. His awareness of his current situation was returning rapidly, and he now remembered seeing the young prince before and gasped in surprise; he had been one of the crew on the space station that had been sucked into the singularity.

He continued to concentrate his attention on his mission and wondered what more mischief would be put in his way. He resolved to be impervious to any more pain, threats or diversions, and in a flash he remembered Baba laughing at some absurdity, Lua buying him a beer when they first met, Lyle and their laughter, and the planet Gaya. He gasped again as a torrent of memory flooded his awareness.

Then by the sheer force of his will, he kept his attention squarely on the fact that no matter what, he was going to meet the...meet the...? Strangely, the identity of the perpetrator of all this eluded him, but he would not be knocked off the scent. He sat in silence and waited.

*   *   *   *

There was some movement in front of him, and he opened his eyes. He sucked his breath in and his head craned back to look into the eyes of Tanea or Lua, who looked imploringly over at him. It must be Lua, he thought. He said nothing, merely gaping at the figure before him. Her look turned to one of irony, laced with affection, and she handed him a soft woolen shawl, which he wrapped around himself.

Dressed in red silk and perfused with an exquisite aroma, she sat down opposite him on the floor. "You see, I am here too. This is my place and I have gone to the ends of my powers to get you here." She smiled warmly and shot him a look of such love that he felt any resistance to her cave in, he had to look away it was so intense. It augured a sexual and emotional longing in her which left him helpless in its potency. His memories of Lua powered back into his consciousness and he looked restlessly around him.

Kel looked at her and asked, "Who are you?"

"I am your queen, your empress, and your love. You and I have been destined to be together since the inception of time. We were parted eons ago and have been disturbed and agitated ever since, fretfully looking for each other over the vastness of space and time. And now I have found you and will never let you go again, my love."

"So who was parted, who were we?"

"Celestial beings my love, living in a heavenly realm and close to the source of all things. You then became fascinated by the physical realm and I have been seeking you ever since." Lua leant forward and held out her hand for his.

Kel took her hand and felt a surge of desire so strong he had to free himself of her grasp immediately. Tears welled up in his eyes and he swallowed hard.

"Slowly, slowly you will understand the intensity of our relationship. It's a little too much for you now, as you have been lost for a long time in the realm of the physical. You are here to stay with me for a while in this lap of luxury. The prince was just a test, to see if you were ready to re-enter our world. And you are—more than ready. You are one of us, my love. This drama has been set to get you here, and here, finally, you are. My heart is bursting with happiness. You are about to experience a level of sensual and emotional love beyond your wildest dreams."

"So who are you?"

"I am your Lua, my love."

"So who is Tanea?" Kel asked.

"A physical vehicle in order for me to manifest, to obtain your realm and find you."

"So who or what is the paramount power here?"

"There is no such thing in this realm, my love, we are merely together—together, forever, in a way unknown to the human senses. Don't you see—your restlessness has always been a longing for what you left long ago."

"You said something about the source of all things. What is that?" Kel watched her every move.

"That is outside and beyond any reflection on it. You must not weigh yourself down with such an inquiry. It is an experience beyond the intellect's grasp. It is, in fact, that which poses the question. Come with me and you will understand my answer."

"There is someone here, like you, who I have come to meet. I am on a mission and I must meet with him. His identity somehow eludes me." Kel was more in command of himself now, and less under the strange and exotic power that exuded from Lua.

"You will meet and understand all soon enough. Come with me and rest awhile, and I will weave you a story of unbelievable intrigue. Come into my heart my love; let me show you the pleasures of our realm. Trust me. You will not be disappointed."

He kept his gaze on the woman opposite him. Something was wrong. But he was more than intrigued by the story she had told him, which definitely had a smidgeon of sense to it—his eternal restlessness, his fidgety mind. He sought some way to test her, and two things rang with great clarity in the recesses of his mind. He kept them there and made a conscious effort not to openly think about them. This Lua had appeared, he realised with a jolt, some minutes after he had remembered her.

"Where did we first meet this time around?" Kel asked.

"On a beach. I bought you a beer," said Lua, smiling at the memory.

When you told me your story, I said something to you in disbelief. I said, 'Pull the other one, it's got…It's got what? Does that ring a bell for you?"

The woman thought for a moment and said calmly "I cannot remember. Do you not trust me? I will do anything to prove who we are."

"What is my name?" he asked curtly.

The woman paused for a second, and looked away. For the first time she seemed unsure and looked up, as if asking for guidance. She slowly caste her gaze down and looked him squarely in the eyes and said, "Kelsie."

"Nice try! Great likeness and a good act, but not good enough. Bloody hell, you nearly had me there. You are not Lua!" and he shot the woman a friendly smile, and closed his eyes.

✳   ✳   ✳   ✳

When Kel stole a peek minutes later, she had gone. He now settled back into his concentration, determined to meet whoever had directed that little bit of theatre.

Then it came with a bang—the Doctor! Yes the Doctor! That was it. Jesus I'm in a black hole, that mad bloody scientist. I'm still here and with it. Don't forget this, don't, don't, don't. He would not move until he met the Doctor. His mission was to talk him out of destruction, and if this failed, to stop him. He resolved not to forget this, no matter what, and he sat in the silence of this pure white orb, still and immovable.

After some minutes Kel laughed, and called out, "You have to do better than that, Doctor. I have seen through this little game of yours. That was not Lua; all this is a device of your making. You are no longer going to get into, or fuck with, my mind. Come and meet me, you coward. I dare you to!"

Silence.

"Stop your miscreant games Doctor. It's over. I am at the centre now, you have to meet me." Another pause, then Kel continued, "I know that that is Duncan, Carter's original, you are holding in the dungeon of this fairyland you've weaved around yourself here. So please do not insult your, or my, intelligence any further with this foolishness. I am not moving or saying anything more until we meet. I, like Duncan before me, come with a message from Gaya, that is all. Surely you must want to know why you cannot ignore me? Why I have been able to get so close? You cannot afford not to know, believe me. Your very continuance depends on me. Ignore me at your peril!"

He focussed his mind on meeting the Doctor and a silence descended in the orb.

There he sat and waited, and after what seemed like some hours of this intense concentration—when the physical pain of stillness had abated—he became aware that his body had gone, and that he again existed in some ethereal state. He kept his attention on getting to the centre, on meeting the Doctor, and not a thought interrupted this deep and arduous state.

So pinpointed was his mental concentration that he could be ignored no longer. It came to a point as if in a dark vacuum, and his soul sought an outlet. He sat on the edge of an explosion and managed to contain it, and keep his attention on his quest.

Energy passed through Kel at tremendous speed, and he was propelled outwards in every direction, like lightning looking for a channel. He exploded out of himself every which way and expanded to a realm that was neither out nor in. His conscious being became finer and subtler in the thick of this increase, this magnification of himself. The expansion reached a limit, and creaked to a halt. Kel was aware of himself and this most subtle level of expanded being, but he could focus on nothing for he was everything that was.

There was a brief pause of stillness in this outermost boundary of consciousness. He had totally let go, no longer being defined by parametres of anything physical or even mental. At its outermost point it had consisted of the subtlest form of energy, and in this form he could take the shape of anything, and illuminate it, but he stayed quiet, and free of any imagining that could create any distraction to himself.

The inward rush of sensation started slowly, but soon Kel was being propelled at enormous speed into himself. His state of mind now recoiled from its total surrender to space, and the contraction brought his powers of discrimination back into focus. With it came his understanding and acceptance of his present journey, and enabled him to see his ability to focus on any one thing, to take the shape of the smallest particle. He was what he was seeing, the observer and the observed. He was the totality of all the dimensions in the flow of time.

With a jolt he realised that everything that he is, is a conditioned state, programmed by habit and memory to gain pleasure and avoid pain. The only way to transcend it is the will to know the truth and the courage to surrender to it absolutely. This all occurs in the act of observing, and he now knew the way to completion of his quest.

He had mindfully transcended the state of consciousness to its very limit, to its finest most subtle extreme. His return to consciousness had empowered him with a crystal clear intention of what he now had to do. He knew that the Doctor could no longer place any illusion in his way. He sat still in this profound state of realisation and reached a previously unknown level of surrender and relaxation, and could wait forever, if need be.

.

ETERNITY'S WINDOW

Kel felt the solidity of a seat beneath him, and realised he was embodied again. He opened his eyes and was in a room with a strange distant echo to it, like muffled voices off in the distance.

"Who are you?" asked the voice.

When Kel blinked, he found himself sitting opposite the Doctor, who was dressed in white, as was he. The room was also white, so too the table that separated them.

"Doctor Ernst, I presume," said Kel.

"Yes," said the Doctor impatiently.

Kel took but a second to orient himself, "I am a messenger and I bring a plea from the planet Gaya. To please leave them alone to determine their own fate."

"You are a nuisance and must leave, or join me. Otherwise I will atomise and dispose of what little is left of you."

"Why haven't you done that already?"

The Doctor ignored him and said, "I need Gaya. It is the ground-seed for a new universe I have created."

"What right or authority do you have to impose your will on these people?"

"The certainty that I can achieve this absorption."

"That's just willful domination, Doctor! Are you unable to see that you have the potential to be so much more, more than just a despot?"

"Don't patronise me, you fool! You have no idea who you're dealing with, do you?"

"Ah come on, here's a group of people dedicated to doing something worthwhile, and making a difference. I repeat, what right do you have to impose your will on them?"

A wry smile flickered across the Doctor's face. "Your hollow plea has no effect on me. The people of Gaya did not respect me for who I am. In fact, they were outrageous for their lack of respect. I am not going to let them off the hook that easily. Now I repeat my first question, who are you?"

"I am from the beginning of the second millennium, and they tell me I am a previous incarnation of Lyle. I am here to ask you to re-consider, and if that has no effect, then to stop you. If I do not go back, you do not exist!"

The Doctor laughed a derisive and contemptuous laugh, and in this action he hardly moved; it was like the hiss of a snake. "I am surprised you have been able to come this far, but you have achieved the impossible—an interview with me. Why do you think that is so?"

"Because without me going back you know your very existence is threatened. I am a previous incarnation of you, and so it has fallen to me to either eliminate or enlighten you." Kel kept the Doctor's cold stare.

"Bah!" hissed the Doctor. "Your so called 'enlightenment' can only be achieved by those who desire it, remember? So no preaching please. God, what a bore!"

Kel grimaced, and crossed his legs quickly.

"That re-incarnation business is nonsense, just because they have a machine that can measure the energy of death, bah!" the Doctor spat out again. "The arrogance of humanity! What a self-absorbed, greedy state you lot are in!"

"Doctor, listen…"

"No, now you listen to me. I have discovered a power of immeasurable dimensions, and I am able wield it as I wish. I can play with these dimensions, this form, and what you believe to be your souls. What can an insignificant piece of conscious flotsam like yourself do to obstruct my course?"

"Number one, I won't go away. Number two, you don't exist without me, believe me, so insignificant I am not; your game is up; without me you are nothing!

The Doctor took one deep breath and looked over at Kel with the hint of a smile, a sympathetic smile towards one so painfully disillusioned.

"And number three," Kel continued, "you are acting like a lifeless and soulless being. Can't you see that this power you have discovered is not being used by you, it is using you!"

The Doctor hesitated for the briefest of moments, then laughed and said, "I would make your existence very uncomfortable if you continue to annoy me. You are either with me, or against me."

"That's fascism, Doctor, and it always destroys itself in the end. With all this power you have a chance of actually doing something positive in the universe, and that is so rare. If you show compassion now you have a chance at immortality—otherwise you're doomed. Can't you see that?"

The Doctor laughed again, "First I get Gaya, and then guess what? I come for your age through the timeless realm of anti-matter. Your world, your sun, and your universe will be mine, at the speed of light—as will everything in between, so your existence or non-existence is of little consequence to me."

"Oh my…"

"By then it will be clear who I am. There will be no other power but me; so you see, this ridiculous conversation is a waste of time."

"Oh my god! Your ego has its sights set on godhead, and you'll end up the greatest slave in any realm or dimension. You are being used, Doctor, don't be a fool!""

"Utter nonsense!"

"This power is using you to cause havoc because that's its nature, that's all it knows."

"I can tell that you have spent time with that superstitious Baba, and his archaic mythology," said the Doctor, "and you call me a fool."

"And you are going to be its servant until the end of time," Kel persisted, "Use your power for good; let Gaya go."

"No," said the Doctor, and their eyes locked together in stalemate.

The Doctor broke the silence. "Everything is in place; even now I have some influence on Gaya, and was aware of your coming before you turned up here."

"Then why do you ask who I am? You don't even know my name!"

"Your name is of no use to me. I was aware that something was on its way here, so I deployed some minor delaying tactics to keep you away. You see, it is possible to use a person's negative energy against them."

"Bloody voo-doo!"

"Maybe! But you are a tenacious individual. Anyway I already have some control on Gaya, I am already there!"

"Well," Kel said, "I am here now, to stay if need be, so you see your delaying tactics didn't work. They failed."

"Ah, but you see, I have Duncan here, and through him have been able to get at his twin, the humanoid Carter, without either of them realising it. Do you realise how many pathways of power are being opened to me?" said the Doctor, his eyes at once evil and exultant.

"So, you can control an organic robot from a great distance," Kel spat back. "So what?"

"I cannot, as yet, get to the originals through the humanoids that were with me on the station, but we are working on that, and will soon have an army on this proud little planet of Gaya—my army."

Kel suddenly thought of Carter, how much he liked him, and an anger burned somewhere deep inside.

"Those that are with me will be exalted. I can control consciousness, as I am the puppeteer! Carter works for me, without even being aware of it. So any ideas they may have of bringing conflict against me are futile."

Kel remembered his spin in the Briefing chair; the loss of energy at the end of his maiden space flight that put an end to his relationship with Lua; the delay when he first traveled out of body, and the shadowing of Carter on his way to Baba's.

A dull thud echoed around the bare walls as Kel thumped his fist on the table. He stood, briefly, and then sat slowly down again and took a deep breath. "It's hard enough for all of us to deal with an ego, but a pathetic, self-interested monster like you is unacceptable, totally unacceptable, do you understand?"

"You have become tiresome with your silly comments about stopping me. I don't care whether you go back or not. If Carter was anywhere near you when they lifted you out of your body, you probably don't have one to go back to."

Kel sat still, staring intently at the Doctor. "I am never going away, I will be there at every turn to haunt and distract you. I am your worst nightmare, make no mistake. You are something to do with me, and your actions lack compassion and mercy...and are, I repeat, unacceptable. Do I make myself clear?"

"I sit on the threshold of eternal consciousness and unlimited power," replied the Doctor, calmly. "I am about to break into your world and swallow up everything; you could help me if you wish. Your reward would be beyond your wildest dreams. You could then spend time with Lua, that other, as you put it, organic robot. Until you tired of her, that is."

"I could never be with you, you morbidly self-absorbed shithead! And you listen to me. If I don't go back, then you don't exist, it's over! You are not yet the master of the past, and that past is here to destroy you."

"You are unaware of my power," sneered the Doctor. "I keep you in a pocket of energy while the forces of creation rage around us, and it is only my interest in you that stops you from imploding into nothing at the speed of light."

"Doctor, you are using consciousness for your self-willed desire. Please, please, please re-consider."

The Doctor laughed, shaking his head.

"The worst part of us humans is our greed. It nearly destroyed my world. Can I ask you to look into your soul and re-consider?"

"No," said the Doctor.

"You have also attracted the attention of a power source that will reek havoc on all existence. Please think what you are doing, I implore you, for your sake and ours."

"For my sake, bah! I accessed the limited consciousness of you wretched human beings in order to manifest, and now I am here—I have woken! You have no idea what you are talking about. I am consciousness!" The snake was back, and the final hiss of the Doctor's sentence affronted Kel's ears.

"You do not exist without me, and you are not yet at the throat of my world. Only the fire of our dying sun will put an end to the Earth, and you cannot control my consciousness because I am, and let's face it, you are not. Your very existence is questionable." Kel sat back, calm and still.

"Existence is nothing without me," said the Doctor.

Kel said nothing.

The Doctor lifted both hands in a gesture of giving and said, "There are a million emotions and feelings going on here in my world at this very moment; there is also the most amazing scientific discovery going on as well. The consciousness that opposed me here is dead and gone, that which surrendered to me exults in itself. I will share just a fraction of it with you. Then we will see who is, and who isn't! Here, have a taste."

Kel suddenly felt a rush of extreme ecstasy; so great was the feeling he had to shut his eyes and bend forward and hold his abdomen to stop himself exploding. It was a mixture of happiness and sadness, of comedy and tragedy. Tears flooded his eyes. It was a relentless tsunami of excitement and ardour, and he gasped at its power over him.

"Join me," said the Doctor.

Kel looked deep within himself and saw that these extreme feelings were not his, they were part of him, but they were not his experience. He was sucking on them like a...."You parasite," gasped Kel, still holding his belly. "You have nothing yourself, so you suck it out of others, like a..."

"Look deeper, this is just the experience of a few. Think if it were the experience of billions, and as you get stronger, of universes. Think of that, the intensity of it!"

The tidal wave of passion continued and was unremitting, and Kel was becoming drunk with the emotions that coursed through him. Hundreds of dramas swirled through his being leaving nothing still. He was intensely alive, and madness loomed large. The drama within reached a peak and was unbearable, and he was about to appeal to the Doctor to halt this power that surged through him like a locomotive on its way to heaven or hell, when the intensity suddenly abated. Now a feeling of power, some control in the midst of this passionate madness. Invincible, a peace descended on Kel, and everything about him became still. A great power loomed, readied for his acceptance.

You know this isn't right, you know this isn't real; don't sell out, no, no, no! Kel's mind clawed its way back into his awareness, and sought not to reason, only to act. He screamed loud and hard, summoning whatever energy reserves were available to him. He screamed and screamed to exit himself from his illusion. "No!"

Immediately he found himself back with the Doctor. Neither of them had moved.

"We have a word for you where I come from!" Kel said with a grimace.

The Doctor raised an eyebrow.

"You're a wanker!" Kel spat the words out, and took two deep breaths. "You have nothing so you drain life out of those around you.

You exult in others to provide you with a vestige of life. You care only about your pitiful, self-absorbed little self, and I want nothing to do with you. Do I make myself clear?"

The Doctor stared at Kel, still and emotionless. He then flung a hand out to the side and snapped his fingers, and a large portal opened up with a flash. Beyond it was a swirling cauldron of luminescent light, its intensity overwhelming. Kel looked away.

"There is your demon. I accessed and created this in order to manifest," said the Doctor.

Kel strained to look into the light.

"Welcome to the new beginning. Therein lies your future, and the future of everything and everyone you have ever known. It is the realm of anti-matter, a superhighway to your world, and soon we'll be on our travels—sooner than you, or those fools on Gaya, think."

"We're not going anywhere, believe me." Kel cupped his hands over his eyes.

"You see you have in ways unbeknown to yourself, assisted in this new beginning. The fact of you being here gives me a route there, to your world, in ways and means that are being investigated right now, at the speed of light. And I must say, I like your spirit; if your world is filled with such spirit then this creation will be all-powerful. You could say that I have orchestrated all this; you being here now is no mistake."

"You bloody sicko! We have succeeded in getting here, and now we are going to stop you," said Kel. He got up and edged his way forward towards the bright glare of the portal, shielding his eyes from the fierce light. He bent slightly at the waist and held one hand out in front of him, unsure of where the realm of anti-matter started."

The Doctor stood and approached the portal, and looked into it wide-eyed and triumphant. "All that you regard existence to be is but an effect of this," he said, waving an arm at the light. "One billion and one particles of matter to one billion particles of anti-matter. When they collide and cancel each other out, that which is left over is existence, or rather, what appears to be existence to your limited senses. Just a slight lopsidedness in favour of matter that enables existence to be."

"We are not just a lump of matter as time will tell soon enough," said Kel, turning to face the Doctor.

"Ha!" cried the Doctor contemptuously. "Time is just the fact that matter decays more slowly than antimatter. That's all. It's just like a scientific test gone wrong because the agents of the experiment do not cancel each other out immediately." The Doctor now turned to face Kel, "You are a mistake, that is all," and he laughed.

"Our only mistake is producing a mutant like you. The best part of you got lost somewhere in the wiring between Lyle and your faulty circuits. You are the mistake, and mistakes can be rectified."

The Doctor maintained eye contact, inches away from Kel. "Now we have to find some game to entertain you with."

"You are not going to get rid of me, Doctor. Ever!"

"At the end of this universe there will be a condition called maximum entropy," the Doctor continued, "and at that point all the processes of nature will halt. Energy will be uniformly spread throughout the cosmos. Time will cease, for there will be no direction for it to travel in. This is our definite destiny—this absolute randomness."

"So fucking what! Are you listening to me? I am not going away."

"The fate of existence after that cannot be computed because there is insufficient data, but I will be there. Do you understand me? I will be there. You will not be, so enough of your empty threats, and do not insult me any further. That is a warning, your first and last."

Kel looked at the portal, then at the Doctor. He had no idea what to do next.

"Trust me! Don't spit on me! I have found the way. If you trust me everything can be yours." So saying the Doctor placed an arm on his shoulder, and Kel felt its weight and gentle pressure.

Kel closed his eyes and sought guidance deep within himself. He suddenly remembered the six-syllable mantra he had been given and said it to himself, expecting nothing in return. At that moment Baba's face appeared in his mind's eye and said, 'He is now in a body and is yours. Be quick, do what you must. Now!'

Without a moment's hesitation Kel flung his arms around the Doctor and held him in a bear hug, lifting him just barely off the ground.

The Doctor's look of surprise soon turned to scorn and disdain, and he smiled imperceptibly. "You fool!" he said, "You have no idea what you are dealing with, do you?"

Another moment passed and his look turned to shock, horror, and disbelief as Kel started to edge his way towards the portal. The Doctor was under the power of another. He had overlooked something, something that cannot be measured. And that which cannot be measured now held him in its grip.

"Put me down you fool!" he screamed, and struggled with all his might, twisting and kicking Kel where he could. "This can't be, no, no, no," he pleaded, "Tell me what you want?"

"Nothing! It's too late. Soon you will be nothing," said Kel.

"Please stop, listen, no you cannot do this, no, no, no, I will let Gaya go. I promise, please, please!"

"You are mine, Doctor," said Kel, using every ounce of concentration and strength to keep his grip on his panicking captive. Slowly he moved on, impervious to the pleas and lashings of the Doctor.

Suddenly the whole room shook as a roar filled the air. Kel lost his balance and fell on one knee, his grip on his prey intact. Something was awakening; he must be quick. He struggled on, edging closer and closer to the brink of oblivion.

His opponent, gaining in strength, had now calmed a little. He stopped biting and kicking, and his attention became more focussed, calculating.

The room shook once more—a terrible shake, and another roar of some energy. Kel knew that the moment must be now. Inches away from the portal, he could move no further.

As he prayed for strength, his armlock on the Doctor was suddenly broken, and in shock and horror he found himself locked, chest to chest with the Doctor. He looked slowly up into his adversary's eyes and a shockwave of fear blasted him from the inside out. He was looking into the eyes of the most terrifying sight, for where the Doctor's face had been Kel now looked into the eyes of the demon. Its look was one of absolute scorn, hate, and disdain. This was evil incarnate.

Kel as if instructed from above did not look away, yet his guts screamed with fear and he could not move for they were locked in mortal combat. The eyes and face he looked into were part human, part reptile, amphibian and insect. The head was scaly and angular, diamond-like, merciless and cold-blooded. Kel stared into this abyss of darkness, paralysed.

"I am with you, no fear." Baba's voice suddenly emerged deep in the recesses of Kel's consciousness, "This beast knows only itself, can only recognise hate and fear. Ignore it and you will defeat it. No fear, I am with you. It cannot harm you. Remember who you are."

Encouraged, Kel locked on to the demon's stare of hate, and blew away what fear he could. A psychic battlefield had opened up between them, and from the corner of his vision he saw a stream of red lights hurtling towards him from the outer edge of the demon's deadly stare. His observation of them caused a stream of white lights to emanate from a region above his eyes, and these sped off to meet the oncoming missiles, destroying them with an explosion that shook the two bodies locked in deadly duel.

An army appeared in front of Kel's vision through the intensely angered eyes of the demon—an army of such ugly proportions that he felt everything in him tug him towards retreat, but he held his ground, and the fear passed through him. Goblin-like faces on squat bodies, shouldering weapons of destruction and in disciplined platoons started its advance. As they did so a brilliant swirling light, like a giant white-hot discus emerged from a place beneath Kel's chin, and hurtled on towards the aggressor's army. Another thunderous explosion and a blinding flash of white light left nothing unscathed except the eyes and the face of the demon. The explosion had been nuclear, light, heat and energy had burst out of a vacuum, and the effects were devastating, blasting and annihilating everything in Kel's field of vision.

Kel realised that many unseen dimensions existed between them, and in a flash of light the demon separated from Kel's chest and retreated. It grew to enormous size, and a battlefield created. Kel, no longer locked in its embrace, was left holding the sagging body of the Doctor, while the demon stood before him at the portal of anti-matter, of oblivion. It roared defiantly, and brandished multiple arms, each bearing a weapon of destruction. Its mouth sprouted tusks, hungry and all devouring, and what lips there were twitched convulsively. The noise shook everything around.

Kel let go of the Doctor's body and covered his ears, holding them tight. He took a deep breath. "Just do it," he told himself, stepping over the Doctor's body and approaching the demon. Baba's voice stopped him dead in his tracks.

"Stay with the Doctor, and throw him in the pit after you cut the demon's head off. Now you must seek the supreme-most power in yourself. Look up and rise above."

Kel looked aloft and made a simple plea for help and an answer hit him with laser-like speed and intensity. "Recognise yourself now, and forever!"

"I do," said Kel.

"We are the same!" demanded this divine presence.

Kel hesitated for a moment, and in that moment experienced the total sorrow and joy of the Absolute. Unbearable he recoiled from its intensity, gasping for breath. A dim orange light enshrouded him, and he looked up and confirmed, "We are the same."

Tears burst from his eyes and a searing shaft of light from above hit him on his forehead. Emerging from his embodied state like a spark from a flame that then exploded into the light of his consciousness, Kel found himself surrounded by a dark, phantom-like cloud that clung to his body like a monk's habit. Energy then burst out of his chest and he found himself holding a long staff in his right hand. Instinctively he gripped the staff, and felt its sleek, cold and menacing smoothness.

Free of his body, Kel faced the demon and approached it, encompassed with an absolute calmness, at total peace now, without a hint of any thought or feeling. In the background of his mind he knew himself to be Kel, but something far greater still was with him.

The demon dispassionately regarded this human form in front of it, and raised its weapons as if to let them fly all at once. Kel held up his left hand, and the beast stopped in its tracks, as if paralysed. There was another blinding flash of light somewhere above them, and Kel raised the staff, screaming at the top of his voice. A war cry.

At the moment Kel hoisted the staff vertically and screamed, the area above them swirled and reeled. Clouds of three distinct colours dominated the sky like an unfurling banner: a white, red and black whirlwind spun ominously above them.

A white and red light merged and ignited a streak of lightning, which hit the raised staff with the sound of a thunderous whiplash. A curved blade of searing sharpness was fashioned on to the outer edge of the staff.

All at once from every appendage of the demon, a missile of differing trajectory was hurled in Kel's direction and filled the whole scope of his vision. There was a cacophony of sounds from each weapon, and the demon reared back and screamed—one terrifying, piercing shriek of naked aggression and evil.

Kel pointed his spear at the oncoming salvo, and spun it around in a wide arc. Within a fraction of a second all the incoming missiles were annihilated by the reflection of the spear's intense light. A mighty explosion shook the ground beneath them as each incoming missile was incinerated by the spear's mysterious power.

The demon roared, outraged by the impotence of its weaponry, and the two faced off again. The demon moved forward towards the still form of Kel, so tiny with his bladed staff still held aloft. It looked down at its opponent, arrogant and angry, and its tail swept from side to side, keeping its massive body in balance. Kel kept still, his spear pointing towards his adversary's piercing eyes.

The sky above them swirled again like a whirlwind and from it shot a white lightning bolt which hit the staff from above, and another blade, this one double edged, and glinting with razor sharpness, stood parallel to the other atop the staff. A strange sensation reverberated through Kel, and his conscious body tingled with the ecstatic righteousness of divine power. He held the staff in front of him parallel to the ground, and stared wide eyed at the ornate, effulgent and razor sharp blades atop it. He then saw some movement in front of him.

In one swift movement, Kel pointed the staff towards the approaching beast; it stopped dead in its tracks. There was complete silence as the demon now considered its final charge, to destroy and obliterate this obstruction to its will, the will to destroy and dominate. It's eyes focussed on Kel's form with the concentration of eons of stillness.

The ominous darkness overhead now loomed even blacker, and soon it was pitch dark. Kel could see nothing. A sudden clap of thunder shot a red bolt of lightening through the total blackness and struck the staff with a lightning smack, producing a third blade on the staff. Now three blades shone with a blinding intensity, illuminating Kel below. He knew this to be the ultimate challenge, the trident, its light the ultimate light.

He looked at the enormous beast before him, whose concentration had been focussed on Kel's tiny form, and for a fraction of a second a reflection entered his field of attention, a reflection that drained him of every ounce of energy. It was a doubt, and the surge of power dimmed within him. God no! Not now, not now! You can rise, you must rise! It is just doubt, don't falter. But it would not let him be, and suddenly Kel was momentarily helpless and alone. "I am not worthy," struck a devastating chord in his heart, and he faltered.

"No! Rise up!" demanded the voice in his head.

"This is too much, too much," he answered as fear now gushed through Kel's being like a torrential river. His legs shook, yet he did not retreat, he stood his ground and resolved to go down fighting. *What's happened? Where's my power?*

"You!" this presence boomed in his head, and a crack of a thunderbolt jolted him from his dread and apprehension. He felt an intense burning sensation between his eyes and held aloft the trident, and an earth-shattering roar rocked all the worlds as the demon reared back for its final assault. "We are the same!" the silent voice intimated again, filling Kel's consciousness with the divine word.

Kel looked directly above his head, grit his teeth, and said, "I am You," and then, in one gut wrenching, all encompassing moment, pushing all fear and doubt out into the void, "I am God."

Immediately an exquisite power was upon him, and an eerie silence descended upon this fight to the death. The dragon leapt, claws and jaws all embracing the tiny body before it, and in one clean sweeping motion, the trident swept around its final arc.

So pure was the intention of its bearer that nothing could stand in its way. It cut through the neck with ease, silently severing the demon's connection to consciousness.

Within a fraction of a second, a deafening, desperate shriek filled the air as the beast sensed its own end. And then a deathly silence as the demon's head fell to the ground, its giant body sinking slowly on its haunches, collapsing halfway into the portal. The atmosphere sizzled and crackled around them as the beast's body balanced precariously on the edge of absolute mass, and Kel returned to himself. The trident was gone, so too the robe and he felt deep within himself, in the bowels of his being, a presence stir, something dark and evil. *The Doctor! Get rid of the Doctor. Now!*

An intense flash of light forced him to open his eyes as the demon's body finally disappeared into the dazzling kaleidoscopic jaws of the portal. Kel found himself standing on its edge, absent-mindedly staring at the play of intense light over the Doctor's body in front of him. It moved, the Doctor was back. *Now! Now!*

He quickly sat behind the body and tried to shove the Doctor over the edge of the portal with his feet, he kicked hard but was too late; he had waited a second too long. The Doctor was definitely back and rapidly gaining in strength. Now Kel was alone, totally, no voice in his head to help him, and no divine presence. He had made the costly mistake of delay, and as he sought desperately in his mind for a final resolution, shoved with all his might to push the Doctor into oblivion forever.

The Doctor grabbed him, and the evil that had risen deep in Kel, now confronted him. "I am now the full power of existence and you will submit to my will," said the Doctor in a voice hauntingly calm and seductive. "Otherwise, in you go and an end to you."

"I ain't listening to you any more," said Kel, attacking with his full force, and gaining a neck hold on the Doctor. They grappled clumsily, light careening around them as they twisted this way, then that.

"In you go," said the Doctor.

This isn't working, thought Kel, struggling to complete his quest and finish off the evil in his arms. Then one memory appeared over the ocean of time. He remembered a wrestling move his older brother had taught him—to flip his opponent over—and he remembered squealing in delight as he flipped his elder sibling. In desperation he tried it now, and pulled hard at his opponent away from the portal. The Doctor's strength continued to increase at every second. His sense and control of gravity were returning and he soon would be able to wield it.

As Kel heaved his now writhing opponent away from the portal, he screamed one question at the Doctor, "What is my name?"

No answer from the Doctor.

"What's my name?" yelled Kel again.

This time the Doctor answered, his breathing steadying. "What use is your name? You know, and this is confirmed—you don't have a body to go back to, you are already dead!"

Kel felt a chill race through him, but he would not be put off track. "My name is Kel," he screamed, and as the Doctor was distracted by this simple fact, Kel abruptly changed direction and managed to flip the Doctor's body over his hip. And over they went, off out of the portal into the totality of the unknown—both of them.

For a moment Kel knew that this was not part of the plan and he heard a piercing scream from the Doctor, and a deafening roar behind it, like an echo of the beast he had defeated. Then there was an intense flash of light, then silence, and then nothing.

LOST & FOUND

Seven pairs of eyes peered out of the observation deck into the dark night around the singularity. The window of opportunity would be open for another eight minutes, and they were more than a little worried; Kel had been gone far longer than they estimated, and they feared the worst. Now Lyle and his team were constantly updating their calculations, pushing the window to the limit. The closer it got, the more intricate and difficult became the calculations.

Tanea was present too, her business finished on Gaya. She looked concerned and stared blankly at the black mass ahead of them. Lyle stood next to her, elbows leaning on the shelf of the observation window, chin resting on the palms of his hands. They said nothing, and the seconds ticked by.

"Theoretically there is no time in there—how could he be gone for so long?" said Lyle at last, agitated, straightening up and hopping from one foot to the other. "Oh my God Tanea, what have I done, what have I created here?"

Tanea gently rested her hand on his arm. "It's not over yet, I bet you at this moment they are making their escape." She stole a look at the seconds ticking away.

"Something is happening," someone shouted from the control centre behind them. Seven heads bobbed up in startled surprise.

"The mass is starting to lose power," the same voice echoed. "We need to get out of here, something's going to blow!"

Lyle looked at the read-out screens above the observation deck, eyes darting from one screen to another.

"What about Kel?" demanded Tanea.

"No sign, we need to get out of here and fast, she's going to blow!"

"Damn!" said Lyle and Tanea in unison.

"Work out the flight plan to get Kel back now," said Lyle and then at the top of his voice, "Now!"

Everyone around him except Tanea, sprinted off, and he said, "Get me in contact with Baba, now!"

Within seconds he heard Baba's voice, steady and stern. "Lyle, get Kel's body back to where you found it as quickly as you can. That is all, very quick, like a laser. He has done the job what he had to do and now it is in the hands of God. Be quick and get out of there. You have some moments but be quick. Just send him back, now."

"Launch Kel's craft immediately," cried Lyle

"But sir?" replied the captain of the ship about to transport Kel's body back.

"I said immediately dammit! Launch and fire off around the mass before it blows," cried Lyle, and he turned and swept his gaze toward the mass, then up at the control panels, his eyes wild with the moment, and he cried again, "Now!"

Within seconds Kel's craft was launched, and it sped off skirting the event horizon, building up speed for its whiplash jump back in time. Aboard it lay the body of Kel, and a highly trained skeleton crew to adjust to the rush to pierce through the space-time continuum. They set a course for the twenty-first century, and there was no stopping them now.

An abyss of intense red light emanated from the singularity, and the seconds ticked away as all eyes on board scanned the dials registering the energy that pulsed out of this celestial rogue.

"We've picked up a conscious life form," rang out the voice behind Lyle. "I'm putting tracers on it. We are making the jump in eleven seconds—tracers have locked on to life form. To which ship do I dispatch life form? Take your seats…Now!"

"Oh shit," cursed Lyle as the observation deck sped off for its jump, out of the way of the singularity's implosion into itself, the moment the portal to anti-matter shut completely. That would be the instant when all matter still held by its jaws would catapult out into space around it. "Haul it in," he cried, and he and Tanea landed in their seats just two seconds before they jumped to hyperspace.

The two craft made the jump simultaneously. The crew of the observation ship watched the explosion of the mass, as the window shut down and the illicit source of gravity released its plunder, all in one miraculous moment. It was a thunderous explosion of unbounded magnitude that created a shockwave and sent a shudder through all present. They rode a wave just in front of the line of fire. Tanea and Lyle looked over at each other, eyes wide, half smiling.

Lyle now anguished over his decision to haul in the life form. Had Kel's body left without its general, its consciousness?

"The life form? Is it Kel?" he called.

There was a long moment's silence.

"No, it's Duncan. Duncan is back."

Lyle and Tanea were out of their seats in a second. They turned, faced each other and embraced.

"My god, he did it, Kel did it" said Tanea.

But the thoughts of everyone on board were one. 'Where the hell was he?'

✳   ✳   ✳   ✳

Lost in an ocean of the timeless and dimensionless, a oneness without a second that spans forever. Some movements, then stillness, like the pause between the lud and the thud of a heart.

There is a mysterious miracle that happens from within this formless matrix, which can only be described as a self-willed desire to know the self. A self which is already perfect, and whole, and eternal. This is the single thread that unites all existence. It is pure awareness, the child of God. Formless and nameless, it spontaneously transforms into individual beings, into an energy that is searching for itself, and which in time initiates and completes its self-expression. It rises through all life forms and seeks higher and higher forms of expression, and its journey is forever

When the energy and desire for self expression is strong enough, there is a moment of reflection on the self in which the 'I' comes into focus, and at that instant the universe comes into perspective, and is created in our minds as something that appears to be real. It is the birth of the ego; the knowledge of an individual self, which masks an unfathomable force within us, a power beyond belief.

I am this power; I must get back. I must move on. Something stirred in this stillness.

Once an individual being is born there is a restlessness—a constant search for happiness and wholeness that is already the core of our being. But the die is cast: happiness appears to be outside of ourselves, and we are attracted, and attached to the pursuit of it. The mind in its restless search for pleasure, in truth, only seeks the master of itself. Here and now in this potential, a restlessness stirred, and looked outside itself, looked upon its vast body as a mystery. Not ready, not ready, I must get back, I must move on; this thought persisted.

It is a mystery more secret than secrecy itself that the soul can only take possession of itself by the individual simply being itself, and discovering that it is, in itself, the entirety of existence. Kel now floated in the matrix of this entirety, this formlessness, aware of the restlessness that did not belong, and he rose quickly to a single thought that he already was, I already am.

He saw himself as alone and vulnerable, and reached for the cloak of separation to protect him from the uprooting, from being lost in this singularity.

Follow that light! Surrounded by the light. Too much, focus on light, hold one bit in check and there, I'll be there. Yes that's it. That's mine…Held tightly to his ethereal heart he grasped his innate tendencies, the latent predisposition that guides a soul towards its destiny, as a miser would grasp his belongings; the dearest possessions of a soul seeking its own fulfillment. The greater light of total freedom spells insanity if the soul is not ready. Keep with the little light, a beam now. Follow it, keep it in sight.

The stateless state of Kel then burst through the realms on the innermost border of immortality into the world of spirits that stands between the physical and the eternal.

Fast movement now.

It is possible to become enamoured by this spirit world for eons and eons before the enlightened state of purity is breached, or a return to the physical achieved, but for Kel it posed no danger. He was astride a power of awesome magnitude that no being, ethereal or otherwise, would transgress. Kel's first inkling of reflected awareness since his jump into oblivion was like a dream; he saw himself on the back of a being of bright golden hue, and more or less of human form. On its back, where the shoulder blades should be, a silver white light glowed brightly to the left and right, as they shot through the night of spirits like a laser, flashing by and pushing aside any energy that might impede its progress. They surged through this realm, riding effortlessly on a current towards the flow of time, and finally burst out into the light of the physical universe.

He was now on his own, a pinpoint of light, yet faster than light, and aware of no energy around him other than the enormity of space. He pierced through and alongside opalescent galaxies that appeared to him as images. Some as in a war, or play of the gods, this one like a chariot, another like a raging beast with a lion's mane atop its head, another like a couple locked in embrace. The last play of light he was to witness in this dream resembled a cauldron, and he was headed for its outer edge, and then he was in deep sleep.

✳   ✳   ✳   ✳

Kel heard the sounds of waves lapping gently against the shore, and a muffled murmur of a voice. He felt the ground beneath him; he was on his back, his head resting on something soft. Slowly opening his eyes, he saw the twinkling lights of a sky full of stars, and wondered where he was. The taste in his mouth was strangely fresh after a sleep, and he swallowed and suddenly smelt a familiar scent of a tropical flower, a sweet perfume adrift a warm and gentle breeze. He then noticed above him an old acquaintance in the sky—the Plough, the Big Dipper of the stars, and he sat bolt upright, shocked and startled.

"My god!" he said, looking around him, realising he was home.

Shakey and Ken-eye talked quietly over at the bar, and the moonlight rippled over the sea; no one else was around. Kel looked at the moon—it must be after ten. He put his head in his hands and tried to remember, and formulate some idea in his mind as to what had just happened to him. Glad of the silence and solitude, he thought hard, and searched his memory high and low to make some sense out of his wild thoughts, and then his dream came slowly back to him, and his eyes widened, startled. The girl, the journey, Baba, his quest, the talking plants and a fight he had had, but the last part of the dream was a blur, and yes—the angel—he thought he had seen an angel.

He stayed for some time consolidating each memory, before it would be lost to the ether. What a mystery! He shook his head, got up and took some moments to orient himself to being upright, holding his hands to the side to get his balance. He felt dizzy, his legs wobbly, and he sat down again quickly. Could this be just a dream? He got up slowly and staggered over to the bar.

"Kel, you look a little shakey man, you okay?" said Shakey.

"Something wrong?" put in Ken-eye.

"How long have I been over there?" Kel asked a little hoarsely.

"You went home earlier and then we noticed you had come back and was snoozing quietly, about twenty minutes ago," said Shakey.

"Yeah, right after Shakey is done talking to another pretty woman!" said Ken-eye.

"Was it the girl, the girl from earlier on?" Kel asked.

"What girl?" Shakey replied looking a little concerned. "Are you okay man? You look like you've seen a ghost."

"You guys would not believe, you just would not believe," said Kel and he turned to head down to the shoreline but stopped suddenly. "Shakey, give me that shaving mirror of yours."

Shakey reached back and unhooked his little mirror, and handed it to Kel. "Not believe what, man? Sounds like you been born again!"

Kel peered into his mouth and his new white teeth were mirrored back to him. He whooped with joy. "There you have it," he said, "Look at these, they're new, it's all true."

Shakey peered in, unsure of what he was supposed to see. "I didn't know you had such nice choppers, man!"

"Man, you have been dreaming, and you've been to the dentist too. Amazing what they can do nowadays," said Ken-eye, laconically.

"You would just not believe what I've been through," and Kel suddenly felt extremely alone. There had been no time to even say goodbye. He missed Gaya with a passion that gripped him in its intensity. It had been like heaven. Had he been successful? How did he end up here?

He turned and made his way down to the water, his legs still wobbly. Shakey watched him go, and laughed, nudging Ken-eye, who laughed along with him, slapping his thigh in mirth.

Kel stripped off his tee shirt, dove in and swam parallel to the shore. The water felt good, and he remembered the water channels of Gaya, "It was real, it was real," he said over and over to himself.

He lay on his back in the warm sea staring up at the stars, and wondered where in the universe he'd been. 'Towards the constellation Virgo,' he remembered. Gazing up he remembered the fight with the Doctor, and confronting a beast of terrifying proportions.

He emerged from the water a little way along the beach, and sat looking out to sea. He still felt alone, but the empty feeling had gone, and one of great fulfillment swept over him like a wave. He remembered the giant walking over the sea—a recurring dream he had had as a child, and wondered why he should think of this now. This, and a patchwork quilt of thoughts, jostled in his brain, demanding attention before they might disappear into oblivion.

"You lost?" said the voice in the night.

Kel had not heard anyone coming and he turned, a little startled, his eyes searching in the darkness.

"Remember me?" said the voice.

Kel yelped, and jumped to his feet. "Lua!" he cried.

They ran to each other and embraced. A tight embrace of lost, and found, and longing. They kissed, and Kel remembered the sweet liquor taste of her mouth. This was his Lua.

He looked at her intently in the moonlight, "What happened?" he asked.

"Mission completed! You did the job Kel; the hole folded up. It shut down the second we jumped to hyperspace; otherwise we'd be mincemeat. How did you do it? Can you remember?" Lua asked cupping Kel's face in her hands, stroking his cheeks, lifting herself up onto her toes and kissing his brow.

"I just remember a fight, a wrestling match if I remember correctly. That's all—oh yeah, and Baba was there inside my head, it seemed, and one hell of an ugly something, like an enormous serpent. Kind of like cosmic warfare. The rest before that is just a blur, though I am getting flashes of some pretty weird stuff going through my head."

Lua hugged him close and said, "Kel, my love, I cannot adequately convey the gratitude and good wishes that all of us feel, and send to you from Gaya. Thank you so much. Your bravery and selfless service were a beacon to us all."

She paused a moment and looked down before continuing, "Kel, you have to decide whether you want me to stay or not, and you have five minutes to do that. Sorry to be so blunt, but you know what a rush this star travel business is."

"Please, please stay, Lua. You'll make all of this so complete," and Kel waved his arms at the world around him.

"You're sure?" Lua asked.

"Without a shadow of a doubt."

"What else can you remember from the mission?"

Kel thought hard and deep. "I think I saw Duncan, he was safe but imprisoned, and the Doctor had a way to get here through the realm of anti-matter. He had a mind to dominate creation. Everything seemed so real in there. That's all I can remember at the moment."

Lua unhitched herself from Kel's embrace and got out a credit card-sized transmitter like the one he had received on first contact. She looked over at him and said, "We checked to see if you had any kids, and you didn't."

Kel chuckled, and then suddenly remembered something else. "O yes—the Doctor had a way at getting at Carter, and Lyle's suspicions were correct. He had targeted this age. 'We come for your age next', he said, something like that."

Lua nodded and waited in case anything else would surface in Kel's memory, but that was it. She then spoke into the disk for a couple of minutes, and paced the beach like a busy mother on a cell phone. Kel heard, 'yes, there's a memory imprint...Yes, he had found a way; this age was next'.

She finished and held up the disk in front of her eyes, which had tears in them. Looking over at him, she smiled, and then blew on the disk as if she were scattering the seeds of a dandelion. It disappeared in an instant.

"So that is that. I go when you go, or rather we both go together." She laughed, and pulled Kel to walk with her, arm in arm along the beach.

"What happened your end on the observation deck? Were you there?" Kel asked.

"You were gone a lot longer than anticipated, and we caught the window, and the hole folding up just in time. I was out of recovery and strapped in next to your body on the ship. Tanea was on the observation deck with Lyle." Lua paused and looked down, picked up a shell and examined it.

"And then?"

"Baba was apparently in the deepest of trances right up until the hole started folding. When we couldn't find you, Lyle spoke to him and he told us to get your body back pronto. Your consciousness was, he said, 'in the hands of God.'"

Kel looked thoughtful. "When was it decided to let you come here? I thought that would have been a major transgression of cosmic law."

"When we discovered from the microfile records of births and deaths here that you had no marriage or children. And something happened at the Replication Unit when you came to say goodbye to me. Apparently I opened my eyes and saw you, and that was the transgression—an absolute…. What do you say?"

"Cosmic botch up."

"Yes, something like that. You were so embedded in my consciousness at such a delicate time that the only way to resolve it was for me to be with you. Otherwise it would have been forever unresolved. The team at the unit was relieved when the decision was taken to allow me to stay here. To be honest, they were glad to be rid of me, and everyone guessed what your answer would be." Lua slipped her arms around his waist and drew him close.

"So what happened to me?" Kel asked, and suddenly stopped dead in his tracks, slapping his forehead. "The Doctor told me that I was already dead. It's the last thing I can remember. My body had been dis-

posed of. Come on Lua let me have it all. Am I in some dream world
with you now, or is this heaven—or what?"

Lua looked away for a second. "I am not supposed to say this but
what the hell, it doesn't matter any more. There's no-one looking over
my shoulder. Daljit switched the I.D. plaques on the life support systems between you and Duncan. This was a precautionary measure initiated by Lyle. Well, Carter, under the influence of the Doctor,
attempted to curtail your life function, and ended up curtailing Duncan's body."

"Oh my God, what happened to Duncan? Did he get out?"

"Yes, he must have, and now he'll inhabit Carter's body. Carter was
put into stasis the moment he came to, after Matthias walloped him
one. Duncan's going to wake up to a black and blue chin in a humanoid body. Another first."

"How ironic," said Kel, "What do you mean, 'must have', what
happened after the hole folded?"

"You disappeared into anti-matter, and ended up in your body here.
The last thing we knew, before we made the jump, was that a conscious life sign emerged from the singularity as it began to fold up. I
thought it might be you but the observation ship hauled it aboard and
my darling, I spent the entire journey here wondering if the most interesting part of you was left back on Gaya."

Kel said nothing.

"How the hell you got back is totally out of the realm of logic and
reason." Lua sidled around and stopped Kel in his tracks, and they
kissed in the moonlight.

"So you're sure the life sign coming out of the hole was Duncan's?"

"It must have been," replied Lua.

"So what would have happened if I hadn't have turned up here?"
Kel asked.

"We didn't bring your physical body down until your conscious
body was back, although we didn't have to wait long in orbit up there,"
and Lua pointed a finger aloft. "You, whoever you are, made it in dou-

ble quick time back to your body. You are obviously inseparable! And our calculations were correct, you headed straight for here."

"Did you set up the two at the bar or what?" Kel asked, laughing.

"Yes, I set them up, kind of. I told them we were going to do a massive magic mushroom trip that would liberate you, but you can get back at them if you want," she replied mischievously.

"How?"

Lua dug into the pocket of her cotton shorts and produced a little cloth bag. It contained the herbal mix that Baba had given Kel, and a gnarled and knobbly pipe. There was also a small scroll that he opened and read. It was from Baba, and the writing was meticulous and gloriously old fashioned in its style, even for Kel—like a medieval script.

'My Dearest Kel,

I told you you would get back, and trust that all is finished now. Whatever you saw and experienced in your quest was in your own mind, the images you saw were created by you, as was the stage and the play. The actors were employed by the bloody mad Doctor, and the audience was you. So whatever you saw were just symbols of something going on which can never be perceived by any human sense, you created the images to represent the Deities, and they played their game out in you. This goes on forever Kel, so relax and enjoy the game. I will always be with you, and you are in my heart.

Good job, well done, see you down the road, ha ha!

I am well by the grace of the Lord and wish you the same, Om namoh Shiva ya.

Love from Baba

Kel kissed the parchment and held it to his heart, and he looked up at the stars and thanked them. Then he held the pouch up in front of him.

"Oh boy, oh boy, This will blast those naughty boys at the bar big time, and serves them right," and he laughed. His spirit danced and swaggering hormones skipped and jumped around his system.

"So you have a freshly revived body, new teeth and a passionate humanoid on your hands," said Lua. "But you cannot go back to any regular dentist you've seen before, too much of a phenomenon."

"What about you? You are more than a phenomenon."

"I am programmed to fool the best of them, so don't you worry about a thing. Life is going to be very interesting," said Lua grabbing Kel's waist and pulling him to her again. She kissed him passionately yet slowly, tasting every morsel of his being.

Kel's head spun and they locked in a tight embrace.

"Anyway," Lua continued, "We can go to California for starters. I have to check out a Stanford University there, where they are experimenting with anti-matter; then to a research unit in Japan at a place called Tattemura, or something like that, to do likewise. I heard you can speak Japanese—that'll help. And then I'd like to see India, Kel, I want to go to India."

"I'm broke," Kel said.

"Don't you remember, Kel? We have a million bucks in the bank. Payment for your services."

Kel looked stunned and then whooped with joy, incredulous that he had forgotten this major detail. "Jeez!" he said, spinning around and falling on the sand. He looked up at the stars; some black clouds beginning to shroud their light. Lua lay next to him and nestled her head against his shoulder, both staring up at the firmament above them.

"It's enough to get by," he said.

"I know one thing might interest you," said Lua, serious now, "I spoke to Tanea on the way to the observation ship, and apparently Lyle had made arrangements to go and live near Baba in the mountains once this was all over."

"What about Tanea?"

"Weekend visits most likely. Something was different about Tanea; she seemed more forgiving somehow, less rigid. Anyway, Lyle must be one very relieved man, and all community rules go out the window with him moving away like this. This is a new paradigm. He will live away for a bit and she will stay in close contact, and continue their relationship. You don't know how revolutionary that is for Gaya."

"I have a good idea, believe me. I spent a lot of the time on Gaya in friendly banter and argument. Most of it in fact."

"Yes I heard, and now Lyle is going to be with Tanea, and here I am with you. How strange this life is! He must be so relieved! You cannot imagine the amount of pressure he was under after the Doctor created the singularity," said Lua rolling over on top of him. She was surprisingly light.

"After meeting the Doctor I can imagine just how relieved he is." Kel closed his eyes and remembered Tanea. "She was one tough mama, Tanea, but I liked her a lot. Can you imagine how shocked I was when I arrived on Gaya and was met by her, the image of you."

Lua silenced him with a kiss.

"Lua," he said.

"Hmm," she replied.

"Did I really save the universe?" He heard himself ask the question and laughed, slapping his forehead.

"Yes Kel, you did—with a little help from your friends," Lua turned towards Kel and looked serious. "What do you think you've understood with everything that's happened to you?"

Kel looked out to sea and whistled softly. He fell silent, and Lua put her hand on his shoulder. "There is a God and its closer to me than I ever realised, but it's still a mystery. It's like a child of light that just wants to play. It's dancing in me; it is me. That's about it!"

Lua put her mouth to his ear. "You are beautiful!"

Kel turned to face Lua. "I experienced a kind of singularity of a different sort, an infinity of nothingness which is the heart of everything.

The very stuff that keeps all this life together. I found myself in it, and it was in me, and yet couldn't find myself anywhere."

"Maybe that's the self I said you'd have to meet when I first approached you. You must have been frightened, getting that close?"

"It was the unknown I was always conditioned to fear and control. But it's a love of unbelievable proportions. I think I've finally embraced it. It's actually who I am. Fear is no longer my master, though I don't think this little saga is over yet!"

"Hmm" said Lua.

"This nomadic soul of mine is just energy, burning its way through the dramas of life, attached to this and that, learning its lessons. It's like watching a bloody film."

"Yes," laughed Lua, "Like your Hollywood. So who's watching the movie?"

"That's the mystery to me, but I now have a definite inkling. As far as you know, is anything real?"

"I think our love is, the rest is as you say, a mystery!"

Kel felt at that moment, as he looked into Lua's eyes, that no barrier existed between them. He was complete with her, seamless and totally free.

Lua looked out to sea, the waves were becoming choppy and a squall was in the making. "Now let's join the boys, have some fun, see what happens, and then go to that little shack of yours you call home, and get to know each other a little better. I want to convince you how real I can be."

"What do you mean?" Kel asked.

"Never mind," replied Lua, and she stood and pulled Kel up. "And remember you have this," and she tugged at the bead that he wore around his neck.

Kel untied the thong, on which it hung, and held it up before his eyes, marveling at the uncanny resemblance to the bead that Ken-eye had given him before his quest began. "This very same night," he muttered. He clasped it in his hand and planned to give it to Ken-eye, along with a tale or two to tell.

He trudged up towards the bar, Lua just behind him, her hand hooked onto the back of his shorts.

✳   ✳   ✳   ✳

Meanwhile back at the bar, Ken-eye was on one of his verbal tirades, and Shakey stared down at the beach. "I think Kel's going a little crazy," said Shakey cutting short Ken-eye's argument, "I think he's down there talking to himself."

"My, my," said Ken-eye, "my, my," and he cocked his head towards the beach. "No," he said, "there's someone there with him."

Shakey peered into the darkening night. "You're right, it's the girl who set him up. Man, he does look blissed out. They're coming up this way."

"Well I do hope I can share in some of that bliss," said Ken-eye. "And she owes me a beer too. The night's looking up, Shakey, the night's looking up."

At that moment the scene behind Kel and Lua lit up, as a lightning bolt hit the sea behind them with a smack, followed immediately by a clap of thunder that roared and resonated with everything around. Lua turned and looked behind her; Kel shuddered for an instant and continued up the beach, looking forward to a cold beer, a chat, and the night with Lua.

Afterword

I would like to acknowledge the debt I owe to all the spiritual teachers in whose company I have been fortunate enough to be in. Especially to Swami Vinayagananda of the Kulu Valley, see (sarsaibaba.org), Duncan Callister and Andrew Cohen. And my heartfelt thanks to the the teachings of Ramana Maharshi and Nisargadatta Maharaj.

About the Author

Keith lives with his wife in Northern California. He is an ex diplomat with the British Foreign Service, former float tank owner, and former spiritual junkie. At present he works at the local General hospital as a Physical Therapist, and dreams of living in the northeast of Brasil.

0-595-22527-6